EWART HUTTON

People

HARPER

Harper
An imprint of HarperCollins*Publishers*
1 London Bridge Street
London SE1 9GF

www.harpercollins.co.uk

This paperback edition 2015
1

First published by Blue Door 2014
Copyright © Ewart Hutton 2014

Ewart Hutton asserts the moral right to
be identified as the author of this work

A catalogue record for this book is
available from the British Library

ISBN: 978-0-00-812423-6

Typeset in Minion by Palimpsest Book Production Ltd, Falkirk, Stirlingshire
Printed and bound in Great Britain by
Clay's Ltd, St Ives plc

MIX
Paper from
responsible sources
FSC
www.fsc.org
FSC C007454

FSC™ is a non-profit international organisation established to promote
the responsible management of the world's forests. Products carrying the
FSC label are independently certified to assure consumers that they come
from forests that are managed to meet the social, economic and
ecological needs of present and future generations,
and other controlled sources.

Find out more about HarperCollins and the environment at
www.harpercollins.co.uk/green

WILD PEOPLE

Ewart Hutton was born and raised in and around Glasgow before slipping south to university in Manchester, and then on to diverse occupations in London. He has won numerous awards and prizes for his radio plays, which have been produced for BBC Radio 4, RTE and Radio Clyde. *Wild People* is the third Glyn Capaldi novel. The first, *Good People,* was shortlisted for the Crime Writers' Association's John Creasey (New Blood) Dagger in 2012.

Also by Ewart Hutton

Good People
Dead People

For all the scattered ones – family and friends.

1

I was bad juju again. But this time they had learned from experience, and had tucked me away out of sight. Unlike the previous fiasco in Cardiff, when they tried to pull a PR trick and highlight me as a hero in an attempt to deflect the mess that had really gone down. No, this time they knew better. This time they treated me like the crazy uncle in the attic, and used the equivalent of nine-inch coach bolts and a heavy-duty plank to keep me secure behind the door.

I didn't care, because this time I had real injuries.

The medicos were mostly concerned about the after-effects of the concussion that had knocked me out. I wasn't, because that was nothing more than clinical record by the time I surfaced from it. The real bitch for me was the cracked ribs. Especially since the fuckers had only just started to heal after the Evie Salmon investigation. The contusions didn't help either. The fact that my face looked like a twisted biochemist was trying to cross a yellow tomato with an aubergine. With stubble, as it hurt too much to shave.

They had shipped me off to a specialist hospital in north Shropshire. I only found out later that I was in a secure and private wing that they kept reserved for damaged cops and high-echelon gangsters who had been mysteriously injured in the course of turning Queen's evidence.

I was hurting.

And as I started to adjust to it and come to terms with the physical side of the pain, the emotional trauma took over. But no one would tell me anything. They shushed me and said I needed to reserve all my mental strength for the recovery process. But even in a tight, shut-down place like that I was picking up the broad brushstrokes through a kind of osmosis.

Something terrible had happened.

I had quickly checked out the fundamentals. I still had my arms and my legs, my cock and my balls, and could move the parts that were meant to be moved. I could still remember that a tangent was the product of the opposite over the adjacent, and my date of birth. So it wasn't me.

It wasn't too hard to figure out after that. Although I was still refusing to accept it.

Until I had to.

Two days into it and they deemed me fit enough to receive a visitor.

DCI Bryn Jones knocked diffidently and shuffled his big bulk uncertainly into the room. It was crepuscular, the blinds were drawn, and I could tell that he wasn't ready to be sure that he had the right occupant. Until he started to adjust to the light and his expression screwed-over involuntarily at the sight of my face.

I shuffled to sit up. He gestured for me not to bother. It was the signal I had been testing for. This was unofficial. He was on his own.

'It's a stupid question, but are you okay?' His exploratory smile didn't mask his concern.

I nodded lumpily, keeping the movement within the safe parameters I now knew to work to. 'Thanks for coming.'

'Everyone in Carmarthen sends their best,' he lied.

'Will DCS Galbraith be coming?'

He knew what I was asking. 'Not yet,' he said softly.

He had answered my question. I had to accept it then. I was a Cop Who Had Killed a Girl.

I was Bad Karma.

'They haven't told you?' he probed.

I shook my head gingerly.

'It would have been instantaneous.'

The suppressed knowledge crashed to the surface. And there was no relief in the acceptance. 'Tell me about her, Bryn.'

'What do you know?'

'Her name was Josie.'

He shook his head gently. 'Jessie.'

Fuck. I felt the tears rise. I had killed her, and I hadn't even got her name right.

'Jessie Bullock.'

'What age?' I asked, dreading the answer.

'Nearly eighteen.'

My multicoloured face collapsed.

He looked miserable as the messenger. 'Don't blame yourself. It was an accident. We're all sure there's nothing you could have done about it.' He paused, waiting for me. I stayed silent. 'What do you remember?'

I lay there, looking up at the grid of ceiling tiles, but knowing that I would have to relinquish the numbness I had previously found there. 'I've been in car crashes before. There's usually an instant when you recognize the inevitability of it, and time locks down, and everything shunts on towards the moment.' I shut my eyes and went back to it again. 'But not this time. There was no build-up, Bryn. No recognition that we'd just entered an event. This was like suddenly finding yourself blindfolded and taking off in a rocket that you didn't even know you were travelling in. There was no lead-up sequence of things starting to go wrong. It was as sudden as that.'

He nodded. 'They say that your seat belt saved your life.'

'Why didn't hers?'

His expression saddened. 'She wasn't wearing one. They found her outside the car. She had been thrown. Her neck was broken.'

I shook my head. I looked at him intently. 'She had her seat belt on, Bryn.' It wasn't meant to be a plea, but it came out like one.

'Put your seat belt on.'

After Bryn had gone I went back to that night in the car park in the woods in the rain. The girl had been pulled. But they had already fucked up. They had been too eager. Broken out of cover too soon. We were standing around in the drizzle, heavy drips coming off the trees, while they reorganized themselves. They were going to have to go chasing into the woods now, relying on blind luck. This was bullshit. I wanted out of there. I offered to take the girl off their hands and drive her back to the police house in Dinas.

Why hadn't I got to know something about her? Concentrated, made more of an effort. Instead of just using her as a ticket out of that mess.

'Here's how it's going to go down,' I told her as I led her back to my car. Knowing better than to hold her. But poised, ready to grab her above the elbows if she made any move to run. 'I'm going to drive you to Dinas. There will be a woman police officer there to look after you' – I avoided using the word *process* – 'until we bring the others in, and then you'll all be taken to either Aberystwyth or Newtown.'

'How are you going to do that?' she asked.

And that was the only time I really saw her. I looked down at her then. In the pale second-hand gleam of a headlight reflecting off a car's side window. A wan teenager with a sharp nose and a curled wisp of damp hair dangling over her forehead under the hooded top. Curiosity framed in her expression.

'Do what?'

'How do you know there are others to bring in?'

'Are you saying you were on your own out there?'

'I'm not saying anything.' We had passed out of the light and I couldn't make out her face any more, but from her tone I got the impression that she wasn't being cute. Simply matter-of-fact. Saying it as it came to her. Knowing that it was up to us to do the work.

She also hadn't seemed concerned. This only came back

5

to me now. She had just been arrested, but she showed no sign of anxiety. No nervous bravado reaction, no fear, only curiosity.

I stopped at my car and opened the rear door for her. Another opportunity missed. I could have used the interior light to study her. But I didn't, I used it to make sure she fastened her seat belt.

'Put your seat belt on,' I instructed, and she complied.

I flashed on the ways I could have fucked up. But I wouldn't have driven too fast on that road. I didn't know it well enough. And it was dark, and it was one of those rains that filmed the windscreen. I would have been extra careful.

'I'm Glyn Capaldi. What's your name?' I asked into the rear as we drove away.

'Josie.' I thought she had said Josie.

'You don't strike me as a thief, Josie,' I said, my eyes on the rear-view mirror, my tone telling her that I wasn't being mean, letting her know that I was prepared to listen if she wanted to talk.

She stayed silent.

And she remained silent. The radio turned right down to velvet static, only the windscreen wipers and the wet tyre hiss as a backdrop. I would have heard it. I was sure of it. One of the few things I was certain of. At no time did I hear even the faintest hint of her seat belt being unbuckled.

I wasn't used to this road, but I had driven it enough times to know about the bend. To treat it with respect. I had approached it with anticipation, doing all the right things, dropping down to third gear, braking evenly, starting the turn.

6

And then the car had stopped turning. A huge jolt, which I later realized must have been the offside front wheel hitting a rock on the verge after the tyre had blown. Then take-off.

Did she scream?

Am I going back into a voided memory and inventing that?

But her seat belt was on. And the rear door was locked.

How could they have found her outside the car?

Could I have missed anything in the build-up?

Emrys Hughes had called me. He was the local uniform sergeant, and acted as if Dinas had been his patch ever since his ancestors had crawled out of the sea complete with gills, Stalin moustache and truncheon. I could understand that he would have mightily resented it when my boss DCS Jack Galbraith had decreed that he was going to be sharing his demesne with me. I could even sympathize. Although empathy didn't stop me from rubbing his nose in it from time to time. Sparking up Emrys Hughes had been one of the pastimes that helped to ease my way through a long Mid Wales winter.

'Morning, Glyn.' His tone was cheerful and friendly, and I was immediately wary. His usual greeting was 'Fuck you, Capaldi.'

'Emrys.'

'I was wondering how busy you are.'

I was at my desk in Unit 13 Hen Felin Caravan Park, which doubled up as my office and approximation of a home. I didn't have to look anything up to know that my caseload comprised a con couple, male and female, who were claiming to be from Social Services and targeting pensioners, and an outfit who were knocking off touring caravans. On the computer screen I had the latest swatch of missing person reports. Customers of varied form and function whose last-known coordinates made it possible that they could have been heading into these latitudes. I had a female Latvian student, a middle-aged Turkish Cypriot businessman, and a dyke from Brighton with a completely shaven head, including eyebrows, who was described as bipolar.

'Snowed under,' I told him.

'Good.' The bastard hadn't even allowed my reply to register on his consciousness. 'So how would you feel about helping make up the manpower on a stakeout that Inspector Morgan has asked me to organize?'

In the normal course of events I would have told him straight out where to stick his stakeout. But Jack Galbraith had recently instructed me to mend my bridges with the local force, conveniently ignoring the fact that he was responsible for alienating them in the first place by dumping me in Dinas to act as his command outpost in the empty quarter. Get onto sweetheart terms, he had told me, just in case I ever needed the back-up, because, in the current state of the relationship, any emergency call from me would have most of them reaching for the cudgels so that they could have their go at me before the opposition bagged all the fun.

Which meant that I now had to add finesse to my avoidance tactics. I sucked in a deep doubtful breath. 'It's looking like my diary's pretty stuffed-up here.'

'You'll be free on this night.'

'How do you know?'

8

'Because Inspector Morgan's already cleared it with DCS Galbraith.' I heard the smug chuckle spread down the line.

I checked my annoyance. He'd been playing with me, it was already a done deal. 'What's the operation?' I asked.

His voice dropped low. 'You'll find out on the night. We're keeping this close to our chest. A need-to-know basis, we don't want the targets getting wind of it.' Jesus, he was taking this way too seriously. I'll bet he was even having Special Forces dreams.

I looked out of the caravan's window. We were having a run of good early summer weather. The tops of the exposed boulders in the low-running river were bleached dry and streaked with wagtail guano, the deep green leaves on the alders that fringed the bank were a celebration of chlorophyll, and the sky thrummed blue with small groups of puffy prancing white clouds. I just knew that it was going to end up raining on the night.

I called Huw Davies, a local uniform cop I had made friends with. Huw kept away from the politics and the back-biting, but was an astute enough observer to be able to go to for an overview. 'Have you got any information about a stakeout operation that Inspector Morgan's corralled me into?'

He chuckled. 'You too?'

'It's supposed to be a secret.'

'Oh, it is, everyone that's been told has been made to promise not to tell anyone else.'

'Okay, so it's a golf club locker room kind of secret?' I ventured.

'That's right.'

'So how come no one has made me promise not to tell?'

He laughed. 'Because no one talks to you.'

'I promise not to tell anyone, Huw.'

'Have you heard of the Monks' Trail?'

'Vaguely. Remind me.'

'It's a long-distance footpath that starts near the village of Llandewi. There's a purpose-built car park in the woods at the beginning of the trail. That's where the problem is. Some of the cars that have been left there have been vandalized and broken into while their owners have been off hiking or mountain biking. Certain local worthies have got it into their heads that this is bad for tourism, ergo their businesses, and have bent Inspector Morgan's ear.'

'We're gathering all this manpower and going on a stakeout for vandals?' I let him hear my amazement.

'Correct.'

'There's something quite endearingly reassuring about this, Huw. That this is the extent of major crime in the area. But is it really worth the time and the effort?'

'Feral youth.' I heard his amusement.

'What?'

'They've somehow fixed on the notion that it's down to gangs of wild drug- and booze-fuelled kids from Swansea or Liverpool driving in to target our community and heading back with their bags full of swag.'

'I take it you're not sharing this apocalyptic vision?'

'I think we'd have come across a bit more noise and a lot more damage. And they're not taking our virgins with them.'

'Have you got anyone in mind for it?'

'I could probably point to a couple of people, but I'm

keeping my head down. I don't want to be seen as the one who pissed on Inspector Morgan's crusade.'

I registered the warning.

Feral youth?

Back in my hospital bed I tried to square that with what little I remembered of Jessie Bullock. I couldn't. No snarls, no attitude, not even a visible piercing.

I had been prescient. It did rain on the night.

Those of us who weren't already in their assigned places assembled in a hut that was shared between the local Boy Scout troop and the Women's Institute, as evidenced by the rope knot posters and a tea-making roster on the walls. The floors creaked, and I imagined the memories locked into the fabric, a combination of suppressed unfocused juvenile lusts and home-made scones and jam.

Everyone was in mufti, and most of them had somehow managed to over-emphasize the fact that they were out of uniform by making their outfits look like disguises. A room full of charged and eager hyper-civilians.

Morgan briefed us from the raised dais. I had only ever seen him in uniform before, a stiff and disapproving man with a widow's peak over a crinkled washboard forehead. Tonight he looked incongruous in a pale blue anorak and a knitted ski cap, his voice raised to overcompensate for the lack of visible rank badges.

He ran us through it. Two vehicles had been planted in the car park to act as honey pots, a swanked-up BMW 3 Series coupé, and a Subaru Impreza. Two surveillance vehicles were already in place, a camper van at the far end, and

11

a Ford Transit covering the entrance, which could also double up as a blockade vehicle if the bad guys attempted to leave the car park in a hurry.

The police house in Dinas was going to be used as a reception and holding area, from where the detained suspects would be distributed to the larger centres.

The rest of us were assigned to roadside stations where we would park out of sight and cover all the routes leading to the car park. If any suspicious vehicle went past us we were to call it in to Morgan. But we were to wait for his signal before we moved.

'Any questions?' Morgan asked, his wrist crooked in front of his face as he made a big deal of checking his watch.

I put my hand up. I knew I should have kept quiet, but I couldn't help it. Out of the corner of my eye I saw Huw Davies give me a significant look.

'Sergeant Capaldi?'

'It's the bait vehicles, Sir.'

'What about them?'

'Aren't they a bit . . .' I searched for a nice way to put it. 'Aren't they kind of out of place?'

'What's your point?'

'It's just that I can't imagine the kind of people who would normally drive that type of car to be the sort who would leave it in the middle of the countryside while they go off for a long healthy hike.'

He smiled nastily. 'You're probably right, but the people we're targeting tonight don't know that.'

'Sir?'

'They're only interested in the bling, Sergeant. They don't

12

care what motivates people to come out here. That's why we've carefully chosen these particular cars.' He smiled superciliously. 'I think you'll find that they're going to be more interested in the Subaru or the BMW than any old Land Rover or Vauxhall Corsa we could have left in there with a *no-nukes* sticker on it.' He was rewarded by an all-round chuckle.

'Yes, Sir.' I bowed out.

The teams paired up preparatory to leaving. I was left conspicuously on my own.

I sat in my car in my allocated slot in the dark and listened to the carillon of heavy drips on the roof from the tree canopy, with the occasional heavier note of dislodged beech mast. The radio was turned down to low static with the odd interference jump.

This was bullshit, I told myself again.

'Go, go, go!' Morgan's voice whipped out. And, despite my deep-seated cynicism, I felt the familiar lurch of adrenalin and excitement kicking in as I reached out to start my car.

There were two other cars fishtailing down the access road to the car park in front of me. I pulled up at the entrance and tried to make sense of it. The far end of the car park was illuminated by headlights which were focused on the surveillance team's camper van. The two honeypot vehicles were off to the side, still in the dark, and being ignored. On the other side was the dark hulk of an abandoned and burnt-out car that ruin had made unrecognizable.

I got out and slipped a high-visibility police raincoat on. I walked across the car park until I caught up with a straggler on the edge of the group that was concentrated around

13

the camper van. A loose semi-circle of people had formed, and I could make out Emrys Hughes and Inspector Morgan in the midst of it.

'What's happened?' I asked.

'We've caught a kid,' he replied breathlessly, still meshed up in the excitement of the chase.

'What about the rest of them?'

He shook his head. 'I don't know.'

I moved towards the semi-circle in time to catch Morgan saying, '. . . spread out and move into the woods.' My heart sank.

He caught sight of my hi-viz jacket and scowled at me furiously. 'I didn't give any orders about breaking out of cover, Sergeant Capaldi.'

I looked at the floodlit mêlée that had been created, but thought better than to remark on it. 'I'm sorry, Sir. I just thought we had a result.'

'We got one of the little buggers,' Emrys Hughes chimed in gleefully.

I made a point of looking round significantly. 'Have we got their vehicle trapped in here, Sir?'

'They've parked somewhere else,' Morgan announced crossly. 'They didn't drive in, they came down out of the woods.'

I turned to Emrys. 'How many were there?'

'Don't know yet. We caught this one trying the handle on the surveillance vehicle.'

'She was a scout,' Morgan added his wisdom, 'the rest have scattered. We're going to have to go into the woods after them.'

14

'They're city kids, they won't know how to handle it in there, they'll all be terrified of the dark,' Emrys raised his voice reassuringly as some of the faces around him began to look distinctly unenthusiastic.

I saw her for the first time then, close to the camper van, hemmed in by a couple of big cops, her back to me, hooded top up. A plan formed. A route out of this debacle.

'Why don't I take this one back to Dinas, Sir? Out of your way.' I shrugged apologetically. 'Sorry about the coat. I'm a bit too bright for a chase. But I can free your hands up.'

He thought about it. 'Okay,' he agreed reluctantly, 'but I want you back here after.'

'Of course, Sir.' I moved away from him and towards Jessie.

Only now I knew that I wasn't going to make it back, and I was about to lead her on her death march.

It took two more days before Jack Galbraith turned up at the hospital. My relief was mixed. On the one hand his presence meant that I was probably in the clear. He wouldn't have risked the taint by association otherwise. On the other was the still nagging feeling that I might not deserve to be. Jessie Bullock was dead after all.

I had also started to speculate on another more radical scenario.

He strode in with Bryn Jones in tow. I sat up straighter in bed. They had opened the blinds by now, the room was lighter. He took his time scrutinizing me. 'Jesus, Capaldi, you look like someone stuck your head in a cement mixer.'

I had checked the mirror. The bruising on my face had faded down to shades of apricot and plum. 'It's getting better, Sir.'

15

He sat down and made a big show of staring at the bedside table. 'Where are the fucking grapes?'

'I think you're meant to bring them, Sir.'

He flashed a grin at Bryn Jones. 'I reckon he's on the mend.' He turned back to me, his face serious. 'Who's been to see you?'

I nodded towards Bryn. 'DCI Jones. And my friend Graham Mackay brought my mother up from Cardiff.'

'They haven't let the press in?'

'No, Sir.'

'Good. They've been fucking pestering me. Bastards.' He grunted and returned to his original tack. 'Has Inspector Morgan been?'

'No, Sir.'

He scowled. 'Sanctimonious fucking hypocrite. The least he could have done was come and see how you were getting on. A *thank you* might also have been appropriate. If it wasn't for his chicken-shit operation, that poor girl would still be alive.'

'Did they catch anyone else that night?'

Jack Galbraith batted the question on to Bryn, who shook his head. 'No, they chased around for hours. Half of his men ended up getting lost.'

'Inspector Morgan will not be repeating the operation,' Jack Galbraith pronounced.

'What more do we know about Jessie Bullock?' I asked.

He opened a thin file folder he had been holding. 'She's local. She lived with her mother at the Home Farm of a big estate called Plas Coch up the hill above the car park. They run it as some kind of religious retreat.'

'It's strictly secular, from what I heard,' Bryn corrected.

'Whatever.' Jack Galbraith shrugged loosely. 'She had finished school and was intending to go to university in the autumn.'

I looked at Bryn. 'Could they have charged her with anything?'

'I've talked to some of the people who were there that night. They started mouthing off about an attempted B & E, but when I got them calmed down, all it appears she did was touch the door handle on the camper van. She may have been trying to open it, or she may have been totally innocent. We'll never know now because the stupid bastards over-reacted.'

'What a fucking waste,' Jack Galbraith exclaimed. He fluttered the file folder at me. 'Nothing's official yet, so don't celebrate too prematurely, but it's looking like you're going to be exonerated. There's still the coroner's inquest to get through, and we're setting up an internal enquiry, but everything I've looked at is saying it was an unavoidable accident.'

'Your offside front tyre blew on the bend, which was the worst possible place for it to happen,' Bryn took over the story. 'You lost your steering, it would have been impossible to correct it once it started to go. The car took off, cleared a brook beside the road, hit the ground and turned over a couple of times. It looks like Jessie was thrown clear on the first impact.'

'Do they know what caused the puncture?' I needed the answer to this question for my alternative line of enquiry.

He shook his head. 'The tyre shredded. There was no way

of piecing it back together to find out. Whatever it was, it caused it to blow big time. The theories are either a sharp stone on the carriageway, or a latent fault in the tyre.'

Jack Galbraith came back in. 'You're fucking lucky, Capaldi, your seat belt saved you.'

'I know, Sir.'

'What's the long face for then?'

'She was wearing her seat belt, Sir. I saw her put it on. And the rear door was locked.'

He exchanged a look with Bryn. 'And we believe you, but something must have happened to change that. Something that was out of your hands.'

'All you can tell the coroner is what you know,' Bryn said gently.

'How much longer have you got in here?' Jack Galbraith changed the subject.

'A few more days of observation, unless I have some kind of a relapse.'

'We're putting you on sick leave,' Bryn announced.

'You can come back to the bright lights of Carmarthen and lick your wounds. We'll find you some sort of accommodation,' Jack Galbraith offered magnanimously.

I thought about my alternative line of enquiry. 'Thank you, Sir. Would it be okay to go to Cardiff? I've got family there.'

He shook his head slowly. 'Cardiff is still out of bounds.'

'Even though I'll be off active duty, Sir?'

'That makes you even more vulnerable. It's for your own good. There are a lot of people there who are still clutching sore balls because of you, and would just love to truly fuck you up.'

I nodded, accepting his protective wisdom. 'Then, if it's all right with you, I'll stay in Dinas, Sir.'

He frowned in surprise. 'Jesus, they didn't say anything about it affecting your brain.'

'I thought you were desperate to get out of there?' Bryn asked, also surprised.

I didn't want to tell them the real reason. That I didn't want Jack Galbraith being close enough to make me nervous while I considered the alternatives to the official line. 'I think I want to stay where it's quiet for a while,' I explained meekly instead.

They exchanged another look, managing to hide most of their shared incredulity. They both got up. 'Just don't talk to any reporters, Capaldi. Not until this thing has been cleared away.'

'I won't, Sir.'

I waited until they had got to the door. 'Sir . . .'

They both turned.

'I've been doing some thinking. Do you think that there's any possibility that it could have been a deliberate set-up? That it wasn't an accident?'

I kept it casual, but I needed to know if there was anyone else pursuing this line.

2

The coincidences seemed to be just too loaded.

I had been lying there for days wallowing in guilt and anguish until something in the kick-ass side of my brain took over and said, Wait a minute, stop playing the helpless victim and look at this in another light. A tyre bursts on you, bad news, but it happens. Invariably you pull over to the side of the road, fix the bastard and get your hands dirty. But when the one crucial tyre explodes on a wet surface, at the very worst point on a killer bend and you go flying off the road, you have to start questioning the likelihood of all those factors coming into conjunction without perhaps a little assistance.

Jack Galbraith turned back to face me. 'We thought about that.'

'We checked it out. It was definitely an accident,' Bryn amplified.

'No disrespect, Capaldi, but who would go to all that fucking effort to waste you?'

Who indeed?

I racked my brains for people with grudges. Sadly there were plenty of takers. I then factored in the possession of enough intelligence and resources to have come up with a scheme like this that had left no trace, and that narrowed the field down quite considerably. To zero in fact. I could think of no fiendish Professor Moriarty type who I had crossed badly enough in my past.

But it was occupying me. Keeping my brain engaged. And, more importantly, deflecting my sense of guilt. If someone else had caused this, I could concentrate on retribution rather than morbidity. I could act rather than mope. I was a cop after all. I could use my métier to find out who had been behind it.

I started by putting a call in to Kevin Fletcher in Cardiff. I had been his mentor when he had first joined the force. We had worked together when we had both been detective sergeants, although he had since risen to the rank of detective chief inspector, while I remained a DS, with the added distinction of now being a disgraced emissary in the boondocks. We didn't like each other these days, but I reckoned that he owed me one for unintentionally giving his career another upward shunt recently.

'Glyn!' His tone was ebullient.

'Hi, Kevin, can you talk, or is this a bad time?'

'Absolutely no problemo.' His voice was raised over a background of clinking glasses and conversations. I could picture him in his element, networking with the movers and the sharks in a swanky boozer. His tone dropped to sympathetic. 'Are you okay? We heard about the accident. Fucking shame.'

'It's a terrible thing. And thanks, I'm getting better, but I need a favour, Kevin.'

The brief silence was like a security grille crashing into place. 'And I'd love to have you back here working for me, don't get me wrong. Like a shot, if the decision was mine to make. But it's a political thing.' In the background I heard a couple of his cronies laugh, and I wondered what gesture he'd just flashed them. 'You're still a raw wound down here. The head honchos wouldn't consider it.'

I gritted my teeth to cover my gag reaction at all that faux sincerity, and tried to keep my voice sunny. 'I'm not looking for a transfer, only some information.'

He chuckled benignly. 'That I can do, if I'm able.'

'Can you ask around discreetly to see if there's any talk out there about anyone having a special interest in me.'

'Special interest?' His voice was alert now.

'A big chip on their shoulder. It might be someone I put away, or it might be a more tenuous connection. Perhaps someone I put inside has died in the nick, and a relative might be holding me responsible.'

'As in revenge?'

'Something like that.'

He sewed the pieces together. 'You think the accident might not have been an accident?'

'I'd just like to reassure myself.'

'Leave it with me.'

Give him credit, he acted quickly. Pity he didn't do it in my interest.

'Capaldi!'

'Sir?' As soon as I saw Jack Galbraith's number come

up on the caller display I knew that Fletcher had finked on me.

'A little bird has told me that you are about to take off on a flight of fucking fantasy.'

'I just thought I'd check out the opposition, Sir. There are some twisted people out there.'

His voice rose. 'And I told you we already had.'

I held the phone away from me and ate shit. 'Yes, Sir.'

'The possibility has been checked and discounted.'

'Yes, Sir.'

'Get this, Capaldi, you are currently non-operational. So you are either going to be on sick leave getting up to whatever you do with your sheep or your fucking elks or whatever else you use to relax with up there, or I will haul you back to Carmarthen and have you collating endless reams of useless shit. Understood?'

'I understand, Sir.'

Contacting Fletcher had been a calculated risk. But, even if he hadn't shafted me, I had always known that probably, and sooner rather than later, I was going to have to take this thing underground.

Which is why I declined the offer of a police driver to take me home and asked Mackay to come for me instead. Without my mother this time.

They had allowed me to take light exercise for the last couple of days, so although I was still stiff, I wasn't too woozy on my feet by the time he came to fetch me. And, now that it had arrived, my discharge wasn't the huge relief I had been anticipating, because, in a way, it felt like leaving sanctuary. Back out into the big world where no one gave a shit what the exonerating evidence said. I was a cop and I had crashed a car and killed a young woman coming into her prime, who had been entrusted to my care. Blame accrued.

You could never call Mackay a ray of sunshine, he had too much black history for that, but he certainly brought freshness back into my life, like the proximity of running water on a very hot day. My institutionalized days had turned me stale.

Mackay and I went back a long way, to childhood holidays in Scotland, where his family was entwined into the Capaldi clan there. I had been enraptured by the wild Mackay brothers, and he and I had become close friends despite the geography that separated us. Our life paths diverged when I joined the police force in Cardiff, and he went into the army. After that, whenever we did get together, big trouble inevitably seemed to flare up on our periphery, and I discovered I had lost my appetite for mayhem. Our nadir came when he took up with my ex-wife Gina. Now she had dropped him through the trapdoor in favour of a younger Australian version, he had retired from the SAS, and we had reconnected, with him taking on the self-appointed role of my protector.

He still carried that baby face that was so redolent of Glasgow, although there were now a few crinkles around the corners of his eyes. He ran initiative training courses for corporate executives from his farmhouse in Herefordshire, and this occupation was reflected in his lean fitness, the weathered face, and bleached sandy hair that he wore short.

I climbed into his familiar old Range Rover while he put my bag in the rear. He caught me looking at my face in the

24

vanity mirror as he climbed into the front seat. It was improving. Now it just looked like an accident involving some suspect tanning products.

'Even with the sympathy vote I still wouldn't fancy you.' He grinned.

'At least I don't look like a fucking vegetable hotpot any more.'

'Try an eye-patch and a sling. The damaged look brings out the need to nurture in the ladies.'

'Until they find out the whole story.'

His smile shifted and he dropped into a slow sympathetic nod. 'How are you feeling?'

'Confused.' He waited me out. I gave him a wan smile. 'I've been repaired. They've let me out to catch up with my life again. But all that's been changed. There's a dead girl, Mac, who's stopped going anywhere.'

'But it's not your fault.'

'People keep telling me that.'

'Accidents happen, Glyn.'

'This may not have been one.'

He tried to keep his expression blank, but I saw this hit home. He knew me well enough by now not to probe. I would tell him when I was ready. Or not.

He started the car and looked across at me, his smile trying to lift me out of the moment. 'Home James and don't spare the horses?'

'Can we go the long way round?'

He frowned, he didn't have to ask where. 'Are you sure you're ready for it?'

'I'm not being morbid. There are things I've got to

25

check out. And I'd like you to be there. I'd appreciate your overview.'

'It's a long detour. Are you sure you don't want to go straight home?'

I smiled at his concern. 'Home's a fucking caravan, Mac. It can keep. It's not as if it's going to have sprouted comfort and high style in my absence.'

'At the risk of too much repetition, you can always come back with me. You're meant to be on sick leave after all.'

I shook my head. 'Thanks, Mac,' I said gratefully.

He shrugged but dropped the issue. I knew he wanted to keep me away from there. He thought it was in my best interest.

As far as I was concerned, my best interest lay in finding the equivalent of a hidden machine-gun nest up there.

Something tangible to blame.

We approached from Dinas, the opposite direction to the way I had been driving that night with Jessie. It was also daylight, and the weather was dry.

We had dropped down into a small level-bottomed valley. The road was a narrow two-lane affair that followed the curving profile along the foot of a low, steeply raking, rocky escarpment. The brook coming down off the watershed followed the same course on the other side of the road. The far side of the brook was marshy, tending into rough pasture and then rising slowly to conifer plantations on the side of the hills.

As we got closer to the fatal bend, Mackay slowed down, looking for somewhere to pull off the road.

'Can you carry on and turn round and come back at it the way I would have been travelling?' I asked him.

'Sure.'

Driving in this direction we were on the inside of the bend, close to the face of the escarpment. As we rounded it slowly I looked over past Mackay at a small mound of dead flowers and soft toys on the opposite verge, another example of the kind of tacky public grief shrine that had entered the national psyche following the death of Princess Diana.

'You going to be okay?' he asked, seeing where I was looking.

I nodded. 'Don't worry, as far as I'm concerned that's just a heap of shit. You'd think if people were really sincere about paying their respects they'd at least have the grace to get rid of the fucking supermarket packaging.'

'Don't let it get to you,' he instructed, sensing my tension.

'I won't.'

He turned the car round. I concentrated on the approach. The brook was on my side of the road now, about a metre below us, and narrow here, reed-fringed, the peat in it giving it the slow slick look of dark oil as it coursed between rounded boulders.

I took it in. A road sign giving warning of a sharp bend. A sinuous inside curve to the road ahead before it turned sharply to disappear around a projection in the escarpment. I realized that I was holding my breath.

'Take it at the speed you normally would,' I told him.

My eyes flicked between the speedometer and the road as he dropped down to third gear and swept round. Just under thirty miles an hour. In the wet and the dark I would

27

probably have been going slower. But still fast enough for take-off.

Mackay parked and we walked back to the bend. I tried to ignore the low pile of wilted flora in its cellophane and the forlorn sodden teddy bears.

A grouping of fresh striations on a hefty boulder in the verge showed us where the front offside wheel had made contact. This was the launch pad. I looked across the brook. The wreckage had been cleared up, but the ground was still scored and turned over in the places where my car had made its tumbling contact.

It had been quite a leap.

'You're not thinking of going over there, are you?' Mackay asked, reading my mind.

'We've come this far.'

'I don't think you should.'

'Come on, Mac, don't be such a fucking mother hen.'

'There's no sense in it.'

I looked at him pointedly. 'You're the first guy arriving on the scene. In your headlights you see my car over there, on its roof. You make an instant assumption. More people arrive, they see Jessie's body thrown from the car, no front tyre, a mangled wheel, and that same assumption keeps trotting itself out. That assumption then turns into an explanation. Case closed.'

'What are you trying to say?'

I pointed across the brook. 'Everything's been cleared away. There are no distractions left. So let's take a fresh look.'

'It wasn't just an assumption, Glyn. You told me yourself, everything stacked up to it being an accident.'

28

I smiled at him. 'That's what was reported. Now it's time to take our own look.'

I was stiffer than I thought. He had to help me down the bank and across the brook, both of us getting our feet wet in the process. I followed the pattern of the cartwheels my car had made in the soft ground, reaching the spot where it had finally come to rest. I looked off to the side. In the direction of where they had found Jessie. A shape I hadn't seen from the road.

As I approached I saw that it was a small cairn. A recent pile of stones. I looked around for the source. This was all grass and sedge. These stones had to have been fetched from the brook. Someone had put effort into building a crude but sensitive memorial. The sight of it made my stomach lurch.

I was the one who had something to atone for and what had I done?

I'm starting now, Jessie, I'll find out for you, I floated out a silent promise.

I looked back at the road, trying to visualize myself approaching on that dark wet night.

How could they have done it?

'There were no signs of it being anything other than an accident, Glyn,' Mackay, standing behind, reminded me softly, tuning into my thought process.

'There wouldn't be.'

'Sorry?'

I turned to face him. 'If it was done professionally, they wouldn't leave any evidence.'

He pulled a face, torn between sympathy and frustration. 'That's a cop-out and you know it. The ultimate conspiracy

29

theory fail-safe. Look, I know it's natural to want to find an outside cause. But believe me, I've seen it before; trying to invent an absolving scenario is only going to fuck up the healing process.'

'Help me then.'

'How?'

'Tell me that it couldn't be done. Put your hand over your heart. Convince me that it's impossible.'

He frowned. He knew I'd trapped him. 'Anything's possible,' he admitted grudgingly.

'So how would you have made this one happen?'

'I wouldn't. I'm a civilian now.'

'Humour me, Mac.'

He stared at me for a moment. Shook his head. He knew I wasn't going to drop it. 'That's why you wanted me to bring you here?'

'You've got the expertise.'

'You can be a manipulative bastard, Glyn.'

'I think someone deliberately hurt me, Mac. Killed that girl. I think they might have been trying to kill me.'

He looked as if he was about to protest, but dropped it. He started to look round, and then shifted his eyes sharply onto mine. 'This is an invention. You have to understand that. This is no kind of truth. I'm spinning you a fairy tale here. All we're doing is entering the land of possibility.'

I gave him the acknowledgement his expression was looking for.

He turned slowly, taking in the panorama, gradually increasing his circle. I shuffled along beside him, keeping quiet, respecting his concentration. He took off at a tangent, aiming for a small stand of Scots pine at a point where the ground started to rise up to the denser conifer plantations. I followed him. From time to time he paused to take a bearing on the bend.

He stopped at the pine trees and sighted a line back the way we had come. 'They could have set up here.'

'They?'

'It would need two of them.' He held up a hand to stop me asking any more questions and dropped into a crouch to investigate a small mossy mound between two of the pine trees. I stood behind him and tried to work it out for myself as he slowly stroked and parted the moss and grass, dipping his nose down from time to time and sniffing deeply.

From here we were about a hundred metres away from the road. My car would have been directly side-on when it reached the apex of the bend and the tyre blew. Mackay was obviously working on some kind of sniper theory rather than something having been planted on the road.

He lay down in a prone rifleman's position and sighted along an imaginary barrel. 'This would have been the optimum position.'

'Did you find anything on the ground?'

He shook his head. 'They're not going to leave a casing behind. And it's been too long, and this ground's too springy to have retained the mark of anyone having lain here.'

'What were you sniffing for?'

He shrugged. 'Powder residue. You never know.'

'You think it was a rifle?'

He looked up at me. 'I don't think anything. This is your story.'

'Okay.' I nodded, starting to run with it. 'So I'm side-on to them when they fire. Is that to stop me seeing the muzzle flash?'

'They'd have used a suppressor. They'd already have sighted-up with the laser, so they wouldn't have to worry about you seeing that.'

'Wouldn't they have used a telescopic sight?'

'Yes, a scope with a laser designator to set up the target initially. And the main reason they'd have set themselves up to the side here would be to make the target easier to hit.'

'I'm presuming the target's my front nearside tyre?'

He nodded. 'The side wall of a tyre presents a better profile.' But he was distracted. Still working through the mechanics of it. 'The gun would have been pre-sighted and locked into position here with a tripod and clamps, ready to fire when you came along. There's plenty of cover, it's remote, no livestock, so the chances of anyone nosing around are scarce. They could even have set the gun up a few days before, camouflaged it and waited for the moment.' He sighted along his imaginary barrel again. 'The car's always going to be slowing down for the bend, so its speed is broadly predictable. And over this short range they could accommodate variable wind speeds and directions.'

Something he had said before suddenly made sense. 'They needed two people to set the tyre up as a target?'

'Right. One here tuning the rifle and the other one driving a car, probably with a paint stripe on the tyre to get the exact mark. On a quiet road like this they could drive the simulation target backwards and forwards until they were sure they'd got it right. Then lock the thing down so that when it's fired it's always going to hit the same place.'

32

'It sounds easy.'

He smiled. 'Everything is in fairy tales.'

'Would they have used an exploding bullet?'

He shook his head and tried not to make his smile too superior. 'Too dangerous, even in fairy tales, and even if you could get hold of one. Probably a hollow-cavity bullet. It would fragment on impact, shredding the tyre, and making it virtually impossible to trace in this sort of terrain.'

Even if anyone had been looking. Which they hadn't. It had been designated as an accident, not a crime scene.

He got up slowly, brushing dry grass and pine needles off himself. He was gazing back towards the road, his face distracted again.

'What's the matter?'

'I could be completely wrong, of course; they could have used the cobalt zirconium ray.'

'What's that?' I asked eagerly.

He turned his grin on me. 'Another myth I just invented. That's what I need you to hold on to. This is a story, not an explanation.'

I nodded my acceptance. But both of us knew I was going to totally disregard his rider.

The pied wagtail I had anthropomorphized into my special little friend wasn't around when we got back to Unit 13. I felt an irrational twinge of sadness that he wasn't there to welcome me home. I was used to him bobbing around on the rocks in the river outside the large rear window of my caravan, although, if I was being honest, I had to admit I was never sure that I was seeing the same bird every time.

Mackay wanted to fuss around making things comfortable for me. Much as I appreciated his friendship and kindness, I needed to be on my own to reflect on what he had told me. He left when I played up fatigue, mentioning that the drive, the fresh air and the emotion had taken its toll.

I took on board his disclaimer that it had only been a story, an invention. And okay the details might be totally wrong, but that didn't matter. What was important was that he had demonstrated that it could have happened. Someone could have set out to shut me down and make it look like an accident.

But who and why? I came back to it again. Who, as Jack Galbraith had so succinctly put it, would go to all that fucking effort to waste me?

Were there other possibilities? Could someone have deliberately set out to target the girl? Or could it have been a random hit? But both of those scenarios seemed as unlikely and as implausible as someone trying to waste me.

Because, what could a teenage girl have done in her short country life to warrant that sort of terrible attention? And who would set up a random hit in an area so remote and deserted that they were more likely to end up assassinating an otter than a person. No, random shootings were a strictly urban feature. If someone was that sick and determined to take out a stranger in a car they would have set up their kit on a motorway overpass, or a crowded city street.

So, if it was specific and deliberate, that left me or the girl.

I reminded myself that Kevin Fletcher had never come back to reassure me that my name was not on a butcher's order in Cardiff.

Had I been too quick to dismiss the possibility of a Professor Moriarty?

I set the mental sieve finer and went back over my past cases. I had been involved in a number of murder investigations that had resulted in prosecution and a subsequent life sentence for the perp. But why target me? I had always been part of a team. It had never come down to me being the one brilliant brain that had brought the bastards to justice. No convicted murderer had ever screamed, *I'll get you, Capaldi*, across a shocked court-room as they dragged him from the dock.

What about the ones I had booked who had died?

Two suicides, one on remand, one inside after sentencing, both of them clinically depressed junkies already well on their way down the dead-end road. One serial car thief who had received his moment of illumination in prison, when the sharpened end of a toothbrush had been rammed into his ear to let him know that he hadn't been as hard as he had thought he was. The kiddie molester who had jumped off a railway bridge to get away from me just as the delayed 9.13 to Swansea was coming through.

And Nick Bessant. The pimp who a farmer had executed for desecrating his son and his daughter. The farmer I had led to Bessant's lair in Cardiff, thinking I was doing something for justice and common humanity. Which was the reason that I was at this moment sitting in a cold, damp caravan in the middle of the boondocks looking out the window in the hope of seeing the return of a small fucking bird.

It was impossible to believe. No one could have mourned any of those trashed-up lives that much. Okay, they had mothers. But I didn't think that love or tenderness could have been anywhere in the air at the moment they were being fucked into existence.

And even if one of them had someone who was carrying a torch for their memory, it was way too sophisticated for that world. If they had stooped to revenge it would have been boiled-down battery acid in the side of the face, or a bunch of hired scagheads with pickaxe handles. Something course and mean and demonstrative.

It was a jaundiced view, but I was feeling blue and bitter, and my excuse for it was twofold. First, someone had tried to kill me, and secondly, I now had to let these low-rent bastards back into my thought process again.

EDGAR FISKE!

The name crash-landed on my consciousness. A name I hadn't even run past idle recollection in years. Edgar Fiske had once threatened to kill me.

But it had had nothing to do with me being a cop. When had it been? I racked my memory. But he was back in my head now, looming up too close to make out background details like time or place. A thin-faced young man with short curly sandy hair, freckles, and thick-rimmed tortoiseshell glasses actually quivering on the bridge of his nose as his anger boiled tears and flecks of spit out of him.

I am going to destroy you, Capaldi. I don't care how fucking long it takes. One day you're going to know what it's like to die.

It was uncanny. I wasn't even paraphrasing. They had come back to me after all these years. The very words he had used.

3

I reached for the phone. But it had been so long since I had called that I had to fetch my diary and look up the long number.

'*Pronto!*' A confident young girl's voice.

I had two nieces. I hazarded a guess. 'Graziella?'

'*Si.*' A hesitancy.

'*Ehi, e Zio Glyn da Galles.*'

The receiver clattered down. I heard the receding cry, 'Mama . . .' as she ran away.

I had often wondered whether, if my parents had given me an Italian name, I might have made my home in my father's old country, like my sister Paola. Something rolling like Giancarlo. Waving to all and sundry in my silk suit in the sun in the piazza sucking up spaghetti con vongole, instead of my single-syllable Brythonic moniker pre-destining me to grey skies and scrub-topped hills.

Paola lived in a village above San Remo with her husband

Roberto, a plumber who hated me. I had never found a reason for that hatred, which both my sister and my mother, trying to keep extended family cracks smoothed over, told me I was imagining. The only thing I could pin it on was that I had once informed him in a spirit of bonhomie that Paola and I used to share a bath as children.

'Naked!' His reaction had surprised me.

And it should have warned me not to respond with a quip, that underwear only got in the way of soaping down the fundamentals.

Whatever it had been, Roberto had inculcated a terror of me in his children, so that Graziella's reaction hadn't come as a surprise.

'Glyn!' I don't know whether it was the richness of her adopted language, but Paola managed to put a lot of expression into merely saying my name. Like anxiety and *What the fuck are you calling for?*

'Hi, Paola, you all right?'

'How's Mum?' she asked anxiously. As usual, she couldn't imagine a call from me without an image of our mother face-first at the bottom of the stairs, or straining to hear the last hopeless echo of the defibrillator.

'She's fine.'

Even over the phone I felt her de-stress. 'I was sorry to hear about the accident.'

'Thanks, but I'm fine now.'

'Mum says you're on convalescent leave?' She was probing. The worry being that I might be trying to swing some Mediterranean recuperation, and she was already preparing herself for Roberto's reaction.

I put her out of her misery. 'Do you remember a guy called Edgar Fiske?'

'Edgar Fiske? What on earth brings him up?'

'He was stalking you at teacher training college?'

She gave a small laugh. 'Well, *stalking* is putting it a bit strong.'

'That's the word you used. When you came home once and told me about it. You were really upset, said you couldn't say anything to Mum or Dad.'

'Glyn, I don't really remember that, and what's it got to do with anything now?'

I had hoped for a more sinister recall from her, but I ploughed on anyway. 'Colin Forbes, my friend from Splottlands?'

'I remember Colin. What about him?'

'We went over to Bath and sorted it out for you.'

'Sorted what out?' she asked, puzzled.

I felt that it was time to add a rider. 'I was eighteen. I wasn't very subtle in those days. My social skills weren't too highly developed.'

'Tell me about it,' she chuckled. 'But what did you sort out?'

'Didn't you ever wonder why he didn't bother you again?'

'I got a new boyfriend.' She paused. 'Are you trying to tell me something different?'

I winced at the crassness of the memory. Feeling the shame now in the retelling. 'We boot-polished his private parts and took a Polaroid photograph and told him we'd post it on the student noticeboard if he didn't leave you alone.'

'Glyn!' she screeched. 'How could you? That was horrible.'

'It worked,' I protested righteously.

'No it didn't. Going out with a rugby player worked.'

I didn't try to correct her. 'Have you any idea where Edgar Fiske is now?'

'Why? Are you going to apologize?'

I thought of the set-up in the Scots pine stand. 'I think it may have gone past the time for an apology.'

'I think you should. God, Glyn, that was such a horrible thing to do. Poor Edgar.' She was silent for a moment. 'Edgar and his partner Michael are running a little gallery and tea room in Yeovil. You'll find him in the telephone book.'

'Edgar Fiske is gay?' I asked, surprised.

'Of course. That's why he was pretending to be interested in me at college. He didn't want the trainee PE teachers finding out and making his life a misery.'

A tea room in Yeovil? Suddenly it looked as though Edgar Fiske had lost his sting.

Okay, gay men could be vindictive too. But not usually if their life had settled into a comfortable and contented pattern, which would appear to be the case with Edgar Fiske.

Back to square one. With Edgar Fiske disposed of, there was really no one I could think of out there with a big enough grudge against me.

Was I going to have to consider Jessie Bullock again?

No. It couldn't be. I shook my head to reinforce it. She was an eighteen-year-old girl from the foothills. The Mid Wales equivalent of fucking Heidi. And the Heidis of this world didn't draw down the wrath of professional snipers.

Now that I was home, had no pied wagtail, and had run up against another brick wall, I found that I wasn't yet ready for the isolation. I didn't want to be here alone when the night came down.

Dinas, the town that Jack Galbraith had exiled me to, hadn't quite achieved the tourist bonanza it had hoped for when it had promoted itself as having more abandoned Primitive Methodist chapels per head of population than anywhere else. Consequently the Chamber of Commerce was currently debating whether to give up on failed religion and to try and ride the coat-tails of the town's dead lead-mining legacy instead. It was that kind of vibrancy that kept the tumbleweed moving.

I bought some basic foodstuffs in the convenience store and made my way to The Fleece across the empty market square, past the Victorian gothic clock tower, and the statue of a shepherd with a tilted traffic cone on his head.

The Fleece had been a coaching inn until a smarter and more enterprising town had stepped in and pinched the mail trade. The place now doubled up as my unofficial city desk and recreational centre. Its owners, David and Sandra Williams, who had both spent some time out in the wider world, were also the nearest things I had to best buddies in Dinas without feathers.

I went in through the door to the rear bar. It was early, and the place was quiet enough for David to be making a show of polishing glasses behind the front bar. He held one up to the light with the scrutiny of an ever-hopeful opal miner.

I saw myself in the mirror behind the bar. My gait was still stiff, and the jolting motion it produced, combined with my discoloured, unshaven face and the plastic carrier bag of groceries, gave me the look of an old lush on automatic pilot treading the well-worn nightly path to the beer tap.

I sent out a silent prayer for this to please not be the future I was seeing.

David turned round. He did a jerky double-take when he saw me. 'Jesus, Glyn . . .' He ducked his head into the service entry between the two bars and yelled, 'Sandra!' He emerged smiling. 'We weren't expecting you. You should have called and I'd have come over and got you.'

'Thanks, but I need the practice.'

He took a step backwards and appraised me, following it up with a wince. 'You're not a great advert for the health service.'

'Don't knock it, you should have seen the *before* pictures.' I climbed stiffly onto a bar stool.

He started pulling me a beer and looked at me seriously. 'We were all fucking devastated, you know that.'

I nodded. 'Thanks for the card.' It had been signed by David and Sandra and their cat, and by two of the old regulars who had probably thought they were putting their names to a petition to repeal the Corn Laws.

'We would have come up to the hospital, but Emrys Hughes said you weren't allowed visitors.'

I smiled ruefully. 'They didn't want Joe Public seeing the levels of luxury and excess their taxes were keeping me in.'

He chuckled and let it run out to a questioning expression. 'Do you want to talk about it?'

I lifted the pint glass he slipped across the bar. 'I'm not going to avoid it.' I took a drink. It tasted good, and it helped me avoid it for the time being.

'Glyn!'

I swung round on the stool to see Sandra coming through from the kitchen, her apron balled into one hand. She caught me into a hug, her cheek pressing tightly against me. I smelled old shampoo and cooking oil in her hair.

She pulled back to look at me. She had tears in her eyes. 'It's so good to see you home again in one piece.'

The door to the front bar opened, interrupting the return-of-the-prodigal tableau. Four young-farmer types entered in a whirl of noise and motion. One by one their sweeping glances lit on me, and their animation wilted. It was as if all the juice had been suddenly sucked out of their batteries. They stared at me like they were one entity for a moment, before carrying on to the bar in whisper mode.

David moved away to serve them. Sandra was watching me anxiously. 'I gather there's been talk?' I quipped, trying to lighten the moment.

'It'll pass. They just need something to gossip about.' She touched my hand comfortingly.

Right, until the next time I was seen to fuck up. I had been in this situation before. As an outsider I made a convenient Jonah. Why blame global warming when you had me in town?

I took my beer over to a corner table.

'How are you doing, Capaldi?'

He startled me. I spun in my chair to see Emrys Hughes standing over me, a sheepish smile on his face.

He looked awkward. Trying not to shuffle from one foot to the other. I had an image of this shambling bear of a man crowded into a small lift with a posse of diminutive female

Chinese acrobats, knowing that any movement of his was going to nudge tit. If he had been feeling guilty for being partly instrumental in what had happened to me I could have felt sorry for him. But I didn't credit him with that degree of sensitivity. What was probably cutting him up was having to be in my proximity now that I was even more of a social leper.

He put an envelope down on the table. 'This was left for you. I've been holding onto it.'

Sergeant Capaldi. The handwriting was neat, cursive, and probably female. 'Thanks. You could have dropped it off at the caravan.'

He pulled a face. On reflection, I think it was meant to be sympathetic. 'It might be hate mail. I wouldn't have wanted you coming home and this being one of the first things you found.'

I smiled up at him. 'Thanks, Emrys.' What was the deal? I asked myself. My wellbeing didn't usually loom too large in Emrys's repertoire.

Then it struck me. Seeing the anticipation in his face. He knew who had written this. He wanted to be in attendance when I read it. He wanted to watch my reaction. He and his cronies probably had some sort of sweepstake running.

He made no move to go. 'Thanks, Emrys,' I repeated.

He still didn't budge, his smile frozen in place. 'Emrys?' I said quietly.

'What?' He bent forward to hear me better.

'If you don't fuck off now I'm going to thank you very loudly for sending me the sweet flowers and then stand up and give you a great big kiss on the lips.'

44

His head shot back like a sprung trap. He coloured. 'You don't have to be like that, I was only trying to do you a favour,' he said crossly.

I waited until he had left the bar before I opened the envelope. It was a card with a printed header, but I honed straight in on the handwritten message.

Dear Sergeant Capaldi,
I hope that your injuries are not too extensive, and that your time in hospital will be short. This is just to let you know that I hold you in no way responsible for the tragic accident that has resulted in the loss of my daughter Jessie.
Wishing you a speedy recovery.
Yours,
Cassandra Bullock

Jesus! I put the card down carefully on the table to mask my emotions. I started to get teary. Torn up by the fact that this woman could have taken time out in the middle of her grief and devastation to write this. To comfort me. A stranger.

And that's when it came to me. The catalyst that snapped me out of my egocentricity. What I had missed seeing. What my self-centredness had blinkered.

Forget Edgar Fiske. Forget the convicted murderers and the dead lags. Forget Nick Bessant.

I had overlooked the facts that made it impossible for me to have been the target.

Which meant that they had been out to kill Jessie Bullock.

Maybe not Jessie precisely. I pulled back and rejigged it. I gave it more thought and revised the specificity down.

45

Maybe the target had been more general, like whoever I had ended up carrying in the back of the car.

But definitely not me. Because, once I'd ditched the persecution complex and thought about it analytically, I had to conclude that I couldn't have been the target. Okay, so Morgan's so-called security blanket hadn't been exactly tightly banded with razor wire. In fact, it had been as leaky as a spiked hose. So anyone who had been at all interested would probably have known that I was part of the operation. But they couldn't have anticipated the role I ended up giving myself.

Because what was crucial was that my offering to transport Jessie had been an opportunistic whim. When they had set up that gun in the stand of Scots pines they had no way of knowing that it would have been me driving. What they could presume was that the operation would produce at least one kid travelling to Dinas in the rear of a police car. They didn't care who the driver was, it was the passenger they were after.

I returned to Jessie again. Was she a random victim? Or had it been somehow arranged that night that she would be the one that we caught? I couldn't answer that. I left it hanging. Hopefully at some point I would find a hook for it.

And this all now made terrible sense of things. The locked rear door, the fastened seat belt. Whoever had created the accident must have taken her out of the car and cold-bloodedly broken her neck and flung her away like an abandoned manikin.

I felt a chill creep over me. What would have happened if I hadn't been unconscious? Would they have broken my neck too? Or torched us both in the car? Because those people were after only one consequence and I was certain that they wouldn't have hesitated to kill me if I had gotten in the way of it.

Who could do that to someone who wasn't much more than a child? What kind of person could shut down all humane and nurturing instincts like that? What kind of training in the poisoned arts could produce that kind of soul?

The corollary intruded. What the fuck could she have done in her short country life to warrant such a dreadful reprisal?

I looked at the card her mother had sent me again. The printed heading read *The Ap Hywel Foundation*. I knew I was going to have to visit Cassandra Bullock. I only hoped that she was going to remain as generous and forgiving when she saw me in the flesh.

I got up early the next morning, dragging all my protesting stiffness out of bed in the dark. I shaved for the first time in days, watching my face reappear in the steamy mirror. I stared at myself. Had I changed? I felt that I was underscoring a new start. The old lush was setting aside his torpor.

I needed some background before I met up with Cassandra Bullock, and had arranged to meet PC Huw Davies at the car park at the start of the Monks' Trail where we had arrested Jessie.

I arrived deliberately early. I wanted to have some time there alone. It was an area that had been cleared, levelled and gravelled at the foot of a wooded hillside. It looked bigger in the daylight, but that might have had something to do with the paucity of traffic and activity compared to

47

that night. There were three empty cars parked at random intervals around the perimeter, along with the junked car I had seen before.

The sun hadn't cleared the hill to the east, and the air was cool and damp and smelled of leaf mould and ferns. I circled the car park on foot. The waymarked trail started at the far end, rising up and curving away through the sessile oaks. I returned to the information board and experienced a sense of disappointment, although I didn't know what I had been expecting.

I couldn't bring myself to read the historical and bio-diversity notes on the board. There were illustrations of birds, insects and flora, and the graphics showed the trail winding up through the woods, past a pool and waterfall, and onto the ridgeway above the village of Llandewi. A smaller-scale inset map showed the entire length of the trail traversing the Cambrians and bifurcating to join up with other long-distance footpaths. It made me wonder where the occupants of those three parked cars were now. There was something inviting in the prospect of losing yourself up there in all that space and sky.

Huw Davies turned up dead on time in his marked police Land Rover.

'Sarge.' He nodded and I could see him appraising me for damage.

'Thanks for this, Huw.' I shook his outstretched hand. I had already warned him that this was unofficial. 'Ever walk the trail?' I gestured at the information board, kicking off on small talk.

He shook his head. 'I leave that to the leisured classes.'

'I thought you liked being out in the wild wide-open?'

'I do.' He nodded towards the start of the trail at the far end of the car park. 'But this is channelled. It's the safe path through the jungle. All marked out to make sure you don't trespass. I prefer to spoof it.' He smiled wryly. 'It's a load of sanitized bullshit, you know.'

'What is?'

'Starting the Monks' Trail from here.'

'Why?'

'Because it's a recorded historical fact that the track the monks used to use came from the coast and passed through the village of Llandewi on its way up to the ridgeway and on over the mountains.'

'Why did they change it?'

He shrugged. He still hadn't dropped that wry smile. 'A cynic would say it's because Llandewi didn't fit the image they wanted to project.'

'Not pretty enough?'

'The place is a mess now. Totally depressed. The way all these communities go when the lifeblood gets sucked out of them. In Llandewi's case, it was the sawmill closing down about ten years ago.'

I made a point of looking up at the trees. 'I would have thought that there was still plenty of product around.'

'Not for construction timber. The stuff from Canada and the Baltic's undercut them. The local softwood's all carted off to the pulp mills now.'

'So, the place sounds ripe for juvenile crime?' I offered, getting down to it at last.

He pulled a face. 'You'd think so. But they're an apathetic

bunch round here. And everyone's in the same boat, no one's got anything worth nicking.'

'What about the thefts that happened in the car park here that Morgan's cronies got so worked up about?'

He turned sombre. 'After what happened that night I leaned on the local bad boys and they've all denied it. And I believe them.'

'And we know it wasn't Morgan's marauding city hoodlums?' I left it as a question.

'It's stopped now, Sarge.'

I gestured for him to go on.

'Since the raid, there have been no more vehicle break-ins or vandalism.'

We both looked at each other carefully. I voiced the conclusion behind his statement. 'You don't think Jessie Bullock had been responsible for the previous ones? On her own?'

'I can't answer that. Maybe whoever was behind it got frightened off.'

'Was she a troublemaker?'

He shook his head loosely. 'I'd seen her around. But only as a face on my patch. She'd never come up on my radar before.'

'Tell me about the stuff that happened here.'

'Essentially it was all low-grade. They weren't after nicking the cars themselves, or even things like the alloy wheels or the cycle racks. Windows got broken, and some stuff got nicked – CDs, floor mats, dangly mascots – the sort of silly useless shit that gets left in cars. The kind of things that were worthless, but could have been taken as souvenirs or trophies.

50

The only thing of any real value that was ever taken was a portable satnav. And some of the cars got things spray-painted on them.'

'Such as?'

'*Property is theft,* was a favourite.'

I shared his smile. 'You got any anarchists or radical Marxists in Llandewi?'

'Not that I know of, and definitely not among the baseball-cap brigade.'

'Jessie Bullock was obviously an intelligent kid. Could she have politicized the local bad boys?'

'I told you, she'd never come up on my radar. When kids like her start hanging out with the rough, I make a note of it. It didn't happen with her.'

'It has to be local though?'

'I agree. But it was all juvenile stuff, Sarge. That's what I tried to tell Inspector Morgan. This was kids posturing. It didn't warrant shock and awe tactics.'

'Any chance of getting sight of the reports on the car park break-ins?' I asked.

'I'll email the file references to you.'

'What about the names of the local bad boys?' I tried.

He shook his head. 'Sorry.' He took pity on my expression and elaborated: 'You're meant to be on sick leave, Sarge. I don't want you to get into trouble.'

'Thanks, Huw.' We both left the name Inspector Morgan unsaid.

I watched him drive away. I knew I was procrastinating. Now I had nothing between me and my confrontation with

51

Cassandra Bullock. Except for the insurance policy that the coward in me had built in. I had never called her to arrange the meeting. There was a chance, which a part of me was clutching at, that she wouldn't be available.

As a cop I was used to difficult encounters. That sombre walk down a hallway as you wondered how you were going to be able to tell a mother that her husband had gassed himself and their two young children in his car. Or getting parents to sit down as you attempted to prepare them for the awful fact that the body of their toddler son had been found in a river snarled in the roots of a tree. But never before had I had to face the mother of a young girl whose death I had been partly responsible for. Because, even if my third-party hypothesis was correct, I had to accept that I had been the one who had delivered her to that final appointment.

I drove away from the tree shade of the car park and out into the sun. It was a glorious morning, but it didn't help Llandewi. Huw had been right. The village was a mess, and the sunlight only highlighted the faults.

It was a linear village, curving along the base of the hill, and the state of some of the buildings gave the impression that they had slipped down from a higher point on the slope and never recovered from the journey. The place bore all the marks of neglect, an all-pervading sense of *why bother*. Roofs with missing or slipped slates, walls cracked and algae stained, peeling paintwork and a few faded people on the street staring at me listlessly as I passed. And, the saddest sight of all, the local pub boarded up.

I turned left out of the village and started the drive up into the hills. The full glare of the sun was in my face, it was an angel's ascent, and I left Llandewi mouldering behind me. I drove between stone field walls and rumbled across the cattle grid where the estate wall started on my left, and the land opened out on my right into unfenced scrub and heather moorland that rolled up to the ridge, the hillside sprigged with the occasional gale-tormented hawthorn.

Huw had shown me the route on the map and described what to look out for. But I was still unprepared for the gates to the Plas Coch estate. The Ap Hywel pile, as he had put it, with just a trace of class-warrior irony. The lichen-flecked grey stone piers were massive and capped with pineapple finials on ornately moulded capstones. But it was the gates themselves that made me stop. They were a contemporary take on early Georgian ironwork, but powder-coated the blue-green of copper sulphate. Architecturally it had been a risk, but it worked. The whole thing declared money, taste and artistic daring. What a contrast to Llandewi.

I carried on as instructed until I reached the end of the estate wall, and another entrance, more modest this time, with *Home Farm* picked-out on slate on a gatepost, and *The Ap Hywel Foundation* inscribed into a brass plaque beneath it.

I turned into the driveway and my nervousness began a scampering arpeggio up the scale. I felt like I was arriving with an undigested anvil in my gut.

I went down a neat gravel track that was lined with young chestnuts, following an undulating line of rhododendrons on my left that delineated the grounds of the big house. The track was descending gently and I soon saw a long slate roof and the tops of deciduous woodland behind it. This would be the Home Farm, and I knew from the map that the trees were part of the same woods that rose up from the car park.

The track widened out into a big gravel turning area in front of an exquisitely maintained whitewashed stone long-house. But I didn't have time to take it in properly as I had arrived unannounced into activity.

I parked and tried to work out what was happening before I got out of my car and made a fool of myself.

Two women were sitting in front of the entrance door to the farmhouse at a rectangular wooden picnic bench with an open parasol over it. A man with a camera raised to his eye was backing away from the table at a crouch, taking photographs as he went. A younger woman in a short red coat was standing off to the side, and, as I watched, I saw that she was directing both the women's actions, and the photographer's positions.

Had I crashed a fashion shoot?

I took a more studied look at the women at the table. The older one grabbed the immediate attention. The lines on her face and the heavy mane of silvery grey hair worn in a loose and careless chignon betrayed her to be probably in her sixties, but she was strikingly handsome, her features radiating a combination of confidence and humour and just something in the corner of her eyes that made you think that she might be holding in more knowledge than she was letting out.

Was she too old to have had an eighteen-year-old daughter?

The other woman was slighter, probably more than twenty years younger, her un-styled hair still dark, her sharp features

54

heightened by the small, round, wire-rimmed glasses she wore, and the way she screwed her face, as if she was over-compensating for lenses that weren't quite working any more.

It was the older woman who saw me watching them. She nudged her neighbour, and, when she had her attention, nodded towards me. I felt immediately guilty. By the time I was out of the car both of the women at the bench were standing and the photographer and the younger woman had stopped in place and were looking at me.

I dragged a voice up out of my dry throat. 'I'm sorry to interrupt. I'm looking for Cassandra Bullock.'

'I'm Cassie Bullock,' the younger of the two women at the bench spoke, a quick anxious glance at her companion, her tone apprehensive.

That anvil was still there pinning me to the spot. I closed my eyes. I couldn't help it. The silence was rapt, electricity fried the air. 'I'm Detective Sergeant Glyn Capaldi.' *I killed your daughter.*

55

4

Cassie Bullock poured me a glass of water from a jug on the picnic table. I had already registered the deep shadows around her eyes. Only now did it click that she was dressed all in black, a lamb's wool sweater over tight leggings.

The older woman had taken charge as soon as I had introduced myself. 'I'm Ursula ap Hywel,' she had announced, getting up and approaching, putting herself between me and Cassie, a protective block, her hand held out to shake. 'I live over there —' her gesture casually encompassing the vastness of her estate.

I shook the proffered hand. 'I'm sorry to interrupt. And I don't know whether this is a bad time . . .?' I suggested, part of me wanting her to tell me that it was.

Instead she turned her head to Cassie. 'Is it?' she asked gently.

Cassie shook her head almost imperceptibly. She spoke past Ursula, a small tremor in her voice. 'It's very kind of you to come, Sergeant.'

And now we were alone, Ursula ap Hywel having retreated diplomatically, efficiently shepherding the other two along with her. Back to the big house, I supposed. But, before she had led them off, she had taken me aside and whispered, 'Be kind. She's putting on a brave face, but she's still very fragile.'

I took a grateful drink of the water.

'You look as if you needed that,' Cassie observed.

'More than you know.'

'I did mean what I said in my note. I don't blame you in any way.' She held those dark-rimmed eyes on me as if she were trying to force herself not to look away.

'That was very kind of you.'

'I imagined how terrible you'd be feeling.'

'I was. That's why I felt that I had to come and tell you to your face how dreadfully sorry I feel for your loss.'

Her eyes flickered and she waited me out for a moment. 'And . . .?' she asked softly, sensing the incompleteness in my declaration.

I steeled myself. 'The *and* is the difficult bit.'

She nodded as if she understood. Or was she still numbed by grief and working on automatic responses? 'Come inside. I'll make us some tea.'

I gestured at the photo-shoot props on the table: the jug of water, glasses and a bowl of fruit, apples and bananas. 'Shall I help you carry these in?'

'Thanks, but they stay outside.' She managed a small smile at my flicker of puzzlement. 'You don't know about the Foundation?'

I shook my head. 'No, sorry.'

'You know you're on the Monks' Trail?' she asked.

'I know about the footpath, I didn't realize I was actually on it.' I sensed that we were both relieved by this temporary diversion.

She stood up. I got the impression that she was forcing herself to stand erect, when all she really wanted to do was fold up and crumple. I followed her out into the turning circle, from where we could see both ends of the house. 'The path from the car park comes up through the woods over there—' she pointed as she described, 'and then runs past the front of the house, and carries on up over there. It's a very old trail. It was one of the ones Cistercian monks from the mother house at Clairvaux used to use to travel between the coast and their satellite abbeys in Mid Wales.'

I nodded attentively. I didn't spoil the moment by mentioning that I had been told that the route had been diverted and prettified.

'Well, we think that the original building up here at Plas Coch was built by the monks as a shelter or a hostel on the route. A sort of way station. So, we're just continuing that tradition.' She nodded at the picnic table. 'We provide the basics for passing travellers to help themselves to. Usually it's produce from our own gardens, but we're a little bit short at this time of year.' She tried out what she thought was a laugh. 'And we never quite run to bananas.'

'You work for the Foundation?'

'Yes, I'm sort of the housekeeper and warden.'

'You keep the table stocked?'

She produced another warped laugh. 'There's a bit more to it than that. We run a retreat here. But we're not affiliated to anything in the religious sense. People come and stay for some non-denominational spiritual healing.' She walked back to the door. 'Come inside and I'll show you round after we've had that tea.'

'I'm not intruding?'

Her tour-guide persona dropped and she looked at me solemnly for a moment. 'No, I think we both need this.'

She pushed open the low, wide oak front door, and stood aside to let me through. I stopped on the threshold, adjusting to the surprise. Instead of the dark hallway I had expected it was a fully vaulted space with a red-and-black tiled floor and flooded with light from the two-storey glazed bay at the far end that gave out onto a formal knot garden, edged with low clipped box hedges, that filled an inner courtyard formed by a cloistered arrangement of glazed and timber-boarded, single-storey contemporary buildings. It was a similar sort of architectural juggling as the gates at Plas Coch.

She led me through to a comfortable stone-flagged kitchen, explaining that this was her private quarters. I heard the hesitation as she suppressed the word *our*. Another adjustment she was having to practise without cracking-up.

'How long have you been working here?' I asked as she busied herself with a kettle at the Rayburn.

'Fifteen years.'

So Jessie would have been nearly three, I calculated silently.

'You can talk about her, Sergeant,' she read my thoughts, 'that's what we're here for.'

'Please, call me Glyn.'

She nodded. 'Ursula tells me that it's good for me to talk about her. That I've got to celebrate that she had a presence on this earth.' She closed her eyes forcefully. 'It's so very difficult to think of her life as something that's over. Stopped.' Her knuckles went white on the handle of the kettle.

I waited for the tears. 'Shall I go?' I asked softly.

She shook her head, opened her eyes and forced a wan smile. 'No, I've got to start adjusting to this.' She unclenched her hand and went on as if I had already asked the question: 'Yes, Jessie grew up here. She had no real memory of anywhere else.'

'Where were you before?'

'London. A single mother. Despairing about my future, and then a wonderful piece of serendipity arrived. I was introduced to the ap Hywels, who were starting up the Foundation and were looking for someone to help them run the Welsh side of it.'

'The Welsh side?' I asked.

'We've also got health clinics in Sierra Leone.' She spread her arms to take in the kitchen. 'I got this, and the rest is history.'

'I don't mean to be indelicate . . .'

She looked at me questioningly.

'Jessie's father?'

She let a reflective beat pass. 'Dead, I'm afraid.'

We sat there drinking tea and eating biscuits with the photograph albums in front of us and she told me the tales behind the pictures, seeming to relax into the memories as the pages turned over. Jessie's life at the Home Farm. The guinea pigs, rabbits and ponies. The first days at school, the nativity angel, followed by promotion from first shepherd to the Virgin Mary. The picnics by the pool below the waterfall and on the moors, the beaches at Newport and

Aberdovey. Jessie the child, growing up from skinny stagger-stepping topless and gap-toothed, to a serious, attractive young woman getting ready to move out into the wider world.

'I wish I had taken a little time to know her,' I said regretfully.

'You might not have liked her.'

'No?' I asked, surprised.

'She was at a wilful age. I'm afraid we argued quite a bit. It's one of my real deep regrets now.' She smiled ruefully. 'The young think that we've never been their age. I was looking forward to her getting out there, finding her feet and mellowing. And then coming home and us becoming friends again.' She fought back the tears.

'I'm so sorry.'

She put her hand over mine briefly, sniffled and managed a weak smile. 'Don't be; we can't stop the things that are meant to happen.' She shifted her hand to the cover of one of the photograph albums. 'As Ursula continually reminds me, I've got all these wonderful memories. I want you to fix these happier times in your mind, and take them away with you as well.'

I nodded. 'Why do you think she was down there that night?'

Her face went rigid and she stared at me before she slowly started to nod. 'We've come round to the *and*, haven't we?'

'You don't have to talk about it.'

She studied me again. 'But you do, don't you?'

I nodded again.

She was contemplative. I thought for a moment that she wasn't going to answer me. 'I don't know why she would

61

have been down there on that particular night. It wasn't unusual though. The pool and the waterfall are just above the car park. That was one of their favourite spots.'

'They?'

'She had lots of friends. She was a popular girl.'

'It was raining that night.'

She gave a slanted smile, another memory had returned. 'They were youngsters. They didn't care.'

'Did she have a boyfriend?'

'She had friends who were boys. I don't think she had learned the patience to work at a steady relationship yet.'

'Would you be prepared to give me a list of Jessie's friends?'

She thought about it for a moment before she leaned across the table towards me. 'No, Glyn, I wouldn't,' she said softly. 'They've all been dreadfully hurt as well. I think it's time to put a line under it and leave them to heal.' She scanned my face. 'Why is this so important to you?'

I had tried to rehearse this moment. I had anticipated the question and experimented on the soft lies to answer it. But now that it came to it I felt that I owed this woman the truth. 'This is only my own opinion,' I warned her. 'There will not be any kind of official investigation into this.'

She gestured for me to go on. She was frowning now.

'I think that there's a possibility that Jessie's death wasn't an accident.'

I waited for the shock. I waited for anger or incredulity. Instead she stood up and slowly walked to the window and remained there with her back to me.

'Cassie?'

She turned round. Even backlit as she was I could make out the tracks the tears had coursed down both her cheeks.

'Are you all right?'

She nodded tentatively. 'I don't want to talk about it. All I want to say is that living here has taught me that there is no such thing as the unexpected. We're too small in the chain to begin to understand the reasons behind things. We're too limited. All we can see is ourselves at the fulcrum point, and that's a distorted view. I want you to ponder on that, Glyn, and to try to take some comfort out of it.'

Fucking bullshit!

But of course I kept that to myself.

Cassie recovered her composure and showed me Jessie's room. I think I was expected to take comforting vibes from it, rather than look for clues of malice. But I couldn't get a real feel for it without ransacking it, and that wasn't on the cards with Cassie beside me, nervously straightening the covers and the battered teddy bears on the bed. Going through another one of her self-imposed therapy sessions, I realized.

Superficially I picked up that her music tastes ran to Indie bands, and her bookshelves showed a certain age progress, ranging from an anthology of famous ballerinas, the entire J.K. Rowling canon, the Brontë sisters, to edgier stuff by Palahniuk and Houellebecq. No evidence of radical Marxism in the collection, although there was the famous poster of Che Guevara on the wall, which was balanced to a degree by one of Johnny Depp. And no visible dope paraphernalia or extreme counter-culture memorabilia. There were five dusty wooden African statuettes on top of the bookshelf, the sort of tat that was sold in market stalls across tourist Europe.

I wouldn't know an ordinary teenager if they parachuted into my soup, but Jessie, from this evidence, seemed to fit into the spectrum. But what had I expected? Death threats written in blood pinned to her corkboard beside a crumpled photograph of the netball team?

I pleaded pressure of work and turned down Cassie's invitation of a tour of the rest of the Foundation. Something told me it would be useful for her not to know that I was currently off active duty.

I drove back up the farm track to the road thinking that I was no closer to knowing why Jessie could have been the target of a hit. That level of violence was just all too far removed from this neat corner of loving rural tranquillity.

The woman was standing in the middle of the drive as I approached the exit onto the road. She didn't try to flag me down. She knew I would stop. She stood there with her hands in the pockets of her short red duffel coat, a self-satisfied smile on her face that wasn't far off qualifying as a smirk.

'Hi, Glyn, I'm Rhian Pritchard.' She had moved round to my window after I had stopped the car, and, as a gentleman, I had lowered it. She put her hand in and I automatically shook it. If I had known what was about to go down, I would have said fuck politeness, put my foot down, and driven off.

I had recognized her. She was the one who had been directing the photographer. She had blonde hair tied into a high arcing ponytail, which, with the red duffel coat and skinny jeans with turn-ups, made her look in her mid twenties, although she was probably older. Her face was pale, like someone who didn't get too much sun and wind with their daylight, but its geometry was pleasant, a composition of complementary curves to the cheeks and the chin, and a good nose that would probably flare when she laughed. But that irritating smile really fucked up the shape of her mouth.

'Nice to meet you.' I gave her my dumb-cop smile. I reckoned she was one of those people it was best to start out on the bottom rung with. Let them lead with their preconceptions.

She gestured her head back towards the Home Farm. 'Is this business?'

'I can't say, I'm afraid.'

'You're a long way from Cardiff, aren't you?' Her smile didn't waver.

'What makes you say that?'

She passed me a business card. *Rhian A. Pritchard, Freelance Feature and Investigative Journalist*, it read above a Cardiff address and an NUJ membership reference. 'I did some research while I was waiting for you to finish up with Cassie.' She mimed typing with two fingers. 'A little bit of Google here, a little bit Cardiff press contacts there.'

And still that fucking smile. 'Why would you want to do that?' I asked, struggling to keep it dumb and pleasant.

'This is a PR gig, it's boring. A puff piece. How wonderful is the Ap Hywel Foundation and all who fucking sail in her. I could do with working on something with a bit of meat on it while I'm up here. Like what is a hero from Cardiff doing swanning around with the rednecks?'

I tried out a firm manly smile. 'No thanks. Not interested.'

'It'll make a good story. Human interest. Tough city cop

finds rural peace. Fuck!' She leaned her head back, inspired. 'If we could get a shot of you pulling out a lamb.'

'You've missed the season.'

'We'll think of something with an equal schmaltz rating.'

'No, we won't. And I've got to go.'

She picked up enough from my voice to step away before I drove over her toes. I caught her in my rear-view mirror as I turned onto the road. She was waving. That smile telling me that she had latched onto this and wasn't going away.

The last thing I needed. My Cardiff disgrace resurfacing.

Jack Galbraith would have me counting the puffins on Skomer Island.

Rhian Pritchard was going to be trouble. I could sense it. That face and attitude screamed devilish persistence, although she probably thought she was radiating cute pluck. She was a byline junkie. I had met the type before. Looking for a hot story under every pair of eyebrows, anything to swell the cuttings file that she hoped was going to land her that regular slot on a national magazine one day.

Why did our paths have to cross? Now she was out to use my head as a fucking career stepping stone and press me deeper into the ooze on the way.

I stacked her away in the groaning pile of future problems when I got back to Unit 13. I logged into my computer. Huw Davies had been true to his word and had emailed the file references to the break-ins and vandalism at the car park.

I opened them up. It was all dross. Huw had been right. This was all low-grade criminal activity. The worst thing that had been done had been the breaking of the cars' windows. And that was probably as much to do with vandalism as it was with the petty thefts, because they had never demonstrated any intention of stealing the vehicles. And, apart from one portable satnav, the list of the stuff that had been stolen was banal. A travel rug, CDs, a lucky tortoise mascot, an insulated coffee container . . . It went on in that vein. As Huw had said, trophies, junk to reinforce the memories of the outlaw trips.

Who was going to kill anyone for a portable satnav?

Cause and effect.

None of the shit that had been taken could possibly have been the cause that had led to the effect of Jessie's murder. None of those trinkets and baubles could have warranted anything as extreme as that.

Given the tat value of all the other stuff, I even idly wondered whether the reported satnav had actually been stolen, or if someone had used the opportunity to scam his insurance company.

That warped logic clicked on another step.

If someone could have reported something being stolen that hadn't been, what about something being stolen that hadn't been reported?

I felt the old familiar clutch in my kidneys as new possibilities opened up.

Something so valuable to its owner that the effect its loss had created was Jessie's death. Something so valuable and so illegal that its theft couldn't be recorded?

But what the fuck would something as precious as that be doing left in a car park in the middle of nowhere, frequented by mountain bikers and ramblers and the ghosts of dead monks?

I sidelined that question as irrelevant. It called for too much detailed information. What was important here was the concept. Something of value that couldn't be brought to the attention of the police after it had been stolen.

But why kill Jessie? What would be gained?

A punishment? Or to scare whoever was holding on to it to give it up?

Or had they already tried to get rid of it?

I got on the phone to Huw.

'A hypothetical question, Huw. You have a punter who is walking along a railway line and he comes across a parcel that has obviously fallen from a train. He looks inside and finds . . . Let's say a camera. An expensive camera, in its original packaging, no owner's name. So where does he take it?'

'If he's local, he brings it to me.'

'Let's say he's been away for a bit and picked up bad habits. And his wife's just given birth to triplets and he needs instant cash to buy disposable nappies and fags. Where would he take the hypothetical camera?'

'Why do you want to know?'

'I'm on sick leave remember, Huw. I'm keeping my mind active, researching cottage industries between jigsaws and sudoku.'

'Bullshit, Sarge.' But he laughed. 'You've met him.'

'I have?' I was surprised. I had no memories of any encounters with a neighbourhood fence.

'Yes, our boy Ryan.'

Ryan Shaw. The local low-rent dope dealer. 'Christ, Huw, is he a crook-of-all-trades? Renaissance Hoodie?'

I heard him laugh down the line. 'We don't have enough of the spread round here that you had in Cardiff that enables them to specialize.'

I thanked him and hung up. I had had one previous encounter with Ryan, and he had not been a very happy young hoodlum at the end of it. So much so that he had complained to Emrys Hughes. Because Ryan was also a local snitch.

He was protected. I was going to have to be careful how I approached him.

Orchard Close, Maesmore. Not much had changed. A supermarket trolley had joined the junk installation on the former front lawn outside number 3, Ryan's house, which he shared with his mother and sister and at least one baby that I knew of.

I was glad to see his purple VW Golf was creating its usual obstruction on the pavement. Because, as I had no official business to go knocking on that front door with, I was going to have to wait for Ryan to come out to me.

It was heavy dusk by now. I calculated the distance I needed and parked a few houses down, facing in the same direction as Ryan's car. I kept out of the pool of the street light. I didn't think that he would know my car, but I didn't want to take the chance. Curtains twitched in the house I was parked outside of, but I didn't let it worry me. If you lived near a dope dealer you got used to strange traffic, and usually you learned not to complain about it.

When it was dark enough I slid over to the passenger's side and got out of the car without closing the door. I had already de-activated the interior light. I checked that the street was empty in both directions before making my way up the pavement on the other side from Ryan's house until I was opposite his car. I checked the street again, and then flowed across it, sinking into a low Groucho Marx stride, and dropping to a crouch at the rear of the VW.

I tied the end of the string to the towing ring and bundled the rest of it with the attached tin cans under the car, out of sight. I made my way back to my car.

Now all I had to do was continue waiting. Ryan could do two things to fuck my plan up. He could decide to stay in for the night, or, if he did elect to go out, he could do a three-point turn and head off in the opposite direction to where I was waiting for him.

In the end he obliged me on both counts.

The night had cooled down to chilly, but he still appeared in just a tight white T-shirt and cinched black jeans to show-case his pumped physique. He got in his car, gunned the motor and headed down the road in my direction.

KLANG! KLANG! KLANG!

I had tied the tin cans to a four-metre-long piece of string, so by the time they started rattling, and he had reacted to what sounded like his straight-through exhaust trailing the ground, he was a couple of car lengths short of me when he stopped. As I had anticipated, he left his door wide open and the engine still running when he jumped out and ran to the rear to investigate his mechanical prolapse.

I glided up, switched off the engine and took the car keys out.

He was still snarled up in the confusion of the moment. He had found the cans. He heard his engine stop. There was too much happening here, and it took him a beat to react. When he did turn, I could tell that he hadn't recognized me in the dark.

'What the fuck . . .?' he growled threateningly, trying to make sense of this.

'Shouldn't leave your engine running like that, Ryan, it fucks up the atmosphere.'

Curtains were twitching all around like Aldis lamps. He stared at me malevolently. I could almost hear the tumblers in his brain clicking through the recognition process.

'You!' He pointed at me. 'You're fucked! You were warned off after the last time you tried to mess with me.'

'This is just between you and me, Ryan.'

'Says who?'

'If I thought you were going to report me, I wouldn't help you.'

He chuckled nastily. 'And how are you going to fucking help me?'

I dangled his car keys. 'You're going to have a hard time finding these otherwise.'

'That's fucking theft,' he whined indignantly.

'Which is exactly what I wanted to talk to you about.'

'Are you trying to fit me up?' he asked suspiciously, his mind shifting into another gear.

'No, I want your professional advice, that's all. You talk to me nicely, and I give you your keys back, and walk away.'

He digested it. Probably wondering what particular branch of his profession I was talking about. He nodded his head carefully. 'Okay. I'm not promising anything, mind.'

'Did you know Jessie Bullock?'

'Never heard of her.'

'Oh, come on, Ryan,' I snorted impatiently, 'she was only the biggest piece of fucking news around here since the glaciers retreated.'

He shrugged, unconcerned about being caught out in the lie. 'Okay, I might have heard the name.'

'Did she or any of her friends ever give you something to try and sell for them?'

He looked at me calculatingly. 'Like what?' He was trying to work out what I knew.

'Something valuable.'

He couldn't help himself. It was embedded in his nature to brag. It was only the tiniest twitch, but I caught it. He smothered it with a big faux doubtful frown and a shake of the head. 'Not that I remember.'

The bastard knew what I was talking about. I had my first small open chink into this thing. But what leverage was I going to be able to use on this guy to open it wider?

'Thanks, Ryan.' I tossed him the keys. 'Remember the deal.'

'Yeah. Thanks for nothing. And you can untie those fucking cans before you go.'

I complied. No point in upsetting him any further. Because, if I had my way, I was going to have a lot worse in store for him in the near future.

I even waved sweetly as he roared off.

5

As half expected, he finked on me.

Talk about honour among fucking thieves, I thought, as I listened to Inspector Morgan tearing me off a strip down the telephone line. But Morgan I could tune out. He had the whingeing drone of an ineffectual schoolteacher which whisked me in spirit back to the non-attentive zone at the rear of the classroom.

Jack Galbraith wasn't quite so easy to sideline.

'Sergeant Lazarus, I presume?'

'Sorry, Sir?' He also was on the phone, so I couldn't use his expression to gauge what was coming.

'Am I speaking to the man who miraculously got up off his sickbed and went out into the world to fool around with one of Inspector Morgan's stoolies?'

'I think Lazarus was raised from the dead, Sir.'

'Don't give me fucking ideas, Capaldi,' he growled. 'I detest talking to Morgan at the best of times, so having to listen through another rant from him about your transgressions is nudging my patience and tolerance into the red sector. What the fuck were you doing?'

'I've just been talking to local people who might have known Jessie Bullock, Sir. I think Sergeant Hughes misunderstood and over-reacted when he reported it to Inspector Morgan.'

'Hughes? Is that that idiot sergeant up there? The one that looks like a wax museum's take on Stalin, with the personality to match?'

Who was I to speak ill of a colleague? 'Yes, Sir.'

'Fucking prat.' He came back to me after a pause with a new note of reservation in his voice. 'This nosing around about the Bullock girl sounds a bit unhealthy to me.'

'It's helping me to come to terms with it, Sir. Rounding her out into a real person.'

'That helps?' He sounded sceptical.

'Yes, Sir.'

He gave it a reflective pause. 'If you're going to step on Hughes's toes, do it subtly for Christ's sake. Don't give him any excuse to run bleating to Morgan again. Just make sure you keep me out of that particular loop.'

'Yes, Sir.'

'And don't let your interest in the girl get obsessional.'

I promised that I wouldn't and decided it was time to put my head down and be a good boy for a couple of days.

Until Jessie's funeral service, to be exact.

Mackay turned up in the morning as we had arranged. Not very happy about it, but resigned to my intransigence. I knew he was trying to ease me through to the sunny side of a morbid phase he thought I was caught up in. So, while it was all about me, I had decided to take advantage.

He held the camera I had provided limply, and listened sulkily while I went over it again.

'Isn't it a bit sick, taking photographs at someone's funeral?' he complained.

'Come on, Mac,' I protested. 'One way or another, I'm the guy who made this thing happen, so it would be a lot fucking sicker if *I* was seen filming it.' He was still morose, so I tried a tactful approach. 'And people record funerals now, they're up there with weddings, christenings, Bar Mitzvahs and . . .' I couldn't think of another example.

'Stasi mementos?' he suggested cynically.

'Just photograph the mourners . . .' I had almost called them guests. 'I need a record of her friends. Something I can use later to identify individuals. And I want to see who groups with who.'

He shook his head dismally. 'I don't know where you're fucking going with this.'

'Trust me. I've got my reasons.'

The fine weather was holding. The hawthorn blossom was finally out in the hedgerows, tiny red flowers were fighting a losing battle with docks and nettles in the verges, and the lambs were getting a little plumper and sadly a little less manic.

It was a good day for her funeral. It was an even nicer day to be alive, I reflected guiltily.

We drove up the hill from Llandewi and joined the tail-end of the queue of cars shortly after we crossed the cattle grid at the start of the boundary wall of the Plas Coch estate. Mackay got out at one point while we were waiting and started listing: 'BMW, Jaguar, Audi, Audi, Mercedes. And I can make out at least one Bentley up near the front. What kind of fucking playground is this, Capaldi?'

'I don't know. This is most definitely not local farm-sale traffic.' I didn't get it. This was more like the kind of machinery you saw parked in the members' enclosure of an exclusive Home Counties polo club.

Slowly we moved on up to the main gates. A couple of uniform cops were security checking the cars as they went through, which was the reason for the hold-up.

'Hi, Sarge,' PC Friel, one of Emrys Hughes's sidekicks, bent down to look across to scope out Mackay.

'He's with me,' I said. 'And what's with the cordon stuff?'

'There are some important people here. Politicians and celebrities. Inspector Morgan wants them reassured that we're running a tight operation.'

I jerked my thumb at the line of cars waiting behind me. 'This will chasten them all nicely. Teach them a useful lesson in patience and humility. Probably something they're not used to.'

The starfucker gleam dimmed in his eyes. I had pricked his mondo-celebrity bubble. He waved us through quickly, his eyes anxious now and turning towards the waiting traffic.

Mackay moaned audibly.

'What's the matter?'

'Celebrities! Now I'm not only going to be playing a voyeuristic ghoul, I'm going to look like the fucking paparazzi as well.'

'Don't worry about it. Exposure's oxygen to them. Just tell them you work for *The Tatler*.'

'That's the point. I'm going to have to smile at the fuckers. Against all my socialist principles.'

We were diverted down a side track off the main drive before we got a sight of the big house, and parked where we were directed. Still grumbling, Mackay separated to go off and start taking photographs. I walked towards where people were congregating in front of an old chapel that harked back to the days when landowners built their own direct conduit to God to cut down on the commute and regulate the clientele. It was small, rectangular, stone built and buttressed at the corners, with simple lancet windows, and had lost its roof long ago, but money had obviously been spent to preserve it as a comely ruin.

As I got nearer I started to recognize faces, and was cross with myself for being impressed. Senior politicians of all hues, television pundits, actors, and a couple of novelists I could name. They looked like they had been displaced en masse from a fashionable London gala event. They were all immaculately dressed and radiated well-practised charm, confidence and power. The local mourners stood out like wallflowers that had strayed into a bouquet of tight bud roses.

I spotted Emrys Hughes and Inspector Morgan arrayed in dress uniform and full solemnity. Morgan gave me a cursory nod of acknowledgement that warned me to approach no closer. It suited me.

Rhian Pritchard was in her element working the crowd. She waved across to remind me that I was still in her basket, but wasn't going to be bothering with me today with this feast of the famous to pick at. She also had her photographer working for her, which was going to help to stop Mackay from looking out of place.

At the front of the chapel I saw through the open gothic archway that Jessie's simple wicker coffin had been placed on a shrouded bier at the centre of the building. A single white lily stood in a vase at the head of the coffin. It was all very understated, but the cynic in me wondered how much effort had gone into creating that effect.

An absence that had been niggling at me suddenly clarified itself. Apart from Rhian and her photographer, this was all a middle-aged to elderly crowd. There were no young people. Where were all the friends of Jessie's that her mother had told me about?

As if on cue, a stirring in the crowd drew my attention to a procession that had appeared on a path between huge rhododendron bushes. At the head of it was Cassie in a black coat, no hat, her head down, and a small bouquet of primroses in her hand that could not deflect from the obvious misery in her gait. Her other hand was resting on the arm of a very tall and elegant man in a beautifully-cut grey coat, wearing a sad patrician's smile, and a striking head of long white hair swept back behind his ears.

Behind them I recognized Ursula ap Hywel flanked by a middle-aged man and woman, and, behind them, what must have been Jessie's friends, a mixed bunch of local youth, looking uncomfortable with the occasion and the attention.

They arranged themselves along the front of the chapel, Cassie and her male partner to the front. A ripple of expectancy went through the crowd, damping conversations down to dispersed random coughs. A crow cawed into the one moment of pure silence.

The man began to speak about Jessie. A deep rich baritone voice with an educated South Wales accent. He talked with an easy familiarity. It was evident that he had known her well. I saw Cassie's hand tighten on his coat sleeve. He wasn't a funeral director, as I had first supposed. He had obviously been chosen to give her eulogy.

I sidled up to a uniform cop I vaguely recognized. He nodded at me warily. It was the effect I had on local cops.

'Who's he?' I whispered, gesturing towards the speaker.

'That's Rhodri ap Hywel.'

Ursula's husband. The owner of Plas Coch. Foundation benefactor. I slotted him into place. 'What about the couple who were walking beside his wife?'

'The Stevensons. They look after the place.'

'How come there are so many big names here?'

He shrugged. 'Don't really know. Probably friends of the ap Hywels'. They spend most of their time at their place in London. And from what I've heard, they get a lot of famous people staying at the Foundation.'

I nodded reflectively. I looked across at a woman who had been nominated for a Best Supporting Actress Oscar in her last film. Her name escaped me. Was she one of the Foundation residents? Her dark Prada outfit was a far cry from a fucking jug of water on a picnic table.

I was aware that another cop had appeared beside the one I had been talking to. They started conversing with each other in funeral undertones. I scanned Jessie's friends, looking for something in their faces that might trigger a

79

signal, until I realized that I had just overheard a familiar name.

I nudged the guy beside me. 'What was that you just said about Ryan Shaw?'

He looked at me, surprised. 'You haven't heard?'

'Heard what?'

'Ryan Shaw's dead.'

I felt myself freeze. I had been staring at Jessie's wicker coffin when he said this. Talk about fucking transference!

I sneaked off into the gloomy middle of a rhododendron bush to call Huw Davies. From here I could just make out the teary and desolate voice of one of Jessie's friends adding her contribution to the occasion from the direction of the chapel.

'Why didn't anyone fucking tell me, Huw?' I had to keep my frustration quiet.

'You're on sick leave, Sarge. And Ryan Shaw was outside of your jurisdiction.'

'What happened?'

'We don't know exactly, but it looks like one of his dope buying expeditions went tits up.'

'Where was this?'

'They found his car in Cheshire. They're working on the assumption that he was on his way back from Manchester.'

'Had he had an accident?'

'The car was found on a track leading to a worked-out sandpit. It had been burnt out, with him inside.'

I did a quick mental exercise. Having met Ryan twice I could dismiss suicide. And guys in his business didn't drive down deserted tracks in the hope of spotting a rare orchid or an elusive bittern. 'Did the fire kill him?'

'I don't know. You'd have to ask Emrys Hughes. He's been appointed the liaison officer to help out the Cheshire force with what we know this end.'

'Let me know if you hear any more on that front.'

'One thing . . .' His voice went sombre.

'What's that?'

'There's talk that he'd been tortured.'

It's hard to emerge from a rhododendron bush nonchalantly, but I did the best I could while still stunned and fogged with the revelation of Ryan Shaw's messy end. Our unfinished business hung there like an abandoned bridge project. Now we were never going to reach the other side. Not without hiring a fucking medium.

It could just be coincidence.

He was in a risky profession. He was a cocky bastard. He may have tried to stiff the wrong guys. Shit, knowing the reputation of some of those bastards, he may even just have sneezed at the wrong time.

No! I realized I was shaking my head. People were giving me strange looks. No, there was an umbilical line here. This was no coincidence. The orbits of a low-life like Ryan Shaw and an intelligent vibrant young woman like Jessie Bullock shouldn't have meshed, but I was convinced that there had been a wave interference in there somewhere. These two deaths were connected.

But torture? Why go and stage Jessie's death as an elaborate accident, and then prepare something as crude as this for Ryan Shaw?

Because it worked in the same way! The explanation lit a warm glow in my belly. Ryan Shaw being torched and butchered by Manchester hoodlums fitted as well into his milieu as Jessie's accident had into hers.

In its simplest terms, no one was going to feel the need to go looking for another explanation.

Except me.

But to get there it looked like I was going to need to get into the good graces of Emrys Hughes. The Cheshire police weren't even going to give me the time of day if I tried turning up on my own without any authority.

I drifted around the back of the mourners. A reedy youth's voice started declaiming something by Dylan Thomas and fucking up the rhythm.

I caught sight of Emrys at a corner of the crowd. He was still as tight up to Inspector Morgan as a remora fish to a host shark's jaw. There was no way I was going to be able to prise them apart; I was going to have to tackle Emrys later, when he had unzipped himself from his liege lord.

The formal assemblage was still in place in front of the chapel. Cassie and Rhodri ap Hywel to the fore, Jessie's school friends progressively stepping forward out of the line behind them to add their contributions to her memory.

I didn't bother trying to concentrate too hard on them all. Mackay's photographs were going to act as my reference. Although, without someone to translate the images into real people, they would be useless. And Cassie had already told me that she wasn't prepared to hand her daughter's friends over to me. I needed to identify the soft target. The person

I could go to with those photographs and get names and hopefully background from.

Who was the most approachable kid in that bunch?

I had to try and see through the funeral personas. Their expressions were stiff and stilted and they were all uncomfortably dressed for the occasion. No one knew the correct procedures. They were in pasty-faced shock. They had believed themselves gloriously invulnerable. Death wasn't meant to sidle in amongst them and shuffle one of their own out of the dance. Many of them were betraying traces of real grief and confusion.

It was a heartless world, because I knew that the sensitive souls were the ones to concentrate on.

I homed in on a girl towards the end of the line. She was standing beside the boy who had just finished giving us the Dylan Thomas mutilation. She stepped forward to present her piece, but crumbled, shook her head and retreated back into the line where she slumped against the boy. He acted surprised, his first reaction was to shy away, but then he reconsidered and put out an awkward and self-conscious arm to support her. Even with her head bowed I could see that she was crying.

He was gangly with an unruly thatch of light brown hair that resembled a freeze-frame shot of a volcanic eruption. His Adam's apple was pronounced, and his face was long and angular, still caught in the transition between child and man.

She was wearing a clumpy outfit comprising what looked like school uniform trousers and an unmatched shiny polyester jacket that was too large for her. Her hair was dark

83

brown, worn too long and naturally wavy without any attempt at styling. From what I had seen of her face before she broke down, her features had been chubby, too many pronounced curves, which would probably smooth themselves out with age, but for now made her look as though she had been modelled from putty. The tears weren't helping her complexion.

As I watched, the boy looked round and shot an expression down the line. I saw three boys further down catch it and try not to grin through their rigid funeral face masks. The expression had been a wince, head pushed slightly back, to announce, *What the fuck can I do about it?*

I knew from that gesture that the girl wasn't popular.

Which made her perfect for my purpose. She would hopefully be open to an offer of inclusion, and I wouldn't have to fight my way past her loyalties. And, I quickly justified to myself, it was only cruel if she knew why I had targeted her.

I angled round to the rear of the crowd, getting into position, ready to move in on the girl when the formal side of the occasion broke up. This wasn't going to be long in coming, as an empty hearse had now driven up slowly and stopped at the side of the chapel.

The last of Jessie's friends in the line stepped back after delivering their piece. Rhodri ap Hywel half turned and nodded to the line. 'Thank you,' he declared solemnly, before turning to face the rest of us. 'The family and invited friends will now be going on to the crematorium. But I'd like to remind you that you're all welcome at the celebration of Jessie's life at the Home Farm this afternoon.'

The crowd started to unravel. Dylan Thomas Boy, who

84

had been standing beside the girl, detached himself from her without a look or a word, making for the group of boys he had gestured to. I saw her watch him leave, a half smile of false hope that he might turn round again hanging on her lips. I moved towards her.

'Sergeant Capaldi?'

I couldn't ignore it. I had to turn round. Rhodri ap Hywel was approaching me, his hand proffered to shake.

'Good of you to come. It was greatly appreciated.' I shook his hand and followed his eyeline to where Cassie was being comforted by Ursula ap Hywel, the Stevensons standing respectfully a little away like good retainers.

'It was the least I could do,' I told him.

Up close he was even more imposing. Wealth not only bought good clothes and fantastic grooming, but it also laid down great bedrock for confidence and personality. I knew it was a performance, but, despite myself, I felt flattered that this man had picked me out to talk to. Or perhaps it wasn't all a front. There was a quality about him, the same as his wife, the sense of a deep intelligence that promised to share itself with you, if you were prepared to open up sufficiently, and trust enough to let it in.

Careful, I warned myself. Stay rooted. First my earlier flaky reaction to all those celebrities, and now to this charming, urbane man. I was in danger of being starfucked myself.

'You obviously knew Jessie well,' I observed, trying to keep half an eye on where the girl was heading for.

He smiled ruefully. 'I watched her grow up here. I wouldn't lay claim to have been anything as important as a father figure, but I'd like to believe I stood in as a favourite uncle from time to time. I think Jessie knew that she could trust me.'

'She confided in you?'

His eyes flashed merrily with his smile. 'If she did, it would have been in confidence.'

I nodded, accepting his rider. 'How would you best describe her?' Something warned me not to talk about her in the past tense.

'Wild.' He said it with an expression of controlled amusement. As if he was waiting for me to react. I didn't oblige. I knew he was going to tell me anyway. 'I mean that in its non-pejorative sense. Jessie was natural. She went her own way. She wouldn't allow herself to be contained by received opinions.'

'What about moral codes?'

His expression flickered briefly as he wondered where I was trying to take this. 'I think Jessie always reflected very carefully before she acted.'

'That makes her sound very mature. And yet her mother said that she didn't have a boyfriend. She didn't think that she'd developed the patience to form meaningful relationships.'

'We're talking about two entirely different things here, Sergeant.'

'We are?'

'Perhaps Jessie was aware of the distorting effect of sexuality. Perhaps she was waiting for a time when she would feel more in control.'

'An interesting kid,' I said, shutting the subject down. Something in his manner had just made me realize that he had approached me with another agenda than to shoot the breeze about Jessie.

'Yes,' he nodded wistfully, and then turned the full force of his bright blue eyes on me. 'I'm on a secret mission.'

'Yes?'

'My wife Ursula agrees with me, but Cassie doesn't know.'

'I'm intrigued.'

'I don't mean to be hurtful, Sergeant.'

I met his eyes full on. 'Go on.'

'The wake we're holding for Jessie this afternoon is meant to be a celebration . . .'

It clicked. 'And you don't want the man who killed her turning it into a dirge?' Was he lying about Cassie not knowing? Was she behind this? Did she think I would upset Jessie's friends? Not only by my presence, but with the possibility of awkward questions?

'I wouldn't have put it as brutally as that.' His expression turned thoughtful. 'Believe me, this is not meant personally.'

'No offence taken.'

He held his hand out again. 'I like you, Sergeant Capaldi.' I shook it, but I didn't ask him to call me Glyn. I wasn't ready to be that forgiving. He treated me to another winning smile. 'Come round and see us. Let's get Jessie put to bed, poor lass, and then we'll start again. A new footing?' He raised his eyebrows, making it a question.

'I'd like that.'

He inclined his head to the side. 'Who's the photographer?'

I followed the gesture. Mackay was standing off to the side of the dispersing crowd. How had Rhodri ap Hywel known to connect us? CCTV cameras on the front gates?

'A friend.' I gave it my best shot at looking vulnerable. 'I hoped no one would mind. I thought it might help me. Having a record of the occasion.'

And why was he interested?

The crowd had dispersed by the time he left me. Only a few remnants of local wallflowers lingering by the chapel. The celebrities had probably been whisked off to lunch in Plas Coch. I had lost sight of the girl. In fact all the youngsters seemed to have gone.

I caught up with Mackay. 'Are we finished?' he asked, not disguising his impatience.

'Which way did the kids go?'

He managed a deeply pissed-off sigh. 'Probably the car park, the same as everyone else.'

I ran to the car park. Most of the expensive cars were still in place, so it looked like I had been right about the celebrities being treated to lunch. But other cars were manoeuvring for the exit. Locals, for the most part, judging by the age and condition of the machinery. A car drove past and I recognized one of the kids from the eulogy line-up scowling in the back seat. Parents. Their parents were taking them home.

Had my girl already gone?

'What the fuck are you playing at now?' Mackay caught up with me; he was getting genuinely angry.

I held a hand up to calm his tirade. 'Look for youngsters,' I instructed.

He picked up on my urgency and shifted into sight-hound mode. 'There are four boys over there.' He pointed off.

I looked over. It was Dylan Thomas Boy and his three mates piling into a beat-up Vauxhall Corsa. Fuck subtlety. I pulled out my warrant card and ran towards them shouting, 'Police! Police!'

It worked like a paralysis ray. They froze. One of the boys was caught half in, half out of the front door in the act of squeezing into the rear seat. They watched me approach, each one of them visibly racking their brain for any past infringements that might have caused this.

The driver stepped forward. 'It's insured, MOT'd and—'

I waved my warrant card in front of his face to shut him up. 'What's your name?' I asked DTB. They were all looking apprehensive, but he was the only one who had turned sickeningly pale. I made a mental note of it.

'Dai,' he stammered, 'Dai Lloyd.'

'Where's your friend gone, Dai?'

He frowned, puzzled. 'What friend?'

'The girl you were standing beside.'

'She's nothing to do with me,' he protested, colour swirling into his blanched face like cochineal in yoghurt. His mates, seeing that my focus had shifted away from them, and that it looked like I wasn't going to be chopping their balls off, slowly took up a catcall. 'Louise . . . Louise . . . Louise . . .'

'Louise who?' I asked Dai.

'Louise Black.' He turned to his mates. 'Come on, you bastards, shut up.' He appealed to me. 'I was only standing beside her. That's where they told me to stand.'

I looked around. 'Is she still here?'

They conferred wordlessly. One of them shook his head. 'I think I saw her going off with one of the teachers.'

I got out my notebook. 'Can someone give me an address please? Or even better, a telephone number?'

I walked away with an address. I was halfway to my car before their synaptic relays switched back to normal and they started joining up the dots. It started as a series of random yelps, before they called out in ragged unison.

I turned to face them, already knowing what to expect.

Dai was the spokesperson. 'You're the one who killed her.'

I caught Mackay's anxious sideways glance. I gave him a private nod to reassure him. Their faces were locked into an open-mouthed blend of incredulity and hostility. They looked like they'd just had the myth of vaginal orgasm explained to them and realized that they now had a future of having to work hard at their fucking.

'It wasn't fun,' I announced.

What else could I say?

6

From where I was in Hen Felin Caravan Park it didn't come across as a big explosion. It was very late, and I would have missed it if I hadn't been standing in front of the large rear window staring out into the night. Taking a break from the photographs Mackay had shot for me, printed off the computer now, and spread out on the Formica-topped table in the dining nook.

A sudden fatty yellow flare-up spiked with carmine petals, the sky too dark to make out any smoke. From the direction of Dinas. The soft crump as the lagging sound wave caught up.

What the fuck was happening here?

I whacked the blue flashing light onto the car's roof and took off for town. Not so much to clear traffic at this dead time of night, but to warn the people at the other end that I was one of the good guys and to let me through to the heart of things.

91

I followed the illuminated skyline to the activity in Chapel Street, which led off the market square. The retained and volunteer firemen of the Dinas force had already mustered, their red-and-silver appliance stopped diagonally across the street. I slowed down to pass through the small clusters of onlookers and parked at an angle to form a secondary barrier. It looked like I was the first cop on the scene.

It was a short street of mainly commercial premises. The unit on fire was roughly in the middle of a three-storey Victorian brick terrace, shop fronts on the ground floor, with maisonettes above, although currently about half of the shops were vacant. Times were so hard these days that even the charity shops were packing up and going out of business.

Dense black smoke was pouring from the broken windows on the first- and second-floor level above Don's Den, Dinas's takeaway kebab and pizza joint. Above the roof, inside the smoke, there was a dancing flare of light shuffling through the yellow end of the spectrum, indicating live flames at the rear. The front door had been smashed open, and I could make out shadowy activity inside. Outside, two firemen were playing a hose into the first-floor windows, and another two hoses snaked through the covered passage beside the shop to the rear of the building. The arc lights that had been set up there gave the end of the passage a spooky glow.

The smell of damp smoke, charring timber and melted plastic was quickly embedded in my nostrils and clogging the back of my throat.

A fireman ducked out of the front door. His helmet told me that he was in charge. I went up to him with my warrant card open. He looked drawn and concerned.

'What do you want me to do?' I asked. This was his show, I knew better than to ask non-related questions at this stage. Investigation would come later.

'Get those people back.' He pointed towards the onlookers. 'I want this street evacuated and cordoned off.'

'Any other teams coming in?' I asked. We needed to know what sized gaps to allow in the cordon.

'Yes, two more appliances and an ambulance.'

'You've got injured?'

'I don't know!' he blurted out helplessly.

'Are the occupants still in there?'

'They're not outside. We haven't accounted for them.' He stared at me red-eyed and harassed. 'We can't get in. The rear door and the door from the shop to the interior are made of steel. And the jambs. And there's high-tensile bars over the rear downstairs windows. Why would they do that?' He looked at me, imploring an answer he knew I couldn't furnish. 'We're going to have to use cutting equipment. And I don't know if there are people in there. There's no town gas here, but that's a commercial kitchen, so there's going to be fucking gas cylinders.'

'Isn't that what caused the explosion?'

He flashed me a look of annoyance. 'I told you, the place is locked up tighter than a nun's twat, so, at the moment, Christ alone knows what fucking caused it.'

I backed away, leaving him to his distress and organization. It wasn't the time to argue. But I was sure I had witnessed an explosion. From street level you wouldn't know it though, with the big shop window still intact. Those steel doors must have contained the blast and forced it upwards. That's why

93

all the upstairs windows were broken. It had probably taken part of the rear roof off, which would explain the visible flames on that side.

I didn't hold out much hope for the occupants' survival.

I saw more flashing blue lights arriving, reflected in the shop's window. An ambulance, another fire appliance, and two police cars.

I got to Emrys Hughes as he was piling out of his car. 'We need to get this street evacuated and cleared and barricades set up.'

He glowered at me. 'What are you doing here, Capaldi?'

'I live here.'

'You're meant to be—'

I shouted him down. 'Fuck it, Emrys, don't get territorial on me. You need the manpower.' I pointed off at the sight-seers and cranked-up the drama. 'Those people think this is a fucking carnival, but this building could blow up or collapse at any time.'

He pulled a sulky face, but I saw him give in. He barked out orders to his men before he turned back to me.

'What happened?'

I shook my head. 'Too early to tell. But it'll probably be electrical. These things usually are.' At the time it was as good a guess as any. Because we didn't know about the others then.

'Anyone hurt?'

'We don't know yet. Who lived above the shop?'

'The two men who worked in it. They might be brothers. A couple of Arabs or Greeks. They've got weird names and keep pretty much to themselves.'

94

'Well, both the downstairs doors are locked, and that's the way through to the accommodation.'

He groaned. I thought again about what the boss of the fire team had told me. Steel doors. What the fuck made pizza dough so important that it required that level of security?

I conducted the Rennies to a place of safety. Well, the operation wasn't quite as purposeful as that makes it sound. They were a couple in their late seventies, and they lived above their shop, four doors down from Don's Den, in which he mended shoes, cut keys and engraved names and telephone numbers on dogs' collars.

I was meant to get in there and bundle them out fast, but I took pity on their age and their confusion. I let them reclaim their teeth and get changed out of their pyjamas and nightie into warm clothes. I led the way down the tight staircase carrying the budgerigar's cage, stopping from time to time to let them catch up, as they descended at the pace their rickety knees dictated.

Outside, they paused to catch their breath, and I took the opportunity to review the activity. The other appliances had arrived, and an ambulance was standing by. The rising smoke was even denser now, but not so dark, more steam in it, and the high flame flicker from the rear of the building had disappeared. A couple of firemen equipped with bulky breathing apparatus stood by waiting, but from here I couldn't see the sparks of the cutting rigs they were using on the steel doors.

I led them to the barricade and handed them over to the ladies from the WRVS.

'Glyn . . .'

I winced. Rhian Pritchard. I had only just met her, but the implied associations of that voice were already working like fingernails on a blackboard. I toyed with the idea of ignoring her, but, now that she'd seen me, I knew that she'd have the same persistent debilitating effect as a full bladder. Eventually I'd have to give in.

I checked my watch before I turned round. Half past three in the morning. What was she doing up at this time?

She was bobbing at the barricade to catch my attention. The same red duffel coat, her blonde hair contained under a brightly coloured woollen Inca cap with ear flaps and two long tassels, and a smile which at least this time looked like it was happy to see me as something more than a commodity.

'Can you get me over onto your side of this thing?' she asked chirpily, patting the top of the barricade.

'Sorry, not my decision to make – we're under the fire brigade's orders here.'

'I hear there could be two men still in there?'

'This is just a local news story. This isn't going to win you prizes.'

She raised her notebook pointedly and mimed writing. 'Two men trapped in a blazing inferno?'

I tried an outflanking manoeuvre. 'How the hell did you know about this? Have you had a police scanner implant or something?'

'A Cardiff contact called me.'

'About a little story in Dinas? At this time in the morning?' I showed my surprise.

She reciprocated the surprise. 'It's not only in Dinas.' She clocked my blank reaction. Her expression switched to cunning as she started to wonder if she could gain some advantage out of this. 'You didn't know?'

'No. Tell me,' I instructed.

'You'll owe me in future?' she challenged, her expression triumphant.

'It's a deal.' I didn't even bother to cross my fingers. I regarded this as extortion, and consequently retractable.

She held a hand up and started counting them off on her fingers: 'Dinas, Tregaron, Rhayader, Machynlleth.'

I shook my head impatiently. 'What about them?'

'The other Don's kebab bars. They've all been torched tonight.'

Shit!

I turned and walked away, scanning for Emrys Hughes.

'Glyn!' she yelled after me, her voice hungry. But she was ignorable now. A greater need had taken over. 'Glyn . . .' Her voice turned plaintive. 'Remember, you owe me one . . .'

I found Emrys at the other barricade drinking soup from a Styrofoam cup and chatting to an ambulance driver like a cop in attendance at a minor league football match. He held a clipboard up to the light as he saw me approach. 'Is that the Rennies out?'

'Yes.'

He put the soup down and crossed off a line on the clipboard. 'Good. That's the street clear now.' He preened in front of the ambulance driver, making a show of being the supreme authority here.

'Did you know there'd been other fires in other towns tonight?'

'Yes.' He inclined his head towards his shoulder radio. 'The reports have been coming through.'

I took a deep breath to keep my anger in check. 'Why didn't you tell me?'

He made a big show of letting the ambulance driver see him look incredulous. 'I didn't tell you because it has absolutely nothing to do with you. Your help has been appreciated here, but, at the end of the day, you're just another one of the volunteers.'

I felt the urge to strangle twitch the end of my fingers. But reminded myself that I needed this guy if I wanted to make any progress on the Ryan Shaw front. I eased my fury down into a sickly smile. 'This has to be more than coincidence.' I indicated his radio. 'Anyone saying anything about it?'

'Your bosses are already on the case.' He snickered. 'I bet they didn't appreciate getting woken up so early.'

'What about my bosses?'

'DCI Jones called me. He wanted my observations on the scene,' he said importantly.

'Did you tell him I was here?'

'No. Because you're not really here, are you? You're on sick leave.' He flashed me a smile that could have been interpreted as totally innocent or ground-glass malicious.

'What were your observations?'

'I told him it was too early. Said that the fire brigade hadn't gained access to the building yet. I did say that there might be two men in there,' he added as an afterthought.

'Thanks, Emrys.' I forced myself to sound grateful, and suppressed the urge to bring up the subject of Ryan Shaw.

It wasn't the time. He was feeling too regal. Denying a supplication would come too naturally.

I moved to a quiet spot and put a call through to Bryn Jones's mobile.

'Glyn?' He sounded surprised. His backdrop sounded very similar to the one where I was standing.

'I'm in Dinas, Sir, at the scene of the fire.'

He masked his phone. There was a short pause. 'Capaldi,' Jack Galbraith's voice boomed into my ear, 'what the fuck are you doing there?'

'I saw the explosion, Sir. I came into town to help out.'

'That waste of space of a sergeant didn't say anything about you being around.'

'No, Sir, unless you ask him something directly he has a tendency not to volunteer information.'

'What a useless fucking lump!'

'Where are you, Sir?'

'Tregaron. We've stopped at the nearest incident on the way up from Carmarthen. Give us what you've got there that you think is significant.'

'I think it was an explosion. We may have two victims. The kitchen and the access to the accommodation on the upper floors were locked from the inside. The car belonging to the occupants is still here. They're having to cut their way in though, Sir. The doors are steel.'

'It's the same here. And, from what I've been told, that applies to Machynlleth, and I'm still waiting to find someone sensible to talk to in Rhayader. How close are they to opening up at your end?'

I angled myself to where I could see the sparks from the

cutting rig through the shop's front window. 'It can't be too long now, Sir.'

'Get back to me as soon as you can get inside. I want to know what the fuck they've been hiding in there.'

I hung up.

Whatever it was we were going to find in there, I sent out a silent promise to Jessie that I wasn't going to let it distract me from bringing her killers to book. And, in the interests of balance, fair play and non-gender bias, I added another one for Ryan Shaw.

To ward off the slump, I poured more of the Williams's strong Sumatran coffee down me – the special stuff they used on their big hangovers. We were sitting in the kitchen in The Fleece. Sandra was opposite me, wrapped in a dressing gown, her cigarette held out to catch the up-draught from the extractor hood over the hob. It was a well-practised posture. She had cooked me breakfast. David remained asleep upstairs, dead to the world.

She wrinkled her nose, testing the air. 'I can still smell the smoke.'

'I know, it gets into your clothes.'

'Want to borrow something of David's?'

I smiled a no thanks and shook my head. It was light now, still early, but promising another bright day. After I had finished my stint at Chapel Street, I had used my key to get into The Fleece and take a shower, getting the worst of the smell and particulate residues off my hands and out of my hair. Sandra had met me at the bottom of the stairs as I was leaving, the smell of coffee and bacon wafting out of the open kitchen door arresting my departure.

I had told her that happily we hadn't found any bodies.

And then it had gotten interesting. But I didn't tell her anything about that. That bit we were still keeping under wraps.

I had requested permission to be allowed inside as soon as the firemen had done their initial search for victims. I stood outside patiently, wearing a waterproof coat, over-trousers and boots I had borrowed from the firemen, and a helmet that was too large and made me feel empathy with nodding dogs on the back ledges of cars.

The two firemen who had gone in with breathing apparatus emerged through the steel portal and conferred with Boss Fireman. He heard them out, and then raised his thumbs to the rest of us. 'The place is empty,' he called out. There was huge relief in his voice.

But not joy. And that conversation he had just had with his crew had taken longer than was required to deliver the message that we didn't have any bodies. I moved towards him. He held his hand out to stop me in the doorway.

'Can I go in now?' I asked.

'No. I'm sorry, Sergeant, but I'm having this place sealed. No one's getting in here without a HazMat suit.'

'Why?'

'I've been informed that there's a possibility of a toxic spill.' His attention shifted to a call from one of his colleagues. He moved away from me to brief him.

I seized the opportunity, and ducked past the two firemen and in past the open steel door, its leading edge blued and jagged where the locking mechanism had been cut out. I heard a shout behind me. I ignored it; I needed to grab an impression.

It was a mess, but recognizable as a small commercial kitchen. The floor was covered in a black slurry of ash and water, with a ragged pile of more solid scorched and burned debris that had come down through the large hole in the ceiling, which must have been caused by the explosion trying to achieve unity with the cosmos.

The room was bisected by a partition that was now just charred timber studwork above waist height where the blast had blown out the plasterboard. I scanned for big quick facts, and waded through the mess to a couple of free-standing propane gas cylinders. The rubber hoses had been burnt off, but a fast check told me that the stop cocks on both cylinders were fully open.

I heard a noise behind me and an unintelligible shout. I wasn't going to have much longer. I turned my attention on the partitioned-off space.

I took in a heavy-duty extractor hood above a worktop that was a jumble of soggy plasterboard fragments, some kind of an oven, sooty stainless steel and enamel pots, and an electric hob. The floor was littered with broken glass retorts, beakers and melted plastic drums whose contents had leached into the general sludge. The sorts of containers that chemicals came in. Was this Boss Fireman's Toxic Event?

But what clinched it for me was the machine that was bolted down to the worktop, and looked like a cross between an espresso coffee maker and a bacon slicer. It was a tablet press. I wouldn't normally have recognized it, but something similar had had a starring role in a short instructional film the Drug Squad had shown us in Cardiff.

They physically dragged me back into the street. Boss Fireman was furious. 'I am going to report you to your fucking superiors,' he screamed at me.

'You can in a minute,' I said placatingly, holding up my phone which was zapping through a speed-dial process, and indicating that I needed to talk first.

'What have you got for me, Capaldi?' Jack Galbraith answered. I didn't feel particularly flattered to know that I was on his number recognition list.

'No bodies, Sir, the place was empty.'

'That's a mercy. We think it's the same here, thankfully. We're not in yet, but the men on the ladders can't make out any victims.'

'I think it was a drugs lab, Sir.'

'Cannabis?'

'No, no heat lamps or hydroponics. I think they were cooking up stuff and pressing out pills. Maybe Ecstasy or Acid.' I looked at Boss Fireman as I talked. 'I didn't have much time in there, but the equipment looked appropriate. And I saw two intact gas cylinders.'

'Meaning?'

'They didn't blow up in the fire. So they were probably empty. But they had been turned on. My guess would be that they'd been used as an enhancer when the fire was started. Get the gas-and-air mixture up to help the explosion.' That statement made Boss Fireman even angrier. He tried to snatch the phone from me. 'I've got a fire officer here who wants a word with you, Sir.'

He caught something in my tone. 'Have you been a naughty boy again, Capaldi?' Fortunately I heard the smile in his voice.

'Detective Chief Superintendent Galbraith,' I introduced, handing the phone to Boss Fireman, and retreating to give him space to vent his spleen.

Boy, did he sound angry. It looked like he might be using my perceived misdeeds as a release therapy for all the anguish and frustration he had undergone while we waited to gain access to the building. He was ranting away about disrespect, disregard for safety procedures, unprofessional behaviour and unacceptable risk taking.

Then something changed.

He looked over at me, his hard-edged expression blurring. He listened again and winced, and said something I didn't catch in conclusion. 'I'm sorry,' he said, approaching and passing the phone back to me with a look that nearly got close to tender. 'You should have told me about your wife.'

I forced myself to hold my expression. Christ knows what line Jack Galbraith had spun him, but I was going to run with it. I allowed myself a dry shy smile. 'I didn't like to.'

He dipped his head in sympathy.

I kept my meek and grateful eyes on him as I raised the phone to talk to Jack Galbraith again. 'Sir?'

'Don't try and thank me, Capaldi, you know how I hate fucking sentiment.'

'Right, Sir.'

'Just write up your report and any observations you want to throw in, and email it to Bryn Jones.'

'Anything else you want me to do this end, Sir?'

'No, you can stand down. I can see this turning into an organizational nightmare. Four separate scenes of what has to be arson, and we're going to be totally stretched finding enough SOCO people to cover them all. And we're going to have to liaise with the fire investigation officers, and, if what you say is true, the Drug Squad will want to get in on the act as well. So, for now, that useless sergeant and his people can do the basic door-to-door spadework.'

So I was on my own again.

And in The Fleece kitchen the coffee was fighting a losing battle. I was currently drifting along just below the level of total consciousness.

'Glyn . . .?'

Sandra's voice brought me back to the surface. She laughed as I blinked at her. 'You looked like you were miles away.'

I shook my head and smiled at her. 'A bit tired.'

Which wasn't quite true. I had been a long way away. In a place where I was wondering what had caused two hitherto loyal employees who hustled kebabs and pizzas, and doubled-up as manufacturing chemists, to suddenly decide to torch their place of work and make a run for it? Simultaneously, in four separate locations? Or could it have been a coordinated attack by rivals? Was this some kind of turf war?

I reminded myself that I had been cut loose. It was no longer any of my concern.

Famous last fucking words.

7

Now that that exotic interlude was over I could get back to dedicating my skills to Jessie. Although I was almost tempted to send a postcard to my former colleagues in Cardiff who were convinced I spent my time up here sorting out the right end of sheep for hayseeds with two heads and webbed feet to stick their dicks into.

I composed it in my head. *Just been involved with major drugs factory explosion, now chasing down leads on murdered teenager and torched and tortured dope dealer. Fairly typical night. Wish you were here.*

But they wouldn't believe me.

I drove back to Unit 13 to pick up the photographs. Another slump wave rolled in and hit me. It was still too early to go calling, so I closed the lacy, fly-spackled nylon gauze that passed for curtains, folded myself in under the duvet and attempted to conjure up darkness. I tried to pretend that, as I still had my clothes on, it would only be dozing, it wouldn't count as real sleep and I wouldn't regret it.

I woke up three hours later confused and drooling. I had a headache, my bedclothes now smelled like a burnt-out ghat, and the inside of my mouth felt like it was lined with feathered creosote.

I drank some orange juice to vary the taste in my mouth, and then checked out Louise Black's address on the OS Map. The Bungalow, Tynycelyn Farm. It was high, lots of contours, in a part of the terrain I didn't know. But I had picked up enough of the sociology by now to appreciate that, generally, the higher you went, the poorer the farms got. Until you got right up onto the grouse moors, when everything changed, and you were into the fiefs of the helicopter-owning classes.

The approach was up a narrow valley, the single-track road following the twists of a shallow, alder-lined stream. I drove in and out of shadow as the steep side of a scree- and gorse-studded hill cut out the sun intermittently.

I stopped at the entrance track to Tynycelyn Farm. The valley had widened out here as we reached the watershed into marshy upland pasture dotted with sheep that looked like they were waiting for the grass to grow again and give them something to do.

The Bungalow was a crappy single-storey brick rectangle with a low-pitched concrete-tiled roof, and stood firmly at the chewing-gum end of the architectural haute cuisine hierarchy. On a slope behind it, sheltered by a scraggy copse of fir trees, I could make out the original two-storey white-washed stone farmhouse. More hill farm sociology. If Louise and her parents were living in the bungalow it looked like the grandparents weren't ready to relinquish the running of the farm yet.

I left the car at the end of the track. Despite the sun, there was a chill in the wind this high up. I was approaching on foot to appear less threatening. And I was winging it. I had no official reason to be here. I was also working on the hope that Louise, being the same age as Jessie, would have finished school by now, or would at least be at home on study leave.

She answered the door with a baby in the crook of one arm. I tried not to show my surprise. Had I been wrong about her popularity? It looked like it had been magnetic enough at one time to have turned her into a single mother.

She read my mind. Or maybe she had got used to strangers making that mistake. 'I'm babysitting,' she explained. And she wasn't surprised to see me. She must have watched me walking down the track. So, did she have any idea who I was?

I held out my warrant card, widened my smile, and gave her the full nice-guy treatment. 'Hi, Louise, I'm Glyn Capaldi.'

She nodded shyly. 'I know.' She saw me wondering. 'I saw you at Jessie's service. They were all talking about you afterwards.'

She was wearing the same grey trousers with a baggy magenta acrylic jumper which was a small improvement on the previous polyester jacket. Her hair was still a wavy, frizzy mess, and up close her skin was greasy, and she blinked excessively, making her face too mobile. Which, I realized, was because she was trying to compensate for not wearing glasses. Vanity, loss or poverty?

Louise Black was probably never going to be invited to climb up onto the pretty podium. But there was intelligence in her eyes, and a suggestion of reflective awareness in her expression. And she had enough self-confidence with adults not to be cowed by my presence.

'Are your parents in?' I asked.

'No. Dad's out with Uncle Phil dagging the ewes.' My expression showed my ignorance. 'Checking for fly-strike and scouring,' she explained, 'and Mum's gone down to Dinas shopping. I'm looking after Tracy and Tom,' she gestured at the door behind her where television cartoon noises located the missing brother.

I had a dilemma. I had hoped to get to talk to her parents, to get their permission to interview her. If I went ahead with this it could be construed that I had taken advantage of a vulnerable and impressionable teenage girl. Not to mention being a stranger alone in a house with a baby and a child. Given the current sensitivity surrounding child abuse, even an unsubstantiated whiff of it could get me into deep shit.

'I wanted to talk to you about Jessie Bullock.'

'I thought that might be why you're here.' She pulled a self-doubting face. 'I wasn't really a friend though.'

'As far as I'm concerned, that puts you in a better position. It makes you an objective observer.'

She smiled, flattered. 'I'm not going to get anyone into trouble.' It was a statement, not a question.

'I wouldn't expect you to.'

She stood back from the door. 'Do you want to come in?' she asked, opening the door fully.

I looked at her for a moment. I felt guilty. I had already

judged her and been mean and hypercritical. Now, in the full light, with the door open, I could see that there was real character in her face. She was still young. There was time. Given the right influences, she could refine, and, if she could fight off other peoples' limiting expectations, she might be able to make her way confidently in the world.

I decided to trust her. 'I've got a problem . . .' I started.

She heard me out. When I had finished, she pondered, and then weighed me up with an amused scrutiny that was a lot older than her years. At that moment I saw a future barrister in this young lady.

'Tom!' she yelled.

I had passed the picnic tables on my drive up the valley. They were sited in a small clump of silver birches between the road and a loop of tarmac which had been left stranded when the old road had been straightened.

Driving back down here had been Louise's suggestion. So that when she turned up fifteen minutes later with Tracy in her pram, and holding Tom's hand, it could appear to be a completely innocent and chance encounter in a neutral space.

I spread the photographs out on the top of a picnic table while she pacified the baby with a bottle of what looked to be paraffin. Tom just sat himself down on the opposite bench with his back to us and proceeded to jiggle his fingers and thumbs on a small gaming device that would have totally fucked up my eyes.

Louise took a seat on the bench beside me. She looked round at me shyly. 'I saw you watching us. At the service. Did I look really stupid?'

'No, you looked very upset.'

'I've broken my glasses. I couldn't read the piece I'd brought.'

'Which was?'

She pulled a face. 'It was corny.' I prompted her with silence. '"The Road Not Taken" – it's by an American poet called Robert Frost,' she said quietly.

I nodded to let her know I had heard of him. 'It sounds appropriate.'

'It's about choices.'

'Choices Jessie did or didn't make?' I suggested.

She shook her head. She didn't want to be drawn any further, so I didn't push it. I brought her attention to the photographs. 'Jessie's friends?' I asked.

She looked at them in silence for a moment. 'We're all Jessie's friends now.'

'You weren't before?'

She gave a short depreciating laugh. 'Me? Are you kidding?'

'You shouldn't sell yourself short, Louise.'

She pulled a face. 'I'm not. I know where I stand in the chain. I've learned not to worry about it.'

'What about the rest of them? Was she popular?'

'She could have been. She worked at it for a while. Then she kind of gave up, like she couldn't care any more.' She was reflecting. I kept quiet. 'How do you explain Jessie? You know these dumb American high school movies?' She looked at me doubtfully.

'Try me.'

'There's usually the bitchy blonde bimbo with a small group of lookalike followers who are all rich and prom queens and cheerleaders and they rule the roost and put everyone else down. Then a new girl arrives in town, and they set out to destroy her because she's different, and they feel threatened, but she pulls through because she's beautiful and intelligent and unselfish, and ends up putting them to shame.'

'And that was Jessie?'

She smiled. 'Not quite. Jessie was like that new girl in the way that the popular girls realized that they couldn't mess with her. But she didn't identify with any of the others either. She seemed to be happy staying on the outside, just watching us all like we were some sort of experiment. An ant colony or something. Sometimes I got the impression that she was laughing at us.'

'She was a loner?'

'Not really. She let some boys in. We used to call them Jessie's Tribe.'

'No girls?'

'No, not her inner circle.' She dropped her finger onto one of the photographs. 'Sean Thomas used to be one.'

'Used to be?'

Her finger moved to the girl standing next to him. 'Karen made him stop hanging out with her when they started going out together seriously.' Her finger moved to another photograph, and pointed out the boy who she had been standing beside in the line. 'Dai Lloyd's another one.'

I nodded, not letting on that I had already had an encounter with him. 'Is he nice?'

Her exaggerated shrug made me realize I had hit a soft spot. 'I wouldn't know, he doesn't deign to acknowledge me.'

'And?' I prompted, moving us on to spare her blushes.

'Christian Fenner.'

'Which one's he?'

She looked round at me. 'That's the weird thing.'

'What is?'

'Christian wasn't there.'

'And that's weird?'

She looked at me wide-eyed. 'Yes, because he and Dai were so close to her . . . Almost like slaves.'

I flashed back on the scene of the crash. 'Do you know if they built a cairn for her?'

'Yes. Even Sean Thomas was let off the leash to help them with that.'

'Have you got phone numbers for them you could give me?'

She gave me a concerned look. 'They're not in any trouble, are they?'

'No, I promise.' This time I did keep my hidden fingers crossed. Just in case.

She opened up the address book on her phone, and I started to transfer the numbers onto mine. We both looked round at the sound of an approaching car. An old blue Land Rover with an aluminium tilt went past. She waved. 'That's Dad and Uncle Phil.' Tom glanced up, disinterested, before dipping back down into his game.

'Can you tell me more about Dai and Christian?'

Her response was forestalled by the sounds of the Land Rover reversing at speed and the spray of gravel as it skidded to a stop at the side of the road. The driver, his elbow resting on the open window ledge stared at me with impassive, clinical hostility. I started to realize then, that Louise's so-called innocent and chance encounter might not stand up to the test too well.

'Uncle Phil!' I heard her exclaim beside me.

And then I was looking at a younger version of the same man marching round the back of the Land Rover towards me. He was dressed in a pair of faded blue overalls tucked into Wellington boots.

'Dad,' Louise said.

I didn't need the clue, I already knew. His hair was dark brown and mussed from his work and the Land Rover's open windows. His face was lean and sharp and weathered red on the cheekbones and forehead, his lips drawn tightly and clamped to a pale flesh colour.

I read the storyboard. It wasn't the parents who lived in the bigger house, it was his older brother. The two of them now struggling to raise two families on a holding that would have been hard pressed to keep one in comfort. The frustration in his stance was aimed at a world which daily told his children what great things they should be expecting from it. Unfortunately, with my nice newish car and tidy clothes, I was currently Mammon's earthly representative. And he had caught me getting cosy with his kids.

'What are you doing here?' His voice was angry, the question directed at me.

'It's all right, Dad.' Louise tried to intervene.

'Quiet, Louise. Get Tom and Tracy home now.' He turned his attention back on me. 'What are you doing here with my kids?'

I stood up to get on an equal footing. I was taller than

114

him, which didn't help. I held out my warrant card. 'Detective Sergeant Capaldi, I wanted to have a word with Louise.'

'About what?'

'Jessie Bullock.'

'He was the policeman that drove the car that killed her,' Uncle Phil called out helpfully.

Louise's father stared at me with his cold eyes. 'Have you got some sort of official piece of paper for this?'

'No, this was informal.'

'So, you come sneaking round to see my kids when you knew we weren't going to be around?'

'No. I had hoped you would be at home. So I could ask your permission.'

'What does this look like to you, Phil?'

'Pretty creepy if you ask me.' A pair of dogs barked from the back of the Land Rover, adding their vigilante support.

'Dad, it was nothing like that,' Louise interjected.

'I told you to be quiet, Louise. And I told you to get home.'

She looked at me helplessly.

I nodded at her. Smiling would not have been a good idea. 'Thanks, Louise, you've been very helpful.' I turned my attention back on her father. 'I don't know what you're reading into this, Mr Black, but I can assure you that I had no other intentions than asking Louise some harmless questions.' I heard myself sounding like a pedantic prick. I could almost see his point. I was coming across like an invasive force in his world, a missionary trying to showboat the pygmies.

He raised a hand, one finger pointing stiffly skywards between us. 'I'm going to report you. There has to be some rule that stops grown bastards like you pestering young kids.

I'm going to make your life hell, Sergeant whatever-you-call-yourself.'

Here we go again.

How long did I have before the shit hit the fan?

The Blacks were country people. Hill farmers. They weren't impulse buyers, they deliberated over things. They would probably discuss it among themselves first. Make it an extended family issue, throw their grievances into the cooking cauldron and stir them around. Then they would have to work out where to take the complaint to. They would hesitate before they got into dealing with officialdom.

Who was I kidding? I already knew the answer. The clue was in *country people*. They wouldn't fuck around with bureaucracy. I was probably on target with the protracted deliberations, but, when they did decide to act, they would go straight to Emrys Hughes.

I groaned inwardly. Emrys was my conduit to Ryan Shaw's demise. I desperately needed to stay in his good books.

But, as there was nothing I could do about it, I decided to do some anthropological research on Jessie's Tribe.

I found Huw Davies where the Dispatcher had told me he would be, helping Customs and Excise on a roadside inspection for vehicles running illegally on red diesel.

'Can they spare you?' I asked, walking up to him.

He raised an arm and spread his fingers. 'Five?' he shouted at the Customs Officers. One of them raised an answering hand in acknowledgement. He gave me a measuring look. 'I hear you had some fun and games in Dinas last night?'

I held up my hands in protestation. 'Not guilty, Huw. I was only helping out.'

He laughed, but I would have liked to have heard more meat in it. 'So what can I do for you? Are you still researching our cottage industries?'

'I've moved onto people now. I was wondering if you could tell me anything about a couple of youngsters called Dai Lloyd and Christian Fenner.'

He frowned. 'Why those two in particular?'

Huw wasn't stupid. I was going to have to give him something.

'They were close friends of Jessie Bullock's.'

'The poor girl's dead, Sarge. Can't you let go?' he sighed.

'That's what I'm trying to do. Humour me, Huw. I'm attempting to lay a ghost.'

He looked at me searchingly. 'Has this become official?'

I evaded the question. 'DCS Galbraith knows about it.'

He looked away from me to think about it. When he turned back, some of his tension had loosened. 'You want to prove that Jessie had nothing to do with the car park break-ins?'

If he wanted the salve of that conclusion, who was I to disavow him? 'I can't talk about it. I can't involve you,' I said guardedly.

'Except as an information machine?'

I grinned. 'A non-attributable one.'

His return smile wavered, but at least he had dropped the frown. 'Dai's Dai and Marjorie Lloyd's son. They've got Penrhos Farm, a couple of miles from Llandewi. Nice people, good farmers, they keep a tidy place.'

'Has Dai ever demonstrated a wild streak?'

117

He shook his head. 'Not since I've known the family.'

'So, like Josie, he's never come to your attention?'

'Not in the line of business.'

'What about Christian Fenner?'

He studied me closely for a moment. 'Do you carry some sort of jinx around with you?'

'What do you mean?'

'Stuff seems to happen to people you get interested in.'

I shook my head. 'I'm not with you, Huw.'

'Look what happened to Ryan Shaw. And now Christian Fenner's parents have reported him missing.'

I felt a sense of deep foreboding. 'Since when?'

'He didn't come home last night. They haven't seen him since yesterday morning when he went off to Jessie Bullock's funeral service.'

I looked at him in surprise. 'He wasn't there.'

'I know. I've talked to his friends.'

'Can I talk to his parents?'

'No. There's nothing you can say to them that's going to help them. You'll only upset them more.'

I had another thought. 'How was he meant to be getting to the service?'

'Robbie Green, one of his friends, has a car. He was going to pick him up at the Lloyds' place. But, according to young Dai, he never turned up there.'

'Has it happened before?'

'If it has, they've never reported it.' He looked at me closely, a thin film of something like accusation clouding his eyes. 'You hadn't been round pestering him, had you? About this Jessie Bullock business?'

'No, I promise. I've only just heard his name, that's why I came to see you.'

He held my gaze for a moment before nodding flatly. 'I'd better get back to work.'

'Thanks, Huw.' He had turned and started walking away before I remembered. I called out. 'Any more news on the Ryan Shaw front?'

He looked round. I saw the reluctance in his expression. 'Emrys Hughes has got a meeting in Cheshire tomorrow with the force that found the car. There's supposed to be someone from Manchester CID coming over as well.'

'I asked you to keep me posted on that.' I tried not to sound aggrieved.

'I know, but I never agreed that I would.' He smiled to let me know that it wasn't personal. 'The investigation's in Cheshire and Manchester, Sarge, you can't stretch your jurisdiction that far. And you're not operational.'

It was parochial. He didn't want to let me in. Even Huw, who I regarded as the worldly one of the local bunch. Ryan Shaw was their dead petty hood and they didn't want to share him with outsiders.

I nodded my understanding. 'Okay, thanks, Huw.' Was I only imagining relief in his stride as he walked away?

Tomorrow! I went back to thinking about time frames. I might be in luck. The proximity of this meeting might work for me. The Blacks' complaint might not reach Emrys by then. I might still only qualify as an aggravating nuisance rather than an apprentice child molester. But even that lesser evil still wasn't going to get me an invitation to accompany him

119

to Cheshire tomorrow. I was going to have to employ underhand measures.

Because I knew I had to be there in person. There were important questions that Emrys wouldn't think to ask.

I used the Dispatcher again and found out that Emrys was off duty. He was at home recuperating from the all-night session at Don's Den, and preparing himself for the meeting tomorrow.

I hoped he was getting jittery about it.

Emrys may have been all beef and bluster, but essentially he was a homeboy. A lot of guys in his situation would have relished the opportunity to get out to the bright lights and the action bars, and would be practising the brilliantine sweeps through their coifs, but, if I knew Emrys, the quaking would already have started.

I was twitchy to get at him, worried about the Blacks' complaint coming through early, but I forced myself to postpone calling on him until well after lunch. It wouldn't help my cause if I added sleep disturbance to the list of grievances he already held against me.

His wife was outside their house, kneeling down by a flower bed with a small trowel and a trug basket, yellow rubber gloves on her hands. She was a short, narrow-waisted, dainty woman with her hair in a tight perm and lips so surprisingly small and pert that, in profile, they looked like a finch's beak.

I had seen her a couple of times before, on the fringes of social events that the local uniforms, through social convention, had been forced to invite me to, and that Jack Galbraith had ordered me to attend. My only memory of the time we had been introduced was of an image that had intruded on my mind of this tiny woman crushed underneath Emrys's gyrating bulk. And, for some reason that I didn't want to investigate, I had pictured Emrys as a naked full-hefted, huge-hammed satyr, while I had attired her in nothing but a ruched apron, and a genteel, *let's get this over with* smile.

That recall wasn't helping as she got up and approached me at the garden gate with a forced smile of polite curiosity. The pleasantry was all surface, because the snap of her rubber gloves coming off betrayed the same streak of annoyance as a surgeon who has just fucked up a gall bladder removal.

'Hello, Mrs Hughes, is your husband around?'

The smile remained fixed, but she twitched her eyebrows and squinted, turning her face into a question mark.

'It's DS Capaldi.'

'Oh, I'm sorry, *Sergeant*, I didn't recognize you,' she gushed and slapped a hand to her chest, putting the stress on the word to let me know that, in her book, real sergeants didn't arrive in crumpled shirts, khakis, and scuffed yellow Caterpillar boots. I recognized her smile as one of pure dislike.

'Wait here,' she instructed, giving me another withering once-over before she picked up the trug and waltzed into the house calling for her husband in a voice that was honey-coated strychnine.

'Capaldi.' Emrys nodded at me cautiously when he eventually emerged. He was dressed in a grey woollen V-necked jumper, pressed grey slacks, and, his off-duty concession, a crisp checked shirt without a tie. The outfit looked like an out-of-uniform uniform.

121

'I came over to check that you got DCS Galbraith's email?'

He looked puzzled. 'What email?'

I frowned. 'You didn't get it? That's strange. He copied me in. He wanted to make sure you were happy about your meeting tomorrow, and didn't need help with any pointers.'

His face twisted. 'Pointers?'

'Yes, to back-up our end of things.'

'What is there to back-up?' He tried to be hearty, but I could see the start of the fear flicker in his eyes.

'There are three forces involved, remember. They're all going to be passing the blame around.'

He tried on a confident bluster. 'Blame? Shaw was found dead in Cheshire. It's their investigation. I'm only going up there to provide local background on him that might help them.'

I shook my head worriedly. 'DCS Galbraith is concerned about our budget.'

He looked at me blankly. 'What has that got to do with anything?'

'These people can be slick, Emrys. It's a whole new ball game these days. Times are tight. With the cutbacks, the Cheshire guys are going to be looking to squirm out of the full responsibility. They'll be trying to find some loophole that ties us or the Manchester lot into sharing the funding.'

'What sort of loophole?'

I shrugged and made a show of searching for an example. 'Like why didn't we make any kind of effort to stop Ryan Shaw travelling through their patch on his way to and from scoring his dope?'

'How could we have done that?' he snorted. 'How could

we possibly have known when or where he was going, and what he was doing?' He tried looking incredulous, but his eyes were laced with tiny fissures of uncertainty.

I gave him a supportive shrug. 'I know. It's a crazy world. But have we got a paper trail to show that we at least tried?'

His face reddened and he struggled to contain himself. Something told me that he wasn't allowed to swear around the house. 'What about the Manchester police?' he blurted. 'Surely they've got the same responsibility? It was people there he bought the drugs from.'

'Have you ever worked with the Manchester police?'

He shook his head warily.

'They're wrigglers. They're famous for it. They're not known as the greasy pole for nothing.'

'Greasy pole?'

'Nothing gets to climb up, and everything slides off. They spend a fortune giving their guys special training. And . . .' I hesitated and shook my head. 'No, I shouldn't say it.'

'And what?' he insisted.

I pulled a self-reproachful face. 'The other two forces are English.'

He turned away from me and walked to the window. When he turned back his face was drawn. 'Have you ever done anything like this before?'

'A couple of times. I hate to say it, but it's not much fun. You have to stay on your toes. Don't let the other buggers trip you up.'

He looked at me then, the plea rising in his voice like a surfacing sperm whale. 'I don't suppose DCS Galbraith would let you come with me?'

123

I played it surprised. 'Me?'

'If you've done it before, you know what to look out for.'

'You mean, like an advisor?'

He nodded eagerly.

I mulled it over. 'I'm meant to be on sick leave at the moment. But I suppose I could put it to him.' I gave him a conspiratorial smile. 'If it helps his budget, it means I get to stay in his good books. And I'm not exactly overworked these days.'

'You wouldn't mind?' he asked meekly.

I broke into a grin. 'Fuck it! Let's do it for Wales. Let's show the bastards!' I saw the relief flood in, even over the anxious glance he threw towards the door in case his wife had listened in on the profanities. 'Where's the meeting?' I asked.

'Winsford.'

'Did they say anything about showing you where Ryan Shaw and the car were found?'

He shook his head. 'No. They said it was a meeting to collate background material.'

'Get back onto them. Tell them you're coming earlier and you need them to arrange for someone to show us the crime scene.' I flashed him a reassuring smile. 'That'll let them know we're serious, that they're not playing with a bunch of rubes here.' I forced myself not to sound too eager. 'And can you bring me up to speed on the case?'

He looked at me blankly. 'The case?'

'What they've told you about Ryan Shaw's murder. Just so I know what we're all talking about tomorrow.'

'Emrys!' His wife's shriek travelled through the house like a heat-seeking missile.

124

His face dropped. He shook his head.

'Tomorrow in the car then,' I said.

Mrs Hughes appeared at the door and gave me a weird look when I left. She either wanted me to fuck her silly, or she wanted to staple my scrotum to the garage door to prevent me from running away while the steam iron heated up.

I never could read women.

8

8

I got back to Unit 13 to discover that I had turned into Mr Popular. My wagtail still hadn't returned, but I had three messages on the answering machine, and a handwritten note taped to the door.

The note was the most disconcerting. It was from Rhian Pritchard saying that she was sorry she had missed me, but would be in touch again soon. There was a heavily underlined P.S. *Love the caravan. Will add great touch to the story.* Basically she was letting me know that she had tracked me down. There was nowhere to hide. The fact that this woman carried her own sticky tape around, for the express purpose of leaving notes on doors, was another scary example of her dogged persistence.

The first of the telephone messages was from Mackay, asking if the photographs were okay. I saw through it. He was checking up on my well-being. Making sure that I hadn't plugged the myriad gaps in the caravan and turned the gas taps on. I made a mental note to give him a call soon to reassure him.

The second message was from Ursula ap Hywel, inviting me over to Plas Coch for drinks tomorrow night. Nothing formal, she informed me in that rich voice of hers, they were just having a few simpatico people round for a fireside gathering. In any other voice *simpatico* and *fireside gathering* would have had me reaching for the retching bowl, but she managed to add enough of an ironic lilt to it, to not only forgive, but to feel selected.

The third message really surprised me. 'Yo, Glyn, if you get this, try and get over to The Fleece about half six tonight. I'll buy you a beer.'

What the fuck was Kevin Fletcher doing in Dinas?

I speculated idly as I drove over to Llandewi. He'd got religion, seen the error of his ways, and had come to apologize for having been such a shit in the past? He'd returned to his former life in Cardiff and discovered that he missed the boondocks so much that he'd applied for a transfer? He was giving everything up to become a hermit? I knew it was all bullshit, but it passed the time.

From the village I went out on the road that would take me past Penrhos Farm. It was level country here, good grass, well watered, lone oak and ash trees in the carefully tended hedges. The grazing sheep were chunky Suffolk crosses and Texels, a contented Limousin beef herd speckled a pasture, with elsewhere some advanced winter wheat, and a lot of grass in reserve. If Moses had been leading farmers like the Blacks out of exile, I imagined Penrhos Farm would have been their idea of the land of milk and honey.

127

I drove past the farm entrance until I found a field gate where I could pull off the road. I took my binoculars from the glove compartment, put on an anorak and a wool-lined green peaked cap with ear flaps, which, if it didn't success-fully disguise me as a twitcher, at least, hopefully, diluted the cop in me.

I stood by the gate with the binoculars raised and made like I was searching for a stormy petrel, or whatever the fuck kind of bird was rare in those parts. It was a good spot. I could make out the whole of the yard in front of the impres-sive Victorian stone farmhouse and its range of barns and outbuildings.

I was in luck. The same beat-up Vauxhall Corsa that had driven Dai away from Jessie's funeral service was parked in the yard. Its bonnet was up, and two people were bent under it playing with the engine. There was a tractor with a trailer attached, but no other cars in the yard. The entrails were reading well.

I propped an elbow on the top of the gatepost to keep the binoculars trained and steady in one hand, and used the other on the mobile phone. It started to ring out. Dai Lloyd emerged from under the bonnet reaching into his back pocket, and straightened up with his mobile phone in his hand. It was a weird feeling, watching him check the caller display knowing that it was my number he was seeing. I felt a bit like a digital puppet master.

'Hello?' he asked warily.

'Hello, Dai, this is DS Glyn Capaldi, we met at Jessie Bullock's funeral service.'

'Right?' he said hesitantly, covering the phone's mouthpiece and saying something to his mate, who was also out from under the bonnet now. I searched for the name Huw had given me. Robbie Green.

'This is very important. I need to talk to you about your friend Christian Fenner. I may have some news.' I was working on the assumption that he didn't know that I was on sick leave, and had nothing to do with investigating Christian's disappearance.

'What kind of news?' I detected a trace of what sounded like scepticism, and made a mental note.

'Are your parents in?'

'Only my mother. Do you want to talk to her too?'

Shit! The entrails had suddenly sprouted maggots. I didn't need another responsible adult getting in the way and turning this into a situation like the Blacks. 'No, but I do need to see you as soon as possible. Can you get to the car park at the start of the Monks' Trail?'

He conferred with Robbie, who shrugged, but then pulled the car's bonnet closed. 'Okay,' Dai said, 'we're on our way.'

I leaped into my car, and tossed my cap and the binoculars onto the passenger's seat. I was meant to be already at the car park. I started the engine and threw the car into a jerky three-point turn. Thankfully I was driving past the farm entrance as they were coming up the drive. I put my foot down to stay ahead and out of sight.

He hadn't argued. He hadn't tried to put me off. He was obviously curious to hear what I had to say about Christian. But he hadn't been excited, or relieved that there was some news. I put all that together with the sceptical note I had already heard in his voice. I was going to be watching this kid closely.

I was sitting on the hot bonnet of my car making like a patient cop when they pulled into the car park. I feigned stiffness and walked over as they got out of the car.

'You can stay here,' I said to Robbie.

'I'm a friend of Christian's too,' he complained, looking to Dai for support. Interestingly, Dai didn't offer it.

'You're not on my list, Robbie,' I said, leaving him to make up his own mind whether that was a good or a bad thing. And he had the secondary worry of wondering how the hell I knew his name.

I walked over to the Monks' Trail display board and gestured for Dai to follow me. 'Know this place?' I asked, spreading my hands to take in the car park.

'Yes.'

'What does it mean to you?'

He tried to hold my eyes, but he had a problem with his confidence. 'It's where your lot picked up Jessie. You drove her away from here.' There was a slight tremor in his voice. He wasn't used to playing the tough kid.

I nodded, accepting his accusation, and then used silence on him.

'You had something to tell me about Christian,' he said eventually.

'That's right. He's gone missing.'

He registered surprise. 'I knew that.'

'Why?'

'Why what?'

'Why's he gone?'

130

He shook his head. 'I don't know.'

I smiled at him. 'Tell me about Jessie.'

'What?'

'Talk to me about Jessie. Tell me what she was like.'

'I thought this was about Christian?'

'I think you're all tied up together.'

'I don't know what you're talking about.'

'Were either of you having sex with her?'

He flushed, angry. 'You leave her out of this. You're the one who—'

'Yes, I drove the car that killed her,' I raised my voice, cutting over him, 'that's why I want to know about her. I've been told that you were her boys, you and Christian. What did you all get up to?'

He shook his head, trying to contain it. But contain what? Anger definitely. Nervousness. Anxiety. But also fear? 'I'm not staying for any more of this!' he spat at me without meeting my eyes, wheeled and headed back to Robbie.

'Dai!' I commanded.

He turned.

I nodded slowly and pinned him with my eyes. 'I *know*.'

He blanched, anguished, staring at me for a moment, searching my face.

I watched them drive away. What was the baggage he was carrying? What was it he thought that I had on him?

Instinct told me that Dai Lloyd was a nice kid at heart. But it looked like there was something corrosive at work inside him. Or was I trying too hard to make everything fit my own agenda? Maybe I was misconstruing his attempts to

131

cope with grief. Perhaps Christian Fenner's disappearance had been his own way of dealing with it.

But I kept coming back to it as I drove to Dinas. That ghastly look on Dai's face. Why had he been so shocked when I had tried to bluff him out with that *I know*?

I got to The Fleece at quarter to seven. It was still busy with the after-work crowd. The noise level dropped when I walked in, people going through contortions pretending not to look at me. Fletcher was lounging proprietarily against the bar, and I saw him register it. He raised his eyebrows when I walked towards him.

'These fuckers have really clasped you to their bosoms, haven't they?' he quipped sarcastically without lowering his voice, and turned to David behind the bar, 'Get my friend the Wandering Jew his usual, please.'

As normal, Kevin Fletcher looked pleased with himself. He had had his hair cut short, which actually suited his long square face, although it left his ears a bit adrift. He was wearing a very smart dark blue suit in light wool, and a pink shirt with a striped tie that he would want people to think was either regimental or old school.

'What brings you back to these parts, Kevin?'

'Business, old son.' He smiled conspiratorially. It looked like it took an effort for him not to wink. He swept up my freshly poured beer and his own drink. 'Come on, let's find somewhere more private.'

I had no choice but to follow him to a small table in a corner of the quieter back bar. He raised his glass. 'Good to see you, Glyn.'

I followed suit dutifully. 'Cheers.' And then it came to me.

132

What I had been puzzling over, the reason he was here. Don's Den. The arson attacks. The drugs labs. 'What's Cardiff's interest in this, Kevin? I would have thought that it's a bit beyond your patch?'

He beamed. I had obviously asked exactly the right question. 'I'm on secondment. You're correct, this is Jack Galbraith's domain, it's outside Cardiff's frame of reference. I'm covering this one for the Met.'

'The London Met?'

'Fucking right.' He looked even more pleased with himself.

I couldn't contain my surprise. 'What's the Met's interest in crimes and misdemeanours in the middle of Pig Wales?'

He leaned forward and tapped the side of his nose. 'That's what they've asked me to find out for them.'

I got the picture. The multiple drug factories had alerted the Metropolitan Police. But they didn't know whether there was anything here for them that warranted sending a team out all this way. So they were using him as a stringer. Just in case there were reverberations that bounced back down the wire to involve them.

'Are you staying in The Fleece?'

'No. I've got the four towns to cover, so I'm staying at a Voyagers Lodge near Rhayader.'

'Isn't that a bit impersonal?'

He gave a hunched head gesture towards David behind the bar before leaning across the table to talk in a whisper. 'Believe me, after that one experience staying here, impersonal beats gardenia-scented spider fucking sanctuary hands down.'

'Does DCS Galbraith know you're here talking to me?'

133

His smile turned even shiftier. 'We're all on the same side, Glyn.'

So that was a *no* then. That's why he was buying the drinks. He needed my cooperation. 'What do you want from me, Kevin?'

'You were the first cop in there. I want to know what you saw.'

'I sent DCI Jones a report.'

'I've read it. Now I want it from the horse's mouth.'

I didn't bother to tell him there was nothing more to add. 'What do I get?'

'What do you want?'

'Why are the Met involved?' I knew I didn't need this. I had enough to handle with Jessie. But old habits died hard. He had cranked up my interest.

He frowned, thinking about it. 'I can't give you names.'

'Okay,' I nodded, accepting the condition.

'The preliminary report on the chemicals and equipment found indicates that they were probably manufacturing Ecstasy and methamphetamine.'

'Any finished product?'

'No. All that obviously went with them.'

'And still no trace of any of the staff?'

He shook his head.

'What's the thinking? An organized mutiny? That they've all skipped off with the proceeds?'

'That's one of the mysteries. It turns out that, so far, no one's come up with the real identities of any of the staff. Only first names, nicknames, but nothing to link them into the system.'

A couple of Arabs or Greeks. I remembered Emrys's vagueness on that front. 'The company must have been registered.'

'It's a shell. The forensic accountants are trying to trace the ownership, but I've been told that it's probably going to end up at a dead end in somewhere like Belize or the British Virgin Islands.'

'But why here? You'd be lucky if you were servicing half a dozen people in Dinas. Why set up a manufacturing base in a place where there's no market?'

'For exactly those reasons. No one's going to be looking for it. If you don't sell locally, you're not exposed, so there's no heat, no surveillance. You're just another pizza joint in Hicksville.'

I thought about it. It began to make sense. 'Delivery vans can come and go with impunity. They bring in the raw materials and pick up the product.' I pictured the map in my head. 'From here you're pretty well placed to distribute to the whole country.'

'That's right. And close to the ferry ports for Ireland.'

I came back to the Met's interest. 'It's tied to London organized crime?'

He raised his hands, cautioning prudence. 'Could be. As I said, I can't mention names, but there's a possibility of North London Turkish Cypriot involvement.'

I frowned. I couldn't place it, but that was ringing some kind of a bell.

He sat back in his chair and folded his arms across his chest. 'Your turn,' he instructed.

If he was disappointed with what I had to tell him, he didn't show it. He didn't take any notes either. The only thing

135

he wanted my opinion on was the *modus operandi* for the arson.

'I think they probably used the cooking gas cylinders in conjunction with some sort of accelerant.' He nodded for me to go on. 'It's going to take a bit for the gas-and-air mixture to get up to an explosive proportion. If they've got that combined with a volatile accelerant rigged up to a timer, it's going to let them get clear before the whole thing goes up.'

'A professional operation?'

I saw his point. 'They were producing dope, they obviously had some sort of knowledge of chemistry.' But not necessarily the refinements of arson.

'It was pretty well fucking coordinated.'

I realized the significance of that remark. 'They're thinking that the staff might have been abducted?'

'It's a possibility.'

'Those doors were steel and locked. But somehow they manage to get inside, take the staff and the merchandise out, and rig up their firebombs. In four separate locations. Without anyone seeing or hearing anything.' I whistled through my teeth appreciatively. 'Jesus, Kevin, that would have taken some sort of organizing.'

He nodded. 'And where are they now? Our ex-workers.'

Or ex-people? I was thinking ahead of him. 'It was either an inside job, or they wanted to set up a smokescreen to make us think that it was. Or, they didn't want to torch them in situ.'

He leaned forward, interested. 'Because . . .?' he prompted.

'Because then it becomes a mass murder investigation. Too much heat, if you pardon the pun. And fire's a fickle bastard. It doesn't always do what you want it to do. It might not have killed all of them.' Which, if that's the intention, is something they can now do in private, I thought to myself.

He nodded and smiled at me benevolently. 'I asked around. You're still on sick leave. You must be bored shitless around here.' He leaned in closer. 'Do you want in? Unofficially. Want to be my sidekick? Me Batman, you Robin?'

He wanted a flunkey. I knew Kevin Fletcher. He wanted me on board so he could slope back to his creature comforts in Cardiff and still pick up the credit if I turned anything up here. I shook my head. 'No thanks, Kevin, I've got plenty to keep me occupied.'

He studied me carefully. 'You're not still beating your meat over that private vendetta shit you asked me to check out for you?'

'I forgot to thank you for all you did for me on that.'

He shrugged unconcernedly. 'Hey, I had to cover my back. We all know that Jack Galbraith sups with the devil. Sooner or later he finds out all this stuff.'

I smiled nervously to cover up just how close to the mark that had struck.

The luck I had been riding up until now finally crashed on the A483 north of Wrexham.

We were in Emrys's car, leaving the Berwyn range behind to the west, the Cheshire Plain opening up to the north and east. It was an overcast morning, not yet raining, but the weather deteriorating as a wet front moved in off the Atlantic, the clouds of the advance guard already mixing it with the chemical haze over Runcorn.

We had started early and Emrys had been taciturn for the entire journey, replying to my attempts at conversation with monosyllabic grunts. I had been trying to get him to open up on the details of Ryan Shaw's death, but he wasn't playing ball. I put it down to funk. He was obviously brooding about the ensuing meeting. It looked like I had done too good a job on the scaremongering front.

He had begun to loosen up and to realize that we were running early enough to be able to stop for a supplementary breakfast, where I hoped to be able to draw the details of Ryan Shaw's ordeal out of him, over his scrambled eggs and fried tomatoes, when the call came through on the radio.

I had been wrong about the Blacks going straight to Emrys. They had aimed higher. The Dispatcher informed him that Inspector Morgan wanted Emrys to call him. He pulled over into a lay-by on the dual carriageway. And then, to jealously guard his superior's pronouncements from my profane hearing, he got out of the car and into the proto-drizzle to make the call.

Which meant that I could pinpoint the exact moment of revelation. When the back of his head slammed into his creased bull neck, and he wheeled as fast as a man of his bulk could manage, to fix me through the windscreen, an almost pantomime glower on his face. He started nodding then, his expression half wince, half supplication as he agreed with everything his boss was telling him.

He got into the car looking at me like I was the guy who had just finished hammering in the last of the Crucifixion nails and was still whistling while I worked.

I tried a soothing tone. 'It's not like it sounds, Emrys.'

'How is Inspector Morgan expected to look when strange plain-clothes policemen are running around in his jurisdiction disturbing and upsetting children without any reason or authority?'

I didn't ask him to define *strange*. And I guessed he was repeating that more or less verbatim. I did my best to look meek. 'It was completely innocent. I only wanted to ask Louise Black about Jessie Bullock.'

'The poor girl's just been laid to rest. You should be the last person to want to stir all that up again.' He went reflective. Probably recalling more of Morgan's invective. 'And you had your friend taking photographs at her funeral service. What are you up to, Capaldi?' His interrogatory expression froze as another unwelcome messenger was relayed up through the synapses. He crashed his big hand on the steering wheel. 'Is that what *this* is all about? Is Ryan Shaw involved in this fucking game you're playing? Have you been messing me about? Is that why you've wangled your way into this meeting today?'

I met his anger with a neutral expression I was trying to temper with compassion. 'It's too late to take me back now.'

'No, but I could fucking leave you here.'

I held his gaze. 'But you're still not that sure that you don't need me, are you, Emrys?'

He shook his head, real pain in his eyes. 'Why are you doing this, Capaldi?'

I decided to go for the Hollywood, pink-haloed, redemptive arc gambit. Only a slightly contorted version of the truth. 'I'm hurting, Emrys. I killed a young girl. You can't possibly know what that's like. I'm trying in my own way to get to know her.' I gave it a dramatic pause, letting the imaginary violins reach for the stars. 'I'm sorry if I've appeared insensitive, or barged in where I'm not wanted, but it was the only way I knew how.'

He held my stare for a beat before he reached for the radio. The Dispatcher answered his call sign. 'Can you patch me through to Detective Chief Superintendent Galbraith in Carmarthen?' We didn't take our eyes off each other until the Dispatcher came back to ask if he wanted to leave a message as DCS Galbraith wasn't presently available. He flicked his head away to think about it. 'Tell him thanks for agreeing to let Detective Sergeant Capaldi accompany me to my meeting in Cheshire this morning.' He looked at me, a thin smile of grim satisfaction on his lips.

Perversely, I was impressed. I hadn't thought he had it in him. I didn't let him see it though. I altered my expression to a pretence of slightly cheeky nonchalance, but, as a precaution, I reached into my pocket and surreptitiously turned my phone off.

After that, any thoughts of stopping for breakfast went out the window.

We sat parked at the rendezvous point waiting for the Cheshire cops to arrive, staring out of our respective side windows in the rapt attenuated silence of an old couple who each blames the other for the accidental death of the family cat fifteen years before.

The young DC arrived, interrupting my reflections, which had been sparking between Dai Lloyd and Kevin Fletcher and trying to hold the bad notes of Jack Galbraith and Rhian Pritchard at bay.

She was young, dressed for the rain, and pleased to have been allowed out on her own, and she compounded our problems by assuming that Emrys was my driver. I watched him bristle as she came over to me and introduced herself as DC Emma Writtle.

I steered her round to Emrys. 'This is Sergeant Hughes, I'm only here as an observer.'

She wasn't embarrassed. We were just two codgers out of Sheepsville, Wales, after all. 'You put in a request to see the crime scene?' she asked Emrys.

I didn't let him see how much I wanted this. He had it in his gift to say he had changed his mind. He checked his watch. We were still early. 'Okay,' he said unenthusiastically.

We all piled into her car and drove south off the main Manchester road. I opted to sit in the rear, thinking that I was being diplomatic, but then realized that it might have looked to the casual observer, and to Emrys, as if I was being chauffeured.

She slowed down on a narrow blacktop lane lined on both sides with conifer plantations, craning forward until she saw the track entrance she had been looking for. She turned left into it, and nodded at Emrys. It took him a moment to realize that he was meant to get out and open the gate. He glared at me sitting regally in the nabob's seat as she drove through.

The car bumped along a narrow, sandy, unmade track through the trees. We emerged in a clearing where the main track forked right and wound its way through a thinner belt of trees to an expanse of water-filled sandpit. She took the left fork along a more overgrown track through scrub and

141

secondary-growth trees, sodden paper rubbish in the ruts and snagged into brambles. She was taking it slow, looking for landmarks.

'There's where it was found.' She coasted to a halt and pointed to the indentation where an abandoned logging trail forked off to the right. Broom, birch saplings and rosebay willowherb were already well on their way to colonizing it. I got out of the car, pulling my raincoat on as I walked over. Behind me I heard their doors open and close.

The vegetation at the entrance to the trail was crushed, charred and scorched. The immediate surroundings were free of rubbish, a stark tidy contrast with the rest of the area. The sandy ground was churned and rutted where they had dragged the burned-out VW Golf clear and loaded it onto a recovery truck.

'Was the car driven front end in, or was it facing out?' I asked Emma as she and Emrys came up beside me.

'What difference does that make?' Emrys asked.

'Front end facing in,' Emma said.

'If Ryan had driven in voluntarily he would have turned the car round to make getting out easier,' I explained to Emrys. 'If it was facing down that overgrown trail, it means that someone else drove it and left it like that because it was never going anywhere else again under its own steam.' I turned to Emma. 'I'm assuming you checked the tyre tracks?'

'Of course. All the legible ones have been photographed and cast, and are waiting to be cross-matched against the fifty odd million other ones on the road.'

'All?' I asked.

She flashed a dirty grin. 'This place is Downtown Shagville Central.' I caught Emrys's disapproving Baptist scowl out of the corner of my eye. 'We get reports of cruising, dogging, peeping, as well as common-or-garden humping. And if you want rubbish, we've picked up a shedload of that – needles, burnt tinfoil, underwear, a sack of dead kittens . . .' she counted them off on her thumb, looking directly at Emrys now, savouring the shock ripples in his eyes, 'butt plugs, used condoms – plain, ribbed and flavoured – and one discarded prosthesis, an artificial leg complete with a yellow sock and size nine brown leather brogue.'

And none of it, I gathered, was screaming *Eureka!* 'Was the car still on fire when you found it?' I asked.

'No. It was reported in by a man who was out walking his dog. This was in the morning. It had been raining all night.'

I looked round slowly. No neighbouring properties, and the trees and the undergrowth were too dense for anyone driving by on the road to have seen anything. The rain explained why the fire hadn't spread more.

'None of the good citizens of Shagville reported seeing anything suspicious that night?' I asked.

She shook her head. 'The rain either kept them all away or they saw what was arriving and thought it wiser to zip up and scarper.'

'How do you think they knew to bring him here?'

She shrugged. 'Google Earth?' she suggested.

I smiled. She was probably right. 'Who drove?' I pretended to be thinking out loud, hoping that she would rise to the bait. She didn't. 'Was he dead when they arrived, or did they do the business here?' I asked directly this time.

She held her hands up and shook her head. 'I can't tell you that.'

'Okay.' I made another slow visual circuit of the place. It told me nothing new. I nodded at her. 'I think we can go on to Winsford now.'

We followed her to her car. Emrys sidled up to me. 'Did you get anything from this?' he whispered. Despite himself, he was interested.

I gave him my wise look. 'Ryan Shaw didn't do this to himself.'

9

The two cops in the meeting room we were shown into in Winsford looked very settled and cosy together. I got the feeling that we had been invited to an eleven o'clock meeting that had actually been scheduled to start without us at half past ten.

The smile on the man behind the desk was on automatic as we entered, but it contorted as he stood up, letting us see his puzzlement. He leaned across the desk to shake our hands. 'Hi, I'm DI Keith Purslow . . .' Oh shit, I groaned inwardly, yet another DI who was younger than me. He gestured towards the woman sitting at the side of the desk, who wasn't, '. . . and this is DI Bradshaw from Manchester.' No first name or department information offered I registered.

She inclined her head, giving us a vague, thin-lipped smile. And big red glasses we were meant to notice, to deflect attention from the intensity of her scrutiny. A modicum of make-up, no attempt to plaster over the lines that creased the sides

145

of her eyes and mouth. Smooth, sleek, collar-length hair, the label on the colouring product would have read something like *rich chestnut*.

Purslow arranged another chair in front of his desk. 'We were only expecting Sergeant Hughes,' he said, explaining his confusion.

We sat down and I gave them both a woolly smile. 'I'm DS Glyn Capaldi, we hoped you wouldn't mind if I attended as an interested observer.'

'Do you always travel in pairs in enemy country?' Bradshaw asked, her lips curling slightly to let us know it was meant to be a joke. Emrys and I chuckled uncomfortably.

'*Interested observer*? Can you be more specific please?' Purslow asked.

I sensed Emrys glancing at me nervously. I hadn't rehearsed this. Fuck it! I decided to usurp Kevin Fletcher's throne.

'You've heard of the recent arson attacks and discovery of some drug factories in Mid Wales?'

Purslow nodded circumspectly. 'Some.'

'We've been circulated,' Bradshaw observed enigmatically.

'I've been asked to liaise with the Metropolitan Police to check it out at our end to see whether there's any tie-in with their jurisdiction, and to try and figure out how far the distribution network stretched.' I deliberately avoided Emrys's eyes. I didn't want his incredulity blowing this apart.

Both Purslow and Bradshaw consulted the notes in front of them. We were all silent for a moment. Purslow and Bradshaw looked at each other. Bradshaw's nod was almost imperceptible.

Purslow led off. 'Ryan Shaw appears to have been strictly

small time. Are you trying to tell us that he was involved in these factory operations?'

'No. Not directly. But he was an opportunist, and he might have come across some product, or looted some. Perhaps he tried to sell it through his contacts in Manchester, and suffered the consequences?' I looked across at them enquiringly, my expression humble and eager.

Bradshaw wasn't buying it. She shook her head knowingly. 'Shaw had nothing to do with this stuff.' She fixed a penetrating stare on me. 'And the Met have already asked for our cooperation on monitoring its circulation in our patch.'

I held her stare. 'I wouldn't know about that. As I said, I'm working the Mid Wales end of the operation for them. I'm here to see whether it connects with Ryan Shaw's death.'

She shook her head again without softening the stare.

'Okay,' Purslow announced, playing the peacemaker, 'I think it's time to get on with what Sergeant Hughes can give us on Shaw's background.'

Emrys laid out Ryan Shaw's life of mean and petty crime, which had started in primary school when he had first come up on the radar for charging his classmates dinner-money rates to view the pale and magic pudenda of a pair of twins he had enmeshed into his short-trousered thrall. I listened as attentively as the two DIs. This was all new to me too. From junior pimp, he had graduated to breaking into coin-fed gas and electricity meters, rising like a nymph in a stream through the shallows of amateur burglary and clumsy thievery to blossom into the mayfly of Dinas's drug culture. A natural self-preservationist, he had shown neither hesitation nor scruples when invited to enlist as a police informer.

Interestingly, Emrys omitted to mention anything about Ryan's role as the local dealer in stolen property. Didn't he know? Or didn't he think it was relevant?

'Thank you for that, Sergeant Hughes,' Purslow said when he had finished. He gave him a smile and a grace pause before he rose out of his seat into that half-standing paper-squaring routine that flags up the end of a meeting.

We were getting the bum's rush. The bastards were short-changing us. They'd had what they wanted from Emrys. Now, as far as they were concerned, we were empty vessels. But I needed more. The problem was, how to say *whoa fucking whoa* to two superior officers and get away with it.

If in doubt, frame it with a deliberate chump smile. 'Don't we get to hear what happened at this end, Sir?' I asked, breaking the convivial tidying-up silence.

Purslow and Bradshaw flashed each other a glance. 'Why do we need to do that, Sergeant?' Bradshaw asked.

I presented Emrys to them with my magician's beautiful assistant side-arm flourish across my stomach. 'We've given you our end of things. Perhaps we can reciprocate.'

'As in?' Purslow asked.

'I'm assuming the current line of enquiry has Ryan Shaw being killed for something he got up to in Manchester?' I looked at Bradshaw as I said it. She nodded grudgingly. 'But what if it was something closer to home? Someone he crossed on our patch. Perhaps if you could give us the details we might recognize something in them that relates to our home-grown villains. Right, Emrys?' I beamed at him, and for once the great lump recognized a cue and nodded.

Another look passed between Purslow and Bradshaw. Their bones told them that it was bunkum, but now that I had raised it, they knew that it had to be at least considered. They both sat down with undisguised reluctance. Purslow nodded at me. 'Okay, Sergeant Capaldi, you start it.'

'Cause of death?'

'Asphyxiation.'

'Smoke inhalation?' He nodded. 'He was in a burning car and he didn't try to get out?' I pressed.

'The fire damage was extensive, the body was badly burned. But forensics found traces of plastic cable clips melted onto the steering wheel. From that and the position of the body, we think that he might have been secured to it.'

'Apart from the fire-related damage, what other injuries showed up in the post-mortem examination?'

'There was evidence that he'd been tortured.'

'Specifically?'

'As well as the general burn pattern you'd expect to find in a fire like that, the pathologist found severe localized burn areas around the genitals and the nipple regions on his chest.'

'Cigarette burns?'

'Bigger. More intense.'

'Like a blowtorch?' I asked.

'The days of the old blowtorch have gone, Sergeant,' Bradshaw volunteered, 'you can blame all these television cookery programmes. In my patch they're using the same thing on their victims as they use to melt the topping on their crème brûlées.'

'He'd also lost fingernails and teeth, and his eyelids had been cut off,' Purslow continued.

'It makes it easier to drip nasty stuff onto the eyeballs,' Bradshaw explained helpfully. I was aware of Emrys blenching beside me.

'Did he drive there himself?'

Bradshaw laughed. 'I doubt that very much.'

'So these things weren't done at the crime scene?' I asked.

'We've found no evidence,' Purslow said.

'It would have been too awkward out there in Dingly-Dell,' Bradshaw elaborated. 'That's where they took him to finish it. For the more refined work they'd use somewhere like a soundproofed lock-up.'

'So they didn't get what they wanted?' I speculated.

Purslow's stare zoomed in on me. 'How do you work that out?'

'If he'd given up what they were after, they would have killed him where they were working on him. It saves on the risk of having to drive him out there. So, if he was alive when they set fire to that car they were giving him a last chance to tell them what they needed.'

'Or they were just bloodthirsty bastards.' Bradshaw smiled condescendingly. 'They breed them like that where I come from.'

'You definitely know he was in Manchester?' I asked her.

She nodded. 'We've got him on camera in his car.'

'Conventional CCTV or dedicated surveillance?' I asked.

The condescending smile again. 'You don't need to know that.'

'I assume he was there to score?'

'Probably.'

'You didn't pick him up?'

She shook her head.

'Too small fry?'

'No, Sergeant. He would still have been clean when the cameras registered him leaving. Probably on the way to a warehouse somewhere to pick up what he had paid for.'

'Warehouse?'

'They get changed too often for us to keep track. We concentrate on keeping tabs on head office.'

'Which is where?'

She almost laughed. 'Nice try. But no fucking coconut.'

'I assume that all these villains of yours have got alibis?' I should have laced that with a bit of respect, but she was pissing me off.

She smiled patronizingly. 'That's why we're all fucking here, Sergeant,' her voice grated.

Purslow picked up on her irritation. 'So, do you recognize anything from that? Anyone you know that partial to blow-torch and pliers work in your valley?'

I actually made a show of consulting with Emrys before I shook my head.

'Okay, we'll wrap it then. Thanks again for coming.' This time he missed out the paper shuffling and just stood straight up. He led Emrys and I to the door and opened it.

Behind us, Bradshaw said, 'Sergeant Capaldi?'

I turned. Emrys looked surprised when Purslow ushered him out of the room. I wondered when he and Bradshaw had passed that particular signal between them. I looked at her expectantly.

She gave me her best vulpine smile. 'I've got some good friends in the Met.'

'That must be nice for you, Ma'am. Get you cheap tickets to a show when you go up to London, do they?'

She ignored that. 'I'm going to be asking them about you.'

I smiled back at her. 'You know something, Inspector?'

She inclined her head, prompting me.

'I really wouldn't bother. You'd be wasting your time.' I hoped that was ambiguous enough to get us out of the building before she took to the telephone. I gave her what I thought was a nifty little nod as I left the room.

Another enemy for the scrapbook?

I reflected on it as Emrys drove us back.

Ryan had been doomed as soon as the bad guys had picked him up. I tried to put myself into that terrible mindset. When had he started to realize that he was dealing with men with no sense of constraint or compassion? The first signals beginning during the period of wrist and ankle restraints and a hood over the head. Fear and disorientation. But always the clutch at hope, even after it had started. *They will realize soon that I don't know what they think I know. When they reach that point of accepting that I can't tell them anything more, they'll let me go.*

But they were never going to do that. These men had no *off* switch. They were never going to pick him up off the floor, dust him down, and drop him at the nearest hospital emergency unit, intimating new-found respect at his sufferings in their farewells.

No, right from the start, even before they had him, they were going to kill him.

And Ryan was no hero. As soon as he had seen the intent

he would have told them everything. Including stuff they hadn't asked for. Anything to make it stop.

But none of it had been what they wanted to hear. They had always wanted more. Right up until he appeared to have been offered that last opportunity. Even after they had doused him and the interior of the car in petrol. Even in flames he hadn't been able to give them what they wanted.

I backed off.

Or was this nothing to do with Jessie? Was this nothing more than a brutal drugs reprisal after all? Had the little weasel finally welched on the wrong people? Had he been left there at a gateway to the Marches as a warning to other members of the hill tribes?

I didn't think so.

But why go to Manchester?

Because that was his portal into the world of big league criminality. Ryan fed off the bottom of the pond, strictly small scale, a tiny abscess on a sucker at the far end of one of the big drug octopus's tentacles. If my theory was correct, and he had been asked to dispose of something valuable and illegal, he would have to have used his Manchester contacts to try to find the appropriate marketplace.

His Manchester dealer might have been in at the core of the deal, or he might just have been working on a fee or a commission to supply the information. But he would have been the one who, directly or indirectly, had put Ryan in contact with the people who killed him.

And one thing I knew for a certainty was that Detective Inspector Bradshaw was not going to give me that name.

Had they already got Christian Fenner?

Were they working down the list to Dai Lloyd?

A change in the car's rhythm brought me back to the surface. We were driving down a ramp off the dual carriageway. I saw the blocky Little Chef building off the roundabout. Under the shadow of a mound that no amount of grass or bushes could disguise its origins as a slag heap.

'I'm hungry,' Emrys announced redundantly as he parked.

'I've got a couple of calls to make. Order me coffee and pancakes.' I felt a sudden need for sugar. He flashed me a tight-lipped petulant scowl. The idiot thought I was trying to get away without paying. 'They don't ask for cash up front, Emrys, they settle up the bill at the end in these places. I'll even pay for you.'

'They were never going to ask us to share the fucking budget, were they?' he snapped. He, like me, had also been brooding.

'Better safe than sorry,' I replied.

'And all that London Metropolitan Police fucking nonsense. I'm beginning to think you're seriously cracked, Capaldi.'

He slammed his door as he marched off.

I took my phone out. It felt like it had gained more heft. What was waiting for me when I switched this on?

Plas Coch lived up to its name. A red house. Large and attractive, Edwardian Arts and Crafts in style, its roughcast rendered walls painted red ochre, with a steeply pitched weathered slate roof. A round stone tower, part of an earlier building, had been incorporated into the frontage, and an ivy-covered open stone porch continued the mediaeval reference.

154

I parked between a black Range Rover Sports with personalized number plates and a tiny Citroën Méhari with a red-and-white-striped soft top that looked like it had been run up from a discarded Punch and Judy tent. Given our climate and the wealth of the setting, this was obviously a declaration of irony on wheels.

I sat in the car and took my time composing myself. I was still worried. What was Jack Galbraith playing at?

There had been no messages from him on my mobile. No emails when I got back to Unit 13, nothing on the answering machine. What the fuck was he doing with all his pent-up wrath?

There had been a text message from Kevin Fletcher. *Think about it.*

And two missed calls. Numbers withheld.

I ignored Fletcher's message. But I was still wondering about the missed calls. Had I got Dai Lloyd running scared? Before I got out of the car I decided that there would be no harm in keeping up the pressure.

I sent a text message. *I think they got Jessie. They may now have got to Christian. If we leave it much longer I may not be able to protect you.* I hoped I had pitched it correctly. I wanted him nervous, brooding and needing me, but I didn't want him running to his parents to show them a scary message from a cop.

I had lived in houses with smaller living rooms than the porch to Plas Coch. The metal handle to the door bell was like something attached to a weight-lifting machine in a fitness suite. I pulled down on it and heard no chimes. I forced myself not to pull it again. It could be a test of

155

confidence. They could probably judge your social standing by the number of times you tried to ring the bell.

The big oak door opened without a creak and no bats flew out. Instead the man I recognized as Stevenson stood aside and said, 'Please come in.' He knew who I was.

He was shorter than me, powerfully built with a sharp nose, chin, and narrow eyes, which formed a strange coexistence with what was a mainly round face. The top of his head was bald, with dark hair slicked behind his ears like little folded wings.

As he took my coat I picked up on something I hadn't noticed before. There was no trace of the servant in this man. His smile was pleasant, but it was steady, and in place of deference there was a measuring quality in his eyes. Definitely no baboon-arse submission here. He was wearing a blue butler's apron over jeans and a pink striped shirt with turned-back sleeves. On the wall behind him I saw a mounted stag's head with an eye patch and vivid carmine lipstick on the pouted mouth. How much more fucking irony could this house generate? I wondered.

He led me across the stone-flagged hall to a large panelled door. 'What do you want to drink?' he asked, before he opened it. I recognized it now. His voice had a faint hint of a Geordie accent.

'I'm driving,' I told him.

'I'll bring you something that tastes like white wine,' he said as he opened the door.

It was a big room with a high coffered ceiling, surprisingly light in contrast to the dark hall, the light coming from two sets of full-height French casement windows catching the setting sun. The focal point was a large herringbone brickwork inglenook fireplace with a brightly glowing wood-burning stove. Above the carved mantelpiece was a charming naïve school painting of a Hereford bull.

From my first glance I estimated that there were between twelve to fifteen people in the room, in small groups, sitting and standing. My attention was immediately taken by the actress I had seen at Jessie's funeral, who was talking to Ursula ap Hywel and an effetely elegant young man I didn't know. I also recognized a few faces from Dinas. The chair of the local magistrates' bench, and a couple of wealthy farmers.

And no Rhian. I felt the easing of a small tension I hadn't been conscious of carrying.

Rhodri ap Hywel detached himself from his conversation and crossed the room to rescue me from social-gathering oblivion. 'Glyn, I'm really glad you could make it,' he said warmly, shaking my hand.

'This is an amazing place,' I told him.

'Thank you,' he inclined his head and flashed a mischievous smile. 'One of the spoils of capitalism.'

'How long have you lived here?'

'I was born here. My father bought the house.' He smiled conspiratorially. 'To shake off our robber baron past and turn us respectable. He even changed the family name in the process.'

'From what?'

He laughed. 'From plain old Howell. My grandfather started the property development business in Nottingham. But even he must have been hankering after the old country

157

when he called the company Taliesin Developments. When my father took over the business he shifted the operation to London, and named us after the old kings of Deheuborth.' He spread his arms mock expansively. 'Et voila, a noble dynasty is created.'

Stevenson approached with my drink. 'Thanks,' I said.

'Thanks, Tony,' Rhodri said, shaking his head at an unspoken question that had passed between them. I took a sip of my drink. It was more than good. If this was ersatz white wine I had obviously been fooled by the real thing for a long time. We both watched him for a moment as he circulated among the other guests looking more like the host than a retainer.

'Come on,' Rhodri said enthusiastically, taking me by the elbow, 'let me show you how I salve my social conscience.' He led me across the room, nodding smoothly at his guests as we progressed, stopping me in front of a couple of aerial photographs on the wall above a Georgian side table. He used a hand flourish to gesture at them. 'The Ap Hywel Foundation at work.' Both showed bush village compounds with identical large blockhouse structures with a huge red cross painted on the metal roofs.

'Sierra Leone?' I said, remembering what Cassie had told me.

He looked pleased. 'That's right.' He pointed at the photographs in turn: 'Hankale and Tavalu. Where we have our clinics. They're close to the border with Liberia, near a town called Pendembu.'

I grunted pretend knowledge. 'How did you come to choose them?'

'Almost literally with a pin on a map. We're not quite up to Bill Gates's level, so, rather than spread what we had around thinly, we decided to try and do something really good in just a couple of places. It was difficult, but I took advice and talked to people in the field. We narrowed the area down, went out there, and chose to do our work in these two villages.'

'You still go out there yourself?'

'Every year,' he announced proudly.

My eyes dropped to a framed photograph on the side table. This corner was obviously the Foundation's wayside shrine. It was a picture of a younger Jessie, surrounded by a bunch of local children, possessively clutching what looked like one of the carved wooden statuettes I had seen in her room. The African kids were mugging it to the camera, beaming delighted gappy-toothed grins. Jessie was also smiling, but hers was the look of a wised-up starlet posing with a crowd of rube fans, her eyes directed straight at the photographer, demanding *Get this fucking over with.*

He saw me looking. 'Jessie used to come out with us too.'

'Not Cassie?'

'Cassie hates flying.' He was reflective for a moment. 'I think Jessie got something out of it.' He brightened. 'And now it's ulterior motive time.' He clasped me lightly round the shoulders. 'We're always looking for funding, Glyn.' I started to reach for my wallet. 'No, no, no . . .' he protested chirpily. 'I haven't got you here to milk you. I just want you to spread the word among your colleagues. Perhaps think about some fundraising for us. It's a great cause.'

'I will, Rhodri,' I promised sincerely, without informing

him that, amongst my peers, I was not exactly the guy that everyone rooted for.

'Hello, Glyn.'

I recognized that rich voice before I turned round to see Ursula ap Hywel. She was looking at Rhodri, and I caught one of those almost mystical exchanges that vibrate silently between long-term partners. He left with a smile and a pat on my elbow to mingle with his other guests.

'Has Rhodri been press-ganging you into serving the cause?' she asked, looking amused.

'He was very gracious.'

She nodded, agreeing with me. 'Thanks for coming.'

'Thanks for inviting me.' I made a show of looking round the room. 'No Cassie?'

'She's very busy. She's got a full house at the Home Farm.'

'She knew I was coming?'

She laughed mock despairingly. 'No, she really is very busy.' She slipped her hand into the crook of my arm. 'Come, I'll introduce you to someone who can verify that.'

It was the actress. She watched us approaching, her features locking into her public face. I couldn't tell whether a signal was exchanged, but the effete young man beside her slipped away.

'Corey, I'd like you to meet Glyn Capaldi.'

Corrine Sanderson. The name came back to me now.

We shook hands. Or rather I clasped the long fingers she graciously presented. I was aware of her scrutiny. 'Capaldi?' She was researching her memory cards. 'Have you got something to do with San Sano Productions?'

I shook my head regretfully, seeing the bar drop down on my entrance into her world. 'No, I'm a detective sergeant.'

It was virtually imperceptible, but I saw her interest switch off.

'Corey's on retreat at the Home Farm,' Ursula explained. She shifted to Corey. 'I was telling Glyn how hard Cassie has to work to look after you lot.'

'Darling!' La Sanderson threw her head back, tilted it into a press release half-profile, and cawed, 'The woman's an enchantress. Provides us with wonderfully healthy meals, keeps everything so clean, but maintains that wonderful serenity that's the reason we come to the place.'

'This isn't your first time then?'

'Oh Lord no, this is one of my sanctuaries. I come here to get sane, don't I, Ursula?'

Ursula smiled at her fondly.

'You knew Cassie's daughter Jessie?' I asked.

She winged a glance at Ursula that made me realize she had been forewarned. *Beware the cop with the guilt chip.* She had now realized who I was. 'Not well,' she compromised.

'Did she help out with things?'

Ursula stepped in. 'Yes, but you have to remember Jessie was young. Therefore, she was selective.'

'Selective?'

'She liked to be on display. Not for her the unseen skivvy work in the kitchen or scrubbing the loos.'

La Sanderson trilled out a laugh. 'Oh, too true, honey.' She clutched Ursula's wrist. 'What wouldn't we give to have all that natural oomph back again? She used to charm the nose hairs off the old geezers.'

I chuckled. I summoned up a light-hearted image of a clutch of elderly guys on recliners in the Home Farm knot garden, eyes bulged out on stalks, watching Jessie pass through their midst in a classic French maid's outfit. Then the shadow passed over. I had just had an intimation of darkness over Shangri-la.

10

I left the Plas Coch soirée with the addition of a new boulder to the woe cairn. I now had Jessie's effect on the elderly male guests at the Home Farm retreat to factor into the tapestry. Given what I had seen of the ap Hywel circle, these would be influential people. Power players. Could she have nicked something strategic from one of them and passed it to Ryan Shaw to fence?

And Dai Lloyd still wasn't answering his telephone.

It was dark now driving back to Dinas, the windscreen wipers on intermittent. As well as thoughts of Jessie, Ryan and Dai, I still had Jack Galbraith's ominous silence acting as another irritant.

My headlights picked out a road sign indicating a turning off to the left. *MAESMORE 3.*

Cogs turned, ratchets clicked, and I came to a stop. I suppressed all the other chaff. The problem of finding the identity of Ryan Shaw's Manchester connection had shot to the surface. Because I had just come up with a possible solution.

No. 3 Orchard Close looked incomplete without Ryan's purple VW Golf cluttering the pavement in front of it. From my memory of the layout, the kitchen, which was dark, faced the street. But there was a light-show going on in the obscure glazed panel on the front door, and I recalled the television set that was the size of a garage door in the room opposite it.

Ryan's mother answered the doorbell. She was wearing a short, low-cut pinafore top over tight leggings, her enormous bulk trying to jump out of every perimeter and stretchy surface, as if there was a sausage-making machine concealed behind her still trying to pump the meat in. Her big face looked drawn though, dark shadows under her eyes and accentuating her jowls, her dyed-black hair straggly and unkempt.

Her expression turned into a complex stew. She had recognized me as a cop, but who I was, and where to place me, bothered her.

'I've come to offer my condolences.'

My voice tipped the balance. She pointed at me. 'You came round here once before.' It was an accusation.

'I came to ask for Ryan's help.'

'You fucking pissed him off.'

'Who is it, Mum?' A voice I recognized as Ryan's sister's came from the room opposite, raised over the sound of the television.

'It's that pig who came round here once,' she yelled backwards before turning to face me again. 'You can fuck off.'

Ryan's sister appeared holding her baby, who seemed to have grown to the size of a small giant panda. I saw recognition in her eyes.

'I wanted to tell you how sorry I was to hear about Ryan.'

'We don't need anything from the likes of you,' she said, her mother nodding along in bitter agreement.

'I want to help find out who did it.'

Her mother scowled. 'The cops in Cheshire are dealing with it. That's what Emrys Hughes said.'

'That's right, they're treating it as a routine investigation.'

She frowned. 'What the fuck's that meant to mean?'

'I've got a special interest.'

She shook her head, weary of me now. 'Just fuck off, will you?'

But I picked up on the new notes in the sister's expression. Curiosity and cunning. I had hooked her interest. She stepped around her mother to face me in the doorway, passing the baby over in one seamless movement, a thread of drool uniting them for a moment. 'Go back in, Mum, leave this to me.'

'Why are you so concerned? What was Ryan to you?' she asked, after her mother had left us with a last contemptuous glance.

Flannel wasn't going to work with her. She wouldn't be impressed by any puff about doing this in Ryan's memory. I had to convince her with pure self-interest. 'I think the same people might have screwed up a friend of mine.'

She eyed me closely. 'What's this friend of yours doing running around with the same sort of people as Ryan?'

'Don't ask.'

165

She thought about that for a moment. 'Okay, so what do you want from us?'

'Ryan's Manchester connection.'

'You're a cop, you can get that from your cop pals in Manchester.'

'They don't want to share.'

A new light came into her eyes, part wary, part excited. 'What makes you think that I can give you that information?'

'A hunch.'

'What do we get out of it?'

'Satisfaction.'

'We're already paying our taxes and shit for the police to give us that.'

That I doubted very much. 'I don't mean to be cruel, but I'm afraid that what happened to Ryan is no big deal to them. They'll pursue the investigation, but it's all a question of the allocation of resources to meet the level of public outcry. And, let's face it, Ryan hardly fits the sainted victim category.' I shrugged. 'But, okay. If you want to take that chance. They might just get lucky.' I turned to leave.

She called me back. 'Are you one of those bend-the-rules cops?' I knew better than to answer that. We rode out a short silence. 'What happens to them if you get there first?'

'That depends on the circumstances. Whatever way it goes down, I'll do everything in my power to truly fuck them up for us.'

She stared me out, her internal debate at work. She scrunched her eyes shut to punctuate the decision. 'Wait,' she instructed, shutting the door on me.

I stood there on the doorstep trying not to look like a

spurned Jehovah's Witness. I was sheltered by the cantilevered porch canopy, but I could now see real rain coming down at a slant in the street light's penumbra. The street was deserted, one of those silences prevailing that made me wonder whether everyone but me had received a holy instruction to get indoors. It made me feel unloved and lonely.

She opened the door again, startling me out of my maudlin introspection. She held out a small piece of lined paper folded into a square. 'If they find out where you got this from, I'm fucked,' she warned.

I opened it up. A mobile telephone number and an address in Rusholme in Manchester. 'They won't. If they need my source I'll tell them that a detective inspector I know on the Manchester force provided it.' I looked up from the paper. 'Ryan gave you this?'

She hesitated for a moment. 'I had to go up there for him once. He'd got lifted dicking around with some shit someone had swiped from the back of a vet's car. Turned out it was the gear they use to kill horses.' She smiled to herself at the memory of someone's lucky escape. 'Ryan arranged it on the telephone. Told me to go up there and do the business. A bloke named Kim would be expecting me.'

'What was Kim like?'

She shook her head. 'I don't know. There was three of them there. They all told me they were called Kim.'

I thanked her with a smile and walked out into the rain under the streetlight. It was one of those moments when a fedora, a trench coat, and a cigarette would have felt appropriate.

*

I had a telephone number and an address. One of the guys Ryan's sister had encountered there had probably pointed Ryan into his last sunset. All I needed was to come up with a way of finding out which one it was, and persuading him to give me the information that had directed him there.

But how? Kim, whatever his real name was, was dirty on multiple fronts, but DI Bradshaw would make it her mission to ensure that official channels were closed to me. And I already knew that turning up with a charming cop smile wasn't going to work it.

Climb the waterfall ledge by ledge, I instructed myself. Cool Zen-sounding bullshit on a grey wet night. You need it when you've convinced yourself that God's talking to everyone else but you.

I rattled over the wooden planks of the bridge into Hen Felin Caravan Park. The headlights reflected off the windows and wet siding of the empty units as I turned into the row that led to Unit 13.

And a parked car.

Outside a unit two ranks down from mine. I hadn't been expecting it and had driven by too quickly to have made out any detail or occupancy. And there were no lights on in the unit. But there wouldn't be. The park was still closed, the season hadn't started yet.

I pulled up outside Unit 13 and turned my engine and lights off. And waited. If they were a couple out for a shag in a quiet spot my car passing should have spooked them. The rain drummed on my roof and the engine block ticked as it cooled. They would be fumbling for zips and hooks and buttons. Any minute now the car would start up and they would hightail it.

Nothing happened.

I was going to have to check it out. I reached into the glove compartment for my torch, trying to hold down the memory of what had happened to Ryan. I got out of the car and put on my high-viz police raincoat. I was hanging it out as a sign. I wanted anyone out there with bad intentions to think twice and consider the consequences before acting on any impulses or instructions they might have to hurt me.

It was a white Citroën C3 Pluriel. Welsh registration. I walked round it shining my torch inside. Empty. I placed my hand flat on the bonnet. It was wet and cold. Short of seeing grass growing up through the radiator grille that was the limit of my forensic knowledge of how recently a car had been moving.

I turned my attention to the two units it was parked between. I reached out for the door handle of the nearest one and tentatively tried to turn it.

'Boo!'

The shock temporarily introduced my sphincter muscle to my tonsils. I wheeled round with my torch. She was grinning. Rhian Pritchard in her red duffel coat, holding a yellow umbrella. 'Guilty conscience, Sergeant Capaldi?'

'What the fuck are you doing here?'

'Waiting for you.' She pushed her wrist forward into my torch beam to look at her watch. 'You've taken your time getting back from the ap Hywels.'

'What are you talking about?' I gasped, still recovering from my fright.

'Ursula makes sure that they always wind these things up promptly at eight.'

'I had to go somewhere else after.' I checked myself. Why the fuck was I explaining stuff to her? 'More to the point, what are you doing here?' I demanded, figuratively hitching my balls back into place.

'I already told you. Waiting for you,' she repeated patiently. 'And I wasn't the only one. You're obviously a popular man.'

'What do you mean?'

'There was another car here when I arrived.'

My anxiety spiked again. This woman was bad for the nerves. 'What kind of a car?'

She shrugged. 'A small dark one. I didn't see it properly. It took off from outside your place after I'd stopped.'

A small dark one? Talk about the power of journalistic observation. Had it left because it had realized that it wasn't my car that had arrived? 'How many people in it?' I asked.

She shook her head. 'I don't know.' She pointed up the row. 'It went that way and drove down the next row and back over the bridge.'

A small dark car. Dai? Christian Fenner? Guys with haute cuisine blowtorches?

'I think it might have been a youngster driving.'

'Why?'

'The way they took off. They were either kids or bootleggers.'

Or gangsters? I clicked back into the real world. 'What do you want here?'

She cocked her head at me. 'Well, I think the first thing

170

we ought to do is get you in out of the rain. Plastered-down hair like that really doesn't do anything for you.'

I let her make us coffee while I towelled my hair dry. She was obviously going to nose around anyway, so she may as well make herself useful while she did it.

I watched her through the open doorway. She had taken off her duffel coat. The short bulky white Aran sweater disguised her upper figure, but it combined with the skinny black jeans and ankle boots to make her legs look like they went on for ever. This visit obviously hadn't warranted make-up, but she didn't need it, she had a great complexion and her lips were a rich dusky raspberry pink, and, for the first time, I saw that her eyes were a bright hazel. Her blonde hair was down, and I realized I had been wrong about her age. She was probably closer to mid thirties. I must be getting tired, I thought, because the smile I had previously found so irritating was almost coming across as playful and confident tonight.

She came into the living area carrying two mugs of coffee. 'The caravan, Glyn.' She gestured at the bookshelves that covered the side wall. 'It makes great background.' She sat down opposite me.

I shook my head. 'You're wasting your time. I'm not going to cooperate. Stick to the ap Hywels.'

'I've virtually finished the piece on the Foundation.'

'Don't you get to go to Africa?'

She pulled a mock pout. 'They've cut the budget.'

'They must be loaded,' I observed.

'Ursula is. From what I can gather, the Foundation was

set up with money she inherited. But she also keeps a tight rein on the purse strings. So, story of my life, we're going to use their photographs now, instead of a live shoot.'

I shook my head and grimaced ironically. 'Tough shit.' I took a bottle of Highland Park and a glass from the cabinet beside me and poured a shot. I held it up to her. 'I'd offer you one, but you're driving.'

She smiled, her eyebrows arching, and powered up a tablet computer she had taken from her bag. Her fingers flicked over the screen display. She looked up at me. 'Why Glasgow University?'

Oh shit, she had been delving. I shook my head. 'Not cooperating.'

She pulled a chiding face. 'Oh, don't be juvenile, Glyn. You know I can do this without you if I have to. And if I do, that picture of you aged four in the little leather jerkin, with your right hand clutching your future balls is going in the piece.'

I bristled. 'Where did you get that?'

'I went to have a chat with your mother. She's very proud of you.'

My first reaction was anger, but then I remembered it's what journalists do. So I capitulated. 'There's an extensive branch of the Capaldi family in the West of Scotland. I had a support network in place.'

'Why Scotland in the first place?'

'The degree courses are four years. It puts off the inevitable.'

She smiled. We both knew where this was leading. 'When you were twenty-two you were arrested in Spain with a friend on your way back from Morocco.'

'We were released without being charged.'

'And then you joined the police force in Cardiff. There's a connection there somewhere, isn't there?'

'What's the point in this, Rhian?' I asked wearily.

'Don't put yourself down, it's an interesting story.' Her eyes flicked to the screen to refresh her questions. 'No children?'

'No.'

'You married Virginia Rafferty, a primary school teacher?' She looked at me, waiting for elaboration. I didn't oblige. She glanced down again. 'You made detective sergeant very quickly.' She gave me a quizzical smile. 'And then you seemed to stop there?'

'Foolishly they didn't allow me to handle my own promotion,' I quipped sarcastically.

'You applied for a transfer to London?'

I tried to hide my surprise. If she knew that, she must have had access to internal sources. So how much of all my other departmental grief did she know? I smiled wanly. 'I didn't get it.'

'Did you feel you were being blocked in Cardiff?'

I shrugged, noncommittal. I didn't think I was being blocked in Cardiff, I knew it. I didn't fit the politics. But I wasn't going to tell Rhian that the attempted move to London had been a last-ditch effort to try and claw my way back into my marriage. By then I had resurfaced from the drinking, and had tried to prove to Gina that I still had drive and dreams. But I now knew that, even if I had got the transfer, we wouldn't have made it. Because, sadly, the traces of Gina's own disillusionment had broken and parted

173

from the wagon that I thought we were still sharing a long time before then.

'You divorced?'

I nodded. I knew what she was building up to. It was time to head her off at the pass. 'The hostage hero crap in Cardiff was all bullshit. It was a cover-up.'

'A cover-up for what?'

'A fuck-up. My fuck-up. And I'm now serving out my time in the hills. End of story.'

She smiled. 'Not quite.' She turned the screen round to show me. The front page of a local newspaper. I looked away from the headline I didn't want to read. 'There's more stuff like this. It looks as though you've started a new proactive career up here.'

I closed my eyes. 'I'm tired, Rhian. I really don't want to talk about it.'

'I won't mention what happened to Jessie Bullock in the piece,' she said gently.

'It's part of the story.'

'Don't be naïve, Glyn. The story's only as much as the editor chooses to keep in.' She leaned towards me. 'I'll concentrate on drawing out your soft, sympathetic side. You'll have the ladies flocking.'

'That I very much doubt.'

She leaned back and took a slow careful appraisal of me. 'No.' She shook her head. 'No, I don't think so. It suits you, you know.'

'What suits me?'

'Living here. In this sort of country. You've got the kind of craggy look that goes with it.'

'The answer's still no.'

She grimaced despairingly until we saw the obstinacy mirrored in each others' eyes and laughed in unison. She raised her hands in mock despair, and got up to leave before I could wonder whether we were about to relax into something.

'I'll call you,' she said at the door. I watched the umbrella recede into the night as she walked back to her car.

I switched on my own computer and finished my whisky as it charged up. I went into my emails. Out of the build-up there was only one that grabbed my attention. *10.00 tomorrow morning The Fleece, Dinas. Be there. DCS Galbraith.*

So, the tsunami had been gathering its pace out there after all. And now it looked like it was about to crest and crash over me.

I was toying with a doleful bowl of over-milked muesli the next morning, brooding on Jack Galbraith, when Emrys Hughes called me.

'You've been pestering young Dai Lloyd as well, haven't you?' he accused me, his tone crossly righteous.

'As well as what?' I stalled, catching Dai's name and struggling out of my malaise back up to alertness.

'As well as Louise Black, and pissing me around in Cheshire, and that nonsense about the Met—'

'Who says I've been pestering Dai?' I demanded, cutting in over him.

'His friend Robbie Green.'

'So Dai hasn't accused me himself?'

'He's hardly likely to do that, is he?' he stated snidely.

I tensed. 'Why not?' I asked carefully.

'Because he's gone missing. Like his mate Christian Fenner.'

'When?'

'He didn't come home last night. His parents contacted all his friends and then reported it this morning after no one said they'd seen him.'

A small dark one. I thought about the car Rhian had told me about last night. 'Has he got a car?'

'No. Robbie says he dropped him off at the top of the farm drive about eleven o'clock last night. His parents said he never came down to the farm.'

'How do they know?'

'The dogs would have made a racket.'

Another thought flashed up. 'Has Christian Fenner got a car?'

'Enough of that, Capaldi, I'm meant to be asking you the questions.'

'What have I got to do with it?'

'What were you getting onto him about? Did you say anything to upset him?'

'No.' I decided to deflect him with honesty. 'I was talking to Jessie's friends, that's all, trying to find out about her.'

'Are you sure you didn't get heavy with him?' I could hear the doubt in his tone.

'Positive.'

'The good kids didn't do things like this before you came along,' he whined.

'Emrys?'

His voice went wary. 'What?'

176

'Did Christian Fenner have a car?'

He groaned in frustration. 'Yes.'

'What kind?'

'An old Ford Fiesta. It hasn't been seen since he left.'

'What colour?'

But he had hung up.

Thinking about it distracted me as I drove to Dinas, and I almost sideswiped a tractor and trailer on the way in. If Rhian hadn't chosen last night to come out and see me I would have encountered the small dark car. Or had she inadvertently saved me? Maybe it wouldn't have been healthy to have discovered who had been waiting for me.

And now someone else was waiting for me. Jack Galbraith's polished big black Ford was parked conspicuously outside The Fleece, like an establishing shot in a World War II film setting up a looming intimation of the Gestapo.

He and Bryn Jones were seated at a round table set for coffee, their backs into the bay window. They both watched me grim-faced as I approached. Jack Galbraith gestured at the two chairs in front of them. 'Take a seat, Capaldi,' he growled.

I pulled out the chair next to Bryn and sat down.

Inexplicably they both laughed. Bryn Jones stuck out his hand, palm up in front of Jack Galbraith. 'That one's mine I think?'

Jack Galbraith dropped a pound coin into Bryn's open palm. Both of them chuckled at my bewilderment. 'We got so fed up losing fucking sleep over you that we've decided to treat you as a game,' Jack Galbraith informed me.

'We had money riding on what chair you'd chose,' Bryn explained.

Jack Galbraith shook his head. 'We despair of you. Poor Inspector Morgan's going fucking apoplectic over your antics.'

I winced internally. 'I'm sorry, Sir, I know you didn't want Inspector Morgan pestering you . . .'

He waved a hand to cut me off. 'Oh, I sorted that out. I put in a filter. I've got DC Weir answering all of his calls.' He suppressed a grin and held up a cautioning hand. 'But this is an official reprimand and if you were back on active duty these activities would not be tolerated.' He turned to Bryn. 'Remind me what we're reprimanding him for.'

Bryn read from his notebook. '*For behaviour which could be construed as child abuse, and for obstructing one of his officers in their line of duty.*' He looked up. 'Alison Weir says he called another one in this morning. Something about harassment of some youth who has now gone missing.'

'What have you got to say for yourself, Capaldi?'

'I'm sorry to have got you involved in this, Sir. All I can say in my defence is that Sergeant Hughes and Inspector Morgan have misconstrued my intentions.' I played the game and gave them my chastised face. They were going through the motions. But, as I was annoying the shit out of Emrys Hughes and Inspector Morgan, my rebuke looked like it was only going to be a token. Another thought sneaked in to spoil the party. Jack Galbraith wouldn't have come all this way to deliver this. There was something else behind his visit.

'You may be off the books at the moment, but consider this a warning,' he was serious now, 'and don't take it any fucking further, because there's a limit to how far I'm prepared to go to protect you.'

178

'Yes, Sir, thank you,' I said meekly.

'And I'd advise you to keep your head down. The last time I spoke to Inspector Morgan he sounded like he was getting the barbecue pit ready for you.' He smiled again. 'Okay, now that's over, let's get back to the game.'

'Sir?'

'My money's riding on the one where it's meant to look like you've completely lost your fucking marbles and you're looking for a full pension discharge.'

'Sir?' I repeated, bemused.

Bryn leaned forward to speak. 'And it looks to me like you're trying to make yourself so unpopular here that we have no option but to bring you home to us before they lynch you.'

I looked at him in turn, equally bewildered.

'I told you, Capaldi, we're treating you like a game now,' Jack Galbraith explained. 'Since your behaviour is so fucking skewed and irrational, we've decided to have a bit of fun trying to work out what you're playing at.'

'You're not serious, are you, Sir?'

He turned to Bryn, ignoring my plea. 'Because Christ knows we could do with a bit of fun, couldn't we, Bryn?'

Bryn nodded soberly.

I picked up the cue. 'How's the investigation going, Sir?'

'Frustratingly. Okay, we've got four drug factories out of commission, which has to be good, but we're no closer to finding out who was behind them.'

'Could there be more of them?' I asked.

'Not in this particular guise. They were a small chain of four former temperance milk bars turned cafés, which failed,

179

and were bought up for fire-sale prices, if you'll forgive the pun. For all we know, they'll have moved on and will be setting up new units in the wilds of somewhere like Cornwall, Lincolnshire, or County fucking Durham. We now know the problem exists, but without being able to find out who's behind it, we can't snip it off at the head.'

'The forensic accountants still haven't traced it?'

He shook his head. 'Dead ends. I prefer to keep my villains big, bad and visible, the way they look on the wanted posters. None of this ducking, diving and weaving through all those convoluted fiscal fucking mazes.'

'And we've still got the eight employees unaccounted for,' Bryn commented.

'Fucking right, and that's the real worry. That's the scary one. Normally I'd believe that eight people are too many to dispose of. But the scale of this operation makes me think otherwise.' He clucked in frustration. 'How can eight people live and work in hick towns like these, and no one knows their real identities? And then how can they just up and fucking disappear in a literal puff of smoke?'

'I wish there was some way I could help you, Sir.'

He and Bryn shared a glance, and I suddenly knew that I was about to discover the real reason why I had been summoned here.

Jack Galbraith leaned forward conspiratorially. 'Has Kevin Fletcher been in touch with you?'

They had both assumed the air of professional interrogators. 'Yes, Sir.'

'Did he ask you to work for him?' Bryn asked.

'Yes, Sir.'

180

'And are you?' Jack Galbraith asked.

'No, Sir.'

'Fuck!' Jack Galbraith snorted, sitting back up.

'You wanted me to be working with him?' I asked, surprised.

'I could have done with you as a fifth column.'

'Wouldn't that be unethical, Sir?'

'No. When I do it, it's called fucking tactical.'

'I thought the Metropolitan Police would be pooling their information with you?' For some reason, as I said it, I thought about DI Bradshaw in Manchester.

'Ostensibly,' Bryn observed.

'But who knows how much they're holding back from the hayseeds,' Jack Galbraith reflected grumpily. 'So far, all they've given us is that they've matched the product to stuff that had previously been distributed by a North London outfit.'

'The Saltik family, Turkish Cypriot,' Bryn elaborated.

'And that was a mere throwaway. A sop to stop us bleating. By implication, we don't need to know about the clever stuff that goes on at their end. And if they've managed to take that any further forward, they haven't told us.'

North London Turkish Cypriot. Kevin Fletcher had mentioned that too. A bell that had rung then was sounding again now.

But from where?

11

I stood outside The Fleece and watched Jack Galbraith and Bryn Jones drive off for their next appointment in Machynlleth. The bell in my head was still tolling annoyingly. Taunting me for having tucked something important so far away out of reach.

I crossed the square to the convenience store to buy a few things to take home to Unit 13. I started to make a mental list of what I needed. The bell lost its insistence. Allowing the magic to make its entrance. Association. Passing the display in the pharmacist's window, a phrenology head advertising laxatives, of all things.

The head was bald.

Association! A shaven-headed dyke from Brighton.

Back in Unit 13 I went into my computer, and found what I was looking for in a routine bulletin I had received before Jessie had died.

This had been widely circulated. It was out in the open. Had anyone else acted on it?

The bulletin wasn't big on information. A passport-type photograph of a dark-skinned man with a scowl and frizzy hair, cut short and thinning, the open neck of a white polo shirt showing. His name was Kadir Hoca, aged fifty-three, a Turkish Cypriot with an address in Enfield, North London, and they had him down as the owner of an import and export business. He had been driving a late-model, black BMW 5 Series Touring, and his last sighting had been at a service station outside Newtown. Which was why I had received the bulletin. On the chance that he had been heading this way.

And of course I hadn't thought anything about it at the time. Only that he was equally as improbable in these latitudes as the Latvian student or the shaven dyke from Brighton on the same bulletin. But with a possible Turkish Cypriot tie-in to the drug factories, his presence now took on a meaning that was more than merely arcane.

Another problem struck me. If this guy had a gangster tie-in, why hadn't it been mentioned? Why had he been lumped in with the ordinary disappeared citizens?

Because the Met or some other organization didn't want to share their intelligence? Or because they simply had no idea?

I called Bryn Jones with the information. He thanked me for it, but was noncommittal. I couldn't tell from his voice whether this was something they were already working on. But that was Bryn for you.

It should have stopped there. I had done my duty and passed it on. I was on sick leave. Their investigation had nothing to do with me. Nothing to do with Jessie.

Or did it?

I made another call.

'Glyn!' Rhian sounded happy to hear from me. 'Are you calling to invite me back for that Scotch now?'

'I told you, not while you have to drive.'

'Well, we'll just have to work it that when I have it I won't be going anywhere for a while, won't we?'

Was she flirting? 'Let me know when you're ready for that.'

She laughed down the line. 'Oh, I surely will.'

'In the meantime, I've got something for you.'

'You mean there's more?' she quipped.

'I'm offering you a trade. If you'll give up on writing about me.'

'Go on.' Her tone had turned suddenly calculating.

'How about a Turkish Cypriot businessman who disappears on a visit to Mid Wales?'

'How about it?'

'Strange and exotic and packed with human interest, don't you think?'

'What aren't you telling me?'

I wasn't telling her about the possible Turkish Cypriot drug connection. I wanted her to find out if that existed for herself, and to come back to me with it. I didn't have official access to police resources, but Rhian had already shown herself adept at worming out sensitive information. 'Use your skills. I'll work with you on this one.'

'Why?' That one word was clouded with suspicion.

'I'm on sick leave. I'm bored and I've got nothing better to do. And it sounds intriguing.'

'Give me what you've got and I'll think about it.' She was

184

no dummy. She knew I had an agenda. But I had already worked out that that might be what hooked her interest. Trying to find out what I was up to, and then to move one step ahead. The old game of who-is-really-leading-who in this dance?

After I had hung up I sent a text to another partner I was spinning around in the reel. *Dai, call me please, I can help you. Or meet me tonight 8 p.m. Monks' Trail car park.*

Maybe saying *please* would make it work this time.

It was dark when I parked by the entrance to the Monks' Trail car park. I crossed the gravel lot, using my torch to avoid the puddles. Thankfully it was dry now, a few high thin clouds scudding across, caught up in an airflow that was only present as a breeze down here. The rising moon was heralded by a lighter band nudging up over the tree line, causing the shadow of the canopy to creep towards me.

I stopped in the middle where I could be seen by anyone approaching down the access road. If he was coming I wanted him to see that I was alone. That it was safe.

For all I knew he was already up in the woods watching me.

I felt jittery. A sense of foreboding had been growing all day, increasing in direct proportion to the lengthening absence of a call or a text from Dai. It drove me into a recurring abstraction. An anomaly I found myself worrying over like a tongue drawn to a crumbling filling. Why had Jessie come down out of the woods on her own that night? Had she been selected? Had she volunteered? Had she been alone? And if not, who had she left behind up there?

Dai, I hoped, could answer at least some of those questions.

An approaching car with its headlights on high beam brought me back to the present. I overcame the reaction to turn my head away, lowering it instead, and squinted to avoid the worst of the glare. It stopped at the entrance to the car park.

This has to be Dai, I told myself, only he knew the arrangement.

Then the chill touched the nape of my neck. If someone had abducted him they would have seen my text message. The same people who had lifted Christian Fenner? Barbecued Ryan Shaw?

I fought the urge to break and run like fuck for the trees.

The car moved again. Started to describe a slow circle round the perimeter of the car park. As the headlights' glare passed beyond me I could make out that it was a small car.

A small dark one?

The low ambient light level wasn't enough to make out the occupants. It went round slowly like a picador marking a bull. Except that I never felt less like snorting and pawing the ground than I did at that moment. It was driving round anticlockwise. When the significance of that hit me, I felt a chill creep up my spine. They were driving so that the passenger's side was facing me.

Would I see a gun barrel in this light?

My rational side stepped in then to remind me that, if they had really wanted to take me out, they could have done a Jessie and set a rifle up in the woods hours ago. They didn't need to compound the complication by trying to shoot me from a moving car on a bumpy surface.

I wasn't totally reassured, but I held my ground.

The car completed its circuit and stopped. The contrasting silence when its engine and lights went off was intense. I waited it out until the breeze through the trees filled the aural void again. No one got out of the car.

So I was expected to do the walking.

The car was an old, small, two-door Peugeot hatchback, dark, the actual colour impenetrable in this light. Drawing closer, I could make out that the driver was the only occupant.

The window was down. She was waiting for me with a look of sheepish expectancy. She was still holding the steering wheel with both hands. In a ponytail her stiff unruly hair looked like a loofah stuck to the back of her head, and the glasses she was peering through had a bulge of silver duct tape on the bridge.

'Louise!'

'Hello, Sergeant Capaldi.' I detected notes of embarrassment and tension in her tone, and a faint tremor of something approaching excitement.

Poor kid! I read the story as soon as I recognized her. She was teen-love whipped. 'Why didn't you drive up to me?' I tried to pitch it as kindly as I could.

'I was told to check that there wasn't anyone else here.'

'By Dai?' I asked.

She nodded awkwardly. Even in the gloom I could sense her colouring.

'Why did he come to you, Louise?'

'He remembered that you'd asked him how to find me. He wanted to know what we'd talked about. If you'd said anything about him. Or Jessie.'

And to recruit you to his cause, I thought. Knowing you'd

187

be a walkover. I remembered her swooning against his side on the day of Jessie's funeral. She had probably built up a whole golden story out of the fact that he hadn't actually allowed her to fall. 'Why send you here? Why didn't he just call me back?'

'He was worried that his phone might be bugged.'

'Whose car is this?'

'It's my mum's.' She caught my concern. 'It's all right, it's legal, I'm allowed to drive it in exchange for running the kids around for her. Dad tells me I'm good. I've been driving the tractor and Land Rover round the fields since I was twelve.' She was speaking to ease her nervousness.

'You drive fast?'

'What?'

'Was that you outside my caravan last night?'

'No.' She frowned, puzzled.

I believed her. 'When did Dai turn up?'

'This morning.'

'Where is he?'

'I can't say.' She looked at me pleadingly. 'He hasn't done anything bad. You shouldn't be hounding him like this.'

So that was the spin he had used on her. 'He's in danger, Louise. I can help him.'

She shook her head, a small pleat of misery on her lips. 'He made me promise.'

'So what's the arrangement here?'

'I've got to ask you some stuff, and then go back to him.'

Agh . . . I groaned inwardly. Adolescent fucking intrigue. At a time of their lives when everything should be simple, straight-forward and exuberant, they build in all these layers of

188

complexity. Dai had obviously played too many computer games. 'And then, if he's happy with my answers, you'll come back again with another set of questions? Probably meet me at another rendezvous point?' I asked, guessing the procedures.

She looked doubtful. 'I think so.' Even she hadn't quite grasped it. I could picture Dai working through his platforms, giving her his instructions.

I lowered myself to rest my elbows on the windowsill, looking like I was getting comfortable. 'Okay, fire away.'

'He wants to know what's going to happen to him?'

How many of these abstract unanswerable questions had he thought up? I drew in a breath and pulled a deep-thinking face. She looked at me expectantly. Before she could comprehend, I reached in quickly and pulled the keys from the ignition.

'No!' she reacted, alarmed and cheated, the consequences of what I had done roaring in. 'You can't do that.'

I stood up and dangled the keys. 'I already have. Now we're going to drive back to Dai.'

'I can't do that. I told you, I promised him,' she wailed.

'Yes, we can. It's all right, Louise,' I said consolingly, 'all we're doing is cutting out the pointless middle layers of his game.'

'I can't take you there, I'll be breaking my word,' she gasped, close to tears.

'I'll drive. You can say I forced you.'

'You're not insured.'

'Yes I am. A policeman can drive anyone's car,' I lied.

*

189

I had to leave my car behind. I would have to deal with that later. It was vital that we arrived in Louise's car. It's what he was expecting.

Using Louise. It was a classic stalling technique. One that he may not even have been conscious of employing. On the one hand, by sending her out to meet me, he could convince himself that he was being dynamic, while, on the other, citing caution as a strategy, he could hold me at bay for as long as he wanted. He probably knew by now that he needed help, but he didn't want to have to face the explanations that went with it. So he could distract himself from the underlying problem by keeping the balls up in the air.

And now I was about to usurp those controls.

Louise sniffled all the way, only surfacing from her dolour to voice the directions. I had taken her phone so she couldn't send him any sneaky text announcements. Other than that I reckoned that she was too straightforward and too stricken to throw in any wobbles. We went through Llandewi, and then drove south, turning left into a small wooded valley that ran south-east, the foothills of the Cambrians nudging up on our left. After a couple of miles on this she warned me to slow down and take a rough track off to the right.

I made the turn and stopped. The moon was up now, the sky clearer. The track crossed an alder-lined brook on a humped bridge, and I could make out the darker lines of the drystone walls that lined its route winding up with the grain of the contours and into a darker mass of woodland.

'Where's this taking us?' I asked.

'There's an old field shelter up there,' she said miserably. 'That's where he's waiting?' She nodded. 'How far?' I asked.

'About a mile.' She pointed. 'The track goes into the trees, and then round the hill. The shelter's on the left, where it comes out of the trees again.'

Quite a hike, I thought. And you had to get all the way down the road before you even got onto this track. 'Did you drive him here?'

'No, he was on his motorbike.'

Shit! I hadn't factored for that. If I wasn't careful he could make a break for it. Then the more important thought hit me. I tried to remember what Emrys had told me on the phone this morning.

I checked for a signal on my phone. Barely enough. 'Don't move,' I instructed her and got out of the car to make the two calls.

As I listened to them complain I watched the spot where the track entered the woods, imagining Dai watching from there. I was in the shadow of a clump of alders. He wouldn't be able to see me, only the car's lights. Would he be wondering why Louise had stopped down here? Getting even more nervous?

I finished the calls, walked over and opened Louise's door. She looked up at me surprised. 'Get out please.'

'Why?'

'He's only expecting one person to be in the car.'

Her face distorted. 'You can't leave me here.'

I felt like a heel, but couldn't show it. 'It's dry and it won't be for long.'

'It's dark and scary.'

I knelt down to her level. 'Dai's in danger, Louise, I don't want him running again, this is your way of helping him.'

She scrunched her eyes to hold in the tears and swung out of the seat. I wanted to hug her for her bravery and her selflessness, but it wouldn't have been appropriate. I had to stay stern for the good of the mission.

There was a lot of loose stone on the track and I took it easy to start with. If I knocked the sump of Louise's mother's car out, on top of having apparently abandoned her daughter in the middle of nowhere without her phone, it would have the equivalent career effect as running naked and frisky into a packed Soroptimists meeting. On the other hand though, if Dai was watching my approach, I had to be seen to be driving like a country girl who had spent her youth throwing tractors around silage clamps and slurry pits. I compromised by putting my foot down a bit harder and keeping my fingers crossed.

As the track entered the trees I slumped down in the seat as much as possible to approximate Louise's height, my knees wedged up against the bulkhead.

I emerged from the trees and caught sight of the field shelter off to the left and set back from the track, where Louise had placed it. It was stone with a monopitch corrugated-iron roof, and a wide opening in the front wall. Dai was standing on the far side of the opening. He turned his head away to avoid being dazzled by my lights as I swung in off the track. More importantly, as the headlights swept the entrance, I saw that the motorbike was parked under cover, inside the shelter. I stopped in front, ensuring that I was blocking the entrance.

Dai came round to the driver's side. He was wearing a woollen ski cap, and a bulky rust-red quilted anorak, which, with his long skinny legs, made him look like he was trying for a fancy dress prize as a toffee-apple.

'Everything go okay?' he asked, reaching for my door handle.

I was still crunched down in the seat, in the shadow of the field shelter. He hadn't yet seen that I wasn't Louise.

Shit! I had forgotten to deactivate the interior light.

I put the weight of my shoulder against the door as he pulled it open and uncoiled myself as the light came on, banging my knee painfully against the steering wheel. He was caught off-balance. His expression fractured in surprise, he tried to back off, but caught a heel and stumbled onto his backside.

I straddled his legs, my left arm, palm upwards, pushed down towards his alarmed face. I had learned from experience that silence made the best force field.

He shook his head, bewildered, an angry petulance starting to surface. 'What are you doing here?' he stammered, trying to express the unfairness of it. I had cheated. He had worked out all these elaborate rules, and I had ignored them. 'Where's Louise Black?' he demanded, in control enough to use her surname to abrogate any assumed intimacy between them.

I ignored his questions. They were irrelevant. I had to put myself in control. 'Get up,' I commanded, moving back. 'I'm offering you this one chance to help you. You can run if you want to, but that's the end of it, you're on your own after that.'

He got up, still watching me sulkily, brushing the dirt off his backside. 'How are you going to help me?' He was still trying to tough it out.

193

'Why have you left home?'

'You scared me. You said that someone had got Jessie and Christian. You more or less said that I was going to be next.'

'I don't buy that, Dai. If you thought I was playing the nasty policeman you'd have told your parents, or complained to someone like Huw Davies. No, I think what I said only reinforced what you already knew.'

'So what am I supposed to know?' he challenged with a bravado that didn't match the uncertainty in his eyes.

'The reason why Jessie died. Why Christian has gone missing.'

He shook his head, still managing to muster defiance.

'What went wrong, Dai?'

He looked at me blankly.

'What got Jessie killed? What did you take from one of the cars you broke into that turned everything to shit?'

His expression skewed to aghast, his head starting to shake violently. 'I had nothing to do with any of that. You have to believe me.'

His reaction surprised me. He wasn't acting. 'You weren't with her that night?'

'No.'

'Was Christian?'

'I don't know. He never talked about it.'

I walked away from him, round Louise's car, and into the field shelter. It was a trials bike, an off-road thing with narrow knobbly tyres. And no registration plate.

I sensed him come up behind me. 'Where did you stay last night?' I asked without turning round.

'At a friend's.'

I let the lie go. I nodded at the bike. 'Does this go well?'

'You know about bikes?'

'No.' I turned to face him. 'All I know is that you don't have one.'

His face went wary. 'What do you mean?'

'I checked with Sergeant Hughes and Huw Davies. You don't own a motorbike. You were on foot when you left home last night.'

He nodded. 'And then I picked up my bike.'

'So even your parents don't know about it?'

'They didn't want me to have one.'

'So you bought this on the sly?'

He nodded again cautiously, trying to keep up with me.

'With what?'

'What?'

'How did you get the money?'

'It wasn't expensive. Only three hundred and fifty pounds. I saved up.'

'Saved up what? And don't give me your fucking pocket money or the job in your spare time that no one else seems to know about.'

He wouldn't meet my eyes. He stared down at his bike. He couldn't quite believe that this beloved object had betrayed him. 'Christian gave me the money,' he said dully.

'Why?' I could feel it, we were close now.

He was quiet, sorting through and abandoning the new lies. 'It was my share,' he finally said, even more quietly. 'Christian passed it on from Jessie.'

'Share of what, Dai?'

When he looked up I saw that he wasn't far off tears. A raw plea in his eyes. 'What will happen to me?'

I set him up in front of a tape recorder in Unit 13.

I had already heard a brief guilt-garbled version from the rear of Louise's car as we drove down the track to pick her up. And the first of the wailing, when I had told him that he would have to leave the motorbike behind. My conditional promise to have it picked up for him had also established the first of the reward situations. If he was very good and very cooperative someone would go and fetch it very soon.

I had also built up Unit 13 as a sanctuary. Holy tin and pop-rivets, bullet- and evil-proof.

The strained silence in the car after we had picked up Louise and were driving to get my car had an almost measurable tensile strength. Even a wet sniff would have ricocheted. They were both drawn up as tight as bottled foetuses in their separate miseries.

At the car park I left it to Louise to get out and release him from the back seat. I stayed where I was to give them a private moment. I needn't have bothered. She was too shy to even look at him, and he was completely wrapped up in the storm front ahead.

I gestured for Louise to wait there, and led Dai to my car. 'You've forgotten something,' I said to him quietly.

'What?'

'You haven't thanked her.'

He looked over at Louise as if trying to place her in the picture. 'She doesn't mind. She wanted to help.'

I leaned in close. 'Go over and say thank you properly,

196

you selfish little fuck.' He looked at me, alarmed. 'I don't expect you to kiss her, but I want to see at least a touch.'

He stuck to the letter of the law, and managed a one-handed pat on her shoulder, not exactly laced with passion, but it did cheer her up. I wanted to give him some avuncular advice, to tell him that if I had known at his age what I know now, I would go for the Louises of this world every time. But it would have been pointless. He was at a stage in his development where his ideal came with software that generated sassy comebacks, weapon skills, and D-cups with crevasse cleavages. None of the things you actually end up wanting in your life partner.

Back in Unit 13 I made tea while he stashed his meagre possessions in the small spare bedroom. I was living dangerously, harbouring a runaway, when I should have been task-dedicated to returning him to the shelter of his family.

He came into the living area and his eyes went straight to the tape recorder. 'Is this evidence?'

'It wouldn't work in a court of law.'

'Why do you want it then?'

'I want you to feel that you're making a real commitment.' And there was that element to it, but I wasn't going to tell him that I was also laying my escape trail. Getting some hard evidence down in the event that this thing turned truly shitty and I had the need of a magic elixir to extricate myself from it. I picked up my tea and waited for him to sit down. 'You texted your parents like I told you? Said you're sorry and told them you're safe?'

'Yes.'

'Good. It's not going to stop them worrying, but at least

it'll remove the biggest one.' I pitched my voice to go with my caring credentials. 'You obviously came up through school with Jessie, so when did it turn special? When did the real friendship start?'

He frowned. 'I thought you wanted to know about the money?'

'I do, but I want to know how you got to be there in the first place.'

'She saw me playing tennis. She came over and watched me one day.' I nodded for him to go on. 'I'm good at tennis. I played even better that time, when I saw she was watching me. Up until then she'd never paid me much attention.'

'But you had her?'

'You couldn't help it. Jessie was one of the hot ones. And not just to look at; she was smart with it and a bit wild, but in a cool way.'

'Did she have a boyfriend then?'

'She was hanging out with Christian and a boy called Sean Thomas.'

'Who went off with another girl?'

'How did you know about that?' I had surprised him.

'It doesn't matter. It means that Jessie had a vacancy.'

He blushed and shook his head. 'It wasn't like that.'

'Was Christian a friend?'

'Not then.'

'When you started going round as a threesome?'

He looked irritated. 'It was just the two of us. I didn't ask about Christian, and she didn't talk about him.'

'Was she your first?'

He lowered his head, and then nodded at the tape recorder. 'Does that have to be on?'

'Yes.' He had given me his answer, I didn't press him. There was more difficult stuff to come. 'So, gradually, Christian drifted into your life?'

The change of tack relaxed him. 'Yes.'

'Were you jealous?'

'Not after I got to know him. We were completely different. We both realized that Jessie liked us equally, but in separate ways, for the different things we were interested in.'

'Okay . . .' I nodded, 'you had tennis, what did Christian have?'

'His music. He played guitar and wrote songs.'

'Did the three of you end up sleeping together?'

'No!' His denial was too sharp. He coloured and looked away from me. I used the silent tool. He turned back to me, his face still flushed. 'Jessie wanted us to. She said if we were real friends we should share everything.' He shook his head. 'There was no way I was going to get into stuff like that.'

'What about Christian?'

'He wouldn't have wanted to either. He might have done it for Jessie though. But I wasn't going to,' he stated adamantly.

But you didn't walk away from her, I thought to myself. She knew she had them both then. The bond would have been tighter if she'd got them fucking each other, but it was strong enough. She'd thrown out the line and tested it. They were both gut-hooked.

'And you had nothing to do with the break-ins at the car park?'

'No. I swear it.'

199

'What about Jessie and Christian?'

'Why would they do something like that?' he protested defensively.

I didn't push it. 'But you both helped her with the blackmail scam?' I asked instead.

He winced; he didn't like the word. 'We were only helping her get her own back.'

'You said something in the car about a "dirty old woman"?'

'She'd been coming to stay at the Home Farm for years. She was an old lesbian,' I heard the distaste in his tone, 'and she'd been pestering Jessie all that time. Pretending to be all friendly so she could cuddle up and touch her and press against her. Jessie used to hate it.'

'Why didn't she complain to her mother?'

'She didn't think she could. She knew that the visitors paid her mother's wages. She didn't want her to lose her job.'

Or had she identified an extortion opportunity at a very early age? As a child had she seeded her dolls' tea parties with snakes and weasels? 'So she decided to do something about it?' I guessed.

'That's right. She told us it was time to get her revenge.'

'And make a bit of money on the side?'

He coloured again. 'I didn't know about that. Not at first.' I nodded for him to go on. 'You know there's a waterfall in the woods off the Monks' Trail, above the car park?'

'I've heard of it.'

'Well, there's a really deep pool under it that makes a great swimming hole. This old bitch used to go there for a swim every day. Even if it was cold or raining. She was like clockwork, you could time her.'

200

I started to see it unravelling. 'You and Christian were waiting with a camera?'

He nodded. 'A really good one Jessie had borrowed from Mr ap Hywel. It had a telephoto lens. So even though we were in the trees on the far side, it was still really clear.'

'The woman came down for her normal swim . . .' I prompted.

'And Jessie was already there. In her bikini, like she'd fancied a swim and it was just a coincidence that she was there. So they swam around together for a bit. Then Jessie showed her that you could climb up onto a rock and jump in. They fooled around a bit like that, and then Jessie took off her bikini, and started jumping in starkers. After that it didn't take long for the old bitch to peel off too. We started taking photographs then, when they were jumping off the rock together.'

'What was the money shot?' I asked.

He looked at me blankly.

'Did they kiss? Did she try and touch Jessie up?'

He shook his head. 'Jessie used the one we got where they were holding hands. Caught in mid air.'

'But nothing actually happened? She didn't try coming on to Jessie?'

'No, but who's going to know that? Looking at them both bollock-naked like that.' He pulled a face. 'And it's gross. The things Jessie told us she'd tried to get her to do before. She was just getting her own back. She's this big important person in London. Like no one's going to respect her after they see this and hear what Jessie has to tell them, are they?'

'But Jessie didn't do that, did she? She didn't tell anyone.

Instead she threatened her with exposure. Unless she paid up?'

He winced, uncomfortable with it out on the table. 'Yes, but it's going to make her think twice before she tries it on again. And, anyway, I told Jessie that I didn't want anything from it?'

'But you took it from Christian?'

He nodded reluctantly. 'I had to. Jessie would have been mad at him if I hadn't.'

'Who was the woman?'

'She called herself Lydia.'

'Lydia what?'

'Just Lydia. That was her retreat name. It's one of the rules, no one is known by their real name there.'

'But Jessie must have known? If she'd been applying pressure.'

'She hacked into her mother's computer to get it. But she never told us.'

Lydia! Had that name been the death of her?

202

12

There were seven people performing t'ai chi on the grass outside the Home Farm when I arrived the next morning. Mainly elderly, mainly women in baggy pastel leisure outfits, they were following the movements of a spindly young man in judo pyjamas with crusty dreadlocks halfway down his back. I saw that La Sanderson was one of them. She didn't acknowledge me. None of them acknowledged me. The exercises were being conducted in total silence.

Cassie opened the door. Once again my arrival was unannounced. If that caused her a problem she didn't show it. 'Glyn,' she chirped sunnily, 'lovely to see you.'

'And you, Cassie. I hope I'm not intruding.'

'Not at all. Come on in.'

I gestured over my shoulder. 'Who's Bruce Lee?'

She got the joke and smiled. 'That's Rupert. He lives in a tepee in the valley. He helps the residents with exercises and meditation.'

I glanced back at him. He was leaning forward with his weight on his front foot, both arms arcing up, palms facing out, looking like he was having a slow-motion battle with a recalcitrant weather balloon. 'How did he and Jessie get on?' I had already pictured Rupert with a great big spliff in his mouth.

Her smile dipped momentarily. 'Why do you ask that?'

'No reason.'

'You've got a suspicious mind, Glyn.'

'It comes with the job,' I quipped, trying to make light of it.

'It damages you. You should open yourself up to see the best in everyone. Come and have some tea.'

I followed her down the hall and into her private kitchen. It hadn't escaped me that she hadn't answered my question about Rupert. I didn't press it. 'Ursula tells me you're very busy.'

'Yes, we're full. It's unusual at this time of year.' She turned to face me, the kettle poised to pour. 'I think they're all being kind. I think people have booked up to try and help me keep my mind off things.'

'Are you okay?'

She turned away. 'Up and down. Being occupied does help.'

I gave it a pause. 'Have you given any more thought to what I told you?'

The kettle banged down on the range. 'I thought that we weren't ever going to mention that again.'

'I need your help, Cassie.'

She closed her eyes. 'It's over, Glyn. Stop dwelling on it. It's time to move on.'

'I need to find out the real name of one of your past guests.'

'You're deluding yourself. You're a country policeman, all this is beyond you. You're only poisoning yourself spiritually. It's done. Let it go. There is nothing you can do about it. Please, please let my Jessie pass on in peace.'

'Don't you want to know? Can't I even give you the name?'

'No!' She screamed it. She whipped round, her eyes open again, flashing with anger. 'I will not have this conversation. I'm sorry, but you're going to have to go. I really can't take it. I need you to leave me alone. I can't sort out your problems for you.'

There was a tentative knock on the kitchen door. 'Cassie, are you all right . . .?' A man's voice, sounding concerned.

I opened the door on a short elderly man with a crazily lined face and a tilted black beret. I smiled at him reassuringly. 'She's fine.' I turned to Cassie. She shook her head warningly. I knew better than to say anything more. I let him escort me to the front door.

Rupert was still putting his group through their paces on the grass. But this time they did all stop to watch me as I walked to my car, all scowling, as if they had picked up on some sense that I had violated their den mother.

I drove as far as the first corner and parked out of sight of the Home Farm. I got out. I had heard the sound of machinery coming from Plas Coch as I had walked to my car. I didn't let myself reason about what I was doing. I took the path that led to the big house between two enormous rhododendron bushes, following the sound.

205

Tony Stevenson was driving a garden tractor towing a mowing attachment. It looked like the first cut of the year, swirled to avoid clumps of bluebells in the long grass that fringed the rhododendrons. He was driving away from me as I emerged onto the wide swath of lawn. Even using his mirrors the angle would have been wrong, he couldn't have seen me, and with the ear protectors on, and the engine noise, he couldn't have heard me.

But he stopped.

He turned the engine off, dropped the ear protectors to his neck, and swivelled in his seat to wait for me to approach.

'Is Rhodri in?' I asked, walking up.

'No. He went up to London this morning.'

'With Mrs ap Hywel?'

'No, Ursula's here.' He pointed. 'Go round the back, onto the terrace, you'll find her in the kitchen.'

I followed his directions to a terrace with a classical stone balustrade and lichen-pocked flagstones, and a magnificent view down over the woods to the flatlands to the west. The kitchen had three pairs of tall glazed doors leading onto the terrace, and I could see as I approached that it doubled up as an informal living area.

Ursula opened one of the sets of French doors. I got the feeling that she had been expecting me. 'A nice surprise, Glyn,' she announced as I crossed the terrace.

'I hope I'm not interrupting.'

'Not at all,' she said, stepping aside to let me in, and closing the door behind us. 'You've missed Rhodri though.'

'So I gather.' I took in two partly drunk mugs of coffee on the large limed-oak table.

She saw where my eyes had gone. 'Joan's in the laundry. Joan Stevenson,' she explained. 'Will you have a coffee?'

'No thanks.' It was time to stop winging it and to put some kind of plan into action. 'I've upset Cassie.'

She shook her head and smiled resignedly. 'And I keep telling you, you're imagining it.'

'No, this time I really have.'

She saw I was serious. 'How?'

How much could I trust her? Fuck it. I didn't have time for the debate. 'I told her a while back that I felt there was a possibility that Jessie's death wasn't an accident.'

She held my gaze. 'I know, she told me.'

I tried to swallow my surprise. 'She did?'

'Yes. She was very upset. She asked if she could confide in me.'

'And?'

'We both agreed that we felt very sorry for you.'

'Can you explain that please?'

She took a moment to organize her thoughts. 'We think that you've been trying to compensate for the helplessness you feel. The fact that you weren't able to do anything to stop what happened to Jessie. It's understandable that you should try to transfer that awful sense of responsibility you're carrying.' She smiled gently. 'This is all your own theory, isn't it? There is no official investigation regarding third-party involvement?'

'No.'

'What would happen if I went to your superiors and told them about this? What if I asked them to open an investigation?'

'I may be wrong, Ursula.'

'So?' she asked, curious.

'This way we keep it quiet. The retreat, the Home Farm and your guests stay out of the public gaze.'

She weighed this up for a moment, and finally nodded. 'Jessie's death was an accident.' She waited for a reaction. I didn't play ball. 'You've got to give it time, Glyn. You have to allow yourself to come to the understanding that no one blames you.'

I left us hanging there in silence for a beat. Preparing her. 'Jessie was blackmailing one of the Home Farm retreat regulars.'

Her facial composure took a dive. She actually gasped before she started shaking her head denying it. 'Stop it, Glyn,' she commanded. 'We've been indulgent with you up to now, but I'm not going to tolerate accusations like that.'

'It's not an accusation, Ursula. It's a fact. This isn't me playing mind games with myself. I've got a witness.'

She continued to stare at me, her mouth partly open. 'Have you spoken to anyone else about this?'

I knew what she meant. 'No. As I said, I want to keep this quiet. I don't want to make anything official before I'm sure. I've got a witness, but for their own safety I've got to keep them wrapped away until I know more. At the moment all I've got is the retreat name she uses. That's how I upset Cassie. I wanted her to give me her identity.'

She turned away from me. I rode the silence. 'Her?' she asked without turning.

'Yes, she calls herself—'

'No!' she exclaimed, turning to me, her face set. 'No, I

don't want to know. These people are our friends. They come here to try and put a spiritual dimension back into their lives.'

'Ask yourself.'

'Ask myself what?' she flared.

'Was Jessie capable of blackmail?'

She dropped her head. She was fighting a hard internal battle. She looked up, the struggle visible in her eyes. 'If it's true, I'll face it then. But for the moment I want to keep all those friendships intact.'

'You could be protecting a murderer.'

She winced. She closed her eyes. It almost looked like she was praying. 'Will you promise me your absolute discretion?' I nodded. 'And if anything comes of it, you'll come to Rhodri or me before you make anything public?'

I nodded again. 'If that's possible, I promise.'

She wheeled away. Without her saying anything I knew I was meant to follow. She led me out of the kitchen, down a corridor, and into a bright room that faced out onto a topiary garden at the side of the house. It was her study. I recognized her presence in the furniture and the two framed exhibition posters on the wall, a Manet and a Georgia O'Keeffe.

'Stay there,' she instructed, putting me on hold in the doorway. She went across to her desk, leaned over, and booted up the computer. She deliberately kept her back to me. She didn't want me to see her access arrangements. 'Okay,' she called me across. There was a file menu on the screen, a databank broken down into alphabetical segments. 'I'm trusting you to only look for what you need.'

'You have my word.'

She gave me a long hard look. 'I still don't know if I'm doing the right thing.'

'You are, Ursula, believe me.'

She scowled, as if I had lost the right to use her name. 'When you've finished, see yourself out please,' she said coldly.

I was torn between giving her a polite pause to get out of the way, and worrying that she might change her mind. I gave up the countdown to thirty at eighteen and clicked the cursor on the H–M section. I scrolled down through the L's.

LYDIA

I took in a lucky breath and clicked the file open.

BARONESS HENRIETTA ALICE BLOOM

Hettie Bloom!

I remembered now. I had seen her at Jessie's funeral service. Just another one of the sparkling ones in the constellation of stars that had assembled that day. I had deliberately suppressed her because of the bad memories she induced. Not that she would have been able to recall one particular mauling of a young DC in Cardiff many years ago.

I copied down her address. A village in Oxfordshire.

How to handle this?

Hey, team, let's saddle up and go roust a feisty High Court Judge over a murder that she cleverly arranged to look like an accident to extricate herself from a shakedown.

It didn't work. Not even in its fantasy format.

I was going to have to go to Oxfordshire.

A call came through from Rhian before I reached the cattle grid on the road down to Llandewi. I reminded myself that she was working for me now, and pulled over to take it.

'Hi,' I greeted her. There was static on the line.

'Where are you? It sounds like you're in a space capsule.'

I glanced out the window to confirm my location credentials. A large black crow was tipping a sheep turd over with its beak. It hopped off nonchalantly when I got out of the car. 'Is this any better?'

'Marginally. It sounds like you're in an aircraft toilet now.'

'The mile-high club?'

'You boasting?'

'I've often contemplated the mechanics of it.'

'Sergeant?'

'What?'

'You are aware that this isn't one of those special-rate phone lines, aren't you? And that I don't call myself either Tania or Goldilocks.'

I blushed and felt my balls rush cavewards. The power of women to inflate and then puncture. 'Sorry,' I managed to not quite stammer.

She laughed down the line. 'That's all right. It's early days yet, so let's not get too ambitious.'

I turned it to safe shoptalk. 'Have you come up with anything?'

'Kadir Hoca was a bagman for some North London gangsters called the Saltiks.'

'Was?' I didn't let on that the name was familiar.

'He's never resurfaced. His car's never been found either.'

I thought about the eight men who were still missing. Could Hoca have joined them? Could he have been the one who organized the torching and the mass mutiny? And, if so, what did they all stand to gain from it?

'Glyn?' she probed.

'Sorry. Tell me about the Saltiks.'

'This particular branch of the clan is headed up by Mike Saltik, one of the grandsons of a Turkish Cypriot guy called Hakan Saltik who started up the enterprise out of a café he ran as a front in north-east London. The front's grown into a chain of restaurants and takeaways now.'

'And the core business is . . .?'

'Drugs, extortion and people-trafficking.'

'So this guy Hoca is a collector for the outfit?'

'And an enforcer, my sources tell me.'

'What's a North London hoodlum doing disappearing in Mid Wales?'

'Come on, Glyn, give me some fucking credit,' she said with an exasperated sigh. 'Was it some kind of a test, not telling me about the connection to the Don's Den drug factories?'

'Your sources are good.'

'It's not my sources, it's my powers of persuasion.'

'The good guys are still trying to make that connection enforceable. They can't get through the chain of ownership to make the link to the Saltik outfit.'

'Want me to have a go?'

What a gift for Jack Galbraith, I thought. Rehabilitation here I come. 'Could you?'

'I can try.'

I was momentarily tempted to ask her to also try to get some background dirt on Hettie Bloom, but I didn't want my interest in her to be released into the world as yet.

'So, have I given you a good story?' I asked.

212

'As in, do I drop the great Glyn Capaldi exposé?'

'Boring and passé.'

She laughed. 'I'll be the judge of that. I intend doing a bit more in-depth research before I write you off.'

Promises, promises! I cut the connection feeling chirpy.

The crow, perched on a fencepost now, watched me judgementally, returning my thoughts to Hettie Bloom.

But first I had to get to Unit 13 to pick up Dai and ship him off to a place of safety. Luckily, Hen Dolmen, Mackay's old farmhouse on the Herefordshire/Radnorshire border, was not a great detour off my route to Oxfordshire. It was a wonderful old building that had hunkered down over the years to become at one with the landscape, and encompassed the architectural range from Jacobean yeoman to rustic Victorian. It always made my heart feel at ease to see it.

I tucked Dai away out of sight in the well of the rear seats until we were clear of Dinas. It brought back the memory of another refugee I had taken to Hen Dolmen.

I had called ahead. Mackay was expecting us. His sidekick Boyce, who frightened me, hovered in his shadow as usual when the introductions were made.

'Boyce will take you and show you the room you're going to be staying in,' Mackay told Dai.

Dai didn't make a move. Instead he looked pointedly at me. I remembered the promise. 'Are you okay about going up to Dinas with a trailer to pick up a motorbike?' I asked Mackay.

He smiled, recognizing that prior negotiations had taken

213

place here. 'Sure.' He turned to Dai. 'We'll get up there this afternoon, if there's time, tomorrow morning at the latest.'

Dai nodded shyly, mumbled his thanks, and, mollified, went off with Boyce. We watched them go.

'This is getting to be a habit,' Mackay observed, 'you dropping your assorted waifs and strays off.'

'Come on, Mac, you know you love it. It helps you keep in touch with your softer side. And it turns Boyce positively tender.'

'What are you up to?'

So I told him. I owed him that.

He whistled. 'Fucking hell, a High Court Judge as well! How do you propose handling this? You're not even a functioning cop at the moment. Can you make a citizen's arrest of the higher judiciary?'

'I really don't know. First I've got to get face to face to see how she reacts when I bring up the subject of Jessie.'

'You said she used to be a shit-hot barrister, she's in the control business, she's not going to give anything away.'

'I'll know, Mac. Believe me, I'll be able to tell. But that's only the start of the problem. Somehow, I've got to try and find out who she recruited to do the business for her. With her now putting it together that that's my intention.'

'Bullhorn sleuthing, eh?'

'I can't see any other way to work it. I've got to confront her to find out. But then, hopefully, if she knows I'm on to her, she might start making mistakes.'

'She's also bigger trouble. You've managed to turn yourself into a target. Remember, if you're right, she's got rid of annoyances before.'

'I've recorded all this. She'll know that if anything happens to me it'll go straight to Jack Galbraith. And Dai's a witness, and I've told you about it. She's got a huge vested interest in my continued well-being.'

He looked doubtful. 'I wouldn't count on it.'

'She might even break down and confess all.'

He smiled grimly. 'On which planet? She's a professional ball-breaker. It sounds like you could do with some help.'

'Not on this one. But . . .' I let it tail out.

He chuckled sourly and gave a knowing nod. 'Fuck you, Capaldi. Why do you always come here with more than one agenda?'

'It's ergonomical.'

'What else have you got up your sleeve?'

I told him about Ryan Shaw. When I had finished he tilted his head and gave me a quizzical look. 'And where do I come into this?'

'Advice.'

'I don't suppose "Stay well clear" is what you want to hear?'

I shook my head. 'I was looking for something more in the way of what kind of threat scenario I could take up against a well-connected Manchester dope dealer, who might actually be three or more guys.'

'And this is to extract the information pertaining to what got this Ryan guy killed?'

'Correct.' I suddenly remembered and clicked my fingers. 'Ah, there might also be one little complication.'

'What's one little complication in the great scheme of things?' he observed mock expansively.

'They're probably under close surveillance from a local DI.'

'And I'm assuming this DI is not the cooperative type?'

215

'Not where I'm concerned.'

'And your own bosses? Can't they help?'

'They think I'm a big enough fantasist as it is.'

'Doesn't leave you many options, does it?'

'I've thought long and hard about this. I don't like to admit it, but there's no way of doing it without crossing over the line.'

'And you're really prepared to do that?'

'I don't think I've got any other choice.'

He looked at me reflectively before nodding. 'Right.' He thought for a moment. 'One question.'

'Fire away.'

'Where does the High Court Judge fit into this?'

'She doesn't. If I was going to do this, it would be for the sister. She trusted me.'

He grinned. 'Who's the softie now? I'll bet you cried buckets when Lassie died.'

'Lassie didn't die.'

He patted me on the shoulder. 'Stay in that world, Glyn. It's a happier place.'

'You'll think about it?'

'Sure, I'll think about it. I'm great on hypothetical situations. As long as they stay hypothetical.'

'Thanks, Mac. Take good care of Dai.' I stood up and raised my car keys at him in salute. 'One step at a time.'

I drove eastwards, crossing the Wye and the Severn, and on towards the rise of the Cotswolds, and into cushioned England. This was eiderdown country compared to the stiffly folded burlap of the hills of Mid Wales, a soft rolling landscape of meadows, woods and limestone field walls, all delineated like the puffed-up squares of a patchwork quilt.

And, as I travelled, I thought about Hettie Bloom. How she could have made this work.

In her time as a successful defence barrister she had had amicable working relations with more Dark Lords than J.R.R. Tolkien could have shaken a stick at. Okay, she had also done *pro bono* work for charities and disadvantaged kids, but they were hardly likely to have pointed her in the direction of a Special Forces-inspired assassination squad. But all those heavy people whose burdens she had eased? What kind of favours had she been able to call in?

I had also had my own bad time with Hettie Bloom.

Before she had been raised to the bench and made a baroness. When she was still a crack barrister and I was a young DC in Cardiff who thought he was making a difference. Before all the falls.

She was a tiny woman. And she played to that strength. She wore a gown that was too large for her, making her seem even smaller. A frail, birdlike lady up against these huge brute cops.

The case was against the Hussein brothers. They were importing and distributing rip-off big-brand cigarettes on a huge scale. Okay, all cigarettes kill, but these things, a mix of factory-floor tobacco sweepings, wood shavings and chemical binders, would get you there a lot quicker, and bring down anyone in regular close proximity as well.

The old timers had warned me. Watch her, she's tricky. Slippery.

Before I was called up to the stand she had been

concentrating on trying to break down the chain of evidence. Trying to distance the Husseins from the warehouse and the couriers. I was nervous, but also buzzing. This was new and exciting. This was the place where we skewered the bad guys.

I didn't see it coming.

'Tell me something, Constable . . .' As well as being small she had big grey soulful eyes that reflected all the tragedy of Jewish history. Ruth, in tears, amid the alien corn. Anne Frank. She used those eyes to full effect now, looking at me over the top of her glasses, and, holding the same pose, turned to the jury. 'I am going to have to quote here, ladies and gentlemen, so please forgive me.' Burning that word *quote* into their souls. Back to me. 'Is it true that you were heard to say' – she made a show of consulting her notes – '"now we can put this on those fucking Paki bastards"?'

'No.' Clear and concise. All that needed saying. But I fucked up. She had fabricated that quote, and I got angry. 'I never said anything like that.'

A look of wistful consternation crossed her face. She let the jury see it. She consulted her notes again. 'Oh, I'm sorry,' she smiled benignly. 'If you didn't say it, then who did?'

'No one said it.'

She looked at me sceptically. 'Are you telling me that not one of your colleagues called my clients "Paki bastards"?'

Our side tried an objection, but the judge overruled it.

And she had me. I believed in the sanctity of the oath I had taken. And of course they had said it. My silence was damning.

'Constable . . .?' she urged kindly.

'Nothing was ever said like that in the context you're implying,' I tried as a damage-limitation exercise.

'That wasn't quite the question.' She smiled at me warmly. 'But I'll let it pass,' she said magnanimously. Because now she knew she had me. Her ranging shot had struck pay-dirt. A patsy cop who couldn't lie. She leaned in to angle the harpoon properly. 'Constable, is your department racist?'

Of course it was. And sexist, and homophobic. And I couldn't lie.

It wasn't only my testimony that brought the thing crashing down. In the end our case just hadn't been strong enough. But I was never allowed to forget my part in its downfall.

I hung around in a lay-by and ate a sandwich I had bought, to give her time to get clear of lunch before I turned up. The road followed a glycerine-clear chalk stream and entered the village over a humped-back bridge that was straight out of *Three Billy Goats Gruff*. I did some slow tourist circling to get the lay of the land.

It was the sort of place where the village shop allowed you to restock on truffle oil and Sicilian figs, the former artisans' cottages were bankers' weekend nests and the attendant classes were conveniently clustered in 1960s housing stock in the same concealed hollow as the sewage farm.

Welcome to Miss-Marple-in-the-Marsh.

Okay, sweeping generalizations, but Baroness Hettie's house, when I found it, had definitely sprung from the seigneurial mould. Double gables and a linking main range in honeyed limestone, dressed-stone label mouldings and mullioned windows with diamond-leaded lights. Ivy traceries on the walls, and an ancient wisteria above the porch. A flagstone path, dished by generations of feet, curved across an immaculate lawn between rose beds from the wicket gate in the garden wall.

I had a thought I should have had before. Did High Court Judges warrant standing Special Branch protection? Bryn Jones would know. But, if I called him to ask, his subsequent questions would get progressively more awkward.

So I took the flagstone footpath unprepared. And no one shouted 'Oi!' and no one sidled out of the shadows and tried to run an obstruction. Not until I got to the front door, anyway.

The woman who answered it was skinny, neat and elderly with her hair in a tight bun, and the kind of fissured complexion that dried-fruit producers strive for in their products. What was she? Lover, housekeeper or amanuensis?

'Is Baroness Bloom available?' I asked, showing her my warrant card.

She wasn't impressed. 'Do you have an appointment?' It was a challenge, one of those questions that were designed to make you turn around and walk away with your head held low.

'It's extremely important,' I persisted.

'In connection with what?'

I needed to hold back on any mention of Jessie until I was within firing range of Hettie Bloom. 'It's to do with the Ap Hywel Foundation.'

'I'm sorry, but you're going to have to be more specific than that.' She wasn't sorry at all.

'It's a private matter.'

'Mary, who is it?' The voice, modulated to carry, came from inside the house.

Mary turned to call back. 'It's a policeman. He's not in the appointment—'

I took advantage of her distraction and bundled past her into the panelled hall. 'Lady Bloom?' I called.

'You can't just barge in here!' Mary clucked, affronted, behind me.

'Mary, what on earth's going on out there?'

I ignored Mary's protests and walked down the hall to the open door where the voice had come from. The central stone fireplace should have dominated the room. But it didn't. That honour went to the little woman sitting at the antique burr walnut desk in the bay window, the afternoon sun catching her strong profile and side-lighting her frizzed grey hair into a wispy tangle.

She took off her glasses in the practised manner I remembered from the courtroom, using the gesture to study me.

'Do I know you?' The voice also went with the courtroom, that combination of soft interrogation under-sown with barbed wire.

'He pushed past me,' Mary interjected, breathless more from indignation than effort. 'He says it's to do with the Ap Hywel Foundation.'

Hettie looked amused. 'Is this one of Rhodri's novel new attempts at fundraising?'

'No,' I gave her the cold stare. 'This has to do with the death of Jessie Bullock.'

221

13

I didn't care that grim-faced Mary was standing behind me hearing this. I only had eyes for Hettie Bloom. Watching for the flicker. The tell.

And when it came she didn't bother to keep it furtive. Her mouth drew tight.

But her mask remained unreadable.

Curiosity? Calculation? Incredulity? Knowledge? What else was in the mix?

She spoke slowly. 'What has that got to do with you?'

'My name is DS Glyn Capaldi, I was driving the car.'

No recognition. No Cardiff courtroom pang. Calmly, she addressed the space behind me. 'Out please, Mary, and close the door after you.' She made a shooing motion with the back of her hand to forestall any protest. I heard the door close. She used the same hand to beckon me forward. 'I'm very sorry to hear that. It must have been traumatic for you, and I hope that you weren't too badly hurt. And now

I'm going to reverse my original question and ask what this has to do with me?'

Jesus, what control this woman had. 'I don't think the crash was an accident.'

'I asked what this has to do with me.' She had been quick, but I had caught the pause. I had forced a notch into her timing. What was she trying to process? The possible extent of my knowledge?

I decided to make it easier for her. 'I know Jessie Bullock was blackmailing you.'

Those big grey fucking eyes were on me again. She nodded slowly, the rhythmic motion covering the private thoughts. Relays working. Putting stuff together.

'And somehow that has got something to do with the accident that you don't think was an accident?'

'It gave you a motive.'

'A motive for what?' she thrust at me. 'Be more precise, please.'

'To arrange for someone to make her death look like an accident.'

She laughed. She laughed deeply and comfortably and studied me again. 'You're serious, aren't you?'

'I'll find out who you used.'

'Oh, don't be so preposterous, man!' She clicked her fingers at me impatiently. 'Sit down.' She clicked them again when I hesitated, and I took the chair opposite her. She spread her hands, taking in the room. 'I'm not in the business of arranging for people to be killed. Think about it sensibly. Why would I do something so ridiculous? Jeopardize all this, my career, my family, my reputation?'

'Because Jessie Bullock was going to take your reputation away.'

She nodded reflectively. 'Tell me, before the tragedy you were involved in occurred, had you got to know young Ms Bullock?'

'No.'

'Well, you can count yourself lucky. She was a scheming, manipulative little witch.'

I didn't disguise my puzzlement. She wasn't meant to be admitting these things.

She read me. 'As you've already pointed out, she had tried to blackmail me. Now, if young Ms Bullock had managed another ten years in this world she might have become a force to be reckoned with. But, unfortunately for her, she never got past the juvenile end of malicious. She was lazy and conceited and too convinced of her own self-importance. She wanted things to come to her too easily. She wasn't prepared to put in the hard work.'

'I don't understand.'

'She never tried to seduce me.'

I shook my head, still not comprehending.

'She tried to blackmail me, but she hadn't put in the effort, so she didn't have the grounds for it.'

I felt my own ground starting to sink under me like the crust on melting permafrost. 'She could have lied. It would have been made public. It would have damaged you.'

'You forget my métier, Sergeant. She would have been attempting to take me on at my own game. I would have figuratively ripped the little bitch apart.'

'There was a photograph.'

Her eyes went soft. 'Ah yes, the photograph.' She stood up. 'Come with me.'

I followed her down the corridor and into the hall. She opened a door and stood aside to let me enter first. It was a cloakroom with a WC and a wash basin. And a framed blow-up of a photograph on the wall.

'There you are' – she spread her right arm in as big a flourish as the confined space would allow – 'Jessie Bullock. Seventeen years old. Stark naked and street legal. The less said about the crone the better.'

It was actually a joyous photograph. It struck me as I looked that it was hanging here as a celebration.

In black and white. A study of contrasts and similarities. The two of them holding hands, linking the subjects. The cold water giving both their skin a tonic sheen, their nipples distended, their pubic triangles the only formal geometry in the composition.

The camera had caught them in the dynamic of leaping, knees raised, legs pedalling. Jessie's younger body was taut, her small breasts remaining in place, while the motion had flung Hettie's fuller breasts and stomach folds momentarily skywards.

But Jessie's face was the revelation. The child was shining through, caught in the thrill and the fun of the leap, the anticipation of the plunge, the motive and the manipulation behind it temporarily suspended.

'Wonderful, isn't it?' Hettie pronounced behind me.

'Yes,' I agreed, starting to come back to the real world and realize that I was staring at a totally naked depiction of the woman standing beside me. A High Court Judge.

'Think about it, Sergeant. If this was a blackmail tool, would I have it on display?'

'You say she never tried to seduce you?'

'No, she was cocky. I was old and ugly in her book. She didn't want to be bothered with the messy side of the business. Having to actually touch the wrinkly old hag. She was convinced her supreme self-confidence would make me crumble. She thought I was rich, that it would be easier for me to give her some money than go through all the inconvenience of having to deny everything.' She smiled wickedly. 'I soon put her right on that front.'

'Did you tell anyone?'

'No, because I knew anything like that would rebound on her mother. And I'm very fond of Cassie.'

'So no money ever changed hands?'

'No.' She shook her head, her expression going gentle on me. 'I'm sorry, Sergeant, I can't help you.' She touched the back of my hand. 'I can see how you might have wanted it to be me. It's a big burden to carry.'

'If she had tried to seduce you . . .'

I didn't have to finish the question. 'Of course not!' she exclaimed, laughing. 'I've tried to tell you, she was much too dangerous.'

Fuck! Fuck! Fuck!

I drove away from there with my tail between my legs. If I hadn't needed them for the controls I would have stamped my feet on the floor pan in temper and frustration. I had wasted my time, and made a fool of myself in front of a High Court Judge. Who I had seen naked. And neither of

226

those would stand me in good stead if I ever came up in front of her professionally.

I hadn't quite returned to square one, but I had managed to slip back down the longest snake on the board.

I reviewed what I had. I had already been told that Jessie was a manipulator, now I had proof that she had been a wannabe extortionist. What other character flaws lay between those two poles?

And I now had Dai bang to rights as a liar.

And where was Christian?

A call came through from Rhian Pritchard. I pulled off the road to take it. 'Hi,' I chirped, trying to cut out the morose.

'Where have you been? I've been trying to call you.'

'I've been busy, my phone's been off.'

'I need to see you. Can you make it to The Fleece in Dinas to buy me dinner?'

I checked the time and did the mental calculations. 'Seven o'clock? Have you got stuff for me?'

She laughed. 'Wait and see. Don't be so impatient, big boy,' she signed off in a fake moll's drawl.

I keyed in another number. I had an obligation I'd been resisting.

A man's voice answered. Tony Stevenson?

'It's Detective Sergeant Capaldi. Is Ursula ap Hywel there, please?'

'I'm afraid she's not available at the moment. Can I take your number and ask her to call you back?'

'No, that's all right, if you could pass on a message for me, please. Tell her that I was wrong, and that I apologize. She'll understand.'

I shut down the phone. I felt mentally weary. I had charged myself up for the confrontation with Hettie Bloom, and now I felt drained and deflated.

I looked out the window. Something struck me. If I turned my head in a certain way, screening out the tarmac road, I could be looking at a landscape that hadn't changed in hundreds of years. No telegraph poles, no pylons, no mobile phone masts. Just a stone field wall, a weathered five-bar gate, a meadow rising to a beech hanger on the skyline, and fat lowland sheep grazing.

A character out of Fielding could have wandered down from the woods and not looked out of place. Or a kid on a quad bike could have roared into sight and been equally valid.

Things were not always what they seemed.

What was this trying to tell me?

And then it came. Dai hadn't lied to me. He wasn't that good an actor. I had accused him out of pique, because I thought that he had deliberately sent me down this cul-de-sac. But what if he hadn't known himself? What if he hadn't been told that the blackmail scam had never taken root?

But why had Christian told him that the money was his share of that enterprise?

Because Jessie had instructed him to? To stop Dai's conscience making him stray? To remind him of his outlaw status?

It came back to the money. Where had the money come from?

Oh Jesus! Had Ryan Shaw managed to sell the object they had stolen? I shook my head. There was a huge inconsistency.

228

Ryan couldn't have returned to distribute the spoils if he had been killed while still in the process of trying to negotiate the sale.

I groaned inwardly. It looked like I was back on the difficult Ryan Shaw route to salvation.

Things were not always what they seemed.

Was there anything else to apply that to?

Think about it, Sergeant. If this was a blackmail tool, would I have it on display?

I felt the cold clutch of doubt grab me. Had Hettie Bloom managed to work a super bluff? Had I been the victim of a snow job? Was she, at this very moment, erasing the evidence trail and getting the black-ops guys back on standby?

And something else. An unease that had started to resonate like a deep and distantly ominous jungle drum caught only fitfully. Involving something trapped behind a clot in my reasoning and memory. It was like recognizing a face in a crowd, but the identity remained stuck in a mental drawer that wouldn't open. You knew it was there, but you couldn't put your hands on the tools to prise it out.

At least I had an assignation with Rhian to look forward to. It didn't make the troubles or the sense of foreboding go away, but the anticipation, as I got closer to Dinas, shunted them down the list. Changed days, I thought to myself with a grin, remembering my first reactions to her.

I had decided to leave Dai in the safety of Mackay's for tonight at least. I even tried to pretend that it hadn't entered my head that, if he were back staying with me, it might cramp my style.

Because I was allowing myself to build up to that level of anticipation.

I should have known better.

But I was still running on hope juice when I used the rear staff entrance into The Fleece. Sandra Williams caught me sneaking through the kitchen. 'What are you creeping around for?' she asked.

'I want to use your bathroom.'

'Why can't you use the public one?'

'Because there's no hot water, and the mirror's crap.'

'Vain bastard,' she cracked. We had had this conversation before.

I checked myself out in their functioning mirror. I had inherited my father's dark complexion, but luckily not his capacity to grow a full-bore beard in less than twenty-four hours. My eyes had some dark shadowing under them, but there wasn't much I could do about it other than hope it added character. I splashed some hot water on my face for freshness, and used some more to tamp down some of my more erratic hair events.

I looked at my reflection, trying to appraise myself through a stranger's eye. As usual, I ended up grinning inanely at myself.

Rhian was on a stool in the front bar talking to David, a glass of red wine in front of her. I stood for a moment to take her in before she saw me and adjusted her persona accordingly. She was wearing a tight, scooped-neck, navy blue cotton dress which flattered her figure, revealed a treasure trove cleavage and no bra strapping, and stopped well short of her knees. Her chunky Aran sweater was bundled on the stool beside her like a stuffed dead pet she still carried around for sentimental reasons. Her hair was down, soft and mobile. Her face in profile held an attentive natural smile as she listened to David. I realized I could be in danger of getting seriously fixated on that face.

David saw me first. Rhian turned to follow his reaction. Her smile lit up, then wavered back to the slightly mocking setting she used as a default with me.

She turned her cheek to be kissed. 'You're late,' she chided.

'I'm sorry. And thanks for coming to Dinas. It's a long way out of your way.'

'Not really. I had some proofs to bring up to show Ursula. I'm on ap Hywel time.' She poked me playfully in the chest. 'But you're still paying for dinner.'

'I thought you were coming to see me?' I let her hear a twinge of chagrin.

Which made her smile. 'And here I am.' She grinned. 'Multi-tasking. We girls are good at it.' She reached up and mussed my hair.

'What's the matter?'

'It's too flat. Now order your drink and let's go and eat.'

She slipped off the stool, picked up her sweater, and I watched her walk to the dining room as I waited for David to pour me a glass of white wine. She knew I was watching her and put an extra twitch into her backside as she went through the doorway. She was playing with me. I wondered whether I could remember the counter moves.

We settled at a table and went through the preambles of small talk, choosing and ordering, with David hovering over us, beaming like a faux gypsy waiter.

'Well?' I asked when David had left us alone.

She knew what I meant. 'No joy, I'm afraid. The trail's too convoluted. The friend I asked lost it after yet another shell company in the Cayman Islands.'

'But it's probably beyond doubt that the Saltiks are the end users,' I speculated out loud.

'Right, but nothing to hammer the nails in with. I did try another tack though.'

'As in?'

'I worked it the other way round. All four premises were bought as a job lot about five years ago from a property company called Taliesin Developments.'

'How does . . .?' I stared to say. Then it clicked in. 'That's the ap Hywel business.'

'Correct, but don't get too excited. I called Rhodri and asked if he could shed any light on the sale.'

'And?'

She shook her head. 'No, it was arranged by one of his minions. Lawyer-to-lawyer stuff. He told me that the original properties were bought by his father as part of a fire-sale bundle, when the then owner was still running them as temperance bars, and needed to raise some capital. He was apologetic, but, as he said, those properties never formed a vital part of the portfolio.'

'They're North London gangsters, so why buy in Mid Wales?' I asked. I already knew how she would answer.

'Because it made sense. It took them away from law-enforcement pressure and rival operations. It was safe and tranquil and distribution wasn't too much of a hassle.' She laughed. 'They may even have made a small profit on the kebab and pizza front they were using.'

I nodded. 'And, because they already had the ap Hywel connection in London, they decided to look over here for their rural retreats.' I knew all that. But I still couldn't stop myself from wondering if there wasn't more to it.

We made our way through the usual mediocre Fleece dinner, trying to boost it as much as limp parsley and half a tomato as garnish with the chips would allow. Still, she was good company. I persuaded her to talk about herself after I had set the ground rule that Cardiff and I were off the agenda. Her upbringing in Ross-on-Wye, her ponies, Hereford Cathedral School, a false start studying the law, and then a degree in journalism in London. And then a lucky break, aka an uncle in the business, writing features for a paper in Bristol, before going freelance and moving to Cardiff as a part of the package of a relationship that had since foundered.

'You still like Cardiff?' I asked.

'I thought that was a taboo subject.'

'Only when I'm in it.'

She thought about it. 'For now it works for me. It's the right scale, it's vibrant, and I've made some good friends.' She leaned forward. 'What about you? If you had the choice of anywhere, where would it be?'

I opened my mouth to say it. *Anywhere but here.* Then, for the first time, with a shock, I felt that that would be almost a betrayal. I suddenly realized that I was starting to develop a complicated relationship with this place. I compromised. 'Between here and there.' I laughed. 'I don't think there's anywhere in particular I want to arrive at yet.'

'That's a cop-out.'

I shrugged.

She looked me straight in the eyes. 'I think it's now time that you bought me that malt whisky you promised.'

I felt that old amorous flutter in the region of my kidneys. 'Here or at my place?' I managed to ask without faltering or colouring.

She smiled knowingly. 'It had better be here. My taxi back to Plas Coch will be turning up in about twenty minutes.'

I disguised my disappointment behind a goofy smile. 'Okay.'

Her return smile was totally in control. 'One step at a time, okay?'

I nodded. 'Okay.' I called David over and ordered her a Glenlivet.

She looked at me quizzically when he left to fetch it. 'I thought you were drinking Highland Park the other night?'

I reached across the table and put my hand on top of hers. She didn't retract it. 'I was. An eighteen-year-old. And it's still sitting there, back at my place. We've got to leave you something to look forward to.'

I went to bed horny, but alone, and woke up the following morning with company. The big malaise had returned in trumps.

Starting with Mackay standing over my bed shaking me. At that point, not being fully awake, he was more of an annoyance than a surprise. He didn't have a key to the caravan, but I knew he had a way of jiggling the door handle that bypassed the lock.

I blinked back up to consciousness, taking in the dishcloth

grey of the early morning through the window. 'What the fuck time . . .?' I groaned.

'Dai's gone,' Mackay announced.

I sat up abruptly. 'When?' I asked anxiously.

'Sometime in the wee small hours.'

I jumped out of bed and started stumbling into the clothes I had abandoned on the floor last night. 'You and Boyce are fucking ex-SAS, Mac, aren't you rigged to stop that sort of thing?'

'He was a free agent, we weren't detaining him.' He shrugged his excuses. 'He wheeled his bike well away before he started it.'

'Why didn't you call me?'

'I didn't know he'd gone until I got up. And I was going to have to come up here with this anyway.' He tossed what looked like a mobile phone onto the duvet.

'What's that?'

He tried an experimental grin, pleased with himself. 'A tracking monitor. I fitted a transponder on his bike.'

I returned the grin, and picked it up. This might actually work to my advantage. Lead me to Dai's lair. And what else might I find when I got there? 'How does it work?' I asked, turning it over.

He took it from me and activated a button. The screen lit up, and he handed it back.

'Shouldn't it be beeping or something?'

'That's the downside. It's got a short range. We've got to get closer to the signal.'

We used his old Range Rover as it had the rough terrain capacity if we were going to have to go off-road to find him.

As we drove to Llandewi, I tried calling Louise. She wasn't answering. Was there anything to read into that?

Where to start?

At the village, the Lloyd family farm was the closest place with any connection, so we tried a transit past it, and a rough circuit around it, but picked up nothing on the receiving device.

I directed Mackay to the track up to the field shelter that Louise had brought me to. The field shelter had been a rendezvous, not a base, but I had had a thought. What if Dai had come down to there, instead of *up* from the road like I had? This was his backyard. He could have found somewhere to hide out further up in the hills.

We drove up the track, still not picking up any signal, and stopped at the field shelter. Mackay looked at me doubtfully. I got out of the car. The tyres of Dai's motorbike had left a distinct imprint in the mud in front of the shelter. I started walking uphill on the track, my eyes on the ground.

'What are you doing?' Mackay shouted, his head out of his window.

'Stalking,' I shouted without taking my eyes of the track, which consisted of two stony ruts with grass in the middle. Where was the mud when you needed it? 'I'm trying to see if his tyre tracks come down the hill.'

'You're looking in the wrong place.'

'What?' I turned round. He pointed over the stone wall to the side of the track. I walked over. A set of motorbike tracks rose up across the field to an open gateway that led onto the track higher up. He had cut out a corner. He was young, he had a new motorbike, and he had wanted to be fast and exuberant and rip up some dirt.

We carried on up the track. I waited expectantly, constantly glancing at the tracking gizmo, wondering whether the first sign, when we came into range, would be a blip on the screen, or an audible bleep.

I never found out. We never did pick up that signal.

Just as we didn't see the smoke until we were almost there. The wind had been blowing it away in the opposite direction.

The sense of doom hit me like a kick in the stomach.

'Oh fuck,' Mackay mouthed quietly.

I tried to read it as we approached, the track rising up between fenced pasture that had been reclaimed from high marginal land and laid to monoculture grass. Bleak open country. My attention focused on a Dutch barn that formed the end of a small sheep enclosure fronting the single-track road our track was coming up to join.

Part of the curved galvanized roof had been prised off and peeled back, and the green painted corrugated metal sheets of the siding at the far end were now blackened, buckled and slouched where the heat of the fire had deformed the structural steelwork. No flames now, only a column of thick grey smoke rising, and then bending and trailing off in the wind like a departing ocean liner. Or the last gasps of a foundering dreadnaught.

The fire brigade had two units there and an auxiliary Land Rover. Marked police cars were manning road blocks on either side. As we approached, one of these moved to the side to allow an ambulance to leave. You don't normally send ambulances to fires in hay storage barns, I reminded myself.

The ambulance drove off almost casually, no strobe light, no siren.

Because they had had a wasted journey, I willed.

Or because there was no longer any need to hurry?

We turned off the track and onto the tarmac road. A uniformed cop walked in front of his car, hand raised to stop us as we approached his blockade. I recognized Friel. 'Drive round him,' I instructed Mackay.

I braced myself for the lurch, and Mackay drove over the verge and onto the open moorland, skirting round the police car. I was aware of Friel running along the road parallel to us, shouting something. I ignored him. I could now see the front of the barn.

The hay had been almost totally consumed at the far end, the metal roof and walls distorted, where the wind had fanned the flames. The large central opening contained what looked like the stepped side of a ziggurat formed by untouched bales on the upwind side, the other a blackened, formless, smouldering pyre.

Mackay stopped the car abreast of one of the fire appliances. Part of me registered that Emrys Hughes had appeared and was hammering on my door. But most of my attention was centred on the debris that was arrayed on the ground in front of the opening. Mainly soaked and charred hay bales that had been pulled from the stack to prevent the fire spreading, but also a rough semi-circle of stuff that looked like it had been spewed out in an eruption. Large clumps of loose hay and pink baler twine from violently burst bales, bent metal tubing, and a partially melted 12 volt battery casing. And a buckled wheel.

The wheel destroyed any hope I had been clinging to.

I fought back the impulse to scream.

'Move this vehicle, Capaldi, you're causing an obstruction, you have no business here.'

I looked across at Mackay. He had reached the same conclusion. He shrugged sadly. I finally allowed myself to engage with Emrys's anger.

I opened my door. Emrys backed off, still ranting.

'How many bodies?' I asked.

Something in my tone or expression told him I was dangerous. 'Two,' he said, lowering his voice and watching me curiously now.

'Have you identified them?'

'Not yet. They were too badly burned.'

'One of them is Dai Lloyd. The other is probably Christian Fenner.'

'How can you possibly know that?'

I pointed at the wheel, the tyre shredded around the rim. 'That's from Dai Lloyd's motorbike.'

'Dai Lloyd doesn't have a motorbike.'

'Don't!' I gave him the warning. 'Don't even think of fucking arguing with me.'

14

I talked to the most senior fireman in attendance. I wanted his take on it. Emrys hovered, but stayed well clear of me. I think he felt that I had finally flipped, that the spores of a wild psychosis were about to erupt, and he for one wanted clear open ground between us before I started frothing and went running for the nearest meat cleaver.

At first, the fireman told me, they had thought they were dealing with a straightforward barn fire. Then someone had recognized the strewn motorbike debris for what it might represent, and put that into the equation. Someone had driven this up here. Why hadn't they driven it back?

The bodies had been found towards the middle of the stack. Charred and unrecognizable. Why hadn't they tried to get out? The smoke would have killed them quickly, he had reassured me. If they had been asleep at the time they may not have woken up.

He couldn't be absolutely certain, but by the way a section

of the fire had collapsed in on itself, he thought that they might have constructed a hollow among the bales. Some kind of inner chamber. There was fire-twisted stuff that had been found in there with them that might turn out to have been camping equipment. I pondered it. Emrys had told me that this was Lloyd family property. Dai would have had the opportunity to arrange the bales any way he liked. The fireman wondered if it had been a kind of den. I didn't tell him that it had been a foxhole.

And the cause?

There would be an enquiry, but, as far as they were concerned, the cause was obvious. The motorbike. It had been stashed away behind a wall of bales to hide it. Probably before it had cooled off properly. The still-hot engine had caused the surrounding hay to smoulder, and then ignite, the smoke rising to suffocate them. The fuel tank had eventually exploded.

A tragic accident, they all agreed.

But I knew better.

Jessie had been given her automobile crash.

Ryan had had his spoils-of-dope execution.

And now, apparently, the lethal combination of dry hay and a hot motorbike. Dai and Christian had been given the deaths that worked for them.

But this time round Mackay was on my side. He was informed by his sense of guilt. He shouldn't have let Dai run away from his safety.

He wasn't as badly affected as I was though. I was complicit in this. I had been selfish. I had used the scare story to extract what I wanted from Dai. But I should have taken it seriously.

I knew what these bastards were capable of. I should have foreseen this possibility.

I should have protected him.

There was nothing more we could do here. I asked Mackay to drive me back to Unit 13. I had plans of action to put into play.

'What will you do?' he asked me after a long silence as we took the same road as the ambulance down the hill.

'I caused this. I should have taken him home to his parents when I had him. If I hadn't scared him, he wouldn't have run here.'

He nodded slowly, his face strained. 'So, you're going to make a full and final confession?'

'I have to, Mac.'

'Bullshit! Dai was running scared anyway. They both were, that's why he'd made the hideout, that's why his mate Christian was already installed. It wasn't you that drove them here, it was what they thought was coming after them. He'd have run away from his parents again. For Christ's sake, you did your best, Glyn, you offered him sanctuary. He just didn't accept it.'

'What are you trying to tell me, Mac?'

He nodded towards the barn. 'If you get yourself taken out of commission through some misplaced sense of guilt we won't be able to go after the bad guys.'

I tried to absorb the first intimations of what he was offering me before I spoke. I knew that this was going to get an awful lot more complicated on many fronts. But I didn't have time for that now. I nodded, accepting it. 'I've still got to go to Carmarthen. Will you think about Manchester? If what I'm going to try doesn't work?'

'I already have. I've got an old army colleague who works as a special firearms advisor to the police forces in the North West. He may have the contacts who can provide the information we need.'

'Why didn't you tell me before?'

He flashed a weary smile. 'I didn't know then if I wanted you to know it.'

Mackay left me at Unit 13 to go off and tackle his former SAS buddy with the information that Ryan's sister had given me. I stood under my pathetic shower to get the smell of smoke out of my hair and wash off the worst of my visible despair. I dressed carefully. Neat and smart. I could allow no trace of the wild man to show through. I had to present a serious and considered front, that of a man who could be trusted to start an investigation.

Why had Dai left Mackay's? Why had he gone back to Christian? Why had he left home in the first place? Had someone followed him to the barn, or had they always known about it? How much of what he had told me about Christian had been lies? And about Jessie?

These were the questions that were preoccupying me as I drove to Carmarthen.

But there were too many of them to cope with. And no one left to answer them now. Not on our team.

I was like a palaeontologist faced with a jumble of old bones. How to put them together into the semblance of something that had once walked the earth and roared?

Jessie's machinations were at the essence of it. They were the backbone. Start from there, I instructed myself.

I'd believed Dai when he'd told me that he hadn't been involved in the car park break-ins. I still did. But he hadn't managed to convince me when he'd tried to suggest that Jessie and Christian had had nothing to do with them either.

For a start there was the prima facie evidence that we'd caught Jessie that night. Had Christian been waiting in the woods for her to sound the all-clear? Or had she known about the raid all along, and decided to treat it – and us – as a joke? Just push it far enough for the thrill, but leave us with no real grounds to prosecute?

That night was an aberration, but I was fairly certain that they were the ones who'd previously been targeting the car park. I could now see Jessie's malign influence behind it. Christian following her doggedly, but Dai's straight-farmer upbringing causing him to baulk, overriding even her pull. But it had been, as Huw Davies had put it, mere bravado posturing. They were finding nothing of real value, only trinkets and baubles, rubbish for their bandit showcase.

Until, one night, they scored large.

Something they recognized as illicit and valuable. It could have been the diamond as big as the Ritz, or a ripped-off universal cure for cancer, I didn't bother wasting time trying to speculate. Whatever it was, Jessie recognized that dealing with it was way beyond the limits of their experience. They needed someone with criminal credentials and contacts to handle the negotiations for them.

Around Llandewi there weren't too many of them listed in the Yellow Pages, so they cut Ryan Shaw in on the deal.

Meanwhile, back at the Bad Boys' ranch, things would have been in turmoil. They had just been stung by the worst

244

type of opposition. Amateurs! Because amateurs didn't know that there were codes and rules in place. Amateurs didn't appreciate that there was a hierarchy. The control and stability that comes from the understanding of fear is useless when you're dealing with cretins who are blind to the fear.

And shit like this is not supposed to come out of the boondocks. They have no procedures in place for dealing with hayseeds. Where do they start with the pressure?

They are at a loss, until they catch the news of a badly kept secret. That an idiot police inspector is going to mount an operation to flush out the car park thieves. The cops are going to act as their pest controllers and delivery men, all rolled into one. And after that it's purely a question of logistics.

It will be arranged that one of those people will die, so that their associates will know what they are dealing with. To speed up the negotiations by making the alternatives very clear and very stark.

Jessie's death was the neon warning.

The problem was that, again, it came down to the difficulties of dealing with amateurs. The way Jessie's accident was set up was just too good. Neither Christian nor Ryan were experienced enough to recognize it as a signal. So, instead of a spirit of capitulation, Ryan went into the negotiations preparing to play hardball. And they killed him for it.

I went back over my original thoughts on that. By the way he had been killed it looked like they hadn't got what they had hoped to find. But they would have got Christian's name out of him early in the process.

By which time Christian is learning fast, and goes to

ground. But what does he do with the object of everyone's desire? Or had he already given that up in an attempt to save himself? Is that why killing him had become an expedient option?

And why did Dai follow him there? Did he feel the threat catching up with him?

The questions were starting to pile up again.

And why had he fed me Hettie Bloom? If they had really wanted my help, why hadn't he taken me to Christian and explained about the real shit-storm that was blowing their way?

Unless I had gone totally off-beam with this? Could I be applying too much science and not enough folklore? Was I making it all too complicated? Should I be removing the Ryan Shaw element altogether? No gangsters? Had they sent me after Hettie Bloom in the hope that the outcome of that confrontation would cause their fears to go away?

I thought back to yesterday afternoon. I had called Mackay after I had left Hettie Bloom's to say that everything was okay, it had been a false lead, and I was returning to Dinas. But maybe it hadn't been okay for Dai and Christian. Perhaps the last thing they had wanted to hear was that Hettie Bloom had wriggled out of it. Had they been terrified that she could return to concentrating on them?

Did that figurative pile of bones I was scratching my head over contain the remains of more than one creature? Was I trying to attach a pterodactyl's head onto a stegosaurus's body?

Jesus, I was confused!

*

246

'Hi, Sarge.'

I knew the voice. I turned round in the corridor at Carmarthen HQ. Alison Weir, a DC I had worked with, had come out of an office with a bunch of files in her arms.

'Alison, nice to see you.'

'How are you?' There was unmasked concern in the question.

'Fine now, thanks.'

'You look tired.'

'No, I'm okay.' I tried grinning my way out of it. I was meant to look rested, confident and ready to go.

She wasn't convinced. 'Are you looking for DCI Jones?'

'And DCS Galbraith.'

'They're both in the canteen.'

'Thanks.'

She held the silence for a beat. 'I was sorry to hear about it.'

I nodded my thanks. She was talking about Jessie. She was talking about history. I couldn't tell her that my latest troubles were right bang up to the minute. Even though it obviously showed.

I paused outside the double doors to the canteen to recharge. Through the circular windows I could see Bryn Jones and Jack Galbraith at a table by a window, a clear zone of empty tables surrounding them in the otherwise busy canteen. I braced myself and pushed through the doors.

They saw me coming.

'Capaldi!' Jack Galbraith greeted me warmly from across the room, causing heads to turn. I discovered the reason for his bonhomie as I got closer and saw his fork poised over a half-eaten *millefeuille* cream cake. He was in his comfort zone. Bryn Jones had the grace to look guilty about his chocolate éclair.

He waved me into the seat that Bryn had pulled out. 'Have you decided to take us up on our offer of bed, board and street lights?'

'No, Sir, I'd like to make a formal request to be transferred back to active duty.'

'Hey, I didn't see that coming.' He held up his fork to keep me on hold while he retrieved his notebook and made a show of scanning its pages, shaking his head. 'Nope. Didn't get it. How about you, Bryn?'

I remembered their game from the last time I had seen them in The Fleece.

'No,' Bryn responded, smiling, 'the last one I had was him running away to join the Foreign Legion.'

'I'm serious, Sir.'

Jack Galbraith dropped the joviality and studied me closely. 'Why all the hurry?'

'Has the doctor cleared you?' Bryn asked.

'I'm sure that will be a formality.' I took in a breath to steady my resolve. 'I'd like permission to open the preliminaries to a murder investigation, Sir.'

They looked at each other.

I carried on before they could surface from their surprise. 'At this stage I'd only need a small SOCO unit and a couple of uniformed officers, who could be seconded from—'

'Whoa, whoa, whoa!' Jack Galbraith cut me off. 'So, who the fuck's been murdered?'

'Two young men: Dai Lloyd and Christian Fenner.'

248

'When and where?'

'Last night. In a barn fire near the village of Llandewi.'

He turned to Bryn. 'What do we know about this?'

'It was reported routinely. It's with the fire investigation people, but there are no apparent anomalies. We haven't been asked to look into anything at this stage.'

He turned back to me. 'But you think differently, Capaldi?'

I hesitated momentarily, rehearsing how this sounded in my head. 'They were close friends and associates of Jessie Bullock, Sir.'

He groaned out loud. Bryn just stared at me.

'It's too much of a coincidence, Sir. I think they were targeted and executed by the same people who killed Jessie Bullock.'

'Jessie died in a car accident, Glyn,' Bryn corrected me gently.

'Capaldi, we have to make the clear fucking distinction here between crime and tragedy,' Jack Galbraith chided quietly.

'This contains elements of both, Sir.'

He sat up and folded his arms. 'Okay, convince us.'

I had prepared for this moment. I set it out for them as clearly and concisely as possible. Starting off with Jessie's contrived accident, Ryan Shaw's involvement and execution, and on to the immolation of Dai and Christian. I steered well clear of any mention of Hettie Bloom. Introducing a High Court Judge on the wrong side of the barriers would not have been good for my campaign.

When I had finished, Jack Galbraith nodded to himself for a moment, pondering. 'So this is why you've been making

Inspector Morgan's life such a fucking misery?' He looked across at Bryn. 'Neither of us got this one, did we?'

'No, we didn't,' he agreed. His voice was concerned when he addressed me. 'You know we can't act on this, Glyn?'

'It all fits, Sir. I've thought it through carefully.'

Jack Galbraith stepped in. 'You've made it fit, Capaldi. You've started with a conclusion and bent everything into the shape you need to return to it.'

'You're not going to do anything about it, Sir?'

'I'll get onto Inspector Morgan. I'll suggest that he investigates your take on the car break-ins, and that he mentions the possibility that Ryan Shaw might have received stolen goods to the Cheshire police.'

'And what about me, Sir?'

He looked over at Bryn, cueing him with a small nod. 'I think you should consider a course of serious counselling,' Bryn stated solemnly.

I had expected it. I had hoped that I might be able to convince them, but I had always known that this would be the likeliest outcome. On the other hand, if I had gone ahead on my own without putting it to them, I would have been effectively flushing my career down the toilet, and activating the macerator for good measure. As it was, if they knew what I was contemplating next, they would have already arranged for me to be bouncing around the padded cell.

They left me to brood at the table.

Until Mackay got back to me I was in limbo. And I felt no catharsis or any sense of having been cleansed by psychic scouring as a result of my outpourings. I was still clogged with guilt, anger and that insistent sense that I had missed something important.

I closed my eyes. Something jarred. Something Jack Galbraith had just said to me. *You've made it fit, Capaldi.*

Was that where the clot was? Another thing I had made to fit?

Think!

There was either a momentary total lull in all the conversations around me, or I manufactured the silence. Allowing myself to experience only the clang of a metal lid in the servery. Sounding like a kettle going down on a stove. Taking me back to a kitchen at another time when I had been crowded by guilt and anxiety.

You've made it fit, Capaldi. The clot started to dissolve.

Oh fuck!

Cassie Bullock!

I had taken it all at face value. A grieving mother, a spiritual woman in charge of a place in the deep country that people used for refuge. I had created a tableau of sanctity and innocence. I had twisted the true meaning of what she had really been telling me to fit that image.

I hadn't seen it.

That first meeting. Sitting at her kitchen table. Both of us caught up in our separate grief. She had been shocked and upset when I had told her that I felt that there was a possibility that Jessie had been murdered.

But she hadn't been surprised!

That's what had been nagging at me. The suggestion hadn't astonished her. But, instead of querying it, I had made it fit. I had attributed it to the accepting fatalism of her faith.

And then there had been that second time. When she had thrown me out of her house. Because she hadn't wanted to talk about it.

You're just a country policeman, all this is beyond you.

Again, I had put that down to her faith talking. That, in the eyes of her God, we were all tiny and inconsequential. That we couldn't hope to understand the true purpose that lay behind seemingly awful events.

But what if she had been speaking literally?

What if she had been trying to tell me that, as a hick cop, I had no idea of the forces of malice that were at work out there in the bigger world? Cassie hadn't been surprised that her daughter might have been murdered. Was that because, at some point in her life, she had inhabited a milieu where that possibility was a live and credible occurrence? Had she felt that that world had caught up with her again?

And what had she done about it?

I shuddered. Oh Christ, what forces could Cassie Bullock have called into play?

I called Rhian.

'Hi,' she chirped, 'are you calling me for the lucky second date?'

'No. Yes' – I corrected myself – 'but first I need you to do something incredibly important for me.'

She caught my urgency. 'What?'

'I need you to drop everything and see what you can find out about Cassie Bullock when she was in London.'

'Cassie Bullock?' she sounded surprised.

'Yes. I can't explain now.'

'Anything specific you're looking for?'

I thought about it. 'Jessie's father. See if you can find out who Jessie's dead father was.'

I disconnected and found that my hands were trembling. And that all the other people in the canteen were making a big point of not looking at me. And that the zone of revulsion formed by the empty tables around me was now even greater than it had been when Jack Galbraith and Bryn Jones had been sitting here.

How could this change things?

I put it out of my head before it could turn obsessional. There was nowhere I could go with it until Rhian got back to me.

I drove home from Carmarthen under a lowering sky. The clouds were playing at being perukes, hazing the tops of the Cambrians and Mynydd Eppynt, filling the valleys with superfine moisture that filmed on the windscreen and defied the wipers to shift it. It was a day for wraiths to glide about in. It was not a day for the living to be anything other than circumspect. Not that there were too many of them in evidence.

The barn was dripping in the clouds. Everyone had left. Even the smoke had been defeated. The perimeter had been marked out with incident tape, giving the whole compound the look of something junked, tied off and awaiting the arrival of the disposal team.

How would they have done it?

The ground on the other side of the road rose up away from the barn in a series of low ridges. I shifted into Mackay's mindset. They would probably have set up on the first of

253

those ridges, where, by staying low, they would have been hidden from the road and the barn by the topography, old bracken and gorse bushes.

I resisted the temptation to go up and explore. One day, I promised myself, I was coming back here with a forensics team, but I would only fuck things up if I started trampling around up there now.

Had they used the same sniper set-up as they had with Jessie? Keep things at a safe remove? Pin them down if they tried to escape? They could have watched where Dai had stashed the motorbike, known which bales to target to establish the seat of the fire. A silenced rifle and tracer bullets into the hay? Or would they have risked moving up close for the hands-on approach? A thermal lance through the bales, or the old tried-and-tested safety match technology? The ground outside was going to end up so messed around anyway that there was little risk of their footprints giving anything away.

More speculation.

I was getting fed up with this. I wanted real answers.

It wouldn't be fair to call Rhian, she hadn't had enough time yet. So I decided to pester Mackay.

'Any joy?'

I caught his hesitation. 'My guy's come back to me with a name and a home address for your Manchester dealer.'

'Is he called Kim?' I asked, remembering what Ryan's sister had told me.

'No, Patrick. Known as Paddy. Paddy Brady.'

I felt a lump in my throat and the internal lurch as the anvil returned to my stomach. This had now shifted into

254

the realm of the real. With potentially devastating consequences. I swallowed to clear my throat. 'Why didn't you
tell me?'

'I just have.'

'No, when you first heard. So I could get myself ready.'

'That's why I didn't,' he said patiently. 'It's too early.'

'Too early for what?'

'To do anything. I've got things to prepare this end.'

I knew he wouldn't tell me if I asked. 'How long do you
need?' I asked instead.

'Ideally two weeks?' he offered.

'Not a chance.'

'I didn't think so,' he sighed resignedly. 'I'll pick you up
in Dinas tomorrow morning.'

'What do I need?'

'Nerves of steel.' He laughed at his own joke. 'Failing those,
you could try some rubber underpants.'

I stood in front of the barn after we had disconnected. I knew
I wasn't being fair. Mackay had his own life, I shouldn't have
enlisted him to fight my battles. I corrected myself; not just to
fight them, but to organize and choreograph them as well.

Because, in a situation like this, I wouldn't have known
where to start. Desperate measures.

I was up in time to greet the dawn, or the grey, washed-out
light that passed for it in these parts at this time of year. I was
too nervous to eat breakfast. Although I had to reconsider
that decision at ten o'clock when Mackay still hadn't appeared.

'Where have you been?' I asked, trying not to sound too
narky, when he eventually turned up about an hour later.

255

'I said I'd be here in the morning,' he responded calmly.

'I thought we'd be starting off first thing?'

'It's going to be a long enough day as it is,' he explained patiently.

'What do I need to bring?'

'You're fine as you are,' he said, already moving towards the car. He hadn't even looked. I could have been wearing a fucking tutu as far as he was concerned. I realized I had been keyed up for a more dramatic build-up.

I glanced in the back of the Range Rover as I walked round to the passenger's side. It was empty. I had half-expected to see the outline of what could have been a Bofors gun under wraps. There wasn't even a bundle capable of hiding a starting pistol. Part of me was disappointed in a *Boy's Own* adventure kind of way.

'What's the plan?' I asked as he started the engine.

He turned round in his seat and gave me one of those smiles that made him look very young and cherubic. 'There is no plan.'

I thought he was joking.

So I gave him a while to settle in to the driving and repeated the question.

'I told you, there is no plan.'

'Come on, Mac,' I chivvied, 'stop pissing around. I need to know what you expect me to do.'

'How long did I ask you to give me?'

'Two weeks?' I smiled tentatively, expecting a joke to follow.

He nodded. 'That's right. Minimum. And what do we know?'

I realized it was a real question. 'His name. A telephone number. A home address.'

'Correct. A few facts and all the rest is surmise. Is he married? Does he have kids? Does his aged mother live on the premises? Does he walk a dog? Does he wheel his rubbish out himself?'

'What are you trying to tell me?'

'That you need time to do these things properly. Time and patience. You have to develop your intelligence through observation. Watch for the patterns, the rhythms, all the set pieces in the guy's domestic life. What you're looking for is the best place to insert yourself into there seamlessly. You can't do all that in twenty-four hours. That's why there is no plan.'

'So, what do we do without that preparation?'

He flashed a grin at me. 'We hope we're lucky.'

'And if not?'

'We give up. We don't go ahead.' He saw my expression drop. 'Sorry, Glyn, but we can only do what's within our capabilities.'

It was childish to be disappointed because I had been told that failure was a real possibility. But I couldn't help it. I had pinned too much hope on Mackay's abilities, conveniently forgetting that we weren't working to the rules of the wild frontier. Paddy Brady may be a scumbag dope commissar, but the law still afforded him protection from people with nefarious intent. Even if those people were well intentioned.

We drove round Shrewsbury and took the A49 across the Shropshire Plain, and turned east onto the A54 north of Tarporley. We had already passed close to where Ryan's burned-out car had been found, and now we were going to be passing through Winsford. Was this some kind of test of my resolve? I wondered irrationally.

'Shouldn't we have carried on and taken the A556 up to Manchester?' I asked.

'No. That takes us too far north on the M6.'

'Too far north for what?' I asked, intrigued. He shook his head. I hadn't expected an answer. I had the surprising realization that I felt happier. I was doing something. I was riding with my buddy on our way to our very own black-op.

15

We would have been too far north to get onto the M6 and still be able to access the Knutsford Service Area, as it turned out.

Mackay parked on the fringe of the huge lot, and turned in his seat. 'Can I have your phone?'

I handed it over. He took his own out. I watched with interest, waiting to see if he was going to do some clever Commando-type coordination thing with them. Instead he reached over and put them both in the glove compartment.

'What's that for?'

'We don't need the distraction.' He held his hand out again. 'Wallet and warrant card.' I hesitated. He clicked his fingers. 'You can't be carrying any identification.'

I passed them over. He added them, along with his own wallet, to the phones in the glove compartment, and locked it. He produced a small wad of ten-pound notes from his back pocket and held them out. 'Use this to get back here if we're separated.'

'And then what?'

'Wait. I'll turn up. If you're picked up, just pray that it isn't by any cop you once met at a convention who might recognize you.' I thought about DI Bradbury. What would she do if she caught me poaching on her territory? 'And you don't say anything,' he continued, 'not a word. I'll be along to get you out.'

'You're going to break me out of jail?' I asked, only half joking.

He smiled. 'I shouldn't have to. As long as you haven't said anything.'

'How does that work?'

'You don't need to know. No cop below the level of chief superintendent does.'

But I had heard the rumour. 'Is it something to do with the Defence of the Realm thing?'

His smile turned cunning. 'You're not meant to know about that.'

'You're retired, Mac, won't they have changed the system since your day?'

He shook his head. 'I make a point of keeping up to date.'

He took out a small haversack from behind the seat that I hadn't noticed before. Was this the ordnance? Was it full of Glocks and SIG Sauers and smoke grenades? It actually looked more like it contained laundry than hardware.

We went in and had a coffee and a Danish. Just a couple of guys on the road.

Mackay looked me straight in the eyes. 'It's not too late.'

I nodded, I knew what was coming.

'So, are you really sure about this?' he probed.

I shook my head. 'No, *sure* isn't even close to the word I'd use. More like a variation on *wrong, wrong, wrong!*'

'We can still pull out.'

I gave him my anguished face. 'There isn't another way. I've blistered my eyes scanning the fucking runes for one, Mac, but there isn't.'

He studied me for a moment. 'Okay, it's time to go to the toilet.' I recognized it as an instruction. He took a bundle in a supermarket plastic bag from the haversack and passed it to me. 'Put these on in there. Forget the stuff in the pockets for the moment. And meet me outside, don't come back in here.'

I changed in a toilet stall. The bag contained a pair of dark blue workman's overalls. I felt in the pockets gingerly, half expecting to encounter a garrotte and a phial of nitro glycerine. Instead one of them contained a brand-new pair of thin latex gloves, the other a black balaclava, a full-face job, with three stitch-reinforced round holes to cater for the eyes and mouth. It looked like something from the Gimp Shop.

He was waiting for me outside, also dressed in blue overalls. I started to make for the Range Rover. He called me back with a low whistle. His eyes told me not to question anything, to just shut the fuck up and follow his lead.

We crossed the car park away from the Range Rover, and over to an unmarked white Ford Transit van parked near the big trucks. 'Put the gloves on before you touch anything,' he ordered quietly. He made for the driver's side, and I did as I was told and headed for the passenger's door. It was unlocked. I climbed in at the same time as Mackay, and was about to speak when the sight of the crouched figure in the back sent a jolt of shock through me.

Boyce always managed to give me a little bit of a fright. When I hadn't been expecting to see him that turned into something more like terror.

He nodded. He was also in overalls.

I composed myself and nodded back. 'Whose van is it?' I asked Mackay.

'Boyce has borrowed it.'

I recognized the euphemism. 'Aren't we taking a risk, driving a stolen van?'

Boyce leaned forward over the front seat. 'Don't worry, the registration plates are the same as a similar van that hasn't been stolen.' He was the only man I knew who could make a Somerset drawl sound sinister.

'And local,' Mackay said, and then looked at Boyce with a grin. 'It would be some weird fucking coincidence, wouldn't it? If we ran across them, and there we are at the traffic lights, two white Transits, with identical number plates.'

Boyce laughed. I didn't find it funny. 'I thought you said you didn't have a plan?'

Mackay was still grinning. 'These aren't plans, these are basic survival procedures.'

We parked in the anonymity of a large supermarket in Wilmslow and crouched in the back of the van to study the Google Earth images.

We had already driven past the frontage of the private estate. A high, ornamental brick wall fronting the street, curving into the entrance where it terminated in brick pillars that flanked two barrier poles, an entrance and an exit, with a manned security kiosk between them. Not content with the poles, there were inclined steel plates set into the road that could be raised and lowered beneath them. Without any apparent sense of irony, a large dressed-stone plaque, set into the brick wall, proclaimed in incised gold script, *The Haven.*

'That has to be a twenty-four-hour-security operation,' Mackay had commented as we swept past. Boyce grunted his assent from the rear.

'Shit . . .' I had muttered under my breath.

'Don't worry.' Mackay had heard me. He paused while he checked his mirror and made a right turn. 'It works for us. It makes them feel safe in there. And the safer they feel, the more relaxed they are at home.'

'But how do we get in there past that security?'

Mackay used the rear-view mirror to share his amusement with Boyce. 'Who said we were going to use the front door?'

We had two satellite images. One showing the estate in its entirety, the other a blow-up of the section we were interested in. The estate was a rough trapezoid in form, the shortest of the parallel sides fronting the main road. The access road had been set out in sinuous curves to emulate a country lane and wound back round to the entrance, enclosing an open landscaped green in the centre, complete with duck pond. The layout had been contrived to give all of the huge houses their own private outlook over the open Cheshire country-side to the rear.

The blown-up image of our target house was blurred, a pixelated broth, but adequate for our purposes. The building was H-shaped, a cross wing at either end, with a long, linking main range. At the rear, an extension projected from one of the cross wings into the garden, with a wide paved terrace running along the rear of the house to the other cross wing.

Mackay used the retracted tip of his pen on the blown-up image. 'As well as the boundary wall and fence here,' he traced the line, 'there's a brook running along the outside. Hopefully that makes them feel doubly secure.'

'Is the fence electrified?' I asked.

'No. I'm sure the residents would have liked it to be, but they would have had to draw the line at the possibility of putting megavolts through innocent neighbourhood urchins, never mind the outcry if they went and flash-fried Bambi. They have to be content with a five-foot-high brick wall, then another four feet of heavy-duty chain-link fence on top of that, finished off with razor wire.'

I nodded sagely. It sounded daunting enough to me. 'Won't there be security cameras?'

'Bound to be. Motion sensor lights as well. We won't know the set-up exactly until we get in closer. But the one big thing that runs in our favour is that they won't be expecting anyone coming in from the rear.'

'Why's that?' I asked, not seeing the reasoning.

'Because that's the private view they paid all this money for. That's meant to behave itself, not turn against them.' I started to shake my head, not getting it. He smiled. 'Okay, seriously, because there's no road. There's no way to get a vehicle in anywhere close. So there's no way to get loot out.' He used his pen on the larger image, tracing a rough line from the back of the house, across the garden, over the brook, through the fringing woodland and the open fields. 'No housebreaker's going to risk the effort to hump a plasma screen and a home cinema system over that obstacle course.' He turned to Boyce. 'What are you reading from it?'

Boyce placed his big finger onto the long blocky rectangle at the entrance to the house. 'That's a big garage. Looks like dormer windows in the roof. A staff flat, I reckon. So is that just a housekeeper's, or does he employ resident muscle?'

Mackay had already given it some thought. 'Given the occupation he's in, he's bound to have a driver/minder. And they probably live in. We'll see when he comes home.' He turned to me. 'And what about you, Glyn? Is this telling you anything?'

'He's got a fucking hell of a lot of money.'

He laughed. 'And kids.'

'How do you work that out?'

He dropped the tip of the pencil onto a blur in the rear garden below the terrace. 'A trampoline.'

My anxiety level soared. 'Does that change things?' I asked, almost hopeful, now that this was no longer abstract, that they were going to say that they would have to abandon the mission.

'It might add an incentive. He might want to get back to being a fond daddy sooner rather than later.'

'We've got to get in there first,' Boyce reminded him.

And I remembered something. 'What did you mean by *getting in closer*?'

We parked after dark at a busy country pub. I had been watching with growing dismay as we drove further and further away from civilization.

'Couldn't we have parked a bit nearer?' I asked.

'No, this is perfect. A van parked in a lay-by in this kind of neighbourhood gets noticed. It makes the good folk jittery. Here, if we're still parked after closing time, it just looks like we're responsible citizens who've opted not to drive ourselves home after one too many.'

He had an answer for everything. 'So, we're going cross-country from here?'

'Yes. Boyce will take point. You follow, and don't bunch up on him as he may have to stop in a hurry.'

I held up the balaclava. 'Isn't this a bit of a cliché?'

'No, that's what turns you into the Invisible Man. You wear that, and when the police question any witnesses who might have seen you, they'll swear that you were a two-metre-tall bald Nigerian.'

'With a bone through your nose,' Boyce added drily.

I pulled Mackay aside. 'You don't have to do this, you know,' I told him quietly.

'Now he tells me!' He watched my expression fade into contrition before breaking into a grin and clapping me on the shoulder. 'Come on, Glyn, when they torched the barn it got personal. We both know that Boyce is the only one who doesn't have to do it.' He looked across at his buddy standing by the van. 'And you try and stop him.'

Mackay and Boyce both had rucksacks. I had nothing to carry. But I still had a hard time keeping up with the pace. Boyce jogged on ahead of me, hugging the hedgerow for the most part, keeping to a half-crouch in the open country to avoid being sky-lined, stopping from time to time to orient himself, then moving off again before I had had time to catch my breath properly. He moved fluidly, avoiding obstacles as if he was equipped with sensors, while I snagged myself on branches and brambles, and kept missing my footing in the phantom holes that continually appeared in the ground.

There was no moon. The sky was overcast, but the cloud cover was high, so there was a residual tone of quasi light, like life in a charcoal sketch on dark grey paper. Objects in the landscape were silhouetted against the sky, all contrast, no detail.

Boyce indicated he was stopping as we approached the looming mass of a thick stand of trees. Mackay came up beside me. 'Stay here,' he whispered. 'I'll come back for you.' I watched as he and Boyce were absorbed into the darkness of the woods.

On my own, and not moving now, sound started to settle down and take on individual forms. Mainly the breeze, different notes in the trees and the hedge, but also a very low amorphous background hum, a kind of external tinnitus, as if the very darkness was breathing.

It was spooky.

And I had no way of measuring time. Only the yardstick of mounting paranoia.

So, despite knowing that black bears didn't roam freely in this country, the knowledge didn't help when Mackay crept out of the woods like one. My sphincter still attempted to get a piggy-back on my tonsils.

He motioned for me to keep quiet, took me by the wrist, and led me into the woods. We went up a rise, ankle-deep in leaf mould, him somehow seeing the fallen logs to skirt, me just allowing myself to be led like a primitive life form.

We cleared the woods at the top of the rise, and everything changed. We were at the interface with civilization. Below me a grassy bank led down to the brook, and across from that I could make out the boundary wall and fence. The garden was in darkness, but the rear terrace of the house was lit up like an interrogation chamber.

Mackay pulled me off to the side before we sank to the prone position. 'Don't go over there,' he warned in a low whisper, nodding in the forbidden direction, 'there's a big clump of nettles.'

'Where's Boyce?' I whispered back.

'He's off on a recce,' he replied, as if it was as natural as popping out for fish and chips. He handed me a pair of night-vision binoculars. It was a gesture I remembered from childhood. Being given something to keep me occupied.

They had pet rabbits. A luxury hutch on the terrace, comprising a little pagoda for the living quarters, and a wire-mesh run like a miniature Guantanamo Bay. That's where we started to develop our knowledge of the social network of the house. First the two little girls came out to say night-night to the bunnies, along with the impossibly young-looking, very blonde mummy.

Who we later realized was the au pair, when the not so young, but still very blonde, real mummy came out onto the terrace alone in high-heel shoes, glass of wine in hand, to smoke a sneaky cigarette. The daddy of the house had not yet come home.

And neither had Boyce.

Mackay whispered for me not to worry. Boyce, he informed me, was busy creating diversions for future consumption.

The girls, and the au pair, we worked out by the location of the lights when they trooped off to bed, had their accommodation on the second floor, in the roof space.

The action on the ground floor shifted to what we took to be the main sitting room in the far cross wing, judging by the flicker from the giant television screen through the curtains. At half past eleven these lights went off, and the lights in the room above came on. We had had our hunch about the location of the master bedroom confirmed. It had a glazed wall and a balcony running the length of the gable. Overlooking the countryside.

And still no daddy of the house.

'How long do we wait?' I whispered. I felt cranky. I was damp, cold, and nervous. The ground was hard and I couldn't find a position to feel comfortable in.

'It must be his lifestyle,' Mackay opined. 'If this was unusual she wouldn't have gone to bed, she'd still be downstairs fretting.'

'You don't think the security guys could have found Boyce, do you?'

I couldn't see his face, but I heard the smile in his voice. 'Believe me, we'd know.'

'Have you had any more thoughts on how we're going to do this?'

'Home invasion.'

I didn't like the sound of that. 'Come again?' I asked, hoping I might have heard wrong.

'A variation on a home invasion. A break-in with attitude,

as in LA gang culture meets the Visigoths.' I could tell that he was smiling under his mask. Perhaps that was his way of coping.

It wasn't mine. 'That's going to trigger the alarm.' I observed anxiously.

'Exactly. There's no way of avoiding it. That's why the technique has to be crude and fast. As soon as the shit goes up we know that the cops and security are going to be on their way. So we've got to get in and out of there with our man before they arrive. And it won't just be your ordinary plods bearing down on us either.'

'What do you mean?'

'If they've got Brady's place of business under surveillance, that scrutiny's not going to stop when he peels off his nasty dope dealer mask and goes home to the wife and kids.'

He was right. It stood to reason. Bradshaw would have the house wired. I felt like an amateur at this. 'How effective is this normally?' I probed, looking for reassurance.

'I wouldn't know, I was never on any extraction teams. This is a first,' he announced chirpily.

I settled back down into discomfort and anxiety.

At around half past one the external lights came on. The master bedroom lights had been out for over an hour.

'What's wrong?' I asked nervously.

He stayed silent, binoculars pressed to his eyes. I could tell from his stance that he was in rapt concentration. His shoulders relaxed. 'It's okay. It's the security system. The lights have come on to welcome daddy home.'

As he spoke, what looked like a searchlight appeared sweeping the garden at the side of the house before disappearing again. A car turning in the driveway, I realized. This seemed to be confirmed a couple of minutes later when the light went on in the hall, followed by another in the family room.

We followed Brady's slow progress to bed as a sequence of lights moving from room to room, gradually shifting to the first floor. 'Don't you dare go and fuck around with the au pair, you bastard,' Mackay muttered under his breath. During this display Boyce returned, sinking to a prone position beside Mackay. Neither of them spoke, they just watched the house with their binoculars, until the light eventually went out in the master bedroom.

'Well?' Mackay asked without removing his binoculars.

'A driver-come-bodyguard. He dropped Brady off at the front door, and then parked the car in the garage. He lives in the flat above it.'

'What sort of threat?'

'I've wired his front door shut. That should put him on delay.'

Unless he decides he wants to sneak out and fuck the au pair, I thought. I didn't share this with them. I felt enough of a spare prick as it was, they didn't need me chanting lamentations on top of it.

'Glyn . . .' Mackay rocked me awake. Unbelievably, despite the cold damp opposition of the ground, I had dozed off. 'Come on, Glyn,' he cooed softly, 'it's time to make our move.'

I shook my head to get my blood pumped up and buzzing. 'What do you want me to do?'

'You need to come down to the fence with us. We can't talk down there, so I'm telling you what you have to do now. We're going to go in through the hole in the fence that

271

Boyce has cut, and you're going to wait there for us. He's threaded some wire through the cut ends, and when we get back through you're going to pull the fence tight together again. Tie it off, and then follow us up to here. You understand that?'

'Yes. But will it fool them?'

'Hopefully, because they're going to find the other holes in the neighbours' fences that Boyce has already prepared.' He put his hand on my shoulder and drew his balaclava up close to mine. 'It's going to fucking erupt, Glyn. So you're going to have to hold your nerve.'

I nodded my understanding.

'And you may not like what you're going to see. So prepare yourself for it. Okay?'

I nodded again. I didn't trust myself to speak. My mind was racing. Up till now I had managed to distract myself by the sheer discomfort of the exercise, but now the moral dilemmas were limbering up in the wings again.

Mackay had underestimated. It didn't so much erupt as go into total home security supernova. First the external lights flared on when they reached the terrace and activated the sensors. Then the burglar alarm sounded off like a meltdown in a nuclear reactor when they attacked the French doors to the family room with sledgehammers.

Sledgehammers! It turned out they had been carrying short-handled sledgehammers in their rucksacks! Along with wire cutters, night-vision binoculars, flasks of Lucozade, granary bars, and fuck knows what else kind of survival and interrogation kit.

272

The toughened safety glass gave a reverberating boom, and then a huge crash like a cascading city of greenhouses.

Every sense I had was appalled.

Not only were we committing heinous crime, but we were fucking advertising it! *Here we are! Just follow the lights and the noise! You can't miss us!*

I crouched there, peeking over the top of the wall, convinced that we were operating in two separate time modes. Mackay and Boyce were struggling up through that house in cold treacle motion, while all the forces racing towards us had some sort of temporal hyper-drive on their side.

We couldn't take as long as this and get away with it!

I realized I was craning my neck, trying to will my vision around the side of the house to catch the first glimpse of the arriving strobe lights. And all the time I was fighting the impulse to get up and run like fuck away from all this madness.

And then they appeared. In the garden. Two dark figures running, half-dragging something spectrally white between them. Brady! Naked! The colour of the skin on a milk pudding, the only light thing in the night. But dreadfully foreshortened. Oh Jesus! My senses couldn't take it. They had cut his fucking head off!

Mackay was the first over the wall and through the hole in the fence.

'Why?' I tried to ask, but it came out as a pathetic croak.

Which was just as well. Because Brady was struggling as they tried to bundle him through the hole. Not bad terminal motor responses for a guy without a head, I registered. And then I saw that I had confused empty space with the black hood they had placed over it.

They had secured Brady's wrists behind him with a plastic cable tie. But they had had to let go of his arms to get him through the fence, and he was now writhing like a mad thing, trying to wedge himself in the gap. Boyce gave a mighty push from his end. Mackay spun like a matador to augment the momentum as he came through, and add a directional spin, which sent Brady into the brook.

Boyce leapt through the hole and followed Mackay, who was already in the water. But the tone and manner of Brady's struggles had subsided. The surprise of the sudden immersion had obviously shocked him. He was on his knees in the muddy brook, dripping, shaking his upper body, looking like some naked mediaeval heretic who had just undergone a forced baptism.

I finished hauling the wire tight, drawing the ends of the fence together, tied it off, and clambered up the bank and over the rise after them. I glanced back from the top of the bank. Nothing had changed. Everything was still going off like an installation artist's take on the Sound and the Fury. But was I now imagining the sounds of sirens over the alarm?

I was shaking. Coming out of the adrenalin rush. So much so that I was able to look down on my first contracted abduction with something approaching detached curiosity.

He was face down on the leaf mould. Boyce had one foot on the small of his back, and, holding him by his trussed wrists, had levered his outstretched arms up towards his shoulders to a point where he knew better than to struggle. He wasn't quite so white now. He was streaked with mud from the brook, and the vegetable detritus that had stuck to him when he had been dragged up the bank.

Mackay crouched down in front of him. 'It's time to introduce ourselves, Paddy.'

He raised the hood partially, and I saw the duct tape covering his mouth. It only then struck me that I hadn't been surprised by Brady's silence. There had been too much else going on. Mackay started peeling a corner. 'I hope you're going to talk to us nicely.' He whipped the duct tape off one side of his mouth, keeping hold of the flap it formed.

Brady gave a yelp of pain. His head came up. 'Fuck you—'

Mackay whipped the duct tape back and dumped his face into the ground, at the same time as Boyce applied more pressure on his arm lever. Brady ground his face into the rotted leaf mould in his pain and anger.

'I said nicely,' Mackay told him sternly. 'You disappoint me. I thought you were going to be sensible.' He looked up at Boyce and nodded.

Boyce, without losing his leverage on Brady's arm, removed his foot from his back, and used it to nudge one of his legs aside. Brady stiffened, and then started to shake the leg. The yell of pain that he was unable to utter was perfectly outlined in the arch of his spine.

His reaction surprised me. Boyce hadn't appeared to use violence.

'Urticaria, Paddy, it'll sting like fuck,' Mackay said tenderly, and I remembered the nettle bed he had warned me about. 'Mother Nature bites the Bad Guys.'

He sounded so virtuous. Okay, it wasn't quite the Knights of Bushido's practice of sticking bamboo splinters under

275

their victims' fingernails, but Brady had still been subjected to toxic shock. I took control of myself. As long as I remembered Ryan Shaw torched to a crisp in his car, nettles I found I could handle, it was when it came down to the scalpels or the battery acid, or whatever else they'd carted along in their toolkit, that I was going to have a real battle with my scruples.

Mackay put his fingers on the duct tape again. 'That was just a demonstration, Paddy. We know who you are, and we know what you do, and I'm pretty sure that you've played this game yourself in our role, and you know that, in the end, everyone collapses. It's only a question of the degrees of persuasion. So, are you going to be wise and cut out the bollocks part, where you play at being hard and unbreakable? Because, as you well know, if you don't talk, you end up dead – and that's a pretty fucking stupid principle to give all this up for. We're not window shopping. This is the real thing. You're out here now because we need information from you.'

Brady grunted and thrashed in a big body mime of *Fuck you!*

Mackay nodded up at Boyce, who stiffened the arm lock. Brady's body went rigid in the expectation of even more shocking pain as his arms either broke or popped from their sockets. Boyce eased off slightly.

Mackay put disappointment into his tone. 'You're not a fucking amateur. Recognize the inevitability. There is no point at which we say, oh shucks, he's too strong-willed for us, we'll have to let him go. You've been here before. You must know there are only two possible endings. And by now you must have realized that we're professionals. We've done this many times before, Paddy. Which means we always get away. We know when to cut and run. So you can't keep stalling in the hope that the cops are going to come surging to the rescue like the fucking cavalry. Because, long before that time, it's going to be too late for you.'

Something changed.

We all looked at each other. The alarm had stopped. Mackay held his hand up to let the silence register.

'Hear that, Paddy? That's it. Time's up.' His tone turned harsh and disgusted. 'Ah for fuck's sake . . . . Cut his fucking head off,' he instructed. 'We're taking it back with us.'

He was so convincing that he had to clamp his hand over my mouth to stifle my rising protest.

And Brady had also heard that true note. He was now shaking his head, desperately gesturing capitulation, and, even under the mask, I recognized terror. And I smelled it. He had pissed himself.

Mackay gave me a hand gesture that I translated as time being now in very short supply. He waved me in beside him in front of Brady, partially lifted the mask and got a grip on the duct tape gag again. 'We're on borrowed time now, Paddy. My friend is going to ask you some questions, so don't fuck around.'

'Ryan Shaw came to you with something,' I pitched.

Brady cocked his head, surprised either by my new voice or the question. I could almost see him grading his options.

'I want to know what that was and who you set him up with.'

'Are you ready, Paddy?' Mackay gave a tentative tug on the duct tape.

Brady nodded. Mackay pulled the gag partly off. Brady sucked air in deeply before he spoke. 'I had nothing to do with killing that guy.'

'That wasn't the question,' Mackay threatened.

'It was a laptop computer.'

'Whose computer?'

'That's what he wanted me to find out. He wanted to trade it back to the owner.'

'Why did he come to you?'

'Because he didn't know the password, he couldn't—'

'No,' I cut in impatiently, 'how did he know that you could help him?'

'Because he picked up some gear at the same time he got the laptop.'

'Gear?'

'E – Ecstasy,' he elaborated. 'He reckoned the guy had to be in the trade.'

'How were you able to trace the owner?'

'He gave me the registration number of the car the stuff came from. I used my contacts.'

I had a sudden intuition. 'A BMW?'

'That's right, a Five Series Beamer.'

'Belonging to a Kadir Hoca?'

'If you knew this fucking stuff, why put me through all this shit?' He sounded aggrieved.

'Just answer,' Mackay growled.

'Hoca, yes, some wop first name. I'd never heard of the guy, but I put his name out. Turns out he was some big honcho for the Saltik crew in London.'

'Where was the car when they got the laptop?'

278

'Saltik wanted to know that too, as well as where his man was, but Shaw wasn't saying.'

'So you arranged a meet?'

'I was only the fucking dating agency, man. I put them together. I took no part in what they got up to after that.'

'And what did you get out of it?'

He looked up at me sightlessly. 'This! Fucking assaulted, my home bust up, my wife and kids terrified, and now the fucking law is probably tearing through my crib as we speak on the so-called pretext of rescuing me.' He was starting to get cocky again. Boyce applied some pressure to remind him that feudal law still applied. He yelped. 'I got fuck-all out of it. It just meant I kept myself out of Saltik's bad books.'

'He killed Ryan Shaw?'

'His people met Shaw. I had nothing to do with what fucking happened after that.'

'Are you sorry?'

'What kind of fucking question is that?'

And the thing was, he sounded genuinely puzzled that I had asked it.

16

I reckoned I was now one step ahead of them all.

Because, if Ryan Shaw hadn't told Brady where the laptop had been found, it was probably because neither Jessie nor Christian, whoever his contact had been, had ever told him.

But I had figured it out.

Jessie's lair. The Monks' Trail car park.

But that knowledge threw up a few imponderables of its own. Like why had Hoca parked there? And why had he left his car unattended long enough for Jessie to have been able to break into it? I had never known the guy, but, given his profession and background, I wouldn't have put him down as the sort to take off into the woods to commune with the flora and fauna. And then, when he discovered the theft, why hadn't he told his boss where he was and what had happened? Why had they had to try and literally prise that out of Ryan Shaw?

I reflected on all of this as we drove back to the Knutsford

Service Area in the van. It was useful therapy. It took my mind off the recent jangled madness that had shortened both my fingernails and my allotted life span.

And which had finished up with us leaving Brady tied and wrapped, face forward, around a tree trunk.

'Bet no one ever called you a tree-hugger before,' Boyce had chuckled, finding this immensely funny, patting him on the cheek through the mask as we departed.

It was after four o'clock in the morning at Knutsford. Mackay and I had a coffee in the self-service cafeteria, a Hopperesque interior peopled by drawn and lustreless faces. Boyce had gone off to do what he had to do with the van.

'Did you get what you wanted?' Mackay asked.

'It's another piece. I don't know exactly how it fits in yet.'

'Do we take it to this Saltik guy now?'

I shook my head. I was feeling a weariness that was more than just physical. 'No, Mac. We can't push our luck that far.'

'You don't have to be there next time,' he suggested. Probably a polite way of telling me that I put a damper on their true mode of self-expression.

'Someone like Saltik's going to be untouchable. Believe me, there'll be no route to him. But I'll do what I can to get the mechanics he used put away,' I promised him. I was being ambitious. There could be three separate teams involved. But it was time to rein Mackay and Boyce in. I didn't want to be responsible for the bloodbath spreading.

He looked at me cannily, and then nodded, accepting it for the time being. He drained his coffee. 'Time to go,' he announced.

Back in the Range Rover, he unlocked the glove compartment

and I retrieved my things. I switched my phone on. Missed calls from three numbers. Messages from one of them. Rhian's. I went straight to the most recent one. Half past eleven last night.

'Glyn, why haven't you called me back? I'm getting worried. Please call me. It doesn't matter what time.' She sounded distressed. I flashed a look at Mackay, who was pretending he hadn't overheard it.

The other two numbers were Bryn Jones and Emrys Hughes.

I put the phone away in my pocket.

'Aren't you going to call her?' Mackay asked.

'It's quarter to five in the morning, Mac.'

'She said to call anytime.'

'That was before she went to sleep. Think about when you were with Gina. Can you imagine calling her and waking her up at this time in the morning, just to tell her that you were okay, and there's nothing to worry about.'

That brought a smile. We had both shared my ex-wife's moods. 'Point taken,' he said.

After that we drove back to Dinas in near silence, both of us in post-mission fatigue. The dawn started up behind us as we got closer, nothing joyful or dramatic, merely a low spread of washed-out grey through the cloud cover, illuminating the prospect of even heavier cloud cover.

He dropped me off at Unit 13. I offered him the use of the spare bed, but he declined, saying that he had clients to get back to. I had forgotten that he had a business to run. He saw my reaction and told me not to worry. He had set them a solo twenty-four hours initiative exercise up on the moors. He and Boyce would go and round them up after breakfast.

I almost missed the note. It had been stuck to my door, but the damp had got to the sticky stuff, and it had fallen into the upturned milk crate I used as a front step.

Drove up to see why you weren't answering my calls. If I find out you've been out for a night on the tiles, you bastard!!! Seriously though, am concerned. Staying at The Fleece. Love, Rhian xxx

I reread the note. It put a different perspective on things. The prospect of having a lovely crosspatch on the end of a telephone in Cardiff was one thing. The thought of her being a live act in a bedroom near me was another.

The newspaper delivery lorry was dropping its bundles off in the newsagent's doorway as I drove into Dinas. I waved at the milkman in his van. I felt nervous. All the *what-ifs* that went with adolescent jitters.

I used the key to the rear door of The Fleece that David and Sandra kept hidden under the only inverted flower pot in the cobbled yard. I made my way quietly to the reception desk. Three room keys were missing from their hooks. Number two, I knew, housed a regular, a guy the forestry used to cull deer in the plantations. That left four and six.

I plumped for starting with number four, tiptoed up the creaky staircase, and started knocking softly, but insistently on the door.

'What is it . . .?' It was Rhian's voice, a confused mutter, muted even further by the closed door.

'It's Glyn,' I pitched in a loud whisper.

After a short wait she opened the door wide enough to

283

fit her face into the gap. Her hair was sleep-mussed, face puffy, and eyes still adjusting. She held a kimono-type dressing gown clutched tightly closed at the neck.

I gave her what I hoped was a big Tah-Rah-Rah smile.

'Jesus Christ' – she blinked at me through the sleep fuddle – 'I've changed my mind, I want my money back.'

'Hello, Rhian,' I said sheepishly. I was suddenly aware that I had been so busy stressing over the abstracts of this encounter that I had forgotten about the fundamentals of presentation. I saw myself mirrored in her eyes. Unshaven, splenetic hair, wild-eyed, and basted with that reek of damp outdoors slow cooked by a car heater.

'You look awful!' she confirmed.

She steered me straight to the shower. Any thoughts that this was going to turn into a joint exercise were dashed when she backed out and pulled the door closed noisily.

I should have been more Spartan and had a cold shower. The warm water only reinforced how tired I felt. Still it softened me up and pinked me out. I dusted my underpants and the armpits of my T-shirt with some talcum powder I found. For proprieties' sake I also put my trousers back on.

She was sitting up in bed, still wearing the dressing gown, looking stern and chaste. 'I was worried about you,' she announced.

'I'm sorry. I didn't have my phone with me.'

She pulled back the sheets beside her. 'You look exhausted. You may as well get in here. It looks like we're conducting a job interview with you standing over there.'

I made an executive decision and took off my trousers. She sniffed the air. 'Gardenia?' she asked, puzzled.

'Lily of the Valley,' I said, getting in beside her.

'Where were you?'

'Chasing the bad guys.' The yawn rose up out of nowhere. I felt the warmth of her beside me. The softness of the bed. My eyes started to close. I blinked them open.

They must have closed again.

I woke up alone. I came round with the realization that my arm, stretched out beside me, was enclosing empty space. I opened my eyes and saw Rhian, still in the dressing gown, sitting in a chair opposite the end of the bed sipping from a mug and watching me.

She smiled. 'Good morning.' She held the mug up. 'Want a cup of tea?'

'You got out of bed?' I didn't try to hide my disappointment.

Her smile shifted into the amused end of the spectrum. 'The tea wouldn't make itself.'

I sat up against the pillows. 'Are you going to come back in?'

'I thought about it.'

'And?'

'I decided I want us to have a different beginning.'

I frowned. 'What does that mean?'

'When it happens . . .' She stopped herself with a smile. 'If it happens, I want it to be a bit more fluid and romantic. I don't want to look back on it and feel I was overwhelmed by an unwashed hunk at six o'clock in the morning. It would affect the future tenor of our relationship.'

'How?' I asked, genuinely puzzled by this analysis.

'You'd come to think of me as meek and compliant.'

'No, I wouldn't,' I protested. But not voicing my opinion that I didn't think those two words existed in her repertoire.

She inclined her head knowingly. 'So, you're going to have to keep on working at it.'

'Romance?'

She nodded. 'The way to a girl's heart.'

'Don't I even deserve a preview?'

She stood up, put her mug down, and walked round the bed to stand over me. She looked down, calmly watching me for a moment. I couldn't read her expression. Then she bent her head slowly towards me, forcing me to strain up towards her to reach her for the kiss. Making me work for it.

She broke away just as I was getting a feel for the fit of her mouth. 'Satisfied?'

'No.'

She grinned. 'Good.' She sat down on the side of the bed beyond my reach, but left her hand stretched out where I could take it. 'Well, what did you think of my news?' she enquired, changing her tone.

'What news?'

'The message I left you.'

'That's why I came here.'

'No, not that one. The one I left before, on your phone. That's why I got concerned. When you didn't respond to it.'

'I didn't get back that far.'

She inclined her head calculatingly. 'So you don't know yet?'

'About what?'

'Jessie's father.'

'Jessie's dead father?'

She shook her head and smiled precociously, enjoying the opportunity to re-tell this. 'He's not dead.'

'Cassie told me he was.'

Relays started to spark up in my brain.

'How about Nick Saltik?' she offered triumphantly.

'Saltik!' I exclaimed, sitting up. 'That's the guy behind the Don's Den drug factories.' I didn't complicate matters by telling her about his Ryan Shaw sideline.

'That's Mike, his cousin.'

'This guy Nick's not in the business?'

'My contacts tell me that their fathers ran it together after old man Hakan died, but Mike and Nick had a falling out and split up. Nick branched out on his own.'

'Straight or a spin-off of the evil empire?'

'A spin-off. Mike's got the drug and sex business, whereas Nick's more into extortion, money laundering and people-trafficking.'

We were drifting away from the core of this. 'Tell me about him and Cassie.'

She looked pleased with herself. 'My contacts couldn't help me with that. I had to use my initiative.'

'Go on.' I prompted.

'They had an affair in London. Nick was married, so Cassie was kept discreetly on the side. Then she got pregnant and Jessie was born, and Nick decided it was time to get shot of her. His was a dynastic marriage, and she'd become too much of a liability, so she had to be cast off and shipped away.'

I had a sudden horrible thought. My face dropped. 'Please tell me you didn't go to Cassie for this?'

'No, I asked Rhodri.'

Rhodri ap Hywel. Of course. The man who had provided Cassie with her refuge. His property company had sold the temperance bars to Mike Saltik. So, in all likelihood, he had had a business relationship with Cousin Nick as well. Did it stop at property deals? Was there a toxic thread that tied all these people together? 'Was he providing a love nest in the sticks for Nick to keep up his relationship with Cassie and Jessie?'

'No. He said that all Nick's ties with Cassie were severed. She got a pay-off, a place in the country and a job with the Ap Hywel Foundation, and that was the deal.'

I let go of her hand, pulled the covers back and swung out of bed.

'Where are you going?' she asked.

'I need to talk to Cassie.'

'What's the matter?' She looked concerned.

'I'll tell you when I'm certain.'

She stood up. 'You're not leaving me out of this now. You promised me this story. I'm coming with you.' She ducked and paused in front of the dressing-table mirror. 'But first I need a quick shower.'

I was straining to leave. But I owed her. And Cassie had waited this long. 'Okay,' I said, and stopped struggling quite so hard to get into my clothes.

I had been right. Cassie had once been at home with the scorpions. She had flirted with a lifestyle where people could end up dead for reasons having nothing to do with their health. Now I had to discover what I had inadvertently unleashed when I had told her my fears about Jessie.

And how did this new disclosure tie in with Hoca and the stolen laptop?

I waited until I heard the shower running before I made my phone calls.

Bryn Jones went straight to answering machine.

Emrys's phone kept ringing. But I persisted. I knew he would be watching my name on the caller display, willing me to hang up, but I also knew that his conditioning would eventually force him to answer it. It was the way he was made.

'This is a bad time, Capaldi, I'm busy,' he said pompously.

'You called me first,' I reminded him.

'That was yesterday, you never called back,' he said grumpily.

'No one said anything about a Statute of Limitations.'

'What?'

'Forget it. Just tell me why you called.'

'DCI Jones told me to,' he said, excusing himself, in case I thought he might have been trying to be friendly, 'about what we found when we went round to Christian Fenner's place.'

The laptop? Was this going to lead us straight to Hoca? And then Saltik?

'So tell me,' I snapped impatiently, 'let's not wait for the psychic fucking waves to roll in.'

'You don't need to swear,' he said sulkily.

'Just tell me, Emrys!'

'Home recording equipment.'

'What?' It was my turn to be nonplussed.

'Home recording equipment. For his music. Expensive stuff. His parents said they didn't even know he had it, or where it had come from.'

Like Dai's motorbike?

But this didn't make any sense. Jessie, Dai and Christian were all dead. All they had ever stolen from the car park had been rubbish. The only valuable thing that had ever come

289

their way had been the laptop. And they had all been killed before they could profit from it.

The shower stopped running. I hung up on Emrys. I tucked this latest puzzle away in a safe place. It was too distracting.

It was raining. No t'ai chi on the lawn outside the Home Farm today.

'Shall I come in with you?' Rhian asked as I parked the car.

'No. She's not going to want an audience.'

'I wish you'd tell me.'

'I will.' I leaned across and kissed her.

'You're not going to do a runner out the back door are you?' She was only half joking.

'No, I'll leave that for when you start the paternity suit.'

She grinned. 'Be careful what you wish for.'

I was conscious of her watching me as I crossed the gravel drive to the front door. Was Cassie doing the same?

The door was answered by the same elderly little man in a black beret who had seen me out the last time.

'Is Cassie in?' I asked.

'I'm sorry, she's not available.' So she had seen my arrival. He had been despatched to act as a block.

I dropped my head and made a show of looking crestfallen. 'That's a shame. I wanted to share my regrets about Dai Lloyd and Christian Fenner with her.'

'I'll tell her,' he said, trying to push the door closed against the foot I had inserted into the threshold.

'Perhaps I'll see her at the funerals.'

His little face crinkled with the effort as he tried even harder to force the door closed.

'It's all right, Simon, you can let him in.' Cassie's voice came from behind him. He opened the door. She was standing in the hall, a dark tense marionette framed against the light coming in from the courtyard garden. As I approached I could see that she was looking gaunt.

She led me to her kitchen. She made no offer of a seat or a drink. She stared at me, as if trying to burn out my purpose. I used silence. I had already mentioned Dai and Christian. She could put the agenda together.

She broke the silence. 'Don't you dare try to tell me that the fire that killed those two poor boys was anything other than an accident.'

'We need to find out, Cassie,' I said gently. 'We need to stop this.'

She shook her head sharply. 'I don't want anything to do with you. You brought me this trouble.'

'No. It had already happened. I was only the messenger.'

'You drove my daughter to her death,' she exclaimed harshly.

'You lied to me,' I retorted, 'you told me Jessie's father was dead.'

She stared at me. Her face had turned ghastly pale. She hadn't expected this.

'You told him, didn't you? You told Nick Saltik that his daughter had been murdered. You left it up to him to do what he had to do.'

I saw in her face that I had connected.

Vendetta!

The Turks would have their own equally harsh word for it, but vendetta worked for me.

Her expression shifted to stubborn. 'She was his daughter. He had a right to know.'

I let her see that I understood the implications of this. 'You knew how he lived. What men like him were capable of. You must have known the codes they operate with.'

'Jessie didn't deserve to die.'

'You once told me, *We can't stop the things that are meant to happen.*'

She fixed me with her eyes. 'That was before you told me that my daughter had been murdered.'

'Has it helped you?'

She thought about it. 'Whatever has happened has nothing to do with those two boys.'

I saw her real grief and her pain then. Her doubt at her own decisions. What would I have done in her position? I let my face soften. 'No,' I agreed softly. She had answered me. I had gotten what I had come here for. She had suffered enough. I decided to absolve her from Dai and Christian. 'No, that was nothing to do with you.'

A torrent of emotions twisted her face. Somewhere, in amongst the pain, there was a thread of relief. 'The Nick that I knew could never have murdered children.'

'But Mike could have?'

She watched me for a moment. Her nod was almost imperceptible.

'What about Kadir Hoca? Did he ever come here to see you?'

She shook her head. She looked genuinely puzzled. 'I don't know that name.' I described him. 'No. No one from that life ever came to see me here.'

*

I explained it to Rhian, stressing that this was so pre-sub judice that it hadn't even fertilized in the egg it hadn't broken out of yet.

I was driving us back to Dinas. I glanced over at her. I could see she was struggling with something. 'Which part of it don't you get?'

'I can't see why telling you who Jessie's real father was made such a difference?'

'It explains Cassie's reaction when I told her that there was a possibility Jessie had been murdered. It was wrong. There was no real surprise. Because, as it now turns out, she had known people who were capable of it.'

'The Saltiks?'

I nodded. 'What I didn't know, when I told her about my suspicions, was that she would be able to home directly in on the prime suspect. She knew Nick wouldn't have had his own daughter killed, so it had to be down to Mike.'

She frowned. 'But what could he have got out of killing Jessie?'

'I don't know. I can only assume he was paying Nick back for something. But Nick wasn't meant to make that connection.'

She shook her head. 'You've lost me again.'

'That's why it was so carefully staged. He didn't have her shot or strangled, which would have been so much simpler, because he didn't want it coming back to him. He wanted the satisfaction of exacting the blood price, but he didn't want it to escalate into a war, so he arranged it to look like an accident. His honour was satisfied and the thing should have stopped there.'

'But it didn't.'

293

'No, Nick's people torched Mike's Don's Den operation in retaliation.'

'Because Cassie had told Nick what you told her?'

'That's right. I fucked it up. I've set this whole Saltik clan war in motion.'

'You?'

'That's what I've been trying to tell you. I wouldn't accept the blame for the accident. So when I told Cassie about my suspicions, she went to Nick. This had to be gospel. It was straight from a cop's mouth, after all.'

'But you were right,' she protested.

'Yes, but I never dreamt that our Den Mother had the connections that could get this whole chain of death and disaster up and running. Christ only knows what mayhem's going on in London as we speak.'

She reached across to stroke the back of my neck. 'What else could you have done?'

'Accepted the storyboard and the guilt that went with it. Everyone else seemed to have managed to do so on my behalf.'

'I don't think that's the way you work.' She kneaded the base of my skull with her thumb. 'I think that's what I like about you.'

I flashed her a smile. 'Some people call it stubbornness. But thanks.' It was a good intimate moment. Basking in approbation, her thumb gently massaging the nape of my neck. If this was going to be the tenor of our future relationship, I wouldn't be complaining.

I only wish we could have gone on driving.

But Dinas loomed. I stopped in front of The Fleece. 'You

know you can't publish anything yet,' I warned, softening it with a smile.

'I know.' She leaned over and kissed me. She broke away. 'But I can start my research.'

She was part way out of the door when I had my premonition. 'Rhian . . .' She turned with an expectant smile. 'Keep away from those bastards. Research, yes, but don't get close.'

'I know what I'm doing.'

'They're dangerous.'

She waggled her fingers at me before she shut the door. I watched her cutting her way through the air making for the door of The Fleece. I almost got out of the car then. I almost ran up to her and spun her and told her, 'Life's too short, Rhian. I promise you romance in spades, but let's get on with this, just in case one of us gets zapped by a stroke, or hit by a car before we can get together again.' How sickeningly prophetic was that going to turn out to be.

But, instead, I started the car and reversed.

'Glyn!'

I braked. She had called out from the doorway. I lowered my window. 'What are you going to do?' she asked.

I grinned. For a moment I had hoped that she had had the same thought as me. I put my head out of the window and called out to her, 'Get myself exonerated.'

17

I thought about sending an email. But there was a risk that she might not open it when she saw it was from me. I was going to have to call her.

I had to be patched through. There was a tinny background acoustic, and I pictured her hunkered down in the cramped fuggy rear of a surveillance van. 'DI Bradshaw?'

'What do you want, Sergeant?' she answered gruffly.

'I have information regarding the death of Ryan Shaw that we discussed in Winsford.'

'I'm not investigating that,' she snapped impatiently, 'take it directly to DI Purslow.'

'With respect, Ma'am, I think it might be better coming from you.'

'Are you trying to stalk me, Sergeant Capaldi?' she asked snidely. I heard muted sniggers from the backdrop.

'No. It's just that way you can control how much information you want DI Purslow to have.'

'What are you talking about?' Her voice turned pure mean.

'The information concerns someone you have under surveillance.'

I heard the mumble of voices, followed by a laugh. 'Shut the fuck up!' she barked away from the mouthpiece. She came back on the phone to ask, 'Who?'

'Patrick Brady.'

I could imagine a lot of the stuff that was going on in the silence that followed. 'What do you know about Patrick Brady?' she asked evenly. That told me that this conversation was now being recorded.

'Ryan Shaw had a run-in with a crew working for Mike Saltik, a North London hoodlum. Brady was the go-between. If he wasn't there at the meeting, he would have known where it occurred.'

'How do you know this?'

'Brady was the enabler, he knows who tortured and hit Ryan Shaw.'

'And I asked you how you know this?'

'I respectfully suggest that you pick Brady up and turn him over to the Cheshire force, Ma'am.'

'Are you . . .? Have you been playing fucking Commandoes in my patch!' she yelled, suddenly arriving at her black eureka moment.

I cut the connection. Would she act on that information? She would probably have to as she had just been given a material lead in a murder investigation. Which she had recorded herself. In a way, I hoped that she'd withhold it. That way I could call her again. There was a certain scary nervous satisfaction to be had from annoying the fuck out of her.

I let myself float back down to ambient level before I put the call in to Kevin Fletcher.

After that I called Carmarthen headquarters to make sure Jack Galbraith and Bryn Jones were around. I didn't want a wasted journey.

It was still raining as I drove down, but I didn't care. I was carrying the golden key that connected named North London gangsters to the mayhem that had erupted in Mid Wales. Instead of suspicion floating around like a tenuous gnat cloud that could be experienced but not grasped, I now had the link to Jessie's death as a solid entity. This was stuff we could brace our feet against, and use to push back at the bastards. Mike and Nick Saltik would probably be ring-fenced and untouchable, but we might be able to shake some of their operatives out of the tree.

But, more importantly, for me at least, I was restoring my reputation.

They heard me out, both sitting behind Jack Galbraith's desk, each of them backed up against a wide-open window to pull their cigarette smoke out. I knew better than to think this was courtesy, it was because the smoke detectors were sensitive.

'North London fucking hoods,' Jack Galbraith groaned. 'Coming out here and fucking up our green and pleasant land.' He uttered this without any apparent sense of irony as he puffed carcinogens out into the crappy sunless alley behind the headquarters building.

'Shall I call London with this?' Bryn Jones asked.

Jack Galbraith pulled a face. 'Let's get some breathing time in before you do. Work out strategies. This is my fucking fiefdom, Bryn. I'm not having Kevin Fletcher or some swanky crew from the Met striding in here like the US Fucking Marines to try and roll this thing up.'

Uh-uh.

Bryn saw my expression. 'I think we may have a problem.'

Jack Galbraith followed his glance. 'What's that face for, Capaldi?'

'I've already told DCI Fletcher, Sir.'

His face clouded. Typhoon level. 'You told him fucking first!'

'On the telephone, Sir.'

'Why didn't you call us?'

'I thought you'd want this face-to-face, Sir.'

'Is that what your problem is, Capaldi?'

'Sir?'

'Masochism? You give Kevin Fletcher a head start, and then you come here expecting what? My hands round your throat? Does my fucking anger turn you on that much?'

'No, Sir, it's . . .'

He held his palm out to shut me up. He was thinking. I hadn't factored for this reaction. So much for having virgins scattering rose petals in front of my triumphal return procession.

'I'm going to go to London. The Met won't like it, but I'm going to insist that I get to sit in on any interviews with the Saltiks.' He shot Bryn an apologetic smile. 'I know you should be doing this, and you know there's no disrespect intended, but you also know what those supremacist fucks are like.'

Bryn nodded and laughed silently in agreement.

'A rude and unpleasant Jock DCS is going to loosen more sphincters than a nice Taff DCI.'

'No offence taken.'

'I think it would be useful for you to get over to Dinas and talk to the Bullock woman. Try and see if she's being totally straight fucking arrow about her past dealings with Nick Saltik.'

'Right.'

'And while you're there, you may as well broach the ap Hywel people about their business dealings with the Saltik Boys.'

'Are we treating them as friends?'

'Play it by ear.'

He nodded his assent.

'Can I help, Sir?' I asked, trying to pitch my tone between faithful puppy and resolute husky.

He looked at me for a moment before shaking his head despairingly. 'Why, when you manage to come up with the right goods to deliver to us, does there always turn out to be shit on the handles?'

I knew better than to try to answer that.

'Okay.' He came to a decision. 'We've still got eight missing people out there.'

'Nine, Sir,' I corrected him. 'Kadir Hoca's still unaccounted for.'

He frowned sceptically. 'I have my doubts about him. I think he may have gone over to the enemy. Nick Saltik had to have gotten the intelligence on the dope factories from someone on the inside.'

I hadn't thought about that. Did that change anything? I filed it away to consider later.

He continued. 'The other eight are a long shot. They're either in a big pit somewhere, covered in lime, or have gone off on a long journey in the back of a lorry.' He paused to catch his thread of thought. 'If you can get a doctor to pronounce you sane and occupationally fit, you can help out with that.'

'Thank you, Sir. What about taking a couple of SOCO teams out to the barn where Dai Lloyd and Christian Fenner died, and the scene of Jessie Bullock's accident?'

He slumped in his chair, and shared an exaggerated sigh of weary despondency with Bryn. 'I give him his job back, and not only does he want to take over the fucking world, but he wants to drive the cherry picker through it as well.' He turned to me. 'No, Capaldi, you're not going to get to play El Suprendo, Wonder Fucking Sleuth, this time round.'

Drudge work, in other words.

Locate the missing persons in the haystack known as Mid Wales. Even though there was only a low-odds chance that they were even above ground, never mind the daunting geography. But I wasn't too fazed. I intended to interpret the brief loosely, and concentrate on Hoca. Armed now with a working warrant card.

It took me a while to track down the police doctor, and even longer to get him to hold still in one place for long enough to examine me properly and get me officially back in the saddle.

It was dark when I set off for Dinas.

I called Rhian en route. She was already in London. I told her again to be careful, and that I missed her. She muttered some endearment in return, but I could tell that she was getting caught up in her story.

I thought, as I drove, about Jack Galbraith's theory about Hoca. Was that the answer to the mystery? Had he changed sides and become Nick Saltik's inside man? Had he simply met up with his new friends and gone off with them? But, if he had left his car behind for Jessie to break into, where was it now? And why hadn't he taken his laptop with him? That would have been stuffed with information on his rival that Nick Saltik could have used.

Where was the car? If we could find that we could add a plot pointer on his route from the Monks' Trail car park.

But the hypothetical question I put to David Williams in The Fleece later that night had to do with softer ware. Because, I reckoned, this was one way for word to get back to Jack Galbraith that I was out here doing my job.

He leaned his elbows on the bar and put on his wise look. 'Eight people, eh? Are these bodies or pedestrians?'

'If they're already bodies we can forget it, so let's call them prisoners for the sake of argument.'

'Are they trussed up and are there armed guards?' he asked eagerly.

'The question was, where could you hide eight people, so let's not get carried away with the peripherals.'

'It changes the spatial requirements,' he said huffily.

'Let's simply say we need a big space.'

'A barn?'

'They've all been checked out.'

'Cellars?'

I nodded. 'There's the problem. How many fucking cellars are there in this country? How many shipping containers? How many old truck bodies? Abandoned mine workings?

302

And all I've been given is Emrys Hughes's team, and I know he's going to try to hide them from me.'

'You could narrow it down.'

'How?'

'The place would have to be soundproof.'

I shook my head. 'Not necessarily. You could just gag them.' I saw that bouncing this off the vox populi was going nowhere, so I returned to the car question. 'What happens to abandoned cars round here?'

That one stumped him. 'Don't the local council dispose of them?' he asked, not too sure of his ground.

But I had stopped listening. I held up my hand in apology and walked away from the bar to refine the memory that had just surfaced. The night we had picked up Jessie. There had been an abandoned and burnt-out vehicle in the car park.

What if Hoca's car had never left?

It had been dark. I hadn't given it a second thought. I had been too busy racing on adrenalin and dreams of escaping Inspector Morgan's fiasco. It had been an unidentifiable hulk, part of the background.

Had it been there those other times I had been back?

I had no recall. There were usually cars parked there, left by hikers. But had that wreck still been there? I berated myself for not having noticed. But I hadn't been looking. A car park in the middle of nowhere was a natural graveyard for a clapped-out car. It would have fitted. It wouldn't have appeared out of place.

But a new model BMW 5 Series?

Burnt-out and damaged, it might still have passed the

junkyard test. Because people would only be seeing ruin and redundancy.

Could it still be there?

I put my unfinished drink on the bar and left while David was serving another customer. Outside it was that muscled dark that went with heavy cloud cover, and it was even quieter on the roads than normal. It was as if sane and sensible people had all been privileged with a message that this was not a night to be abroad. I instructed myself to ignore unhelpful thoughts. But the damage had been done. I now felt spooked.

I drove down the access road to the Monks' Trail car park with my high beams blazing and stopped at the entrance. Ahead of me, in the full glare, across the car park, the start of the trail and the woods behind were illuminated like a stark woodcut illustration of a Brothers Grimm fairy tale. The peripheral light-spread just managed to define the perimeter of the car park. On my left two cars were parked, and on my right, where the wreck had been, there was another one. Was that it? Its position seemed to have shifted from that in my memory.

Could the same crew who had torched Ryan Shaw's car also have been responsible for this one? My nervous tension increased as I drove slowly towards it. Could Hoca have been inside when it was put to the flames? What kind of a horror story might we find when we opened that boot?

Boot?

That should have been the first trigger that told me how wrong I was. Hoca's car had been an estate model. Instead of thinking too far ahead of myself I should have been registering that this car had intact tyres, and a paint job that still shone in my lights. And was recognizable as a Ford Mondeo.

With steamed-up windows.

I stopped short and dipped my headlights when I realized. But I couldn't quite let it go. I had come this far looking for a wreck. What if it was still there, on the far side of the Mondeo, where my headlights couldn't reach?

I got out with my torch on and walked round the back of the Mondeo. Empty space circled around to the start of the trail.

'Fuck off you pervert!' An angry woman's voice.

I swung round, instinctively training the torch on the rear passenger window of the Mondeo. The white moon of the face that had appeared there shied away from the light. 'That's it, we're calling the police! Fucking Peeping Tom creep.'

I slunk away. It was not my finest hour.

I was up early enough to wave to the milkman again the next morning as I drove through Dinas on my way to Emrys Hughes's house. Which made it the second day running he had seen me at this time in the morning. There would be talk about my tom-catting.

Mrs Hughes answered the door with a scowl, a floral dressing gown clutched tightly closed, and a hairnet to protect her precious perm. She looked like her head had got caught up in the carrot-bagging machine.

'Morning, Mrs Hughes,' I declaimed cheerily. 'Can I have a word with Emrys, please?'

'Do you have any idea what time it is?' she responded icily.

I clucked my regrets. 'Oh for the nine-to-five routine of mere mortals, eh?'

'What can be so important to disturb us at this time in the morning?'

'Duty, Mrs Hughes,' I said, putting a Gestapo snap in my tone. 'Could you just fetch Sergeant Hughes, please.'

Her eyes flared, and, for a moment, I thought she was going to protest, but she hunched her shoulders high instead, harrumphed, spun round and marched off down the hallway with an acid screech of 'Emrys!'

He took his time arriving. He started to speak as he approached me. 'Okay, Capaldi, I know you've been re-instated, but just remember that some of us have been working all this time while you've been swanning around on sick leave.' He held his hand up to stop my response. 'And before you ask, I can't spare any men. They're all tied up on operations. If you've got a problem with that you can go directly to Inspector Morgan.' He finished with a slight exhalation of breath. It was a speech he had obviously been rehearsing.

'The night we picked up Jessie Bullock there was an abandoned vehicle in the car park. What can you tell me about it?'

He blinked in surprise, the question coming at him out of left field. 'How am I supposed to remember something like that?' he protested.

'Think back. Think hard.'

'Okay, okay, I'm thinking,' he whined peevishly.

'It was on the right as you come into the car park. Think two o'clock.'

His face twisted doubtfully. 'Vaguely. I think I remember it vaguely.'

I recognized it as bullshit. He just didn't want to have to admit to me that he hadn't a clue. I thought of another tack. 'The car had been burnt-out. If there had been a fire, wouldn't you have had a call-out along with the fire brigade?'

'Not me. That's Huw Davies's patch.'

I read his face. It wasn't a cop-out. Emrys was a firm believer in strict demarcation lines. I started to turn away. 'Do me a favour: ask around the other guys who were there that night, see if any of them remember seeing it.'

'It was a while ago, Capaldi, there was a lot going on that night.'

I left before he could remind me that it had been an extra special night for me.

I called Huw Davies from the car.

'No,' he told me, 'I don't remember a wreck, and I don't remember a fire there either. I certainly wasn't called out to one, anyway.'

'It was definitely burnt-out, Huw. And it was probably done in situ.'

'It may not have been spotted. It's a tucked-away place. You could torch a coachload of Christian martyrs there and no one would be any the wiser.'

I ran through a quick recall of the geography. 'What about the Home Farm or Plas Coch? Would you see it from up there?'

I sat out the pause while Huw went through the same mental exercise. 'Maybe. But I doubt it.'

'Why?'

'If they'd seen it, we would have know about it. The ap Hywels would have gone straight to the top. Chief Constable,

307

Inspector Morgan, Emrys Hughes, and then me.' He chuckled. 'It's called drip-down recriminations.'

'Who gets rid of these things?'

'Revolution.'

I laughed. 'Fuck off, Huw. I'm talking about abandoned cars, not the caste system.'

'Try the local authority.'

At least Huw seemed a bit more certain than David Williams. And when I got on the phone to the council there was a series of gateways in place that actually led me through to the department that dealt with abandoned vehicles.

'Where was this located, and when was it reported?' the guy I was eventually connected to asked.

'The Monks' Trail car park, near the village of Llandewi, but I don't know when any reports went in, if any.'

'Don't worry, I know the location, and we'd have had reports. The people who use that car park don't like seeing it messed up.'

'So you would have removed it?' I asked, encouraged.

'Oh no, we wouldn't have gotten involved.'

'But don't you dispose of these things?'

'Yes, but not on private land. And without even going into the system I think I can safely say that the car park is owned by the Plas Coch estate.'

'Who you would have informed?'

'As a matter of course.'

Joan Stevenson answered the door at Plas Coch. I had never actually met her, but she knew who I was. She asked me to wait in the hall while she went to see if the ap Hywels were free.

'Glyn, what can I do for you?' Rhodri asked heartily, striding across the hall, after a short wait.

I shook his outstretched hand. 'It's official business today.'

He backed off slightly. 'Should I be calling you "Sergeant" in that case?'

'No, that's not necessary.'

'Good. Do you mind sitting in the kitchen?' he asked, starting to lead the way. 'You're like London buses you know,' he threw back over his shoulder at me.

'What's that?'

'We had one of your colleagues, an Inspector Jones, here yesterday.' He indicated a seat at the table. 'Is this about the same thing?'

'Pretty much. Just cross-referencing details.' I noticed, once again, there was a spare half-drunk mug of coffee on the table, steam still rising.

He saw me see it. 'Ursula's had to take a telephone call,' he explained.

I nodded, accepting the face-saver.

He lowered his voice. 'I gather that that matter the two of you discussed isn't going any further?'

I gave him my chastened look. 'No. And please apologize to Ursula for any distress I might have caused her.'

'You were only doing what you thought was your duty.' He looked at me reflectively and nodded to himself. 'Have you talked to your colleague?' I shook my head. 'Well, to clear the air with you, let me tell you what I told him yesterday.' He read my silence as assent. 'When we sold the coffee bars, we didn't know we were dealing with a criminal organization.'

309

'But you did know Nick Saltik?'

He nodded. 'Yes. His father and my father had done some property business. It went on from there. No big deals. And I'm not naïve, so it's probably not a coincidence that another branch of his family approached us about the coffee bars. But, I promise you, we never went looking for it, and we never knew that we were dealing with criminals.'

'You didn't know Nick Saltik was bent?'

He shrugged and gave me a confessional smile. 'Let's just say that, for my sins, I didn't delve. Call it moral expediency if you like, the sin of omission, but we can't always do business with the likes of the Church Commissioners. I only ever dealt with Nick Saltik as a fellow property developer though. I had no knowledge of or any involvement in his other interests.'

'How did it work with Cassie?'

It took him a moment to work out what I meant. 'He made me an offer.'

'He sold her to you?'

He laughed. 'Nothing quite so colourful. I didn't know the personal issues between them then. He had heard about me starting up the Foundation and suggested that I should interview Cassie for the job of running the place up here. Ursula and I did, and we liked her; she seemed to have what we were looking for, and we thought she'd fit in. But I'm not going to deny that the substantial donation he was offering didn't influence our decision to at least try her out.'

'You knew she was pregnant?'

'Yes, but we didn't know that Nick was the father at the time.'

'You didn't mind taking on all that extra baggage?'

He smiled chidingly. 'We may be property dealers, speculators, running-dog capitalists, but at heart we're nice people, Glyn. We established the Foundation to try and put a bit of balance into our lives, to give something back. So, to answer your question, no, we didn't mind the extra baggage. In fact, without a family of our own, we actually welcomed it.' He brightened. 'Now, what specifically can I help you with?'

'You had an abandoned car on the Monks' Trail car park.'

The question obviously puzzled him, but he nodded. 'We get them from time to time.'

'You dispose of them?'

'Yes, Tony has a man who comes to collect them.'

'The most recent one? Have you any idea what kind of car it was?'

He sat back playing cod flummoxed. 'Hey, now you're asking, and no, I haven't a clue. Is it important?'

'It's just a piece I'm trying to fit in. Did you ever meet a man called Kadir Hoca?' I threw it in from the side and watched his reaction.

He thought about it, but no flicker of recognition. 'Sounds like another one of our Turkish friends.' He shook his head. 'But no. I'd have remembered a name like that.'

'The car was there on the night of the raid, when we picked up Jessie.'

He dropped his smile. 'If you say so.' He frowned. 'Do all these questions mean you're rethinking what happened that night?' He saw from my expression that I wasn't going to answer that. He nodded for me to continue.

311

'The council say you'd been notified a couple of weeks before.'

'We probably had, but it was a busy time on the estate.' He thought about it. 'I remember now. We were going to have it removed, but Inspector Morgan asked us to keep it there for a bit longer.'

'Inspector Morgan?' I didn't hide my surprise.

'Yes, we were going to move it before his raid, but he asked us not to, he said he didn't want anything changed.'

'You knew about the raid beforehand?'

'Oh yes, I'd think that everyone in the local golf club, and the Rotary and Round Table knew about it.'

'Would Jessie have known?'

He thought for a moment. 'I'm pretty sure Ursula would have told Cassie. Is that important?'

I shook my head, tossing the subject away casually. In hindsight it looked like I had belonged to a very exclusive club. The only guy in the fucking valley without advance knowledge of the raid. And I was meant to be on their side.

What else hadn't I been told?

18

So Jessie had given us the finger.

She had been forewarned about what was going down that night, but she had decided to fuck with us anyway. It was in her character. And the squad who had taken her out must have been acting on that probability.

I was on my way to see a man called Phil Connelly. Rhodri had called Tony Stevenson into the kitchen, who had told me that Connelly was the guy he contacted when he needed scrap metal removed.

His yard was close to Dinas and backed onto the river. I had passed the large gates frequently, but, because it was set behind a high mature hedge, it had never drawn itself to my attention. It was tidy for a junkyard, a big parking and turning area, a garden shed to one side, acting as an office, with neat rows of scrapped cars running off behind it. Opposite the shed, behind a low privet hedge and backing onto the river, was the sort of immaculate mobile home that made Unit 13 look like a desert war had rolled through it.

I got out of the car beside an open-bed lorry with an articulated hydraulic grab holding down three flattened cars stacked on top of each other. None of them looked as if it could have been a BMW 5 Series estate in its functioning life.

'Afternoon, Officer, and what can I be doing for you?' A short man with a soft Irish accent and a knowing smile came out of the shed. The flat cap that he wore at a slant looked like it could have travelled down the birth canal with him.

'DS Glyn Capaldi,' I said, shaking his outstretched hand. I didn't bother with my warrant card as he'd already identified my species.

'You don't look like you'll be coming here for a replacement shock absorber for your old Ford Fiesta.'

'You recently took a car away from the Monks' Trail car park for the Plas Coch estate?'

'Tony Stevenson, that's right.' He cocked his head towards the shed. 'I've got his signed release in there, if you want to see it.'

'I'm not doubting you, Mr Connelly.'

'Phil,' he corrected me with a soft chuckle.

'I just need to know what kind of car it was, Phil.'

'And what kind of car would you be looking for?'

'A recent BMW 5 Series?'

He laughed. 'Jesus, Sergeant, I know we've become a throw-away society, but I'm still not finding too many of them things coming my way these days.' He gestured towards the truck. 'It's the middle one there, the one that was on the car park.'

I took another look at it. It was squashed, scorched back to the grey primer, and looked like a car in pupae form. 'What was it?'

'A Peugeot 405.'

The realization hit me then that I had reached the end of the line. I had nowhere else to go. I had no more leads to follow, only my aberrations.

He picked up on my disappointment. 'I'll keep an eye out for your BMW on my travels, if you like,' he offered sympathetically.

'Thanks.' I nodded towards his mobile home. 'It's nice living beside the river, isn't it?'

'Ah, we don't live there any more. The missus wanted a bungalow where she could walk into the town.'

I looked at the immaculate cream-and-white unit with the blue trim around the windows and its privet hedge and flagstone path to the front door. The season would soon be starting at Hen Felin Caravan Park. I thought of all the greasy barbecue smoke to come, the lunatic kids on their BMX bikes, their angry parents, hip-hop and boy bands competing on the sound systems.

'You wouldn't consider renting it, would you?'

He cocked his head and looked at me until he realized I was serious. He scratched his head. 'Well, it would take my site security up to a whole new fucking level, I suppose.'

Silver linings.

I called Rhian after I left him. I wanted to get her take on what she thought it would feel like to be romanced in a junkyard.

315

The call went to answering machine. Well, I reflected, at least one of us was fulfilling our potential.

The next morning I wasn't quite so sanguine about it.

I had sent emails and left messages all of the previous afternoon and she still hadn't come back to me. I lurched for my phone when it rang as I was having breakfast. The caller display deflated me. Bryn Jones.

'Sir?'

'I've just received a call from a DI in Manchester who wants to submit a formal complaint about you.'

I winced. 'What did you tell her?'

'How did you know she's a she?'

'It's always the ladies who phone first thing in the morning,' I bluffed.

He laughed. 'I told her that DCS Galbraith would contact her when he gets back from London.'

'And what do you think his reaction will be?'

'That will all depend on how nicely they've treated him there.' He gave me a few moments to ponder that. 'The other reason I'm calling is because you're the nearest to this, so I thought I'd pass it on to you.'

'What's that?'

'Hoca's car, the BMW, it's just been found in the car park of the Centre for Alternative Technology.'

Coincidence? I had spent close to two days shaking the bushes for this thing, and now it turns up miles away. Locked, neatly parked, and no sign of Hoca, according to Bryn.

I took the back road to Machynlleth past Llyn Clywedog reservoir, trying to put a bit of elemental beauty and

316

grandeur into my day to soothe my anxieties over Rhian's silence, and the implications of the emergence of Hoca's car.

It was parked at the foot of the old slate tip, near to the bottom station of the water-balanced cliff railway that took visitors up to the Centre for Alternative Technology. A uniform was there waiting for two SOCO guys to finish their in situ investigation before he called the recovery vehicle in.

I parked a little away to get a sense of the place as I walked over. The car park was pleasantly informal. They had let sessile oak trees and the top of the bank that dropped down to the river organically delineate the perimeter. It wasn't busy at this time of year.

'Who called it in?' I asked the uniform. As usual, the SOCO guys were keeping their heads down.

'One of the staff. He had to come back and check something late last night and noticed it then. A swanky car like that, he thought it might have been stolen.'

'No one had noticed it before?'

'If they had, they hadn't bothered to call it in.'

I walked round it slowly. How long had this been here? It was dusty. It had been sitting somewhere for a while. But here? It was parked with its front facing the top of the bank. The arcs of the wipers were visible on the windscreen. I told myself that that didn't necessarily mean that they had cut through old dirt.

I called the cop to me. 'It's locked?'

'Yes, Sarge. The SOCO people don't want to open it here in case they contaminate the interior.'

'No indications that it's ever been broken into?'

He shook his head. 'No, it's all intact.'

317

Shit.

There went my theory. I thanked him and walked back to my car. What had I really been expecting? A jagged hole in the rear window? Traces of rare vegetation that only occurred at the Monks' Trail car park? Hoca's severed head impaled on the gear shift?

A weak sun cleared the top of the hill and started to filter its light down through the trees. Caught in the new light, the fresh foliage looked almost translucent, and water-beaded spiders' webs pulsed in the light breeze.

It was turning into a beautiful day. So why couldn't I just put this to bed now and walk away from it? Finally admit to myself that I had been chasing the wrong phantom.

Because, even if it never came to any prosecutions, I had exonerated myself in my own mind. I had a straight and clean storyboard through the tale. Somewhere down the line Nick Saltik had transgressed badly enough for his cousin Mike to have ordered his bastard daughter whacked. Through me, Nick had found out about it, and had shut down Mike's Mid Wales drug operation. For all I knew, this could have escalated into a full-scale war in London.

Why couldn't I be content with that?

Because it all now pointed to Jack Galbraith's hunch being right. Hoca had defected. He had hidden his car in the best possible place to hide a car: a public car park. A remote one with relatively easy access to a train station. And no sign that the car had ever been broken into.

Why couldn't I let it go?

Because I still had my aberrations. My babies were still yelling their little heads off. Bawling for attention. Okay I

318

could probably now account for Jessie, but I still had the missing laptop, Ryan Shaw, Dai and Christian and their money refusing to slot tidily into place.

And now Rhian had gone and disappeared on me.

So talk to me you little fiends.

I took the same route back to Dinas, but this time the weather and scenery had even less of an impact. I was too wrapped up in my thoughts.

The laptop was the real irritant. For it to have been involved in a trading process it had to have been stolen from Hoca's car. But I kept coming round to the big imponderables. Why had he parked at the bottom of the Monks' Trail? Why did his car show no traces of having been broken into?

It came low and fast out of the woods. It shattered my thought process as I caught it in the peripheral field of my left eye, and ducked and braked instinctively. It hit the windscreen with a sound and reverberation that was pure violence. I pulled over to the side, sickened, watching it in the rear-view mirror, shedding feathers as it tumbled like a Dadaist rugby ball.

I hated this. Really hated it. Such a waste. It was a hen pheasant. Some fucker had probably bred this to shoot, but it had pulled through, it had survived the season. It should have been safe.

It fluttered and twitched on the verge, as if some sick bastard was running an electric current through the grass. I picked it up. Avoid the eyes. Always avoid the eyes. The accusation is too much to bear. I pulled its neck. Thankfully, on this occasion, it stayed attached.

I instructed myself to remain practical. I put it in the boot. Sandra Williams would be able to use it. I was shaking.

I couldn't help it. I flashed on the awful moment when someone had snapped Jessie's neck.

I had to sit down on the verge. I took in air in huge gulps, and put my head down between my raised knees.

Why did you steal the laptop? I roared at her internally. *Why did you make this all so fucking complicated?*

And then the realization washed over me. I sat up to let the thoughts coalesce. I stopped shaking. The panic receded.

The answer was simple.

I had been too rigid in my thinking.

I had been fixated on the Monks' Trail car park. A break-in. But what if she had taken it from closer to home? The Home Farm or Plas Coch? What if he had been visiting and his car had been unlocked?

Rhodri had told me that he didn't know Hoca. But he could have been lying to cover up his involvement with the Saltiks. Or Cassie could have been lying. Or he could have been there to see one of the guests at the Home Farm.

But why did he drive off without his laptop?

Fuck that for the moment. Stay mellow. Avoid the complications. Go for simple answers that fit the aberrations.

What's the simple answer to Dai and Christian's unexplained money?

Jessie gave it to them!

Fuck, I was getting good at this game.

And where did Jessie get it?

This was another complication I was about to drop when

320

I suddenly remembered Hettie Bloom. Jessie had tried extortion once before that I knew of, and failed. But what if she had succeeded on the next attempt? Had she been distributing largesse from another blackmail racket?

Who? Who? Who?

The repetition didn't work. No answers tumbled from the sky. I had exhausted this particular revelation session. I knew I was going to have to get closer to Jessie's soul.

Mackay was outdoors when I called him. I could hear a crop of rooks high in a tree behind him. 'Have you managed to dig up enough to fix those bastards yet?' he asked.

'Not quite.'

He laughed.

'What's so funny?'

'The tone you use when you're about to try and ask for stuff.'

'It's only two small things, and I'll repay you somehow, Mac, I promise. And one of them's a personal favour.'

'You want me to go into the playground and tell someone you fancy them?'

'They already know.'

'The lady who was showing concern the other night?'

'That's right. I'm worried about her. She's a journalist. She went off to London to work on the Saltik story. She's not answering my calls or emails.'

'You want me to go to London?'

'No, Cardiff. I want you to ask around the people she knows there. If it looks like there's anything to worry about, my boss is in London. I can get him to put the heat on there.'

'And you don't want to do this in person because you'd

rather hear second-hand that she was only after you for your body?' he joked. He was trying to relax me.

I laughed. 'No, Mac, I'm too busy trying to fuck-up the outlaws.'

'You ought to sort out your priorities, pal. So, what was the other thing?'

Later I sat parked up off the road above the entrance to the Home Farm and waited for the other thing to happen.

I don't know what tactics Mackay used, persuasion or coercion, but it only took another half hour before Cassie's car appeared on the drive, turned, and then drove away down the hill towards Llandewi.

Some of the guests had taken advantage of the fine evening and had set up an impromptu badminton session on the lawn outside the Home Farm. I parked and nodded and smiled familiarly at them as I made my way to the front door, working on the premise that everyone would think that someone else in the bunch knew me.

Simon, Cassie's little helper, opened the door. He was still wearing his black beret, but he had augmented it this evening with a ruche-fronted Mexican peasant shirt and what looked like black harem pants. Lord knows which universe his fantasy worked in.

He regarded me suspiciously. 'Cassie's not in.'

'It was you I wanted to see.' I didn't elaborate, I would have said that to whoever had opened the door.

'Why?' His unease deepened.

'Do you work here, Simon?'

'No. I'm only helping Cassie out.'

'You're a guest?'

He nodded warily. He watched me as if he expected me to break into a spiel about the benefits of double-glazing at any minute.

'Have you been coming here for long?'

He nodded again. For all I knew this uncommunicative little man could have been the CEO of a high-performance hedge fund in his street life, but he was certainly taking his role as taciturn gatekeeper seriously.

'You're fond of Cassie, aren't you?'

'What are you here for?'

'If you've been coming for a long time you must have seen Jessie growing up?'

I saw that hit home in his face. He tried to cover it, but there had been a reaction. 'She was Cassie's daughter, so of course I saw her.' He was uncomfortable.

I dropped my tone to confidential. 'It was you I wanted to talk to about Jessie rather than Cassie.'

'Why me?'

'Because I don't want to hurt Cassie or upset her any more than she has been.' I watched his puzzlement struggle with concern, and backed away from the door. I gestured towards the picnic bench beside the entrance. 'Come and sit down with me.' I reckoned I stood a better chance with him if I wasn't crowding him on the threshold, reinforcing his volunteer sentinel position.

He hesitated for a moment, and then sat down opposite me. I leaned forward into his space, keeping my voice low. 'You know I'm a policeman?' His head moved in cautious acknowledgement. 'You know I carry some sort of responsibility around with me for what happened to Jessie?' He inclined his head with a little more energy. 'Because of that I feel very protective about Cassie.' This time he actually nodded. He could empathize with that. I fixed him with sincerity and just hoped to fuck that he wasn't another High Court Judge in real-life land. 'I'm here because I don't want my colleagues turning up with a search warrant and tearing the place apart. I don't want to have to put Cassie through that.'

His face dropped. 'That's not going to happen is it?' He sounded dismayed.

'I don't want it to. Let me ask you something very confidential.' He leaned in towards me of his own accord now. 'To your knowledge, did Jessie ever try to put you or any other guests here in a compromising situation?'

He turned ashen. 'Is that what this is about?'

I made a show of looking around me furtively. 'We've had complaints.'

'What are you going to do?'

'Jessie's dead. She can't be punished any more. Cassie's the one who's going to suffer if this surfaces. If there's going to be anything incriminating here it's going to be in Jessie's room. If I could convince my colleagues that I've had a look round and found nothing I should be able to persuade them to drop it.'

'And what if you do? Find something, I mean.'

'It doesn't need to see the light of day.' I sat up, raised my voice slightly and shot him a tremulous smile. 'But, if you don't feel you're able to help, I'll understand.'

*

324

The curtains were drawn shut in Jessie's room. To keep the light out, or her shade in? Simon was on my team now, keeping a watch out for Cassie for me, and would let me out of a rear door if she returned. But I would have to work carefully and methodically, so that I could withdraw at a moment's notice and leave the room looking undisturbed.

Okay, technically Simon had voluntarily invited me in, but this was still an illegal search. Nothing that I found here could surface as evidence, or be used in a court of law. But we'd gone way past that option. I was now looking to see if there was anything here that would tell me what had really got Jessie killed.

I stood by the door, switched the light on and slowly worked over the space with my eyes, taking stock. The overhead light made it look harsher than it probably was, but, even with full sunlight streaming in, this would never be a soft room. Partly it was the colour scheme. The wall behind the bed had been painted a pale lilac, but it didn't sing muted pastel, it was more the tint of a dead fish's belly bobbing upturned in polluted water, and the polar white on the other walls was too stark and clinical.

The cushions and the soft toys on the bed, the clunky jewellery and make-up on top of the chest of drawers, the computer on the cheap desk, and the posters on the walls, all looked like props. As if they had been placed there as set dressings to make the place read like a young adult's room, which hadn't quite worked. Because there was no sense that anyone had ever lived in here.

I started with the windowsill that was screened by the closed curtains, and then moved to the floor, sighting under the bed, and using a ruler I had brought with me to rake out the voids under the chest of drawers and wardrobe. All I exposed was accumulated fluff, which I pushed back under again.

The bed had been stripped down, leaving only a bright Indian-print cotton cover over the mattress. I pulled this off and lifted the mattress to check underneath it. Then I went over it carefully, looking for concealed openings or mended tears. I wasn't expecting anything, but I had to be systematic.

After replacing the bed cover, toys and cushions, I started on the wardrobe. I patted down the hanging clothes, turned over the shoes and boots and checked the shelf above the rail. Then the four large square drawers down the side, sifting through the contents before pulling them out to make sure there was nothing concealed behind them. The third one down was totally empty. An anomaly?

I left that thought hanging and turned to the chest of drawers. It had four drawers, two small ones side by side at the top, and two larger ones ranged below them. I applied the same exercise here. All of these drawers were full, or nearly so, and there was nothing secreted behind them.

I went back to the wardrobe. I pulled the empty drawer out and checked behind it again. Nothing. There were a couple of sweatshirts and thermal tops at the bottom of the wardrobe that would have fitted in the empty drawer.

So why leave that space empty?

Because Cassie had wanted to preserve the room exactly the way that Jessie had left it?

I didn't have time to take the analysis any further at this stage, I had to start going through the books. I took them out one at a time and replaced them after checking for hollowed-out voids, or loose papers. As I worked through I accidentally knocked the bookcase with my knee, and three of the wooden African carvings on the top fell over. Rather than disturb the system I decided to leave them like that until I had finished with the books.

The books revealed nothing. I stood up. The wood carvings were variations on anthropomorphic themes and carved from ebony or a look-alike wood. I picked up the first fallen one to put it back in place. It was surprisingly light. As were the other two tumbled ones. I lifted one of the two that had remained standing. It was definitely heavier.

I sat on the bed and looked at it carefully. It was dusty as I had previously noticed. They were all dusty. But the dust was concentrated in the creases of the carvings. Almost as if it had been deliberately applied. I reviewed all five of the carvings carefully. There were abstract representations of human figures, bush animals and stylized birds. All more or less the same in size, but different in their details. Apart from one thing. They all had a series of carved concentric rings circling their bases. The indentations of these were dusty. I shook it and nothing rattled, I peered closely looking for join lines, but could see none.

I held the figurine securely, and tried unscrewing the base. Nothing budged. I picked up one of the lighter ones and hefted them both, one in each hand. They were definitely different weights. I put it down to the species of wood they had been carved from.

I was setting them back up on the shelf when I remembered the famine at Unit 13. It wasn't long after I had moved in, and the cylinder for the gas cooker had run out. I had a spare, but I couldn't unscrew the valve on the empty one. I had been like that for two days, existing on takeaways, until the campsite owner turned up. With one of those looks that combined pity with superiority, he had showed me how the valve unscrewed on the opposite thread.

I tried again with the figurine. It was stiff, but that might have been the clever workmanship, to deter a casual attempt, because, when it eventually gave, it opened smoothly, turning on the precise wooden thread.

The inside was hollow. Had been hollow, I corrected myself. There was now something wedged tightly up inside. I got my forefinger up far enough to touch the obstruction. I felt the end-grain texture of tightly rolled paper.

I had found Jessie's stash.

I didn't count it. Other urgencies had kicked in.

Because I had guessed the significance of the empty drawer.

I parked on the grass at the entrance to the Home Farm drive. It was dusk now. Shadows were picking themselves up off the ground and reorganizing into the dominant light form.

I guessed that Cassie had kept the room exactly as Jessie had left it. Apart from that one drawer. She had had to remove its incriminating contents. Because that was where Jessie would have kept her trophies. Her mementoes, all the useless stuff she had thieved. Cassie had allowed herself to do that much editing to sanctify her daughter's memory.

I was now fervently hoping that she hadn't been able to bring herself to destroy them.

Headlights appeared coming up the hill from Llandewi. I got out with my torch. The headlights' glare made the car impossible to identify, but it was indicating a turn into the Home Farm. I stood in the middle of the drive and switched my torch on, and hoped that, if it was Cassie, I wasn't providing her with a terrible but irresistible temptation.

The car stopped. It was Cassie. Her head came out of the window. 'You're trespassing. Get out of the way and let me carry on,' she shouted, angry and upset.

'I need to talk to you, Cassie,' I shouted back.

'I've nothing to say to you. Just move.'

Any moment now and she would realize that she could drive round me on the grass. I moved closer to keep her confused. 'Cassie, I know about the stuff that Jessie took. I don't care about any of it, apart from the laptop.'

I couldn't see her face. I didn't know what she was going through. The silence extended, only her car's engine ticking over.

'I promise, no one will ever know.'

'You bastard!' She was crying.

I let myself in the passenger door. Her hands were gripping the steering wheel, and her forehead was pressed against the top of it. Her sobs were expressed in the movement of her shoulders. I debated whether trying to physically comfort her would cause even more damage.

'I'm sorry, Cassie.'

'Why couldn't you leave me alone?' she pleaded without moving her head.

'I will, very soon. Do you still have the laptop?'

She raised her head and looked round at me. She had

stopped sobbing, but, in the dim light, the tears had made her eyes look as wide as a lemur's. 'How long have you known?'

'I had it down for youthful bravado, I never thought there was any malice involved,' I answered evasively.

'She would have grown out of it.'

'I know,' I agreed. What else could I say?

'Who else knows?'

'No one. And I promise to keep it that way.'

'If I give you the laptop?'

'I'm not setting any conditions. If you do let me have it, I promise you that no one will ever know how I obtained it.'

She watched me silently for a moment. 'Why do you want it?'

'It belonged to Kadir Hoca.' She shook her head. She had forgotten I had asked about him. 'It contains valuable information on Mike Saltik's organization.'

She studied me again. 'You promise that this is the end?'

'I promise.'

'It's down at the house.'

'I'll come with you.' I could walk back up the drive. I didn't want to take the risk of her changing her mind again.

She started to put the car into gear, but then had another thought. 'Why did he do it?'

'Do what?' I left my response general, not knowing who she was meaning.

'Mike Saltik. Why did he order Jessie killed?'

'He was taking revenge for something Nick had done to him.'

She shook her head, sad and puzzled. 'I talked to Nick.

330

He swore to me that he had never done anything to Mike, his family, or his organization that could have caused him to have done something like that.'

'So who did he think did it?'

'It had to be Mike, no one else knew about Jessie. But Nick had done nothing to cause it.'

'And you believe him?'

She nodded.

A shiver passed through me. It felt as if someone had just activated a salad spinner inside my head. I allowed myself a pause to let all the implications settle down. Suddenly Hoca's disappearance took on a whole new meaning. And the carvings in Jessie's room? I had been so preoccupied that she had been using them as a cache that it hadn't clicked that she had only been a cuckoo. I flashed on the photograph I had seen at the soiree in Plas Coch. Jessie, surrounded by the African kids, clutching one of the figurines like a trophy. Had she known then?

I had overlooked their original purpose.

I thought through it as she drove me down to the Home Farm, and while she went inside to fetch the laptop.

Jessie's death was supposed to have been accidental. But I had fucked around with that. So, what if they had anticipated that possibility and had prepared a back story around it just in case? A fallback. A gangster vendetta fairy tale. Nothing would be able to be proved or disproved, but it would establish a motive. The escalation that had followed my blabbing to Cassie couldn't have been predicted, but, while the attention it brought would have been unwelcome, it would also have served to reinforce the vendetta scenario.

I should have been inured to it by now. They had been blindsiding and distracting me from day one. I should have been able to see through the stagecraft.

But I hadn't. Crucially I had allowed my attention to slip away from the blackmail victim. I had been continually mind-fucked by the managed illusion of the Saltik vendetta.

Cassie came out with a supermarket carrier bag. I felt the heft of the laptop straining the plastic when she passed it to me. 'Do you want the other things as well?'

It took me a beat to realize she was talking about the trophies. 'No. You dispose of them as you see fit.' She nodded curtly and started to walk away. 'Cassie?' She turned around. 'Did you used to go and meet Jessie when she came back from Africa with the ap Hywels?'

She pulled a face. The question had thrown her. 'What on earth are you bringing that up for?'

'Did you?'

'Yes. Joan Stevenson and I used to go to the airport together.'

'Tony Stevenson went over with the ap Hywels?' I wasn't surprised. It's what I had expected.

'Yes, but I don't see—'

'Bear with me. The carved wooden figurines that Jessie was given, did she used to carry them off the plane herself?'

She shook her head, perplexed. 'What has this got to do with anything?'

'Please.'

'Yes. They were very precious to her.'

'Did she get to take them home with her right away?'

She returned to the memory. 'I don't know why I should remember this . . . But no. Tony used to take them to the publicity people in London for photographs for the Foundation's website. They came back up to Jessie in Wales a bit later.' She started to shake her head again. 'I don't know why you—'

I put my hand on her shoulder to cut her off. 'Do me one last favour, please.'

She scowled. 'Why should I?' she challenged.

'Because I want to get the people who ruined your life.'

'I thought you said the laptop was going to do that?'

'I'm not talking about Mike Saltik.'

She stared hard at me for a moment. 'Who are you talking about?'

I shook my head. 'It's too soon to tell you. But I'd like you to go and see Ursula or Joan Stevenson now and tell them that you've been talking to me and that I've said I now know what really happened to Jessie.'

'And if I don't?'

'Nothing changes.'

'Is that a bad thing?'

'It's not if you want to remain the lone sufferer.'

She walked away from me. I watched her go. The future forked off from here. Without turning to look back at me, she took the path towards Plas Coch.

She had chosen the future in which everything was about to explode.

I ran up the drive to my car. I had to pause to get my breathing under control before I called Mackay.

'Mac, what have you got for me?'

'Give me a chance. I've only just got here.'

'You haven't spoken to anyone?'

There was a pause. 'Yes, but I've hardly started.' I sensed a reticence.

'And?'

'The person I've spoken to is worried as well. They've been

334

asking around, and no one seems to have heard from her recently.'

'Okay, thanks. Can you get back up here now? Meet me at The Fleece in Dinas?'

'Now?' I heard suppressed exasperation. 'Don't you want me to ask around any more?'

'No, I can handle it from this end. It's more important to have you up here.'

He sensed something in my tone. 'Do you want me to pick up Boyce on the way?'

I laughed. 'No, Mac, I think that might be overkill.' I hoped I wasn't going to come to regret that decision.

The next call I made continued to ring.

'Capaldi, this better be fucking good,' Jack Galbraith warned when he finally answered. In the background I could hear muted conversation and the tinkle of cutlery and glasses.

'I'm sorry to disturb you, Sir.'

'You will be if this isn't worth it. You've pulled me away from the company of an Assistant Police Commissioner, a Deputy Chief Constable, and a DCS, and the fucking pudding is about to be served.'

'I've got Hoca's laptop, Sir.'

His silence amplified the background noises. A man's guttural laugh punctuated what had to be the punchline of a filthy story. 'Do you know what kind of stuff's on it?' he asked eventually.

'No, Sir, it's password protected, I can't open it.'

'They've got guys down here who'll be able to do that faster than bypassing a pair of silk fucking knickers,' he said, letting me hear a rise in his cadence. For Jack Galbraith that was expressing excitement.

'That's what I thought, Sir.'

'This guy was Mike Saltik's head honcho, right?'

'From what I can gather, Sir.'

'So how the fuck did you get hold of it?'

'I'd rather not say, Sir.'

He groaned. 'Have you been up to your fucking tricks again?'

'He was last seen in Wales, Sir. The computer probably has all the details of the drugs' factory operations here. And there must be stuff on it that the Met would give their eye-teeth for.'

'If this comes back to haunt me, you're going to wish you'd been born a nun,' he warned. 'Okay, where are you?'

'I'll be home very shortly, Sir.'

'That's a caravan, that's not a fucking home. But okay, I'm sending a motorbike team up to you, and they'll courier it up to London.'

'There is one more thing, Sir.'

He sighed audibly. 'Why am I not surprised, Capaldi?'

'A journalist called Rhian Pritchard. She's been investigating the Saltiks.'

'Big tits?'

'Not overly, Sir.'

'But I'll bet she got the heads-up on this before even Kevin Fletcher.'

I avoided answering that. 'I think she's been abducted, Sir. By either Mike or Nick Saltik's people.' I explained about Rhian's disappearance in London.

'Okay, okay, leave it with me. Pressure will be brought to bear. The word will go out that she is a protected person. You get yourself back to that glorified baked-bean tin of yours and wait for my motorbike team.'

'Thank you, Sir.' I hung up. I closed my eyes and concentrated on the chessboard I had set up in my head. It was time to move some more pieces along.

The two guys from the fast motorbike unit who picked up the laptop took one look at Unit 13 and treated me accordingly. They didn't quite spit in the dust at my feet, but their eyes behind their tinted visors gave me the same once-over they would use on fluff.

They roared off spinning gravel into my face.

I took a walk through the caravan. What here was I going to miss? All my books. But they would have to stay. I took the family photographs out of their frames, even the ones with Gina, hid the frames in a drawer, and tucked the photographs into my waistband, under my sweater. I would put these in the car. But I couldn't be seen to be carrying anything else out. Not if I was meant to be carrying on my normal routine.

Would I be going down this route if I hadn't met Phil Connolly? I wondered. If I hadn't been smitten by his luxury mobile home? I took a mental step backwards. I was being premature. The bait might not have been taken. I didn't know it was going to happen yet.

Before I left for The Fleece I went on the Internet to confirm my hunch about Liberia and Sierra Leone.

Mackay walked in about half an hour after me. He was

wet. The weather had changed. Tonight of all nights. Just my luck.

'Aren't we drinking?' he asked, nodding at the cup on the bar in front of me. I shook my head. He ordered a coffee. David trotted off, eager to play maestro on his new all-hissing-all-gurgling espresso machine that the older regulars regarded with the same wary derision that they had once treated draught lager.

'What's this about?' Mackay asked, as we moved away to a quiet table.

'I need to borrow the balaclava again.'

He smiled. 'It's getting into the blood, is it?'

'Tell me about Cardiff first.'

'You didn't give me much time there.'

He had turned away from me, and I heard that reticence again. 'What happened, Mac?'

He stirred his coffee needlessly. 'I've been going over it in my head while I was driving up, wondering whether to tell you or not.'

'Since the conversation's got this far, I gather you're going to tell me?' I felt the lead octopus slip down into the pit of my stomach.

He turned to face me, his eyes pained. 'I decided it was for your own good.' I nodded for him to go ahead. 'The only person I got to talk to in Cardiff was a guy called Alex Rutherford.'

I knew what was coming now. 'A friend of Rhian's?'

'A bit more than that. He lives with her. They're shacked up together, Glyn. That's why he was so worried about not hearing from her.'

I nodded. He knew not to push it. I felt the sourness of acute disappointment, and a sense that something vibrant had been suddenly snapped. So this was the relationship that had supposedly foundered? Had she only ever been interested in me for some kind of a story? I mentally shook my head to clear it. I had to put it aside. We had things to do.

'I'm sorry, Glyn,' he said sympathetically.

'That's okay, Mac. You were right. It's better to know.'

Then I told him what I wanted us to do.

I drove back to Hen Felin Caravan Park on my own. It was pitch black when I trundled across the bridge, windscreen wipers working hard. Very soon the holiday season would start and all the lights would be on here and the place would be transformed into a playground. For some, I thought grumpily.

I let myself into Unit 13. I drew the curtains closed in the living room and forced myself to sit there for half an hour before turning off the lights and moving to the bedroom. I closed the curtains here, and went through the usual motions of going to the bathroom and brushing my teeth. I got into bed, switched the light off, and then pulled on the same dark outfit I had worn on the night we had braced Brady over my bedtime T-shirt. I waited until I had got out of bed before I put on the balaclava.

Getting outside again was the weak point in the plan. I just had to hope that in the darkness and the augmented shadows cast by the alders no one would see me rolling out of the door, and hear the snap of it closing. I slipped under the caravan and lay dead still, trying to sense if anything had changed around me. Had I been heard?

339

It was still dry under there. But I couldn't stay. I waited until I had established that I had created no disturbance before crawling on my belly through the shadows to the next unit over, and then, after another re-establishing pause, to the next unit after that. This, we had reckoned, would be in the safety zone.

But lying prone on my stomach under there meant that I could see nothing.

I had got wet crawling through the grass. The ground under the unit was dry and dead, the air super-saturated with fungal spores, and I felt the cold damp seeping into me. I had to fight off morbid reflections on Rhian. I also had to resist wondering if what I was doing wasn't a stupid waste of time. Lying here cold and miserable when I could have been oblivious in bed.

The light flashed microseconds before I heard the whoosh of the oxygen being sucked out of the sky, and, even under here, the initial heat from the flare-up felt like a warm dab of fever on my cheeks.

Instinct tried to get me to wriggle free and run, but I forced myself to continue lying there until my phone vibrated in my trouser pocket. Mackay's signal. I crawled out at the back of the unit and went to the river bank, everything around me raggedly illuminated by the dancing inferno that used to be my home.

I quartered the skyline and caught Mackay's torch beam lacing through the tree canopy on the other side of the river. I turned on my own torch and started running for the bridge, following his beacon.

The small dark mystery car had finally reappeared. It

turned out to be a black VW Polo. It had been concealed down a dirt track between the trees just along the road from the access to the caravan park. The four flat tyres that Mackay had arranged had fucked up any chance it had had of driving out of there. To reinforce that message, Mackay had the driver bent face-down on the bonnet, his arms locked halfway up his back behind him.

I pulled off my balaclava before I relieved him and snapped the handcuffs on. 'I am Detective Sergeant Capaldi, and I am arresting you on suspicion of arson and attempted murder.'

Tony Stevenson raised himself slowly off the bonnet as I read him his rights, testing his muscle systems before turning round to face me. He was dressed in a pair of dark blue overalls zipped up to his chin, a black army beret tight on his head, his face still smeared with blackout make-up. He looked amused. 'This is a bit of an extreme reaction to bird-watching.' He nodded towards Mackay. 'I want you to arrest this man for assault and vandalism.'

'He was making a citizen's arrest.'

He shook his head; he still looked unconcerned. 'I've done nothing.'

I gestured towards the light of the flames coming off my ex-caravan. 'You know nothing about that?'

'Nothing except that it screwed up my observing a tawny owl.'

'Most birdwatchers use binoculars.'

He smiled. He knew we were playing a game. 'I like to give them a chance.'

'You were followed.'

341

'It's his word against mine. It's a dark night, and I'll have a good lawyer.'

'Paid for by Rhodri ap Hywel?'

His smile just broadened.

'I've checked, Tony. He was your commanding officer when you were both in the TA. It looks like you're still doing his dirty work for him.'

He shook his head slowly, letting me see his contempt.

Mackay gestured towards the car's boot. I opened it. I nudged the petrol can enough to feel that it was empty. 'Even petrol has a language, Tony. Our forensic people will be able to find a signature that will match the residue in that can with what was used to burn down my caravan,' I announced this with more hope in the science than conviction.

He shrugged. 'I think you'd better either release me, or let me make my telephone call.'

I put the call in to Emrys Hughes. He was already in transit, along with the fire brigade. The good citizens of Dinas had alerted him to the sky lighting up. Most of them apparently thought that the holiday season had opened early and that the first wave of the barbarian hordes had descended.

I searched the car. There was no gun. I had done a background check. He was licensed for a hunting rifle, ostensibly to keep the deer on the estate under control. A Steyr Mannlicher SSG 69. The one he had probably used on my front tyre. But it wasn't here.

He hadn't dumped it because Mackay had been watching all his moves. He just hadn't brought it with him. I had hoped to catch him with it. But he hadn't taken that risk. My demise by fire would have been convenient, but it wasn't crucial, the back story was still holding. If the arson didn't work, then so be it, he wasn't going to escalate it to a murder investigation by shooting me.

We heard the sirens approaching. Mackay walked down the track to guide Emrys in. I put a restraining hand on Stevenson's elbow. He turned and flashed me a grin and shook my hand off. 'I'm not going anywhere.'

He was too cocky. But then he knew the calibre of legal representation the ap Hywels could afford.

I took Emrys aside to explain the situation. When I'd finished, he made a point of looking over at Mackay. 'That was a lucky coincidence. Your pal coming round to visit just at the crucial time.'

'Wasn't it.'

'And I see you managed to slip into something comfortable before it all went up.'

I nodded at Stevenson. It was time to get Emrys's attention onto the bad boy. 'He's going to claim he was birdwatching, but Mackay saw him torching my place.'

He shook his head wearily. 'We used to be able to blame the squirrels for fires like these. Little buggers chewed through the battery cables. Before you came along that was our version of juvenile delinquency.'

'I need a favour, Emrys.'

'Why should I?'

'Because we're meant to be on the same side.'

He looked at me doubtfully. 'What do you want?'

I nodded at Stevenson. 'Give me an hour before he makes it to a telephone.'

'How am I going to manage that?'

343

'Take your time getting out of here. Make a show of retrieving his car.'

He looked down at the mud on his boots. 'Thanks a lot, Capaldi.'

Motion-activated security lights popped on as I drove up to Plas Coch. The CCTV cameras would be running as well. I was hoping that I wasn't making a huge mistake here, otherwise my downfall would be recorded in full colour with zoom and pause capability.

I pressed the doorbell and hammered on the heavy cast-iron door knocker. It was now getting on for one thirty in the morning, and I wasn't expecting a quick response. Even though I guessed that at least one person was awake in the house.

The porch light eventually came on, followed by the sound of deadbolts being snapped back. Joan Stevenson opened the door. She was wearing slippers and a sensible dressing gown, her hair was pillow-fluffed, and she was still blinking her way out of sleep.

'Tony's been arrested,' I told her, stepping inside. 'You'd better go and get dressed.'

'Tony! What . . .?' she asked startled, trying to collect her thoughts, forgetting that she hadn't actually invited me in.

'Do as he says, Joan. I'll find out what the problem is.' Rhodri, also in a dressing gown, had appeared in the hall from the direction of the kitchen.

'What problem?' Ursula asked, in yet another dressing gown, coming down the stairs, passing a now fraught Joan on her way up. Ursula's hair was down, a heavy grey tumble spilling over her shoulders. She already had the stern majesty, all she needed was a candlestick prop and she would have made a creditable Lady Macbeth. Rhodri, in his corner, was trying to come across like Polonius. This was starting to resemble a bedroom farce with serious Shakespearian pretensions.

'Glyn's just said that Tony's been arrested,' Rhodri explained to his wife. 'He's about to tell us why.' I recognized that as an instruction.

'He set fire to my caravan. We're charging him with arson and attempted murder.'

Rhodri and Ursula went through a series of shocked and disbelieving reactions. Were they both acting? I played the dumb and meek messenger until they settled down.

'What can we do to help?' Ursula asked. The question seemed to be directed at both Rhodri and me.

'I'm going to wake my bloody lawyer up,' Rhodri stated resolutely, and started to turn away.

'No, Rhodri, you're not,' I told him.

He turned and shared a look of surprise with his wife. 'What do you mean by that?' he asked me.

'You're going to stay here and tell me what I need to know.'

'How dare you!' Ursula snapped icily. 'This is our house. Tony works for us, we have a responsibility.'

'Are you involved in this?' I asked her, turning my back on Rhodri and stretching a hand behind me to shut him up. 'How much do you know, Ursula?'

'How much do I know about what?'

I changed tack. 'A source tells me that the Ap Hywel Foundation was established with your family money.'

'What business is that of yours?' she flared.

'Don't talk to him,' Rhodri commanded.

Ursula flashed him an angry look. 'I have an independent family trust fund.'

I nodded. 'Does Rhodri have access to it?'

'Is this pertinent?'

'Very.'

She looked at Rhodri again. 'The trustees only answer to me.'

'So, Rhodri isn't as asset rich as the surface would suggest. That had puzzled me. Why, when you seem to have everything, do you need the extra?'

She looked confused. Rhodri gave up protesting from behind me and joined our frame. His smile was patient, his voice firm. 'It's time to leave graciously, Glyn. We're not vindictive people. We're still prepared to put this intrusion down to fatigue and PTSD, and not make a formal complaint. Aren't we, Ursula?'

She gave him a look. She wasn't sure what was happening here. Rhodri went to the door, opened it, and beckoned me forward. 'Glyn?' he urged.

'What came first, Rhodri? Was Jessie the egg, or Hoca the chicken?'

He smiled affably, humouring me. 'I'm sorry, but I don't know what you're talking about.'

I nodded. 'You really don't know how you screwed up, do you?' I stared hard into the wise counsellor persona he was trying to project. He didn't blink. 'You didn't realize that, when Hoca turned up here, Jessie, opportunistic as ever, stole his laptop and some sample drug product from his car.'

He closed the door again, using the manoeuvre to cover the flicker that this produced in his otherwise impassive face. I saw Ursula see it too.

I continued. 'That was the stone wall I kept running into. That's what had me totally stumped. Why had Hoca never told his boss that his laptop had been stolen? Because it was important. It would have been full of compromising information. You know why, don't you? Why he never told Mike Saltik?'

Rhodri tried to share a *let's humour him* smile with Ursula. 'You're going to tell us, I suppose?'

'Because he never got back to his car to find out it was missing. He never left here, did he? Not alive. And Tony . . . I assume it was Tony who stashed his car, and then drove it to Machynlleth later? Tony didn't miss it because he'd never known it was there. Neither of you knew that it had turned into a trading commodity.'

He shrugged unconcernedly. 'This is your fantasy, Glyn.' He gave Ursula another one of those smiles, but I was aware that she was now watching me closely and seriously.

'What was Hoca here for?'

'And I've already told you, I have no idea who this Hoca person is.'

'Was it a shakedown? Was it private business between you and him? Was he your fence? Was that the relationship?'

'What on earth would I need a *fence* for?' he asked facetiously, trying another conspiratorial smile on Ursula.

'I'm coming to that. Let's just clear up the mechanics of the thing first. Because this thing would only work if Hoca was acting on his own. If Mike Saltik didn't know that he

347

had ever been here.' I clapped my hands together and pretended to have a revelation. 'Was it unintentional? Shall we be generous, Rhodri, and say that Hoca's death was an accident? He tried to hustle you and something went wrong? A bottle fell on his head? He stumbled into the kitchen knife rack? An electric toaster fell into his bath?'

'Please, Glyn, stop it, you're making a fool of yourself,' Rhodri urged sympathetically.

'And what are you going to tell Mike Saltik? You've accidentally wiped out his top lieutenant? I don't think so. No, you're going to cover it up. No one knew he was here, after all. Hoca is going to become a missing person. Another unsolved disappearance.' I clicked my fingers. 'And then you realize. Eureka moment! And now we're back to my chicken-and-egg question. You have a spin-off. You can now create Jessie's accident and plant a fairy tale underneath it.'

'What does this have to do with Jessie's accident?' Ursula demanded.

'Don't encourage him,' Rhodri protested.

I looked her full in the face. 'Jessie's death wasn't an accident. Your husband and Tony Stevenson arranged it to look like one.' She started shaking her head. I shut Rhodri's protests out. 'And, as insurance, they layered a tale of gangland revenge underneath it. Hoca and Jessie. Mike Saltik would blame Nick Saltik for Hoca's disappearance, and Nick would blame Mike for Jessie's death. Nothing could be proved, of course, but the circle was completed.'

'That's impossible,' Ursula declared, still shaking her head.

'Of course it fucking is,' Rhodri concurred angrily.

I took out the four rolls of tightly wadded cash and threw

them onto the hall table. They had been rolled so tightly inside the figurines that they had retained their cylindrical shape.

'What's that?' Ursula asked.

'Let's ask your husband. How much did you pay her, Rhodri?'

'Pay who?' Ursula asked.

'Jessie.' I nodded at the money. 'That's why she had to die.'

Rhodri shook his head nobly with the look of a reasonable man whose patience was being stretched. His eyes flashed on mine. I caught the smug gleam. He thought I was playing a game with him. Trying to trap him. As if I really believed he would incriminate himself by trying to reclaim it.

And I had another realization. Ursula had never been a party to any of this. I felt sad for her. I was about to fuck up this version of her life for ever.

'When did you realize that it would have to stop?' I asked Rhodri. 'Was she getting greedier? Or did you just think it was too dangerous to continue? Having her knowing all about it.' I answered the question in Ursula's eyes. 'Jessie was blackmailing him.'

'For what?' she asked Rhodri.

'Don't be stupid, Ursula, he's playing games with you,' Rhodri protested angrily.

She stared at him hard. 'She was only a child.' Shock rippled through her expression. 'Were you sleeping with her?'

'Don't be ridiculous,' he snapped with all the disdainful conviction he could muster.

'She found out about his sideline,' I told her.

'Sideline?'

349

'Don't listen to him,' Rhodri commanded.

'Was it Rhodri's idea to set up the clinics in Sierra Leone?' She nodded. It was her turn now to put out her hand to shut Rhodri up. 'You know why he chose that location in particular?' I asked.

'Why?' Her voice was hushed.

'The carvings are too small to hold any profitable amount of drugs. So it had to be a high-value, low-volume commodity. Like illegal blood diamonds, Rhodri?'

'Ursula!' Rhodri pleaded. 'This is pure invention.'

'It started off as guesswork, but you confirmed it when you sent Tony Stevenson to torch my place.' I turned back to Ursula, ignoring his protestations. 'He smuggled them out in the wooden figurines that Jessie was presented with. The charitable foundation was the front, and she was the icing on the cake, the cute little mascot that cut through the formalities.' I turned to Rhodri. 'But you made a big mistake with your choice of cherub, didn't you? She was Nick Saltik's daughter after all. She was genetically disposed to sniffing out the main chance. How many trips before she discovered the deal with the figurines?'

But he had stopped listening to me. Ursula had slumped to sit on the stairs, and was hugging herself tightly like a woman in shock. He knelt in front of her, trying to break through the barrier of her arms. 'Ursula, Ursula . . .' he coaxed.

She raised her head and looked at him. 'Is any of this true?'

'Of course not. Can't you see it? The man's obsessed with extricating himself from any sense of guilt over what

350

happened to Jessie. He's created this fantasy to exonerate himself.'

'The same fantasy that has Tony Stevenson burning my caravan?' I reminded him.

'If you have any proof that Tony did that, then he was acting alone.'

I shook my head. 'No, Rhodri, it won't work. You can't cut him adrift. It always needed two of you. It was teamwork. That's what you employed him for, after all. Butler, handyman and shit-shifter. Tony Stevenson wasn't going to be able to abduct Hoca on his own in your house.'

'Ursula, I'm your husband,' he appealed, 'this man's demented. I swear that none of this is true.'

She turned away from him to look at me. 'Why?' she asked plaintively.

'I don't know.' I shrugged wearily. 'Greed? Debt?'

'He used to gamble.' She spoke to me, but she was staring at Rhodri accusingly. 'He promised me he'd given up.'

'I couldn't help it,' Rhodri protested, 'it got complicated. I ended up owing some seriously bad people.'

'You could have come to me.'

His eyes narrowed defiantly. 'I refuse to be a fucking lapdog.'

'You kill people to save your pride?' I interjected.

He ignored me. The plea in his voice was for his wife. 'I needed an outlet, Ursula.'

'I thought that was what the Foundation was for?' she retorted.

'I knew you wouldn't understand.' His head turned involuntarily and he shared his patronizing smile with me. This was

351

the realm of blokes. The road maps here were designed to be unfathomable to women. 'I needed something with an edge. I needed risk. I wanted to put my balls on the knife's edge.'

'And you failed at that too,' she snapped angrily.

His face dropped. 'What?'

'You've still got your balls, and you didn't win any money.'

'I'm trying to explain a compulsion to you,' he whined.

But she had given up listening. 'Can you prove any of this?' she asked me.

'No, not sufficiently for a court of law.'

'See!' Rhodri declared triumphantly.

'I'll try and save you from the worst of it, Ursula. I'll swear to them that you had no knowledge of what he was doing.'

'What the fuck are you talking about?' Rhodri raged.

'I'm telling Mike and Nick Saltik.'

He shook his head, not believing what he had heard.

'Mike knows he had nothing to do with Jessie's death, and it's the same with Nick over Hoca. It's that tidy circle of deception you created, Rhodri. I'm going to break it. I'm going to tell them that you were responsible for both deaths. And, because of you, they've probably both suffered war damage. And Nick's lost a daughter.'

'You wouldn't!' His voice was hoarse.

'You killed Jessie, you bastard, you killed Dai and Christian. You probably killed Hoca. And you were responsible for another man getting tortured and burned to death. I'm being generous, I'm giving you advance warning of your fate. I'm giving you the chance to run from it.'

He stared at me, his face aghast now as the implications sank in. He clutched my upper arms. 'You said you'd no proof. You're a serving police officer. You can't take the law into your own hands like this.'

'I'm resorting to something more primal than law and order. I'm invoking fucking justice, Rhodri.'

I shook his hands off. I waited for Ursula's eyes to lift to meet mine. I tried to express my sorrow and regret. I touched her lightly on the wrist before I left.

One last small benediction.

THE DUST SETTLES

Rhian never knew which branch of the Saltik clan had been holding her. She had been kept hooded in a series of what smelled like cellars, and only moved around at night in the boots of cars.

Luckily for her, word of her newly protected status filtered down from the Met before she could be turned into a kebab, or shipped out to pleasure a pasha. They dropped her off in East London. Not so luckily, the car was still travelling at the time. She suffered a broken nose and collarbone, a dislocated hip, and multiple contusions and lacerations.

I received a one-word answer to the text I sent asking when I could visit.

Wait.

Jack Galbraith's acquisition of Hoca's laptop was regarded as a masterstroke by the Met. They upgraded the restaurants they took him to, and let him share the billing on the communiqués they were issuing announcing the demise of another criminal conspiracy. Behind the scenes, I gather, they came to a working compromise with both branches of the Saltik operation.

On Nick's part, he gave up the eight victims of the Dons' Den arson attacks who stumbled into a police station in a remote area of Anatolia with disgruntled tales of kidnap, transportation and the deprivations suffered from having been kept confined by armed and lustful goat herders.

Unlike his car, Hoca never turned up. There is an outside chance that he boarded a train in Machynlleth and set out to make a new life for himself in Paraguay. But I doubt it.

Jack Galbraith returned home sated, fêted and happy. Which was fortunate for me, because DI Bradshaw was still on the warpath. I gave him a version of Ryan Shaw and the laptop story which cut out the inconvenience of involving Jessie, and told him I had passed on a lead to DI Bradshaw that had come to me circuitously.

'How circuitous?'

'There was an operation of which I'm not privy to divulge details, Sir.'

'Stop talking like a fucking lawyer, Capaldi. Yes/no answers. Was this a legal operation?'

'There's a very fine line, Sir.'

'That's a no then.' He instructed a call to be put through to DI Bradshaw. While we waited he stared at me with one of those looks of his that pre-empted the invention of X-rays. Bradshaw answered. He listened. From where I stood she came across like an angry bomber pilot.

'And . . .?' he drawled when she'd finished.

Even I heard her astonishment in the silence.

He continued. 'I'm disappointed. DS Capaldi was showing diligence and initiative in directing you to the malfeasance committed by Brady, a man who you had under constant supervision, and yet missed his involvement in Ryan Shaw's murder.'

He put the phone down. He grinned up at me. 'You're not the only one who can talk like a fucking lawyer.'

'Thank you, Sir. Can I come back to work at Headquarters?'

His grin didn't falter. 'Fuck off, Capaldi. You've used up your entire quota of my gratitude.'

Despite my best efforts, Tony Stevenson got out on bail at his remand hearing. Rhodri wasn't in court, but he'd sprung for major league legal representation. Outside the magistrates' court Tony and his lawyers got into a swanky Mercedes with blacked-out windows. I followed them as far as the airfield at Welshpool. Tony flashed me the finger as he crossed the tarmac to the private plane. I never saw him again. Neither did the court.

I had a crisis of conscience to work through. By fucking up Rhodri ap Hywel I was going to be causing a lot of peripheral damage. Ursula's marriage was probably screwed, but she had the wherewithal to restore her life. But Cassie? I tried to meet up with her to talk about it, but she refused to see me.

So, would the threat of exposure to the Saltiks be enough to get Rhodri running rather than actually acting on it?

After a near-miss with a forty-ton articulated lorry, I decided not. It could have been a coincidence, but Rhodri was too dangerous to have as an enemy and leave out there un-neutralized. So, with Mackay and Boyce as minders, and me as an anonymous concerned citizen, I took my tale to the Saltiks.

I didn't move in the same circles to know what happened to Rhodri after that. All I could work with was the peace that seemed to descend. No more huge trucks looming up in my rear-view mirror as I was slowing down for a roundabout.

And, as for Cassie, it looked like I needn't have worried. Plas Coch and the Home Farm were sold to a consortium with plans to turn them into a luxury spa, or a drugs rehabilitation clinic, depending on what version of local rumour you run with. Cassie, last heard, was managing the retreat on the private island in the Caribbean that Ursula's new foundation had bought.

I wondered how Simon would tailor his fantasy to a tropical situation.

With Bryn Jones's help I managed to get SOCO teams to investigate the sites of Jessie's accident, and the barn where Dai and Christian had died. Nothing was found at either of them. With Jessie's I wasn't surprised, it had been too long. Time, the growing season and the weather had all taken their toll. But I had thought that the barn might have thrown up something. I was faced with the nagging possibility that this one might have been accidental after all.

Someone had removed the supermarket trolley from the front garden of 3 Orchard Close, Maesmore. Ryan Shaw's sister answered the door, jiggling her bulk, and rhythmically patting the bum of her baby, who was thrown over one shoulder. I couldn't help myself. I glanced behind her to see if there was a connecting trail of drool leading back into the television room.

'What do you want?' she asked, her tone flat and hostile.

'I've come round to tell you that I'm sorry about Ryan.'

'Thanks,' she said without too much conviction, eyeing me closely, waiting for the catch.

'He asked me to give you something.' I took the bulky envelope from my inside pocket. I had borrowed an iron from Sandra at The Fleece, where I was staying until the tenancy agreement on Phil Connolly's mobile home got sorted out, but, despite my best efforts, the cash just wouldn't lie flat, the bent manila envelope looking like a component from a piece of Scandinavian modernist furniture. 'I was holding this for him.'

She took the envelope and hefted it. She knew what was in there. 'You think I'm stupid?'

I shook my head, smiling, trying to put her at her ease.

'You think I'm going to fall for this?' she asked, trying to push the envelope back at me. 'You think I don't know what fucking entrapment is?'

I held up my hands in denial. 'It's Ryan's. I was holding it for him.'

'Right and I'm fucking Tinkerbell.'

'Is your mother in?'

'Why?'

'Get her to take a photograph of me giving it to you.'

Shit, it was hard work being illegally philanthropic.

Ready.

Rhian's text message finally came through and I drove up to London. I had had time to reflect on things. Very quickly into that process I knew I wanted to make the journey.

Another hospital bed. We had come back to the beginning.

It was a private room and the blinds were set to muted light. There was a dressing on her nose and her face was still swollen and bruised. 'Hello, Glyn,' she said, wincing slightly as she propped herself up against the pillows.

'Hello, Rhian.'

'I'm a mess, so don't you dare turn on the fucking lights. But you should have seen me before.'

I bent over and kissed her forehead. 'I know the feeling.'

She made a show of trying to peer behind my back. 'What have you brought me?'

I handed her the gift-wrapped package. She tested its weight and grinned. She had guessed what it was. She stripped the paper off. 'Twenty-one-year-old Highland Park!' she exclaimed gleefully.

'You'd better keep it hidden, I don't know if it qualifies as alternative medicine.'

She pulled a faux pout. 'You cheapskate bastard. I've done my research. I know they make a forty-year-old one.'

I paused before responding. 'I thought that one would be better coming from Alex.'

She stared at me, a lot of complex things happening in her face. 'You know?'

'I found out.'

She nodded, working through the knowledge. Her smile was diffident and fond. 'But you still came all this way?'

'I've thought about it. What I didn't know back then didn't seem to be worrying either of us too much. I'm prepared to work at some arrangement.'

'It doesn't have to obviate romance,' she insisted.

'No, it doesn't,' I agreed.

She nodded, her face brightening. 'And I'll get to have my town mouse and my country mouse.'

'And I've got a swanky new mobile home,' I boasted.

'And I've got what could be called an accommodating job.' She dropped the whisky box on the bedclothes, took my right hand and guided it inside her top and over her left breast. I closed my eyes. I wasn't necessarily second choice, I told myself. Better to go ahead on the basis that I was the number one guy in my location.

I leaned down to kiss her. 'When you've recovered enough, I'll be waiting for you to come up and work on the Glyn Capaldi profile.'

'You've changed your mind?'

'Yes. On one condition.'

'What's that?'

'The piece never gets printed.' I covered her mouth with mine to shut off any protest.

It was sunny on the day that I moved into my new home. And there, in the back garden that led down to the river, bobbing on a boulder beside the water, welcoming me, was my pied wagtail.

The next day, just to remind me that happiness is fleeting, the letter from the prison arrived.